⑨ *The Leads*

⑩ *Riva degli Schiavoni*

⑪ *The Arsenal*

⑫ *San Michele*

⑬ *Murano*

⑭ *Mestre*

THE RAPE OF VENICE

In the summer of 1796 Roger Brook, somewhat unwillingly, undertook a new secret mission for his master, Mr. Pitt. It brought him in contact with Rinaldo Malderini—a Venetian Senator, who was a disciple of the Devil—and his wife Sirīsha, a beautiful Indian Princess. The mission fizzled out, but the damage had been done, Roger and the evil occultist had met; Fate took charge with terrible results for both.

With his usual prodigality Mr. Wheatley follows the opening with not a few but scores of exciting scenes: a séance, a duel, a shipwreck on the way to India, capture by cannibals on the African coast, being sold as a slave to an Arab potentate, high life in Calcutta, intrigue at a Rajah's court, the kidnapping of a lovely lady, a minor war against a native state, the violating of a harem and a desperate night assault against a walled city. While through it all there runs a passionate love affair beset with the most exasperating complications.

Even that is but half the tale. Fate decrees Roger's return post haste to Europe to renew his vendetta with the Satanist Malderini. He is then immediately plunged back into the vortex of international intrigue.

In the spring of '96 Napoleon's name was hardly known outside Corsica and Paris. By the spring of '97 he had destroyed four Austrian armies, overrun half the Italian States and held the rest to ransom. The thousand-year-old Republic of Venice remained to be dealt with. How Roger played pimp to Buonaparte, robbed Venice of her last vestige of independence, yet saved her as a pawn to be used in a renewal of the desperate struggle of the Allies against the French, makes a tremendous story.

The background in both India and Venice is factual. Against it Roger, the Princess Sirīsha, lovely Clarissa Marsham and the evil Rinaldo Malderini play out their drama of love and death.

THE
RAPE OF VENICE

By
DENNIS WHEATLEY

THE BOOK CLUB
121 CHARING CROSS ROAD
LONDON, W.C.2

First published 1959

© by Dennis Wheatley 1959

For

My good friend

BOB LUSTY

Contents

1	The Shape of Things to Come	9
2	The Unexpected Happens	21
3	A Very Strange Performance	34
4	The Séance	45
5	The Duel	54
6	The Venetian Strikes Back	62
7	Alarms and Excursions	69
8	The Great Temptation	81
9	The Trials of an Uncle	92
10	Clarissa makes her Bed	110
11	Death Reaches Out	129
12	The Will of Allah	140
13	A Bolt from the Blue	151
14	A Lie Comes Home to Roost	159
15	The Golden Age in Bengal	165
16	The Mysterious Elopement	181
17	In Desperate Straits	194
18	A Tough Nut to Crack	213
19	To Cheat the Moon	230
20	With Death at the Post	242
21	The Wrong Side of the Fence	253
22	Within the Enemy's Gates	276
23	Patriot or Spy?	285
24	Half an Hour to Live	299
25	The Uncrowned King	309
26	The Rape of Venice	324
27	The Trap is Set	335
28	In the Trap	357
	Epilogue	371

CHAPTER ONE

The Shape of Things to Come

'PEACE, Mr. Brook; peace. It is that the nation needs, and must soon have if we are to escape anarchy and total ruin.'

The speaker was William Pitt the younger, on a sunny morning in June 1796. He was then only thirty-seven, but looked far older, as for thirteen years he had been Prime Minister to King George III and during them had worked himself to a shadow.

Tall, thin, worn-looking, and dressed very plainly in grey, only his eyes and autocratic manner indicated the iron will which had enabled him for so long to dominate the political scene and guide the destinies of Britain.

As he spoke, his sparse fairish hair, now prematurely grey, was ruffled slightly by a gentle breeze, for he was standing on the battlements of Walmer Castle: a residence he sometimes occupied by virtue of his office as Lord Warden of the Cinque Ports.

His companion cut a very different figure. Roger Brook was twenty-eight, and the sight of him would have gladdened any woman's heart. His deep blue eyes, prominent nose, firm mouth and aggressive chin were indications of the intelligence, resource and resolution which had made him Mr. Pitt's most successful secret agent during the French Revolution. His slim hips were encased in dove-grey breeches and his broad shoulders in a royal blue coat. These, with a gaily flowered waistcoat and the sparkling jewel in his cravat, were the outward expression of his cheerful nature, while the easy grace with which he carried himself showed him to be unassuming but self-confident.

The association between the two men had lasted close on ten years; during them Roger had not only sent the Prime Minister secret reports from many countries but he had more than once been vested with Ambassadorial powers, and as a reward for special services, been given the lucrative appointment of Governor of Martinique.

Like his master, who had become Chancellor of the Exchequer at the age of twenty-three, he had an old head on young shoulders. Mr. Pitt had no secrets from him and gave considerable weight to his opinions, because his long residence abroad had brought him into personal contact with many foreign royalties and statesmen and given him an exceptional knowledge of the policies they were likely to pursue.

9

In consequence, he replied with the candour of the privileged: 'You had best make up your mind to it, Sir, that we'll get no peace with honour till France is exhausted; and as yet she is far from that.'

'I disagree,' the Prime Minister retorted sharply. 'She cannot support for much longer the burden she has been carrying. It is now over four years since the Monarchist Coalition was formed against her. Having had to wage war for so long, and for most of that time on all her frontiers simultaneously, must have placed an intolerable strain on her resources and her people.'

'No worse than that sustained by Britain when she stood alone against a world in arms during the seven years of war that preceded the Peace of '83.'

'The situations are not comparable. Our people were then united behind a stable Government and could draw fortitude from their Christian faith. We had great accumulated wealth, the mastery of the seas and, above all, the strength inherent in centuries-old traditions of service, orderliness and discipline. France, on the other hand, is still in the throes of the greatest upheaval that has afflicted any nation in modern times. For seven years she has been a prey to anarchy and atheism. Every stabilizing factor in the nation has been destroyed, her riches squandered and her commerce ruined. Her collapse is inevitable.'

Roger shrugged. 'I regard it as less likely now than it was in '93; or even this time last year. Look what has happened to your mighty Coalition. Those greedy Prussians gained nothing by transferring their army to the East. Catherine of Russia saw to that. But it does not alter the fact that in the hope of getting a bigger share in the final partition of Poland they betrayed us by making a separate peace. Their treachery led to the collapse of Holland, and last summer Spain, too, was compelled to sue for terms. Now, the recent defeats of the Piedmontese have forced sturdy old King Victor Armadeus out of the war. What is there left? Only Austria and ourselves.'

'I know, I know!' Mr. Pitt waved an impatient hand. 'The defection or defeat of so many of our allies is most deplorable. But it is not now upon military success that I pin my hopes. It is on France's internal condition. With the overthrow of the Monarchy her whole taxation structure fell to pieces. Her government of brigands succeeded in carrying on only by forced loans, the wholesale pillage of private property, and the issue of paper currency secured on the lands confiscated from the nobles and the church. The value of these *assignats* has steadily fallen until now they are scarce worth the paper they are printed on. Armies, even if they are not paid, must be fed, equipped and munitioned if they are to continue fighting, and reports I have received show France's financial situation to have become positively desperate. It is that which makes me confident that the time cannot be far distant when we shall be able to bring her to terms.'

From under the long lashes that many a girl had envied, Roger gave his master an uneasy glance. He had a considerable affection and great admiration for him, but was not blinded to his shortcomings by his abilities.

Beneath the Prime Minister's haughty manner there lay a kindly disposition and his awkwardness with strangers was due only to shyness. He was a brilliant speaker, an able administrator, and a skilful diplomat; but he hated war and everything to do with it. In consequence, although he showed high courage in the leadership of the nation, his lack of military knowledge and grasp of strategy were severe handicaps in the struggle against France. Moreover, so eager was he for a restoration of peace that he allowed his judgment to be clouded by that desire. On the other hand, in the field of finance he was supreme, and after the last great war had in a few years brought Britain back from near bankruptcy to a marvellous prosperity. It was this which made Roger hesitate to challenge him on his strongest ground. Instead he said:

'May I ask, Sir, if through neutral sources you have recently sounded the French Government on the subject of entering into negotiations?'

Mr. Pitt was looking across the battlements out to sea. A frown creased his high forehead, and without turning, he replied, 'I have; and I confess the result was disappointing. Our Austrian allies insist on the return of their Netherland territories. It was with a view to having something to offer in exchange for them that, at a great cost in men and money, I pressed our operations in the West Indies. Despite the furore it would raise in the City, I'd give the French back their rich Sugar Isles if they would agree to evacuate the Low Countries and undertake to cease their subversive activities in others. But it seems that the Directory that now rules the roost in France is not even willing to discuss my proposals.'

The reply confirmed Roger's belief that his master was once more a victim of the unfounded optimism that had led him to hope for a speedy peace ever since the fall of Robespierre. As gently as he could he said, 'Can you be altogether surprised at that? The armies of General Moreau and General Jourdan are more than holding their own upon the Rhine, and all France must be cock-a-hoop at the brilliant successes of the young Corsican General, Buonaparte, these past three months in Italy.'

'I would not be did I not know that France is bankrupt. Her armies are in rags and her cities starving. Military triumphs can temporarily raise the morale of a people, but they cannot be used as a substitute for bread.'

'You must permit me to disagree with you about that,' Roger said firmly. 'Do you recall the report on my dealings with General Buonaparte that I submitted to you on my return from France last April?'

'Indeed I do.' Mr. Pitt gave one of his rare smiles. 'It was largely due to your skilful machinations that Madame de Beauharnais agreed to marry

him, and that he was diverted from his assignment to prepare an army for
the invasion of England by being given command of the Army of Italy.'

Roger made a little grimace. 'It was my knowledge of how ill-prepared
we were to resist invasion which led me to take that course; yet more than
ever now I have the feeling that it would have been wiser to let him risk
destruction in the Channel. It was not of that, though, that I was thinking.'

'I see. You meant to remind me of your assessment of him as the most
intelligent and dangerous of all the French generals. It was a shrewd
appreciation, since he had never then directed a battle.'

'I had had the advantage of seeing him in the field; for I met him when
he was still an unknown Artillery officer.'

'That was at the siege of Toulon, was it not?'

'It was.' Roger gave a sudden laugh. 'It might almost be said that we
won our spurs together. I got myself into a pretty fix, and as Citizen
Representative Breuc was under the necessity of leading French troops in
a daylight charge against a Spanish battery. It near cost me my life, but
later paid most handsomely; for ever since, the little Corsican has accounted
me a gallant fellow and worthy of his friendship. But for that he would
never have discussed so frankly with me last February the project for invading England, and offered me a Colonelcy on his staff. There was, though,
another project on which he spoke to me with equal frankness, and 'twas
to that part of my report that I was hoping to direct your memory.'

'You refer to the Italian campaign. Yes, I remember now. It was his pet
hobby-horse and he had long been endeavouring to persuade the Directors
to accept his plan for it. No wonder he so readily abandoned all else when
given the chance to carry it out himself, and within forty-eight hours of
his marriage jumped out of his bride's bed to gallop off and take up his
new command. Well, he has certainly justified your belief in his capabilities;
but what of it?'

Since Roger's tactful references to his report had failed to ring the right
bell in his master's brain, he felt that he now had no alternative but to
speak out and endeavour, once and for all, to shatter his dangerous
illusions.

'Sir,' he said. 'You have evidently forgotten the salient point that has
reference to our conversation. It is my having informed you that General
Buonaparte spoke to me of Italy as the treasure-chest of Europe. And he
was right. Nowhere in the world is there so much accumulated wealth.
We know, too, that the French Republicans have no scruples in plundering
unmercifully the cities that their armies overrun, by means of indemnities,
forced loans, fines for alleged wrongs, and open looting. I think Buonaparte
too big a man, and too confident in his own future, to exact for himself
more than he requires for his immediate needs; but you may be sure that

one thing he is set upon is to be allowed the continuance of a free hand in Italy. To ensure that he must keep the good-will of the Directors, and the one way in which he can make certain of doing so is by supplying them with money. I would wager all Lombard Street to a China Orange that during these past few weeks treasure convoys despatched by him have carried many million ducats across the Alps into France. And those ducats will buy the food she needs so badly. Yet worse, there is no reason to suppose that this river of gold will cease to flow until Buonaparte's victorious advance is halted. Distressed as I am to disabuse you or your hopes, I am convinced that there is not the least foundation for the supposition that France must shortly collapse as the result of an empty Treasury.'

Mr. Pitt's grey face had gone a shade greyer. Slowly removing his arm from a stone crenellation on which he had been leaning, he walked over to a painted iron table that had on it a decanter of port and two glasses. Refilling them both he drank from his own, set it down and remarked sourly: 'I have often found you a disconcerting person with whom to discuss foreign affairs, Mr. Brook; but never more so than this morning.'

Roger, too, took a swig of port, then murmured, 'I am truly sorry, Sir, but I would serve you ill did I not give you my opinions with complete frankness.'

'That is true;' the Prime Minister laid a friendly hand on his elbow; 'and believe me, far from resenting it, I am grateful to you. Yet, if you are right, and the rejection by the French Government of my overtures implies that you are, it means that we must resign ourselves to another year or more of war. I would to God I could be certain that the nation will stand up to that.'

'What!' exclaimed Roger. 'You cannot mean it! In the last war we stuck it out for twice the time we have been involved in this, and as a nation we still have all those advantages over the French of which you were speaking a while ago.'

'Alas, there you are quite wrong.'

'Wrong! How so? The nation is united under a stable government. The Coalition gives you an overwhelming majority in the House. We are still sustained by our Christian faith. The war may again be making heavy inroads on our resources, but we still adhere to our traditions and are as determined as ever to maintain our rights.'

'Mr. Brook, having lived for so long abroad it is understandable that you should have remained unaware of the changed feeling in your own country. Last October, on His Majesty's going to open Parliament his coach was stoned by the mob.'

'So I heard, Sir, and was most deeply shocked; but I took it to be an isolated act by a small group of fanatics.'

'It was far from that. Thousands thronged the Mall and booed him. No such demonstration against a British Monarch has taken place within living memory. That it should do so is clear evidence that the loyalty of the masses has been undermined by the pernicious doctrines of the French. During the past two years they have spread like wildfire, and every town now has its proletarian club at which agitators preach revolution. Were the franchise universal at the next election there would be a real danger of this country becoming a Republic. So you may rid your mind of the idea that the people are still united.'

Roger finished his glass of port, then said with a frown, 'I was, of course, aware that hot-heads like Horne Tooke had long been creating trouble, and of the near-treasonable activities of the London Corresponding Society; but I had not a notion that sedition had become so widespread.'

'Last autumn the Society of which you speak convened a meeting in Islington Fields. It was attended by no less than fifteen thousand persons, and resolutions were passed at it advocating armed rebellion. God knows what might have happened had I not promptly ordered numerous regiments of troops from their stations in the country to the outskirts of London. Norwich, Birmingham, Sheffield, Bristol, and a score of other cities have become hot-beds of revolution. I am at present holding the masses down only by having suspended Habeas Corpus and having put through a Treason Act making malcontents who speak against the Constitution liable to transportation for seven years.

'You spoke, too, of the Christian Faith,' Mr. Pitt went on, with a shrug of his narrow shoulders. 'It has recently suffered as serious a decline as loyalty to the Crown. John Wesley's teachings detached a great part of the masses from the Established Church. Methodism is a revolt from religious discipline and on doctrinal matters near synonymous with Freethinking. What more fertile breeding ground could you have for complete disbelief? Those who preach anarchy also preach atheism and, alas, thousands, many thousands, of the proletariat have now accepted both.

'With regard to money: in the present war I have had to find vast sums to subsidize our allies. Without British gold they could never have kept their armies in the field so long, and the drain has near ruined us.

'As for myself, 'tis true that I have the backing of a large majority in the House; but I no longer possess the confidence of the people. If ever I now drive abroad I am greeted with shouts of "Peace! Peace! Stop the War! Stop killing our friends! Murderer! Stop sending our money to the foreign tyrants! Give us bread! Give us peace!"'

'Tell me, Sir,' Roger asked, 'what is the cause of this extraordinary change in the people's attitude?'

'The Whig aristocracy is fundamentally to blame. Unlike us Tories, they have never lifted a finger to protect the common people. Democracy means for them equality among themselves and striving to bring the Monarch down to their own level. They prate of Liberalism and the Rights of Man, yet did not scruple to take advantage of the Enclosures Act and increase their own properties by grabbing the land that for centuries had been held in common by the peasantry of each village. Robbed of free tillage, pasture and firewood, the peasants migrated to the towns. There they were sweated, brutalized from being forced to live in slums, and at bad times turned off to starve. Then came the French Revolution, and from it there emerged this wave of agitators who promise that the dethronement of Kings and the murder of the rich will bring about a Utopia. Yet can it be wondered at that any prospect of bettering their appalling lot should light a flame among the slum dwellers? I do not blame them. On the contrary, it fills me with despair that we should have to spend on war the millions that I might otherwise use in wise measures to ameliorate their lot.'

After a moment the Prime Minister went on: 'That is the root cause; but the positive factor that has turned widespread discontent into smouldering revolution is the failure of last year's harvest. Early this year the best wheat was fetching six guineas a quarter—a positively phenomenal price; and bread now costs far more than the ordinary worker can afford to pay.'

Roger nodded. 'I was aware of that, Sir; and that you had taken measures to counteract it. Prohibiting the manufacture of whisky, putting a tax on flour used for powdering the hair, urging the bakers to use one-third barley when making loaves, and having the members of the House set an example by voluntarily denying themselves pastry until the crisis is over, should have gone a great way to restoring the situation.'

'Nevertheless, considerable numbers of His Majesty's poorest subjects have actually died from starvation. Should the harvest fail again this year, I'll not answer for it that events here will not follow the pattern they took in France, and a guillotine be set up in Whitehall as a means of terminating the activities of people such as you and I.'

'Plague on it!' Roger protested. "Twould be prodigious hard if having lived through the Terror in Paris I were called upon to spit in the basket no more than a quarter of a mile from my own Club.' Then he added in a more sober tone, 'I no longer wonder now at your anxiety to secure a peace. Yet I see no way to it short of betraying our Austrian allies and submitting to ignominious terms.'

'That I would never do,' replied the Prime Minister haughtily. 'Nor, did I make such proposals, would His Majesty consent to them.'

'Do you believe, Sir, that the Austrians will stand equally loyally by us?'

'I believe the Emepror has the will to do so, but whether he has the means is another question. Only this week I received from him a request for a further one million two hundred thousand pounds. He asserts that without it he will be unable to pay his troops through to the end of this year's campaign.'

'Is it your intention to let him have it?'

'Legally, I cannot do so without the consent of Parliament, and the House does not reassemble until October.'

'By then he would receive it too late for the purpose he requires it.'

'I had thought to shelve the matter, hoping that by the late summer the French would find themselves compelled to enter into negotiations for a general pacification.'

Roger turned away to gaze out across the battlements. Far below some children were paddling in the gently creaming surf. The blue-green sea was calm, the sun glinting on its wavelets. A few miles out a brigantine with all sail set was heading down Channel. Otherwise the sea stretched unbroken to disappear in a heat-haze on the horizon. Without looking at Mr. Pitt, he said:

'Should it be not France, but Austria, that has to give in through lack of funds, the whole power of the Republic will be turned against us. You must face it, Sir, that before this time next year we would then be at death-grips with General Buonaparte's troops upon these very beaches.'

The Prime Minister sighed. 'Your having brought to my attention this new source of wealth which will keep the French fighting, I dare not ignore that possibility. It is clear, too, that in the Austrian armies lies our only hope of checking Buonaparte's advance, and with it this flow of gold; so it has become more necessary than ever to keep them in the field. Let us go down to my room and from a map endeavour to judge the way in which the campaign is likely to develop.'

Picking up the decanter and his glass, he led the way down a flight of stone steps, through a low nail-studded oak door, and so back to the room in which he had received Roger that morning. It had no great map of Europe—such as one might have expected to find pinned up on the wall of the study of the leader of a nation at war—but Mr. Pitt took from a shelf a well-thumbed atlas and flicked over its leaves until he came to the map of Italy.

It was a patchwork of different colours. The Kingdom of the Two Sicilies, embracing all southern Italy and the great island of Sicily, was the largest. Next in size came the Kingdom of Sardinia, consisting of that island, together with Savoy and Piedmont in the north-west, which, in the previous month, had been conquered by General Buonaparte. The whole middle of the peninsula was occupied by the States of the Church and the Grand Duchy of Tuscany. Above them lay a mosaic of smaller states: the

Republics of Genoa and Lucia, the Dukedoms of Parma, Modena, Mantua and Milan, and spreading over all of the north-east, from near Milan to the Adriatic, a territory as large as Switzerland that was still ruled by the Serene Republic of Venice.

Roger laid a finger-tip on Nice, drew it eastward some way along the Ligurian coast, then twenty miles inland, and remarked:

'That is the route Buonaparte took, and it was up there in the mountains that he carried out the first part of his plan by driving a wedge between the Piedmontese and General Beaulieu's Austrians. Alone the Piedmontese had no chance against him, and one most unfortunate result of their surrender is that it has enabled Buonaparte to open direct communications through Turin with France.'

The Prime Minister nodded. 'Yes, Lord Cornwallis pointed that out to me at a recent meeting of the Cabinet. 'Tis a sad blow, as previously all his supplies had to be brought from Nice along the coast to bases on the Italian Riviera, and were then exposed to constant harassing from Commodore Nelson's squadron working out of Leghorn. Now we are no longer able to aid the Austrians even to that extent.'

'In such mountainous country,' Roger went on, 'and with so many river barriers, one would have thought that the Austrians would have been able to hold him; but I gather that their generals are old in years and old-fashioned in their methods. At all events, the Corsican foxed them by by-passing the Po and forcing the Adda at Lodi. He does not lack for courage and, by all accounts, his capture of the bridge there against great odds was a personal triumph, as well as the second important milestone in his campaign. It scared the Dukes of Parma and Modena into asking him for terms, and the Duchy of Milan, too, fell like a ripe plum into his lap.'

'I am told that owing to the agitators he had sent ahead to spread revolutionary doctrines, the Milanese welcomed the French troops with open arms.'

'The poor fools will soon have cause to rue it,' Roger commented with a cynical laugh, 'as did the Belgians earlier in the war when they opened the gates of their towns to General Dumouriez's cut-throat soldiery. Within three months, the bringers of Liberty had stripped them of all but their shirts.'

'What, in your opinion, will Buonaparte's next move be?' Mr. Pitt enquired. 'Both the Papal States and Tuscany lie open to him and neither could put up a serious resistance. Such easy prey must be very tempting to him.'

'No, he will not turn south. At least, not if he adheres to his grand design, as he expounded it to me. It was to drive north through the Venetian lands, and so into the Tyrol. There, he hopes to join up with the

Army of the Rhine and thence, with the united armies giving him overwhelming strength, march direct on Vienna.'

'One cannot but admire the breadth of such a conception. He must be a remarkable man and is, I gather, not much older than yourself.'

'He is, in fact, my junior, Sir, by some eight months.'

For a few minutes the Prime Minister remained silent, then he said:

'Your mention of Venice reminds me of the main reason for my sending for you; but I'll not enter on that for the moment. Your grasp of military matters has always impressed me, and I would like to hear what you consider General Buonaparte's chances to be of carrying through his great plan?'

'You flatter me, Sir,' Roger smiled. 'But my work has oft necessitated my living for long spells at the Headquarters of Generals commanding armies in the field, and maybe there is some little truth in the old adage that "the looker-on sees most of the game". Even so, I hesitate to make a prediction in this case, because it is subject to so many unknown factors. In the first place, will the Emperor be able to continue the war without the new subsidy for which he has asked you?'

'He shall have it, Mr. Brook.'

'In time for it to serve its purpose?'

'Yes; it shall be furnished to him within a month.'

'Do you intend, then, to recall Parliament?'

'No. I shall send it on my own responsibility.'

Roger raised his eyebrows. 'Should you do that, Sir, surely you would risk impeachment?'

The Prime Minister gave his pale smile. 'It will be ground enough and will raise no small outcry. Did you see Gillray's cartoon based on the stoning of His Majesty's coach? I was depicted as his coachman, driving like Jehu through a hail of bad eggs, carrots and dead cats, while Lansdowne, Bedford and Whitbread strove to stop the vehicle's wheels. Fox and Sheridan, armed with bludgeons, were endeavouring to wrench open its door, and Norfolk was aiming a blunderbuss at the King. All these Whig nabobs will seize on such an unconstitutional act as a fine chance to demand my head; but I doubt not I'll keep it on my shoulders.'

'It is those traitors who should be sent to the block on Tower Hill,' Roger declared, his face reddening with indignation. 'Ever since '89 Fox and the Holland House crew have at every turn encouraged the French revolutionaries by applauding their acts, and striven to thwart your measures for the defence of Britain.'

'The right of the Opposition to attack Government in Parliament is the very cornerstone of our liberties,' replied the Prime Minister mildly. 'So I would be the last to wish things otherwise. And in himself, Charles Fox is a most generous and kindly man. But tell me; what prospects do you consider the Austrians have, given that we can keep them in the field?'

'They should be able to prevent the enemy from invading their own territory, for this year at least; and they have one great asset which should aid them in doing so. That is the fortress of Mantua. It is one of the strongest in Italy. I greatly doubt if Buonaparte would dare to leave it untaken in his rear, and, if well provisioned, it should be able to hold out for several months.'

'Should treachery or incompetence cause Mantua to fall within the next few weeks, what then?'

'Then all would depend upon the Army of the Rhine. Buonaparte's line of communications would be so long and, having to pass twice through the Alps, too hazardous for him to advance on Vienna unsupported. Unless Moreau and Jourdan can, in accordance with his plan, rendezvous with him at Innsbruck by the early autumn he would have to winter in the Tyrol.'

'Can you, Mr. Brook, suggest any means by which we might assist our Austrian allies to prevent the junction of the two enemy armies?'

Roger shook his head. 'I can think of none; other than an attempt to rebuild the Coalition, and thus provide the French with additional enemies.'

'If the war drags on there may come a time when that would be possible; but for the present it is out of the question. However, because I have had great hopes of negotiating a peace with the French this summer, that does not mean that I have altogether ignored the possibility that we might have to continue at war. And there is one powerful state that by skilful handling I believe could be drawn in to our assistance. I refer to the Serene Republic.'

'Venice!' The widening of Roger's blue eyes showed his astonishment. 'Admittedly I have never visited that city but, from all I have heard, centuries of luxury and debauchery have rendered its inhabitants the last word in decadence. Already both the French and Austrians have violated the Serene Republic's neutrality by sending troops across her borders, yet that has not led to her even making a serious protest.'

'It is true that the Senate have not yet defined the position that they intend to take up. But having witnessed the Kingdom of Sardinia, three out of the four Duchies and their sister republic, Genoa, all so swiftly brought under the heel of revolutionary France, you may be sure that they are greatly concerned about the future. I know that to be so, for they now have a secret envoy in London. His instructions are to assess our capability and will to carry on the war, so that they can decide whether to ask us for an alliance and declare against the French, or if it would pay them better to offer General Buonaparte free access to all their strong places in exchange for a guarantee of the return thereof after the war, and of the Republic's continuance as a Sovereign State.'

'Did you grant this envoy an interview yourself, Sir,' Roger enquired, 'or did my Lord Grenville see him at the Foreign Office?'

'Neither of us has seen him; and we are not likely to. That's just the rub. I have been privately informed about him. He is not here to make an official approach to His Majesty's Government, but has been sent only to spy out the land; and from our point of view he could not have made a worse beginning. Like so many of these wealthy foreigners he was already acquainted with several of our die-hard Whig nobility; so he was promptly made much of at Holland House, and Sheridan has appointed himself his bear-leader during his stay in London.'

'In that case 'tis a certainty that those pro-French traitors will send him back to Venice convinced that Britain is near down and out.' With a shrug, Roger added lightly, 'But I'd not let that worry you unduly, Sir. I doubt if the Venetians have a kick left in them; so whichever way their Senate may decide will make little odds to us.'

'On the contrary, Mr. Brook. While the war continues, no chance whatever of securing help in it should be neglected. Despite my sanguine hopes that, within the next few months, peace might be restored, I have never lost sight of that. It is the reason that I sent for you. I desire you to make the acquaintance of this Signor Rinaldo Malderini, and give him clearly to understand that Britain still has great resources and will never agree a peace that does not embody a full recognition of her allies' interests. Before our talk this morning, I had accounted this small commission as merely a precautionary measure, and one unlikely to require following up; but now I regard it as both urgent and of the first importance.'

Roger looked puzzled and far from happy as he said:

'Permit me, Sir, to question your choice of me for this particular mission. I'd need to see the Venetian a number of times to make any worthwhile impression on him. Sheridan well knows my political allegiance to yourself, so 'tis certain he would prejudice him against me and thus doubtful if I would be accorded more than one brief unsatisfactory interview.'

'My choice fell on you largely because I believe you to be in a position to get over that hurdle with ease. You are still staying with the Countess of St. Ermins at her place down in Surrey, are you not?'

'Yes. The loss of my wife in Martinique has made me reluctant to live again as yet in the home we shared at Richmond; so I shall probably continue for some while at Stillwaters, as Lady St. Ermins's guest.'

'Did I not know of your long attachment to her, I should count such an association strange, seeing that she frequently entertains there my worst enemies, but in . . .'

'Your pardon, Sir,' Roger cut in, his eyes suddenly bright with anger. 'Georgina St. Ermins is a woman of exceptional intelligence as well as beauty; so it is natural that she should cultivate the friendship of gifted men who play a part in the affairs of this and other nations. She is in no way governed by politics, and were you not so averse to going into society she would, I know, be happy to welcome you to her house. As for her patriotism, it is beyond question.'

Mr. Pitt made a little bow. 'I pray you overlook my inept remark. I knew only that Fox, Sheridan and others of their complexion enjoy her hospitality, and at times make use of her house to show their foreign friends something of the English countryside. It was that which gave me the idea that she is unlikely to refuse a request from you to ask Sheridan to bring Signor Malderini down for a weekend. Such an arrangement would afford you a perfect opportunity for conversations with him.'

'Lady St. Ermins would, I am sure, oblige me,' Roger replied with a shrug. 'But, in my opinion, even if we succeeded in drawing the Venetians in, as allies, you would find them worthless.'

'You speak without having given the matter due thought. The Serene Republic has lasted near a thousand years, so you may be sure that it will not lightly surrender its independence. Its territories have a population of over three million, so they could put a considerable army into the field; and the Croatian levies that they draw from across the Adriatic are said to be exceptionally brave fighters. Look, too, again at the map. The Venetian lands lie right athwart Buonaparte's only line of advance to the Tyrol. All this makes Venice a potential ally that we should now spare no pains to secure. Like our other allies she will, of course, demand a subsidy to pay her troops, and you have my authority to tell Signor Malderini that it will be forthcoming.'

'Devil take me!' Roger jumped to his feet. 'You can't really mean that with our Treasury near empty, and our taxes so high, you'd actually pay these soft, lazy decadent Italians to make ugly faces at Buonaparte. For I'll vow that's all they will do.'

The Prime Minister's glance became icy, and he snapped, 'That, Mr. Brook, is my affair, not yours. If the war must go on I'll leave nothing untried which may help to bring us victory. All I require from you is an answer to the question: will you, or will you not, do as I wish?'

In an instant Roger's whole attitude changed. Placing his hand upon his heart, he replied, 'Such sentiments, Sir, make me as ever your devoted servant. You may count upon me to do my best.'

CHAPTER TWO

The Unexpected Happens

GEORGINA lay dozing in her great canopied bed at Stillwaters, the gracious Palladian mansion, near Ripley in Surrey, of which she enjoyed a life tenancy under the marriage settlement made by her first husband. She greatly preferred it to White Knights Park, the seat in Northamptonshire of the Earl of St. Ermins, whose tragic death had made her a widow eighteen months before; so she made her home in Surrey for the greater part of each spring and summer.

She was now twenty-nine, and in the full flower of her striking beauty. Although blessed with the voluptuous curves that were considered the hall-mark of a perfect figure in Georgian times, she had not a pound of superfluous flesh, and, on the splendid mounts she kept in her stables, she could outride most men. Her rich complexion, strong white teeth, glossy dark hair and full red lips all testified to her abundant vitality. Her wicked black eyes were constantly alight with laughter, but when she felt inclined, from under their thick lashes she could launch a challenge that even a monk would have found irresistible.

A discreet knock came on the door of the room. She called 'Good morning, Jenny', then sat up in bed and stretched out a hand for the night-dress that she had left draped over a nearby chair. As the figure beside her did not move, she added, 'Roger, my love, did you not hear? 'Tis time for you to leave me.'

'Plague on it!' Roger muttered drowsily. 'Although but half awake my thoughts were set on making love to you.'

Smiling, she leant over and kissed his cheek. 'Then you have left it too late, dear heart. In ten minutes Jenny will be bringing me my chocolate.'

Jenny had been Georgina's personal maid since her girlhood, and it was a long established custom that she should call her mistress a short while before coming in with the breakfast tray. In theory the interval was to give Georgina an opportunity to wash and tidy herself, but in fact it was to give time for her lover, if she had one with her, to make himself scarce by way of the boudoir.

'Really!' Roger protested a shade petulantly. 'That we should continue to behave like ostriches is farcical. Jenny knows that we have been lovers on and off for years. As you have no secrets from her, I'll wager that some time or other you have even told her that it was you who seduced me when a boy.'

'Roger, how dare you! I did nothing of the kind. It was mutual.'

'Nonsense,' he laughed. 'You know well enough that you were my first experience, and I certainly was not yours.'

As a girl of sixteen she had, not altogether unwillingly, become the victim of a handsome highwayman; and being a young wanton by nature had later gloried in the affair, declaring it to be 'a fine romantic way to lose one's maidenhead'. Now, she returned Roger's smile and said; 'You've never got over your regret at not having been the first with me, have you? But that was no fault of mine; and I trust, Sir, that I've given you no cause to complain of me since.'

'On the contrary, Madam. You have given me many of the happiest hours of my life, and none more so than during these past two months. Yet it irks me that we should continue to pretend in front of Jenny instead of enjoying breakfast in bed together in the mornings.'

'What! Have Jenny bring to my room a tray for two, with hot dishes and cold meats to appease your hunger. How, pray, could she explain that in the kitchen? What my servants may guess at I care not; but 'tis quite another thing to give them clear grounds for dubbing me a whore. The price for breaking your fast in bed with me, m'dear, is beyond your purse; for it would be no less than marriage.'

'Damne, I've half a mind to take you up on that! You've had two husbands and I two wives, yet neither of us has had the joy with them we've had with one another. We've the same interests, never had a cross word . . .'

'Enough!' she cut in sharply. 'I was but joking and you are talking like a fool. The very essence of our golden hours is their impermanence, and the lack of obligation on either side. We've long since agreed that were we permanently united the time would come when we would tire of one another; physically I mean. We'd then begin to yearn for pastures new and end like most other married couples, observing the courtesies before the world but cheating, bickering, and disillusioned in private.'

Sitting up, he shrugged his shoulders. 'Alas, you're right. Yet you must marry someone. You owe it to little Charles.'

'Oh, I'll wed again; although not yet awhile. Charles is barely ten months old; so for some years to come he'll reap no ill from the lack of a father. But your case, Roger, is very different. Your little Susan is welcome to a home here for as long as you may wish, but however loving my care of her it will not be her own home; and that she should have. Poor Amanda used her last breath to place her infant in Clarissa's charge and express the hope that you two would marry, I pray you . . .'

'So Clarissa told you of that?'

'Yes. She did so soon after her arrival here with the child last week, and I pray you, Roger, give Amanda's wish your serious consideration. Clarissa is a most lovely young creature and passionately enamoured of you.'

'I know it. Has she not pursued me from the West Indies on the excuse of bringing my daughter to me, although the child was over young to travel?'

'That is unfair. There was less risk in her doing so with a wet-nurse in attendance than to wait until the child was weaned and had to be fed for many weeks on such dubious foods as a ship can carry. You could find no better step-mother than Clarissa to rear your child, and . . .'

'Yes, yes! I grant you that. She is, too, sweet natured and intelligent. I will admit that did I contemplate marriage I'd be tempted to make her my wife. But I do not; so spare me, I beg, further solicitation on her behalf.'

Georgina began to put on the nightdress with which she had been toying. 'I'll not promise that. But now is no time to pursue the topic, and at such an hour as this it was foolish in me ever to have raised it. At any moment Jenny will be bringing my chocolate. Be off with you now, this instant.'

Jumping out of bed he snatched up his chamber robe, and exclaimed in mock distress, 'You drive me from Paradise! How I'll live through the day I cannot think!'

She laughed. 'What a liar you are. You know full well that your mind will be filled with schemes to win over the Venetian. You'll not give me another thought till it's night again and time for us once more to essay a flight to Heaven. But the woman is not yet born who would not love your pretty speeches.'

Grinning, he blew her a kiss over his shoulder before disappearing into her boudoir. Beyond it, through another door, lay the room he always occupied when at Stillwaters. Having rumpled the sheets of the unslept-in bed, he got into it and lay down. As Georgina had predicted, his mind had already switched from her to the members of the house-party that had assembled there the previous afternoon. She had made no difficulty about asking Richard Brinsley Sheridan to bring down the Venetian envoy for the weekend, and both had come accompanied by their wives.

Roger had known Sheridan for some years and, much as he detested his politics, could not help liking him personally. The son of talented parents, the gifted Irishman had early achieved fame. At twenty-three, his play *The Rivals* had scored a great success, a few months later his opera *The Duenna* had taken the town by storm, and at twenty-five his *School for Scandal* had placed him among the immortals of the British stage. During the years that followed, as poet, playwright, producer, manager, and principal shareholder in Drury Lane, he had become the arbiter of London's theatrical world.

A little before he was thirty, realizing what an asset his quick brain and silver tongue could prove to their party, the Whig politicians had persuaded him to contest Stafford in their interests at the elections of 1780, and he had won the seat.

From his entry into Parliament he had given his unquestioning allegiance to Charles James Fox. Now, leading only a rump of Whigs who refused to join the Coalition formed for the better prosecution of the war, Fox was old, embittered and discredited; yet Sheridan continued to support him in his venomous attacks on the Prime Minister and near treasonable advocacy of the policies of the French revolutionaries. Even so, on other matters Sheridan was high-principled and full of good sense; while his fertile mind, charming manner and amusing conversation made him a delightful companion.

His first wife, Elizabeth Linley, had been a concert singer. Her great beauty and golden voice had brought her a score of rich suitors while still in her teens, but Sheridan, himself then only a few years out of Harrow, had won her heart, fought a duel on her behalf and carried her off to France. Their romantic elopement had proved the prelude to a marriage lasting eighteen years and, although towards its end he had caused her much pain by his unfaithfulness, her death from consumption had proved a terrible blow to him.

He was now forty-five, and a year earlier he had married another beauty —this time a daughter of the Dean of Winchester. They had bought the estate of Sir William Grey of Polesden, near Leatherhead, and, as it was only seven miles from Stillwaters, Georgina had ridden over several times to see them. She had told Roger that 'dear Sherry's new young wife was having the effect of an Elixir of Life on him' and, apart from the fact that his face had become very red from heavy drinking, Roger, now having met him again, fully endorsed her opinion.

The couple the Sheridans brought with them were so different from themselves that at first Roger was puzzled by their close association; but during the Friday evening he had learned that Signor Rinaldo Malderini was a rich backer of Venetian theatrical ventures, and that the two men had many mutual acquaintances in the international world of opera singers and ballet dancers.

They were, too, about of an age, but whereas Sheridan had a fine presence, lustrous laughing eyes, a sensitive mouth and well-cut features, the Venetian's appearance was so nondescript that one might have met him half a dozen times yet later failed to notice him in a crowd. He was a bulky man, although somewhat under middle height, deep chested and broad hipped. His complexion was pasty, his cheeks flabby and his face pudding-like, its only noticeable feature being the eyes. These were a pale grey under thick dark brows, and had a curious opaque quality which gave the impression that with them he could, while completely masking his own thoughts, read other people's.

His English was poor, but he spoke excellent French; so during the evening the company had used that language. As yet, Roger had had no chance to talk to him in private, but he had soon taken a strong dislike to him. Before the evening was out he had formed the impression that the Venetian was cruel, cunning and treacherous. He had never felt any enthusiasm for the task that Mr. Pitt had thrust upon him and now he was unhappily aware that having to deal with such a man would make it doubly difficult of accomplishment.

The two wives had proved as great a contrast as their husbands. Esther Sheridan was a typical product of a Cathedral Close; moderately intelligent and well-read, transparently honest and good tempered, good-looking above the average in an unmistakably English way, and still aglow with her own happiness as the young wife of a successful man whom she obviously adored.

The Signora Malderini—or, as her husband always referred to her, the Princess Sirīsha—was the still young daughter of an Indian Rajah. Her tall slim figure was accentuated by the beautiful silk sari she wore swathed tightly round it. The loose end of the garment practically covered her raven hair and in the centre of her broad forehead she had a caste mark. Her face was oval and the colour of pale coffee. In it, her dark almond-shaped eyes looked enormous and seemed to hold all the mystery of the Orient. But their expression was sad, and that was hardly to be wondered at, as she spoke not a word of any language other than her own, so was cut off from communication with everyone except her husband, and he rarely bothered to address her.

It was largely this which, despite Georgina's gifts as a hostess and Sheridan's inexhaustible fund of amusing anecdotes, had caused the Friday evening at Stillwaters to be a little less gay and carefree than was usual on such occasions. During dinner they had all been rendered vaguely uncomfortable by the presence of the silent Princess. She had eaten practically nothing and, apart from acknowledging with a pale smile the courtesies shown her by her neighbours, had played the part of a beautiful ghost at the feast.

A further awkwardness arose when the ladies had left the room. Although the other men had not noticed it, Malderini had, throughout the meal, refused all wine and he now declared himself to be a total abstainer. Such an eccentricity was most uncommon in those days, and almost in bad taste; for the other men felt that out of civility to Georgina's foreign guest they must forgo the pleasure of sitting over their port for any length of time. In consequence, although secretly a little disgruntled, they accepted without protest the lead of Colonel Thursby, Georgina's father, who broke up the session before the decanters were half empty.

At one end of the long drawing-room a table had been made ready for *Vingt et Un*. Georgina, realizing that the Princess would be unable to join in a card game, suggested taking her round the house and showing her some of its treasures. Her husband, through whom the proposal had to be put, had replied with a somewhat ungainly bow:

'I appreciate your Ladyship's thoughfulness, but in India women are brought up to have no other interests than their husbands and, if they have any, their children. That was one of my reasons for taking a wife while in the Orient. If we were still in the East the Princess Sirīsha would, of course, be living in purdah. While we are travelling in Europe that is not possible; but whenever we go into society she considers it her duty to remain at my side, and she derives much pleasure from watching me enjoy myself.'

All the ladies present were hard put to it to hide their shocked disapproval of his selfish attitude towards the lovely Indian girl; but even to show her their sympathy was not easy. Georgina sent Clarissa to fetch from the library some volumes with colour prints of birds and flowers for the Princess to look at, and the other eight members of the party settled themselves round the card table.

From it, two hours later, Rinaldo Malderini had risen the richer by a considerable number of English guineas, and Roger with a shrewd suspicion that the Venetian had detained his wife in the room for a reason he had naturally not given.

For the first hour or so the Princess had sat apparently absorbed in the books Clarissa had brought her; but she had then left Clarissa busily embroidering a pretty bonnet for little Susan and crossed the room to watch the game from behind her husband's chair. Had she remained there that would have given no cause for speculation about her conduct; but from time to time she had moved round the table and stood for a while behind whoever happened to be holding the bank.

Later that night, Roger had discussed the matter with his closest friend, the Lord Edward Fitz-Deverel—known to his intimates as 'Droopy Ned'. Neither of them had actually seen the Princess make a signal to her ugly husband but, such collaboration being the easiest form of cheating ever devised, they agreed it to be highly probable that the Venetian's having come out of the game by far the largest winner could be accounted for in that way.

Roger was somewhat cheered by the probability that the man with whom he had to deal systematically cheated at cards. Trickery in connection with games of chance was prevalent all over Europe. Even in the highest circles it was not unusual; but it could definitely be taken as a sign of an avaricious and unscrupulous nature.

It went without saying that, from whichever side Malderini favoured in his report to the Senate of the Serene Republic, he would expect a substantial present of money. That was a recognized perquisite of any ambassador; but in most cases envoys accepted such gratuities only for recommending a policy that they had convinced themselves was in the best interests of their country. Here, though, was a case in which it seemed that an envoy's greed might induce him to accept a heavy bribe to advise his government without searching his conscience too closely about possible results.

That suited Roger, and he was still deliberating on the size of his opening bid to win the Venetian over when there came a knock on the door. At his call to 'Come in', Edgar, the footman who had been valeting him during his stay at Stillwaters, entered the room carrying two large cans of hot water. Having told him what clothes to put out, Roger got up, shaved, washed, dressed and went down to breakfast.

Only Colonel Thursby was seated at the table. He was a spare, ageing man of kindly disposition and high intelligence. On his retirement from the Corps of Engineers, his faith in the future of machines had enabled him to make a considerable fortune during the Industrial Revolution. He had long been a widower and Georgina was his only child. They adored one another and, although he had two houses of his own, he had for several years past become almost a permanent resident in hers. Roger had a great affection for him and, as he helped himself to a Dover sole from the long array of tempting dishes on the sideboard, they dropped into easy conversation.

'Really,' remarked the Colonel, 'what induced Georgina to ask this Venetian here I cannot think! He has the appearance of an overblown woman who was born ugly, follows some hypochondriac régime which makes it embarrassing for other people to do justice to their wine, and treats that charming young Indian wife of his little better than if she were a slave.'

'I fear I am to blame, Sir,' Roger admitted. 'It was at my request that Georgina asked Sheridan to bring him down. Never having met him I had no idea that he was such a monster; but, between us two, Mr. Pitt asked me to get to know him and endeavour to prise him from the clutches of the Whigs.'

The Colonel's thin face broke into a smile. 'What an intriguer you are, my dear boy. But I know that you serve your master well, so I'll grumble no more at having to support the company of this curiously uncouth Italian. Yours is the harder part, by far, and I commiserate with you upon it. Fortunately I am more than compensated this weekend by the presence here of so charming and erudite a guest as Mr. Beckford.'

He had hardly ceased speaking when Droopy Ned and William Beckford entered the room.

Droopy owed his nickname to shortsightedness, his constant peering having given him a permanent stoop. He was the second son of the Marquis of Amesbury, and something of an eccentric. His foppish clothes and lazy manner gave a first impression that he was a nit-wit, but under them he concealed an extremely shrewd brain. He was considered an authority on ancient religions, had written several monographs on the effects of Eastern drugs, and owned an unrivalled collection of antique jewellery.

Beckford was a millionaire, and the richest commoner in England. Orphaned at the age of ten, his upbringing had been supervised by the great Earl of Chatham, who had chosen the ablest tutors for him; among them Sir William Chambers to teach him architecture and Mozart to teach him music. No youth could have made better use of such opportunities. When twenty he had published his first book *Biographical Memoirs of Extraordinary Painters*. Its subjects rejoiced in such names as Og of Basan and Sucrewasser of Vienna. They had, of course, never existed, and the book was actually a satire on the Dutch and Flemish schools; but so skilfully was it done that many people who posed as being knowledgeable about art were at first hoaxed into accepting it as a serious work. Inspired by the Arabian Nights, he had followed it up with *Vathek*, which was destined to become one of the classics of the English language.

He was a dark good-looking man, now thirty-five. Until two years earlier he had lived mainly abroad, and at times travelled with so many servants that on one occasion he had been taken for the young Emperor of Austria. He was a passionate collector of all things rare or beautiful, and also an omnivorous reader. Having purchased Gibbon's library he had shut himself up at Lausanne for the best part of a year in order that he might read the whole of it. Such prolonged withdrawals from society had given him the reputation of a misanthrope, but the fact was that with such great wealth he needed nobody's patronage, so had the sense to do as he liked; and he was exceedingly particular in the choice of his friends.

His splendid country home, Fonthill, was no great distance from Normanrood, the seat of Droopy Ned's father, and one chance meeting between these two eccentrics had disclosed that they had many interests in common, including a hatred of all blood sports. Largely on that account, Beckford rarely visited at country houses, but Droopy had brought him down to Stillwaters to see Georgina's paintings; for since being widowed she had again taken up her hobby, and during the past year had produced several canvases which were decidedly original in construction and colouring.

One of Beckford's characteristics was an intense impatience to press on with any matter that happened to be occupying his mind; so, as he seated himself at the table, he said to Colonel Thursby, 'Can you inform me, Sir, when the rest of the party will be down?'

'I cannot speak for Signor Malderini,' replied the Colonel, 'but few foreigners are hearty trenchermen in the morning, so 'tis probable that he'll take a continental breakfast in his room. As for Dick Sheridan, he may send for a draught of ale or a decanter of Madeira, but he never joins the company before midday.'

''Twas of the ladies I was thinking, Sir; for now we have the morning light, I'm all eagerness to see Lady St. Ermins's paintings.'

The Colonel smiled. 'My daughter, Sir, is apt to take an unconscionable time with her toilette, so I much doubt if we can count on seeing her, either, until the morning is well advanced.'

Having piled a plate high with kedgeree and poured himself a glass of claret, Droopy looked across at Roger, gave him a mischievous grin, then said to Beckford, 'Mr. Brook has been staying here for some while, and when he does so Lady St. Ermins always shares her studio with him. Until her Ladyship appears he would, I am sure, be delighted to give us his views on art and a sight of his latest masterpiece.'

'Fie, Ned! Shame on you!' Roger exclaimed. 'You know well enough . . .'

'So, Mr. Brook, you too are a painter?' Beckford cut in with quick interest.

'Nay; I'm nought but the veriest tyro, Sir. And then only for brief intervals between long periods when other matters leave me no leisure to ruin canvas.'

'Such modesty becomes you, Sir; but I'd wager that you are belittling your talents.'

'It is the truth,' Roger assured him. 'Even had I, like Lady St. Ermins, had the advantage of studying under Mr. Gainsborough and Sir Joshua Reynolds, I could never have entered her class.'

Beckford raised his straight dark eyebrows. 'I find it surprising that those rival masters should have been willing to give instruction to the same pupil.'

'In this instance, their rivalry was over who could do the most for her,' Roger laughed. 'I'd not impugn their honour by suggesting that it was a case of Susanna and the Elders; but it was not unnatural that two old gentlemen who had long since won wealth and fame should both find a new interest in imparting their knowledge to such a lovely and talented young woman.'

'Of your own painting, though,' the Colonel remarked, 'you have no reason to be ashamed. I thought the portrait you have done from memory of Queen Marie Antoinette, as she was while still living at Versailles, an excellent likeness.'

With eager interest Beckford again looked across at Roger. 'You knew that lovely but ill-fated Queen, then?'

'I did, Sir. Her Majesty honoured me with her friendship, and I saw her with some frequency both before and after she was imprisoned.'

'I, too, continued to visit Paris up till '93, and I was present at both the taking of the Bastille and the execution of King Louis.'

This exchange led to their swapping memories of the Revolution during the remainder of the meal. Then, when all four men had dealt fairly with the selection of chops and kidneys, eggs and sausages, York ham, steak pie and galantines, Colonel Thursby said:

'As Georgina will not be down yet awhile, I suggest we should take a look at Roger's picture, then go round those in the house.'

There was a murmur of assent. Picking up his ebony cane, he led the way, limping a little, to the Studio. There the portrait was duly praised, then they began a tour of the Van Dykes, Lelys and Knellers; but Roger slipped away, intending to go to the nurseries.

As he walked through the long corridors his thoughts turned to Clarissa Marsham. She was a cousin of his late wife, Amanda, and an orphan without fortune. Until a little less than two years earlier, she had lived with an elderly, impecunious and sanctimonious aunt, from which sad fate Amanda had rescued her, and taken her with them as an unofficial lady-in-waiting when he had gone out to the West Indies as Governor-designate of Martinique.

From a gawky girl with a thin face, beaky nose and mass of ill-dressed pale gold hair, he had seen her develop into a young woman of sylph-like figure and ravishing beauty. On two occasions she had declared her love for him in no uncertain terms. He had tried to persuade himself that hers was an adolescent passion, and that she would soon get over it; so he had done his utmost to discourage her, hoping that she would turn to one of the numerous suitors who were eager for her hand. But deep down he had known that she would not do so.

Now that she had returned to England something had to be settled about her future. So far he had managed to avoid discussing it with her, and he was most loath to do so because he found her so bewitching that he feared he might weaken in his determination to keep his freedom.

He was still pondering the worrying problem she presented when he entered the main hall and went up the stairs.

On reaching the landing he saw Signor Malderini and his beautiful Indian wife coming towards him. Instantly he dismissed Clarissa from his mind and decided to postpone his morning call on the children. With Sheridan out of the way for another hour at least, this was too good an opportunity to be missed of sounding the Venetian about his opinions.

Having made a graceful leg to the Princess, he enquired of her husband how they had slept and if all their wants had been attended to. Then he said that, as a guest of long standing in the house, they must allow him temporarily to play host and show them something of its beauties.

Malderini thanked him for his courtesy and the three of them descended the great marble staircase together; but, instead of taking them into any of the rooms, where they might shortly have run into the other party, Roger led them out between the tall pillars of the Palladian portico and down its steps onto the long terrace. The stone vases along it were gay with flowers and below the balustrade the well-tended lawns sloped gently away to a broad lake, from the far shore of which rose woods of silver birch and pine. In the sunshine of the June morning it was as lovely a prospect as could have been found in England.

The vases were filled with many-hued Phlox Drummondi and, pointing at the nearest, Malderini made some remark to his wife in her own language She returned a low-voiced reply, then he said to Roger, 'The Princess Sirisha has a great fondness for flowers. Her name, you know, is that of a particularly beautiful flower that grows in her native country.'

'Indeed,' replied Roger. 'Then let us go to the rose garden and the herbaceous borders. We'll visit the hot-houses too. They contain many tropical plants and the Princess may find there several with which she is familiar.'

As they strolled through the gardens to the west of the house, pausing now and then to admire a vista between box hedges, a fountain, a lead figure, or some specially lovely bed of flowers, Roger made no attempt to turn the conversation to the state of things in Italy. After a quarter of an hour it struck him that he might be shirking the job because it meant working against his own convictions, but he quickly reassured himself, as it was obviously sounder policy to endeavour first to get on terms with the Venetian. That would not be easy, for his heavy features held no trace of bonhomie, and his curious mind-probing eyes no hint of desire to make himself liked. Even so, given a little time, there was every reason to suppose that in the course of conversation he would make some remark about the war, and so provide a natural opening. It was, after all, only Saturday morning, and that strengthened Roger's feeling that there was no hurry yet to grasp the ugly nettle.

They spent a further twenty minutes in a leisurely progress round the glasshouses. Malderini proved very knowledgeable about plants and his conversation with Roger disclosed a quick, well-ordered mind—another depressing indication that, when they did get to business, he would prove a hard nut to crack. To his wife he scarcely said a word and she never spoke unless first addressed by him. Roger felt deeply sorry for her but could do no more than give her an occasional friendly smile. More and more he wished the weekend over and that, having done his best for Mr. Pitt, he would never be called on to set eyes on Rinaldo Malderini again.

It was shortly after they had entered the orchid house that they caught sight of one of Georgina's footmen, and another man, hurrying towards them. The footman pointed Roger out, then the other, who wore a plain riding livery, came through the glass door, removed his hat and, taking a letter from a leather pouch at his waist, handed it to Roger. A glance at the seal showed him that it was from the Prime Minister. With a word of apology to his companions, he tore it open and ran his eye over the single paragraph. It read:

If you have not yet opened the business with Signor R. M. refrain from doing so. I have just learnt that, contrary to my expectations, after spending three weeks as a private person in the other camp, he accompanied his ambassador to the Foreign Office on Friday morning and presented credentials as a Plenipotentiary Extraordinary. Now that my cousin, Grenville, is in a position to put our cards on the table openly, I shall have no further need of you as intermediary. W.P.

Malderini coughed and remarked politely, 'I trust that this urgent message does not contain bad news.'

'The very contrary,' Roger laughed. 'For a friend I had undertaken a most uncongenial task, and one which I was convinced would cost him a lot of money to no good purpose. He writes me now that he relieves me of it; so I could not be more delighted.'

Thrusting the letter into his pocket, he gave expression to his pleasure by dismissing the messenger with a guinea, then cutting some of Georgina's choicest orchids and, with a bow, laying them in the slim brown hands of the Princess.

But he was wrong in his belief that now he would never have cause to remember the ugly Venetian and the beautiful Indian except as the most casual acquaintances, and that he would not be called on to play any further part in the affairs of Venice. Fate, in the person of Mr. Pitt, had woven the first tenuous thread that had brought the three of them together. It was soon to coil and strengthen into a terrible bond that would alter the whole course of their lives, and a time was to come when Roger would hold the fate of the thousand-years-old Serene Republic in the hollow of his hand.

CHAPTER THREE

A Very Strange Performance

THAT afternoon Georgina took her guests into Guildford. The drive
through the well-wooded countryside made a pleasant excursion,
and it had occurred to her that with such difficult guests as the
Malderinis a visit to Guildford caves would serve to while away an hour or
so. The caves were a natural formation but had been occupied by primitive
man from great antiquity.

Provided with a candle apiece and led by a guide, they traversed the
narrow tunnels and halted in the larger chambers, a little awed by the
weird effects of their shadows on the rough hewn walls and ceilings. When
they were assembled in the largest cave there came a sudden sharp cry. It
was uttered by Sheridan's wife as her husband, bored with the caves,
had decided to lighten the solemnity which had descended on the party by
pinching her bottom.

The dim light hid her blushes, but much embarrassed she stammered
out, 'I . . . I thought I felt a ghostly hand touch my cheek.'

Malderini, who was standing near her, shook his head and, speaking
in French as usual, declared in his rather high-pitched voice, 'Maybe it
was so, Madame. If you are psychic you may well have felt the touch of
the long-dead in such a place as this. Yours was not the only cry that I
have heard these past few minutes. The despairing screams of virgins
being dragged to the sacrifice still echo round the walls. I have but to look
at yonder archway to see the bearded priests with their long knives and
the terror on the faces of their victims.'

'I take it, Sir, that you are drawing on your imagination to supplement
your theories as an antiquary about what may have taken place here,'
remarked Colonel Thursby, drily.

Malderini turned sharply upon him. 'Not at all! Not at all! Certain
people have the power to see beyond the veil, and I am one of them. Given
propitious circumstances I can both look back into the past and foresee
the future.'

Georgina, on her mother's side, had gipsy blood, and had inherited the
gift of telling fortunes. She said to the Venetian: 'I, too, have often secured
accurate glimpses of the future, but seen outside their context such glimpses
can, at times, be pestiferously misleading.'

'More frequent practice should enable your Ladyship to assess their meaning with greater accuracy. What vehicle do you use to make contact with the unseen powers?'

'I used to gaze into a goblet filled with pure spring water; but, some years ago, I suffered an experience with regard to my own future which was so unnerving that I decided to abandon such seeking after hidden knowledge.'

'Few decisions could be harder to justify,' Malderini replied somewhat rudely. 'Psychic gifts are rare and should be cherished by those who have them. You should renew your contact with the spirit-world and would be well advised to do so through a human medium. I studied in Paris under the famous Doctor Mesmer and learned from him how to turn the minds of others into far more potent vehicles than crystals, cards, and such impedimenta. It is a fundamental of the Secret Art that all occult operations require the exertion of will, and you would find your powers greatly increased if you brought under your control the subconscious mind of some lesser personality.'

'You speak as though you would have us believe you to be a magician,' Sheridan said in a slightly mocking tone.

'If, my friend, by that designation you imply a person who by will-power can cause phenomena to occur which are ordinarily regarded as impossible, then I may certainly claim to be one.'

'My daughter has compelled me to recognize that some people are gifted with second sight,' the Colonel remarked, 'but I still cannot believe it possible to bring about material happenings solely through the exercise of will, even if given the help of the Devil.'

'Then, Sir, it is high time that someone showed you to be in error,' the Venetian retorted, 'and if you wish, on our return to Stillwaters, I will prove my point by a demonstration.'

'You shall, Sir, by all means,' replied the Colonel quickly. 'I have ever taken the greatest interest in all forms of science, and surely the moving of mountains, or even of molehills, without application of physical force, must be counted a scientific triumph.'

No more was said on the subject at the time, but they had hardly descended from the carriages before Beckford raised it again by saying, 'I can hardly contain my impatience to witness the demonstration that Signor Malderini has promised us. When and where is it to take place?'

'Without preparations of an involved nature, and an opportunity to refresh my memory on certain rituals, it can be no more than a simple one,' replied the Venetian, 'but that I will give you whenever and wherever you wish.'

Georgina was loath to pursue the matter. She had an uneasy feeling that no good would come of it; but, in view of Beckford's eagerness and that others in the party were backing him up, she had little option; so she said, 'Now that we are returned, a syllabub will shortly be served in the Orangery for our refreshment. Let us go there and drink it while Signor Malderini performs his promised marvels.'

In the lofty Orangery a semi-circle of basket chairs was set among the brass-bound tubs in which grew the bushes with their small, unripe, but decorative fruit. Malderini asked for some slips of paper to be brought, then, as they sipped from their cups of well-iced wine beaten up with thick cream, he said:

'Four or five of you will oblige me by writing questions on these pieces of paper. They must be questions the answers to which might reasonably be supposed to come within my knowledge. I shall then mesmerize the Princess Sirīsha and, when her mind has become completely under my control, put your questions to her. As you are aware, in her normal state she has the unhappiness to be deprived of the pleasure of conversing with you because she can speak no tongue other than her own. But, while she is in a state of trance, I shall imbue her with powers which she does not ordinarily possess. Having written your questions add to them the word French, English, Italian or German, and she will give you the answer in whichever language you have selected.'

There was a subdued murmuring as the papers were passed round. Colonel Thursby, Beckford, Sheridan, his wife, and Droopy Ned all wrote out questions. Malderini glanced through them and agreed them to be reasonable ones, then he led his wife to a vacant chair at one end of the semi-circle, stepped a few paces back from her, and asked that complete silence should be observed. As the hush fell, he lifted his plump, heavily be-ringed hands, and began to make a succession of slow complicated passes in front of his wife's face.

After a few minutes her eyelids drooped and closed, her breathing became irregular, her limbs jerked spasmodically and her head rolled about on her shoulders. Suddenly she became rigid, remained so for several moments, then as suddenly relaxed. She gave a heavy sigh and sat up. Her eyes opened again but they now held only a blank stare.

Taking one of the papers from his pocket, Malderini gave her in her own language a translation of the question written upon it. There was a tense moment while the muscles of her throat contracted and her mouth opened and shut soundlessly, as though in a desperate but futile effort to speak; then the words came, slowly at first but coherently, and in Italian she gave a perfectly sensible answer to the question.

The Venetian repeated the process with the other questions and to each she replied in the language requested on the paper. Her English and German were noticeably less good than her Italian and French, but Malderini had clearly implied that the power with which he intended to imbue her came from himself; so it was natural that her vocabulary in these languages should be limited to his own.

It was a most impressive performance and, when the last question had been answered, Clarissa exclaimed, 'How truly marvellous! Could you, Signor, perform such miracles with any of us?'

Malderini regarded her fixedly for a moment, then he shook his head. 'Not with anyone, Signorina. I need to be in close *rapport* with my subject. But, with people who are psychic, such a bond is not difficult to form, and I can tell at a glance anyone who would prove a suitable subject.'

'May one ask how?'

'By their aura. It was not without reason that the old Masters always depicted the Saints with golden haloes. All of us carry with us such an indication of our basic characteristics, as auras vary in colour. Those of born warriors are bright red, those for whom all things grow readily, apple-green. A yellow aura denotes a religious nature and a magenta aura a person given over to evil.'

'Do you really mean that you can see such auras—that we have them now, about our heads, at the present moment?'

'Yes; with what is termed "the third eye". That is the focal point of psychic perception, and it lies beneath the bone in the centre of the forehead. Everyone has it but in most people it is rudimentary. Very few develop it, as I have done by long training, to a state at which I can use it consciously. Both Lady Georgina's aura and yours are blue, indicating the possession of psychic qualities. Hers is the stronger but, with either of you, I could, in quite a short while, establish a *rapport*.'

Clarissa's blue eyes lit up. 'I find the subject fascinating. Would it be asking too much that before you leave Stillwaters you will experiment upon me?'

He bowed. 'If you will later name a time and place, I shall be happy to do so, Signorina. But now I must arouse the Princess Sirīsha from her trance.'

Roger had watched the proceedings with a jaundiced eye. His conviction that the Venetian had made use of his wife the previous evening to swindle them at cards filled him with a lively suspicion that this was another case of secret collaboration between the couple; yet he had to admit to himself that the whole procedure had followed the pattern of a skilled mesmerist operating on a medium. In any case, having seen exhibitions of hypnotism by disciples of Dr. Mesmer in Paris, and on one occasion a woman who, while in a trance, had made a shocking spectacle of herself by writhing about in what were obviously erotic paroxysms, he was fully determined to prevent Clarissa exposing herself to anything of that kind.

He pondered the matter further while Malderini made the passes necessary to bring the Princess back to normal, and it struck him that as the Venetian had spoken to her throughout in her own language, although he appeared to have been giving her only a translation of the written questions, he might instead quite well have been furnishing her with the answers she should make to them. But that did not account for the fact that she had given the answers in four languages of which she was supposed to be entirely ignorant. That meant that, if a deception had been practised, she was as fluent in them as Malderini himself; and it was difficult to believe that if she could speak them she deliberately cut herself off from communication with everyone except her husband, solely to be able to aid him in occasional hoaxes such as this. Furthermore it did not appear, at first sight, that the couple had anything to gain by practising this type of deception.

That amicable but hardened materialist, Colonel Thursby, also had his suspicions. When the Princess had fully recovered, he said in Italian: 'We all owe you our thanks, Signora, for having aided your husband in his demonstration.'

He had hoped that by a spontaneous reply she would give herself away, but her face remained expressionless. Not even a slight movement of her lips suggested that she had been near falling into the trap.

Malderini turned angrily on the Colonel: 'You know very well, Sir, that in her normal state my wife understands no language but her own. And I resent your use of the word " aided". She was no more than an unconscious instrument of which I made use to display my powers.'

'Your pardon, Signor; your pardon.' The older man waved an airy hand. 'Having but a few moments back heard her speak Italian with such fluency, I had temporarily forgot that she was not one. As for my use of the word "aided", I meant only to thank her for having allowed you to throw her into a fit so that you might attempt to prove your assertions.'

'Attempt!' repeated Malderini. 'Again, Sir, you are ambiguous. Do you suggest that I have failed to do so?'

'You can hardly claim to have brought about the seemingly impossible by the sole use of your will-power.'

'How else do you suggest that the Princess Sirīsha was able to speak in tongues unknown to her, and reply to questions normally beyond the range of her knowledge, except as a puppet animated by my will?'

'There are other ways in which . . .'

'Papa!' Georgina interrupted anxiously. 'I pray you carry this discussion no further.'

'Oh, come!' countered Beckford. 'Surely your Ladyship will not insist on our terminating so promising a debate.'

'I was about to say,' went on the Colonel, 'that it would ill become me to challenge the integrity of my daughter's guest; but, as a scientific man, my conscience permits me to go no further than adopt a course at times resorted to by the Scottish Courts. That is to declare that I must continue to regard the existence of occult power as—"Not proven." '

Malderini hunched his bulky shoulders and glared at the Colonel. 'You have said either too much or too little, Sir. You must either withdraw your implication or frankly accuse me of having used ventriloquism to deceive you.'

For Georgina's sake, Roger stepped quickly into the breach. In the honeyed accents of sweet reason, he said: 'You are mistaken Signor. Colonel Thursby implied only what, I think, several of us feel. Astounding as your demonstration has been, its nature was not of the kind we expected. There was, I recall, some talk of moving mountains or molehills, solely by the use of will-power, and you must agree that we have not been witnesses to a substitution of will-power for physical force.'

'Well said,' murmured Droopy Ned, and Beckford chimed in, 'I, too, am of that opinion.'

'Ladies and Gentlemen'—the Venetian made a slight bow to the company in general. He seemed to have suddenly become quite amiable again—'I must admit there is something to be said for the point Mr. Brook has made. Very well. I am prepared to give you proof that will-power can be substituted for physical force. You will no doubt have heard of levitation, as practised by the mystics of India. If, while standing at some distance from the Princess Sirīsha, I can cause her to leave the ground and cross a room without visible means of support, I take it you will acknowledge my claim to occult power?'

There was a nodding of heads and excited murmur of assent; then he went on: 'To perform such an operation is no light undertaking. I must spend several hours preparing myself, and to fast before it is essential. If it is to take place tonight the Princess Sirīsha and I must deny ourselves the pleasure of dining with you. Moreover, I feel that I am entitled to some compensation for the doubts which some of you have cast on my powers.' Turning to Colonel Thursby, he added: 'What will you wager me that I prove unable to carry out this undertaking?'

'Providing we can agree conditions,' the Colonel replied, 'anything in reason. Would a hundred guineas suit you?'

Malderini shrugged, 'I had been told, Sir, that you were a rich man, and I have ample funds. The sum you suggest is a paltry one.'

Taking a pinch of snuff, Colonel Thursby flicked the spilt grains from his cravat with a lace handkerchief, and said casually, 'Make it five hundred if you wish.'

'I'd be happy to share the stake,' said Beckford eagerly.

'And I,' nodded Droopy Ned, raising his quizzing glass.

'I will take each of you for that sum, in addition to my five hundred with Colonel Thursby,' Malderini replied to them with a confident smile.

Sheridan's red face had been getting still redder with suppressed excitement. Suddenly he burst out, 'I, too, must be in on this. 'Tis a feat unheard of outside travellers' tales. I'll stake five hundred that you'll not succeed in it.'

His young wife threw him an agonized glance. Her parents had been most averse to her marrying a man of Sheridan's reputation and more than double her age. As a condition, they had stipulated that he should produce fifteen thousand pounds to be tied up with five thousand that had been previously settled on her, believing that he could not possibly lay his hands on such a sum. To their consternation he had managed to do so; but the whole of the jointure had since gone into the property at Polesden and, large as his income was, his unbridled extravagance kept them perpetually hard up. But he was an inveterate gambler, and now ignored her silent appeal not to join in the wager.

Malderini took his bet, then looked at Roger. 'And you, Mr. Brook?'

Roger shook his head. The canniness inherited from his Scottish mother had saved him from the vice of gambling, and he rarely risked money on chance, except for comparatively modest sums at friendly games of cards. With a bow, he said:

'I thank you, no. The two thousand guineas already wagered should surely be sufficient to compensate you for missing your dinner. And someone must act as an unprejudiced observer to ensure that the conditions agreed are correctly carried out. Let that be my part.'

There ensued a discussion on conditions. Malderini asked that a room should be entirely cleared of furniture, that its walls should be stripped of pictures, and any chandelier taken down from its ceiling; then that its floor should be swept clean of every particle of dust. Later, he conceded that sufficient chairs for the party should be brought back into the room, but he was adamant on the point that the curtains of the windows must be drawn and no artificial light allowed. He stated that the Princess would wear a pure white sari, and they could not contest his argument that, as it was high summer, the light filtering between the drawn curtains would still be ample for them to follow her movements. He stipulated that in no circumstances should anyone attempt to touch her, and protested that, without undergoing a fast of several days' duration, he could not expect to raise her more than about nine inches from the ground. But he agreed to remain at least three feet distant from her throughout, and was prepared to accept Roger, Georgina and Clarissa as judges. Finally, it was settled that if two of the judges were satisfied that, while travelling three yards in a straight line, from right to left in front of them, the Princess's feet had been clear of the floor, he should be declared the winner of the wager.

Georgina said she thought the small yellow drawing-room would be the most suitable place to hold the séance, then she asked Roger, as one of the umpires, to give the necessary instructions to the servants and later assure himself that they had been fully carried out. Soon afterwards the party broke up, and dispersed to rest or to write letters until it was time to get themselves ready for dinner.

Having found the groom of the chambers and given him his orders, Roger decided that he would pay his postponed visit to the children; so he made his way upstairs and along the East Wing which, after years of disuse, had, with the advent of the baby Earl, become again a hive of activity.

The day-nursery was large enough for a dozen children to romp in, yet on Roger's entering it the room seemed quite crowded. The two babies had just been brought in from their afternoon airing and each was having its outer garments removed by its own nursemaid. A smiling mulatto woman who had acted as foster-mother to little Susan since her birth was preparing to give her the breast, and near one of the windows plump, bustling Nanny Bellows, who ruled this domain with a rod of iron, was discussing some point of infant régime with Clarissa.

All five women stopped what they were doing as Roger came in, and bobbed him a curtsey, but the moment Mrs. Bellows straightened up she shook an admonitory finger at him. 'I've told you afore, Sir, this is no time to come pestering my little ones. It's in the morning you must make your visits, or when they've woke up from their sleep in the afternoon; not when we're getting them ready to have their suppers.'

Mr. Pitt's despatch, having relieved Roger of all responsibility in the Venetian business, had put him in a high good humour. With a laugh, he cried, 'It's not them I come to see, but you. Surely you must know that.' Then he threw an arm about her shoulders and gave her a resounding kiss on her apple-red cheek.

'For shame, Mr. Brook!' she exclaimed, torn between a desire to laugh with him and to preserve her dignity in front of the grinning maids. 'One day you'll have to answer for such taradiddles; and to put wrong ideas into the heads of these lazy baggages is no way for a gentleman to behave.'

'Forgive me, Nanny,' he smiled. ''Twas no fault of mine that my visit was delayed. I'll do no more than wish them good appetite, then relieve you of my presence.'

'Be quick about it, then. What an outcry you would make did a clowning bear break in on you while sitting over your port of an evening; but for the babes 'tis every bit as bad a thing that you should peer and posture at them just before their meal.'

Roger went first to his daughter. She was just six months old, a fine healthy child, with his blue eyes and Amanda's auburn hair, which gave her a good prospect of beauty. But she was a solemn little thing, and when he chucked her gently under the chin she gave no more than the suggestion of a smile.

He turned to his godson. The ten-months-old Earl of St. Ermins was a sturdy fellow, and with a tipsy rush of feet could already stagger a few paces unaided. Like Georgina and his father he was dark, and from them he had inherited both gipsy blood and that of King Charles II. The combination almost certainly predestined him to become a rake, but Roger felt that to be no great matter for concern, provided that the boy also inherited the good humour, generosity and sound common sense of his mother and his royal ancestor. He already gave signs of a merry nature, for when prodded in the stomach he uttered gurgles of delight and gamely strove to clutch at Roger's offending finger.

Clarissa laid a hand on Roger's arm. 'Please Roger! Desist, I beg. If you excite him so he'll not be able to keep down his supper.'

'Very well, then'—he turned to smile at her—'but what are you doing in Nanny Bellows's domain?'

'I still count myself responsible for Susan,' she replied quickly, 'and about that I'd like speech with you, when you have the leisure.'

In his more cheerful mood, he now felt that he might as well get the interview over that he had been shirking; so he said: 'I am at your disposal now, Ma'am, if you wish.'

'I'm mightily obliged, Sir;' she lowered her eyes, and added, 'In that case, let us leave the children to be fed and bedded.'

After a word or two with Nanny Bellows, she led the way from the room and Roger, giving a gay little wave which included all the nurses, followed. Side by side they walked away from the nursery regions, then along a broad corridor. Suddenly Clarissa threw open a door and signed to him to pass her. Till then, he had had no idea whereabouts in the house she slept, but this was obviously her bedroom. Before he had time to turn she had given him a push and closed the door behind them.

'M'dear!' he protested lightly, as he turned to face her. 'Is it really necessary to compromise yourself like this? Strap me! Despite the fact that you are looked on much as though you were my niece, tongues would wag mightily did it become known that we'd chosen your bedroom as a place to talk in.'

She was probably unconscious of it, but the dark mahogany of the door against which she stood made a perfect background for her. The pale gold hair fell in heavy ringlets on one side of her oval face. The purity of her milk-and-roses complexion was almost dazzling in the strong light thrown from the window opposite. Her arrogant little nose stood out imperiously above her tilted chin and long slender throat. Beneath the crossed fichus of her bodice, the corset that gave her an absurdly small waist, and the voluminous skirts of sprigged muslin, was a figure that Roger knew to be perfection; for less than six months earlier he had seen her naked.

''Tis the only place in which we can talk with certainty that we'll not be interrupted,' she said quickly.

'And what,' he enquired with a lift of the eyebrow, 'is there in a discussion about my little Susan that demands such privacy?'

'Susan is concerned in this—deeply concerned. Her future well-being may depend on it. But that is not all. Tell me honestly, Roger. Are you in love with Georgina?'

'No more and no less than I was when I first knew her, as a boy; no more and no less than I will be on the day I die.'

'That, then, is a thing apart. It proved no barrier to your marrying Amanda; so should prove none to your marrying again.'

'Not if I had the desire to do so. But I have not.'

Her mouth began to work, betraying her acute agitation. Suddenly she burst out. 'I know it to be unmaidenly! I am utterly ashamed! But since you will not speak of this, I must. Amanda gave your child into my care. Only by invoking the law can you take her from me. It was Amanda's dying wish that we . . . that I . . . that you. . . . Oh, Roger, can we not make a home for Susan together?'

'M'dear,' Roger said gently, 'deeply honoured as I am by your continued attachment to me, I had hoped that our six months' separation would have caused you to feel differently. We went into all this shortly after poor Amanda's death. I told you then that I'd prove a most diappointing husband to you. For one thing, I am too old, and for another . . .'

'Too old!' she interrupted scornfully. 'What nonsense! You are but twenty-eight, and I'm near twenty.'

'I do not mean in years, but mentally. The life I've led this dozen years past, the deceits I have been forced to practise, the sometimes terrible decisions I've had to take, the cynicism engendered by a roving existence in which many women have played a part, all make me unfitted to take a young bride and bring lasting happiness to her.'

'Roger, I'd take you at your word, but for one thing. When I came to your room that night in Martinique, you at first spurned me; yet later, in the dawn, you declared me to be the loveliest thing you had ever looked upon, and vowed that when I'd been married for a while you'd seize on the first chance to seduce me.'

'I admit it; although I added that I'd attempt to only did your marriage prove an unhappy one. Yet I was a fool even to say so much, and did so mainly from an urge to restore your self-respect. I'd have done better to maintain that your beauty left me cold. Then you might by now be married. You were the toast of the Island, and could have taken your pick of the young officers in the garrison or a score of wealthy planters. That you should have thrown these chances away, and continue to be obsessed with a passion for anyone so unworthy as myself, fills me with acute distress.'

''Tis no fault of yours, and I have no regrets. Yet I resent it that you

think me good enough only to become the wife of some young captain
whose dearest wish was to get back to England so that he might once more
enjoy his fox-hunting; or that I would demean myself to become a rich
man's darling. I care not how many women you've slept with; or how
often your secret work has forced you to lie and cheat. To me you are still
worth all the other men I've ever met put together. Amanda did me a great
kindness in rescuing me from a poverty-stricken existence with my Aunt; but,
unwittingly, she also sealed my fate. Although I did my utmost to conceal
it while she was alive, from the very day we met my heart became yours.'

'Clarissa! I beg you to say no more,' Roger protested unhappily. 'Did I
intend to marry again, it would be you I'd ask; for you have much more than
beauty. I'll never forget the high courage you displayed during those dark
days when we were captives of the pirates, and later of the revolted negro
slaves in San Domingo. But in due course I shall go abroad again, and in
circumstances which would make it impossible for me to take a wife with
me. I may be away from England, except for rare brief visits to report to
Mr. Pitt, for years. What sort of a life could that be for you?

'There is no question of your returning to your Aunt. Georgina has told
me that she is more than willing for you to make your home here, and if
you are set on being a mother to little Susan, I'll be greatly in your debt.
But I insist that you should not regard the child as a tie upon you. As I
promised, I have arranged with my bankers to make you a suitable allowance; so you are free at any time to live where you will and, should you
marry, Georgina will do for Susan what you would otherwise have done.
Here, at Stillwaters, you will meet many men; not captains with little but
their pay, or men of fortune with little but their money, to recommend
them. They will be of the stamp of Beckford and Droopy Ned. Wealthy,
cultured, ambitious, titled, and able to give you the position in the world
that you deserve. I beg you to put me from your thoughts, and face life
anew with an open mind.'

For a moment there was a tense silence, then Roger added, 'This
obstinacy can bring you nought but unhappiness. I have done my
utmost to dissuade you from it, but since you are adamant and I am too,
it seems there is no point in discussing it further. That being so, I request
your permission to leave your presence.'

With a sigh, she stood away from the door. 'Go then, and I beg of you
do not despise me too much for having laid my heart bare to you once
again. I'd not have done so could I have found some more material way in
which to show my love for you.'

Touched to the depths, he could think of no words with which to reply;
so, stooping, he took between his fingers the frilled hem of her overskirt,
bowed his head low, and kissed it. Then, silently, he left the room.

CHAPTER FOUR

The Séance

DINNER proved a much gayer meal than it had the previous evening. From the walls of the lofty, panelled room, the gilt-framed old masters looked down on the bare shoulders of the three lovely silk-clad women and the five more soberly dressed men. Although it was still daylight outside, the rich brocade curtains had been drawn; so the candle-light made the women look even more alluring, threw up the spotless linen at the men's throats and wrists, and glinted warmly on the fine silver, glass and china that furnished the mahogany table.

Relieved of the presence of the silent Princess and her uncongenial husband, the talk flowed freely with frequent laughter, but as long as the tall footmen stood behind their chairs, they made no mention of the séance that was to take place later. Yet all of them were eager to discuss it. No sooner had the dessert been placed before them and Georgina's black-clad major-domo, after a last look round, left the room, than Beckford said: 'If there were any takers, I'd readily give three to one up to any sum that he'll not do it.'

For a moment there was silence, then it was broken by Clarissa's clear young voice. 'Had I the means, I'd take you, Sir; but my circumstances do not permit me to bet.'

'That's just as well, m'dear,' remarked Colonel Thursby. 'For you are better qualified to wager on when little Susan cuts her first tooth.'

The others laughed, except for Droopy Ned, who, with his usual shrewdness, had formed a good impression of Clarissa's intelligence. Smiling at her he said: 'Perhaps you have some special reason for your confidence. If so, pray tell us of it.'

'I have,' she replied promptly. 'You all heard Signor Malderini promise, when in the Orangery, that he would experiment upon me and he has already done so.'

'When?' asked Roger with a sudden frown.

Colouring slightly, she looked across at him. 'After . . . after we had met in the nursery, and had our talk about Susan, I sent a note up by one of the footmen to the suite the Malderinis are occupying, asking if he would receive me there. The reply came back that he would.'

A hush had fallen on the company and they listened with close attention as she went on. 'Up in their sitting-room, the Princess took me by the hand and led me to a chair, then he enquired in what way he could be of service to me. I asked him if he could enable me to see into the future. He said he had every reason to suppose he could, if I was willing to place myself under his mesmeric influence. I agreed and requested him to give me a glimpse of my situation in six months' time. He made passes at me similar to those you saw him use on the Princess. After a while I could see nothing but those curious eyes of his. They seemed to grow huge and fill the whole room. Then I became drowsy and fell asleep. When I awoke it was as though I had just come out of a most vivid dream.'

She paused, and Beckford asked eagerly, 'May we know what you saw in it?'

'I've no objection,' she smiled, 'for it was an exceeding pleasant one. I was lying on a pile of cushions under an awning, in the stern of a gaily painted barge. Although it was January, it was as hot as on the best day of an English summer. At first I thought I was back in Martinique, for the banks of the river on which the barge was drifting were fringed with palms. But the oarsmen of the craft, and others were making music on strange stringed instruments, were not negroes; they were lighter in colour and had finer features, so I knew it must be some other distant land. Beside me was a man who I knew had given me his heart, and I could not have been happier had I been in heaven.'

'But this proves nothing,' said Colonel Thursby.

'I think it does,' she countered, 'because the man was one whom I had come to know well in Martinique, and have some reason to believe loves me already.'

'That makes the matter no whit more conclusive. Had you never met Malderini, you might equally well have had such a dream at night, and in it fulfilled the evident wish you have to be married to this gallant.'

'It is my belief that he enabled me to see my future,' she protested stubbornly.

Georgina had been looking at her with troubled eyes and said:

'Be that as it may, I would that you had never indulged this whim to let him practise his powers upon you.'

'And I,' Roger supported her. He had no doubt that the man Clarissa had seen in her dream was himself; but it seemed highly unlikely that either he or she would be going to the tropics, so he agreed with the Colonel that while unconscious she had only given free play to her own desire. Quickly he went on: 'I had meant to warn you against this very thing. One fact that emerges from it is that, having sent you to sleep, has proved that Malderini has genuine hypnotic powers and such powers can be highly dangerous to anyone who has willingly made themselves subject to them.'

'Why should you think that?' Clarissa asked.

'Because, having once established a *rapport*, the hypnotist can at any future time place the subject under his control again, even if it be against her wish. I beg you, most earnestly, Clarissa, to have no further dealings with this man.'

She shrugged. 'Since you wish it, I'll hold no further private converse with him tonight or tomorrow, and he'll be leaving here on Monday.'

'Yes; and God be thanked for that,' said the Colonel bluntly. 'Saving your presence, Sheridan, I've formed no liking for this friend of yours.'

'Oh, he's well enough.' The ruddy-faced *bon-viveur* poured another great dollop of thick cream upon his strawberries, and went on: 'A little brusque and dictatorial in his manner, I'll admit. But he has so able a brain that, although he is not a *diplomat de carrière*, I think the Venetians did well in their choice of him as a special envoy. You'd not have been aware of it, as until recently he has been in this country only as a private person; but their Senate sent him to report on the internal state of the nation, and before we left London yesterday morning he presented his papers at the Foreign Office. I have not found him an easy companion to take about, but his is an interesting personality.'

'Perhaps,' commented Georgina, 'but a far from engaging one, and he treats that poor wife of his abominably. I find him, too, a mass of disconcerting contradictions. He is a glutton for food, yet drinks nought but water. When conversing with him one forgets his ugliness, then those eyes of his suddenly send a shiver down one's spine. He is punctilious in all normal courtesies but, without warning, makes some remark the rudeness of which, were I not his hostess, I would not excuse. To look at, no one could take him for anything but an ugly middle-aged man, yet when with him there are times when I catch myself thinking of him as a self-willed querulous old woman. And now, although Sherry tells us that he is a hard-headed man of affairs, he springs upon us the claim to be a mystic, capable of exercising occult power.'

Beckford looked across at Sheridan. 'I gather, Sir, that since his coming to England you have been much in his company. During that time has he given you many indications that he concerns himself with magic?'

'Nay, not one. Our talk has all been of either politics or the stage.'

'My love,' Esther Sheridan put in. 'Would you not count his having one night, while staying with us at Polesden, gone out to gather herbs by moonlight?'

He blew her a kiss. 'Light of my life, it seems that he did not confide to you, as he did to me, that they were for a concoction which relieves a colic from which he suffers periodically.'

''Tis possible he did not wish to tell you that he required them to work some spell,' Clarissa suggested.

Droopy laughed. 'Then you may burn me for a witch. In my collection I've a sufficient number of strange drugs to kill, cure or temporarily make mad someone for every day of the year; but the drug does not exist that would counteract the force of gravity and enable a person to become suspended in mid-air. That the fellow can practise hypnotism we must now agree; but, with no offence to you, Sheridan, I believe him to be a rogue. I'd vow his attempt will be no honest one; he'll use some subtle trick by which he hopes to cheat us of our money.'

'No offence, taken, my Lord,' came the cheerful reply. 'But it has never yet been accounted reprehensible to win a wager by the use of one's wits. For example, there was that amusing affair at Brighton last autumn, when little Sir John Lade bet the bulky Lord Cholmondeley that he would carry him on his back from opposite the Pavilion twice round the Steyne. To witness the settling of the bet, His Highness of Wales attended, accompanied by his friends and a bevy of beauties. Lade then declared that in the wager no mention had been made of his Lordship's clothes, and, since Cholmondeley could not bring himself to shock the ladies by revealing himself in a state of nature, Prinny ruled that he had lost the wager.'

When the laughter had subsided, Sheridan went on: 'In this present business, had I thought it possible that Malderini could really levitate his wife I'd never have risked my money. I assumed from the first that he was a clever conjuror—that it lay with us to pit our wits against his and, by exposing him as such, make him pay up.'

Roger then made his only contribution to the discussion. 'What you say of winning a wager by the use of one's wits is acceptable. But it is my belief that Malderini staged his demonstration this afternoon with deliberate intent to lure several of us into betting big sums with him.'

'That,' Droopy nodded, 'was my own thought, when a moment back I said I believed him to be a rogue.'

Sheridan stiffened slightly. 'I do not know him well enough to guarantee the contrary; and I would have you remember, gentlemen, that I brought him here at Lady St. Ermins's request; so you must not hold me responsible for his conduct.'

Georgina caught Esther's eye and rose. The gentlemen bowed the ladies from the room, then reseated themselves at the Colonel's end of the table, and commenced to pass the port. Soon they were deep in a discussion of the conditions of the wager, and the possibility that Malderini might win it by use of mass hypnotism.

It was Droopy who produced that idea. In his studies of the East he had read an account of an Indian conjuror throwing a rope up into the air, where it remained rigid while his small boy climbed it, and the explanation given had been that neither the rope nor the boy had left the ground; the audience, having been mesmerized by the conjuror, only imagined that they had done so.

The Colonel declared that he could no more credit the possibility of one person mesmerizing half a dozen or more others simultaneously, to a degree that they were all victims of the same illusion, than he could the lifting of a human body into the air by will-power.

It was at that point that Roger, having made quick work of a second glass of port, asked to be excused, so that he might fulfil his first duty as an umpire, and make certain that the yellow drawing-room had been prepared in accordance with his instructions.

The room, which could be entered both from the hall and from the larger drawing-room, was some twenty-five feet wide by forty long, including the bay of a window that occupied the greater part of its far end. It could not have been better suited to the purpose, as the still good light of the long summer evening on the far side of the drawn curtains made a broad semi-circular band on the parquet below them, and from it just enough light was reflected to enable people to recognize one another when in the room.

Having assured himself that no wires or any other secret apparatus had been installed in the room while they were at dinner, Roger chalked out a line nine feet long across the bay and twelve feet in from it. He then had the servants carry in ten chairs and directed their placing. One was put a yard away from each extremity of the line, and the other eight facing and some six feet away from it in a row across the room.

When he had dismissed the servants he went back into the big drawing-room and found the whole company now assembled there. Taking up a five-branched Dresden candelabra from a side table, he invited Malderini to inspect his preparations. The Venetian accompanied him into the yellow silk-panelled room and, after a careful look round, expressed himself as satisfied. Roger left him to inform the others, replaced the candelabra, and ushered them in.

Once the door was closed it seemed that they were in complete darkness, but after a few moments their eyes became accustomed to the gloom and they could see the outline of the row of chair-backs against the band of pale light below the hem of the curtains round the big bay window. Roger offered his arm to the Princess and led her to the chair facing the right-hand extremity of the chalked line, then asked Malderini to take that at its other end, opposite to her. The rest of the party settled themselves in the row of chairs, the ladies in the centre, Sheridan on their right, and the Colonel, Droopy Ned and Beckford in that order on the left. Roger took the remaining chair on the extreme right, so that he was nearest to the Princess, called for silence, and told Malderini that they were ready for him to begin.

The Venetian stood up and said; 'You will not object, I am sure, to my pinning up the lower end of the Princess Sirīsha's sari; otherwise it will trail upon the ground, and might lead you to suggest that with its folds obscuring her feet she is walking on the tips of her toes.'

Consent being given, he went over to his wife, knelt down in front of her and pinned up the white satin just high enough to show her white-shod feet. Having warned them that they must be patient as it would take some time for him to concentrate his will to the degree needed to lift her by it, he stepped back a few feet, halted and began to make passes at her.

As in the afternoon, she jerked and rolled her head for some minutes, then stiffened and relaxed. Having put her under he stopped making passes and, with his hands hanging at his sides, stood, a dim bulky figure, staring fixedly at her. It was now that his audience had to exercise their patience. The long minutes dragged by—five, ten, fifteen, twenty—while they sat straining their eyes in the semi-darkness; but nothing happened. It began to look as if there was to be no trick after all, but that it was a genuine attempt, and this long sustained effort of concentration must soon exhaust him; so that he would have to give up and confess failure. Yet his breathing was not laboured, and he gave no other sign of fatigue, but continued to stand absolutely motionless.

Suddenly he threw up both his hands, in a lifting gesture. Her hands were on the arms of the elbow chair in which she was sitting. Although Roger could only see their outline vaguely he got the impression that she levered herself up by them. Slowly she rose and her hands left the arms of the chair. Someone drew in a sharp breath. As her figure straightened it was apparent to them all that she had become much taller than her normal height, then that her feet had left the floor.

Malderini began to back slowly away from her, gesturing with his hands as though to draw her towards him. Slowly she began to advance along the chalk line. As they watched her they held their breath. Her body remained rigid, but her feet moved slightly in a slow regular progression, as though she was taking tiny steps through the air.

She covered more than half the stipulated distance and came opposite Colonel Thursby. At that moment a loud clatter shattered the silence of the room. The Princess threw out her arms and gave a piercing scream. Then pandemonium broke out.

The ebony walking stick the Colonel always carried had a crooked ivory handle. He had reversed it, leant forward, swept its crook along the floor below the Princess's feet and, when it met resistance, jerked it hard towards him. Pitching forwards, she crashed full length on the parquet.

Next second Droopy Ned played his part in this little plot that had been hatched between them after Roger had left the dining-room. He scratched the top of a pocket tinder-box with a three-inch magnesium flare and held it aloft, Instantly the darkness of the room was dissipated and everything in it could be seen with almost blinding clarity.

As the Princess fell, her tight sari had rucked up exposing both her legs to the knees. She was wearing calf-length white kid boots, and to the inner side of her legs short, cloth-tipped black stilts were strapped. It was now obvious that Malderini must have adjusted them under her insteps when pinning up her sari and that, had she reached the chair at the far end of her walk, he would have removed her feet from them while unpinning her sari, without anyone being the wiser.

When the fierce light of the flare revealed the scene, Roger found himself staring straight at the Venetian. His face was contorted with insane, diabolical rage. Next moment, howling like an animal, he flung himself at the Colonel. Everyone sprang to their feet, chairs were overturned, the women screamed. The flare went out, plunging the room again in darkness.

There was a short noisy scuffle. Voices were crying: 'Lights! Open the door! Lights! Bring lights!'

Droopy Ned ran to the drawing-room door and wrenched it open. Enough light came through to reveal the scene. Georgina and Clarissa had run forward and were helping the Princess to her feet. Esther Sheridan had flung herself onto her husband's bosom. Beckford had seized Malderini by the coat collar just in time to prevent him assaulting Colonel Thursby. The Colonel, now leaning heavily on his stick, was standing looking at him, a derisive smile on his thin face.

The door had been open only a moment when the Venetian broke free from Beckford's hold and, mouthing curses, again threw himself at the Colonel. Roger was some feet away. In his anxiety to protect the elderly man whom he looked on as a father, he made an awkward jump between them. He was still off balance as Malderini struck out. The blow caught him in the face. He went over backwards and fell with a crash among the chairs.

By the time he had scrambled to his feet, Beckford had again got hold of Malderini and now held him in a firmer grip. Roger, with one hand to his bruised face, and his blue eyes blazing, snapped out:

'Damn you, Sir! You shall give me satisfaction for that!'

With Clarissa's help, Georgina had got the Princess up into a chair. Turning from her, she cried, 'Roger, I pray you let this shocking business go no further!'

Ignoring Georgina, he continued to scowl at Malderini. But the Venetian had now begun to sob with frustrated rage and, between his sobs, gasped out to the Colonel:

'That was a brutal thing to do. Oh, you horrible man! The shock might have killed her. And you ruined my illusion. I suppose you expect me to pay. But I won't! I won't! Why should I, when I should have won had it not been for your interference?'

'You will, unless you wish me to have you barred out of every club in London,' replied the Colonel tartly.

'And you will give me satisfaction for that blow,' added Roger, 'unless you prefer to taste my horse-whip about your shoulders.'

Georgina had come up. Catching him by the elbow she pulled him round to face her and said in a firm voice, 'This matter is deplorable enough already. I'll allow no duel to be fought about it. You'll oblige me, Mr. Brook, by retiring from the room.'

Stepping back, he made her a leg and replied at once, 'Your Ladyship's servant.' But he did not attempt to lower his voice as he said to Droopy a moment later, 'Be good enough, Ned, to act for me and arrange a meeting.' Then he stalked through the door that gave on to the corridor.

Malderini had, meanwhile, staggered back to a chair and collapsed into it. He was now breathing heavily and, after a moment, muttered thickly, 'Send for Pietro . . . send for Pietro. . . . Tell him . . . tell him to bring my pills.'

Sheridan came forward and said quickly, 'Excitement has brought on one of his attacks. He has them occasionally but they are no matter for grave concern. Pietro is his valet, and gives him massage for them. If we can find Pietro, he'll be as right as rain again in half an hour.'

'Clarissa!' Georgina cried, 'Run, please; run to the servants' quarters and fetch Signor Malderini's man.'

Clutching her wide skirts with both hands and lifting them some inches, Clarissa ran from the room. Beckford had just brought in the Dresden candelabra from the drawing-room and set it on the chimney piece; so there was now more light to see by. Malderini's pudgy face had gone grey; his eyes were closed and his breath came with a rasping noise. His wife made no attempt to approach him. Apparently she had not been seriously hurt by her fall, as she sat quite silent. But her head was bowed and with one hand she was holding the end of the sari, which she usually wore over the top of her head, across her face, as though too ashamed to meet the gaze of her hostess and her fellow guests.

After an uneasy few minutes, the sound of running footsteps came again. Well ahead of Clarissa, Pietro erupted into the room. He was a tall, thin, bony, middle-aged man with a shock of black hair. Showing scant ceremony as they made way for him, he ran to his master, fell on his knees before him, and began to babble excitedly in Italian. Malderini muttered something and Pietro thrust a pill into his mouth, then began to chafe his hands.

The Venetian's breathing eased and his eyes opened. For a while he remained seated, then he got to his feet. The tall Pietro stooped and drew one of his master's arms across his shoulders, so that he could support him as he walked. With no word said they crossed the room. Beneath the end of her sari, the Princess had evidently been watching them, for she rose too, and followed. Instinctively the ladies dropped her curtseys and the men bowed as she passed.

Roger, meanwhile, had gone to the dining-room and helped himself to a glass of port. He was, for once, in an exceedingly ill humour, as he loathed being involved in quarrels; yet he saw no way out of this one, which had risen so unexpectedly. Malderini had knocked him down, and that was a matter which no gentleman could ignore with honour. Even an apology could not settle such a case. It demanded that either he must meet the Venetian with weapons or, if he proved a poltroon, horse-whip him. Being an exceptionally fine swordsman and a first-class pistol shot, Roger had no qualms about the outcome of such an encounter; but he felt that, owing to Malderini's now being the accredited envoy of the Serene Republic, the affair was liable to cause the most troublesome repercussions. Gloomily, he finished his wine and, anticipating that the others would by now have congregated in the large drawing-room, decided to join them there.

As he came out into the hall, he saw Malderini being helped up the stairs by his valet. They were about a third of the way up the flight and, their backs being towards him, neither of them caught sight of him. But the Princess, who was following them, had reached only the bottom stair. As he emerged from the dining-room, she turned and her dark eyes held his for a moment.

He had very little doubt that her husband had forced her to play the part she had in the deception; so he felt deeply sorry for her. With a view to expressing his sympathy, he made her a much deeper bow than he would have normally. As he raised his head, he expected her to incline hers, then pass on up the stairs; but she did neither. Instead, she remained poised on the bottom stair, her glance searching his face intently.

It seemed pointless to address her, as he could not expect her to understand him; so he simply stood there returning her solemn gaze. For a few moments neither of them moved, then she looked away from him and up the stairs. Malderini and Pietro had just reached the landing; so they were now out of earshot. Her big almond-shaped eyes switched back to Roger.

Suddenly she spoke in a deep low voice. And she spoke in heavily accented, but perfectly clear, English. 'You will fight him. You must kill him. He is evil; utterly evil. Have care not to look in his eyes. But kill him! Kill him!'

CHAPTER FIVE

The Duel

BEFORE Roger could reply, she had turned away and was running up the stairs as swiftly as her sari would permit. His expression of astonishment gave way to a cynical little smile. Since she spoke English he had no doubt now that she also spoke Italian, French and German. As he had thought possible in the afternoon demonstration, when Malderini had appeared to be reading out the questions, he had actually been giving her their answers. His sending Clarissa to sleep by a few passes proved him to be a competent hypnotist, but all the miracles he claimed to work were fakes.

From their recent encounter, Roger judged that Malderini's wife was his unwilling tool, and did as she was ordered only through acute fear of him or, perhaps, because she lived for the greater part of the time subject to his hypnotic domination. If the latter were the case, the inference was that his semi-collapse had enabled her temporarily to escape from it. After a moment's thought he decided to refrain, for the time being, from disclosing that she had spoken to him. Then he crossed the hall and entered the long drawing-room.

It was still early and Georgina, in a determined attempt to restore a normal atmosphere, had endeavoured to organize a round game. But Droopy and Sheridan had both asked to be excused and her father had gone up to his own rooms; so she had had to make the best of sitting down to a game of ombre with Beckford, Esther and Clarissa.

The first hand was being dealt as Roger came in and, giving only a glance at the group seated round the card table, he joined Droopy and Sheridan, who were talking in low voices in a corner.

'He'll fight,' Sheridan was saying, as Roger came up. 'He must; he has no alternative.'

'But is he in a fit state to do so?' Roger asked. 'I saw him a few minutes back being half carried up the staircase by his man.'

Sheridan shrugged. 'He is suffering only from a temporary indisposition. I've seen him in a similar state on two previous occasions, and on both he has reappeared looking as strong as a horse in the morning.'

'Then, if his health permits, he must give me satisfaction,' Roger declared firmly.

'We'll give him half an hour to recover himself; then I will go up and see him,' Sheridan volunteered. 'The odds are that he'll ask me to be his second. If so, in the circumstances, I can hardly refuse.'

'In that case it will be for you and me to make the arrangements,' said Droopy. 'Mr. Brook has already asked me to act for him.'

Sheridan bowed. 'Charmed, m'Lord, I can think of no one with whom I should be happier to settle the formalities. And now, gentlemen, I suggest we leave this painful subject and kill time by taking a glass of wine together.'

The three men walked quietly through to the dining-room, collected a decanter of wine and glasses, and took them to the library. For a good half-hour they sat there talking mainly about Sheridan's theatrical activities; then he left them to go upstairs.

He was away for about twenty minutes and, when he rejoined them, said at once, 'Malderini is already quite recovered, and he says that if you insist upon it he will fight.'

'I do,' Roger replied, standing up. 'And I'll withdraw now so that you can discuss details. The Colonel never seeks his bed before midnight, so I'll go up to his room. You'll find me there, Ned, when you're in a position to tell me what has been settled.'

Colonel Thursby's private sitting-room held many indications of the way in which he had made his considerable fortune. There were models of machines that he had either invented or improved, and maps of the great canal system that he had aided the Duke of Bridgewater to plan, and most of the books on his shelves were works on engineering. There was also, beside the mantel, a rack holding a row of long-stemmed clay pipes, and the Colonel was puffing quietly at one.

Roger was not an addict of the weed, but he enjoyed an occasional pipe with Georgina's father; so, while he told him how things were moving, he took down the churchwarden that had his initials on it and began to fill it from the Colonel's tobacco jar.

The Colonel nodded. 'So Dick Sheridan and Lord Edward are arranging a meeting. Well, we can only hope that no harm comes to you from it.'

'As I am the challenger, the choice of weapons lies with him,' Roger replied. 'But either way, I don't think you need be greatly concerned about me. If it be swords I have little to fear. He must be at least fifteen years older than myself, and he is anything but an agile man; so I doubt not I'd make rings round him. With pistols, too, the odds should be in my favour. Unless he's an expert marksman, I'd wing him before he gets a bead on me.'

'I hope he chooses swords. A duel with pistols is always a chancy matter. Even a man who has never fired one in his life may score a lucky hit; and if you were seriously injured, I should be distressed beyond measure. The more so as it was my act in exposing his trickery, and then you protecting me from his assault, which have led to this.'

'I pray you don't give that another thought, Sir. You had every right to unmask the rogue, and no one could have foreseen that he would knock me down.' Roger drew the flame from a taper onto the tobacco in his pipe, then added, 'Frankly, though, I'd give a lot for this imbroglio to have taken some other turn, so that I'd not been forced to challenge him.'

'Since he struck you in the face, you had no option.'

'That's just the rub; and why, though I doubt his doing so, I hope he will choose swords. As I told you at breakfast, Georgina asked him here at my request, that I might have a prospect of winning him over to Mr. Pitt's interest. Were I still saddled with that I'd be in an unholy mess. But by a stroke of good fortune, later in the morning I received a despatch from Downing Street relieving me of further responsibility in the matter. Even so, should I chance to lay him low for some weeks with a pistol bullet, that would sadly prejudice the negotiations he is about to open with the Foreign Office. If, on the other hand, we fight with swords, I'll almost certainly be able to disarm him, or, at worst, give him a slight jab in the sword arm. Then there'd be no fear of regrettable repercussions afterwards.'

For some half-hour they talked on, but in a lighter vein, then Droopy Ned joined them. Peering with his short-sighted eyes at Roger, he said:

"Tis to be at six o'clock tomorrow morning by the little temple on the far side of the lake, I fear, though, you may be somewhat disconcerted by his choice of weapons. He has chosen pikes.'

'Strap me!' exclaimed Roger. 'You can't be serious, Ned.'

Droopy nodded. 'I am. Sheridan did his utmost to persuade him to accept more orthodox weapons, but he said that, being a studious and peace-able man by nature, he had never used a sword, and that an astigmatism of the eyes prevents him from shooting straight. He can hardly be blamed for selecting a weapon which will make the chances between you more even, and I did not feel that I had sound grounds for standing out against it.'

'No . . . no; I suppose not. But pikes, Ned! Where will we get them?'

'There are a score or more to choose from among the arms that decorate the walls of the billiards room.'

'So be it, then. What about a doctor?'

'Knowing Dr. Chudleigh to be the household leech here, I've sent a note down to the village requesting him to attend upon us. Beckford refused to act with Sheridan as the Venetian's other second; so the groom who is carrying my note to Dr. Chudleigh also bears one from Sheridan to Major Rawton at the Red House. I gather the Major is a fire-eater of the first water, so the odds on him refusing Sheridan's request are negligible. It remains only for you to provide yourself with another second.'

Roger turned to the Colonel. 'If you would honour me, Sir?'

'Certainly, my dear boy,' came the prompt response. 'Did I have to wait here to learn the outcome of this meeting, I'd be consumed with anxiety; now at least I'll learn it the moment it becomes apparent.'

They talked on till the clock chimed twelve, then the Colonel's two visitors wished him 'good-night'. Droopy told Roger that he had arranged for his man to call them both at five o'clock and, after agreeing to meet down in the hall at a quarter to six, they separated to go to their rooms.

While undressing, Roger's thoughts were no longer on the duel, but on Georgina. As he was to be called at five o'clock there was no way in which he could conceal from her that it was to take place, and he knew that she would be greatly distressed about it. Resigning himself to a protest of expostulations and argument, he put on his flowered silk chamber robe and went through to her.

She was sitting up in bed and had a book open on her lap, but she was not reading. He had hardly closed the door of the boudoir, before she asked impatiently, 'Well! Have you made an end of this wretched affair?'

'Not quite'—he gave a disarming smile—'but I hope to have before you wake in the morning.'

She stiffened, 'You mean that . . .'

'I mean, my love, that, through this pestiferous fellow, I am forced to suffer another and greater injury. On his account I'll be able to spend no more than an hour with you tonight; for I must get a few hours' sleep and am to be called at five o'clock.'

'You insisted on fighting, then?'

''Twas not my wish; but I had no alternative.'

'Oh God! What fools you men are!' Georgina burst out. 'You call such meetings seeking satisfaction, yet only too often it's the offended party who gets skewered for his pains. There's neither justice nor fairness in it; for, right or wrong, the victor is he who's had most experience with weapons, and many an honest father of a family has met his death at the hands of an impudent young blackguard, because he felt in honour bound to call him out.'

'In this case the blackguard is the older party, and I'd be much surprised if, by this time tomorrow, Susan finds herself an orphan.'

'Lud, man! I'm not scared for you. At least, no more than any woman would be for her lover when he's about to expose himself to some chance injury. Pitted against a man so formidable with arms as you, the poor wretch will be lucky if he gets off with a month in bed nursing a slashed face or a punctured lung.'

'Nay; I've no intention of causing him grievous harm. I mean to disarm him if I can.'

She gave him a puzzled look. 'If you will be so easily satisfied, it makes this meeting even more senseless. Surely you would have done better when you got up from the floor to return him blow for blow. He'd not have hit you a second time, I'll be bound; and you could have left it at that.'

'Had we been in Russia, that is just what I would have done. The nobility there indulge in fisticuffs at the least provocation, and even use their canes upon one another. Like yourself, and I admit with some reason, they maintain that duelling settles nothing, and that the men of the western nations who resort to it are crazy. But . . .'

'Then I vow these Muscovites, whom we look on as barbarians, are more civilized than ourselves.'

'Maybe, m'dear. But, as I was about to say, our customs are different. And when in Rome . . .'

'Oh! Roger, I know the stupid conventions that form the code of so-called men of honour well enough. Yet only the weak follow convention slavishly; and, in this instance, the blow was intended not for you but for Papa. Surely it was a case in which you could have composed the quarrel, instead of deliberately flouting my request that it should not lead to a duel?'

He sighed. 'I'm sorry; truly sorry. Had the circumstances been slightly different I would gladly have acceded to your wish. The kernel of the matter was Sheridan being present. The others we could have bound to secrecy with a reasonable hope that they would hold their tongues, at least to the extent of making no mention of the fact that Malderini knocked me down. But you know Richard Brinsley even better than myself. It's not in his nature to refrain from telling a good story; so every detail of this affair will be all over London by Monday afternoon. Within a week, I'd have been forced to resign from my Clubs had I not insisted on the Venetian giving me satisfaction.'

'I had not thought of that,' Georgina murmured. Then her lovely face was lit once more by her warm smile and she said, 'You are excused, Sir; but not from having kept me talking for a part of our precious hour.' As she spoke she held out her arms.

Punctually at a quarter to six, Roger joined Droopy Ned and Colonel Thursby down in the main hall. They had there three types of pike for him to choose from. Having handled all three weapons, he chose the heaviest, on the assumption that, being stronger than Malderini, it would more easily enable him to beat down the Venetian's guard. Droopy took the two rejected weapons back to the billiards room and returned with the pair to the one Roger had selected. Then they set off for the rendezvous.

It was a slightly misty morning which promised another lovely day. As it was a Sunday, none of Georgina's platoon of gardeners was scything the lawns or replanting the borders. Those who looked after the glasshouses would do their airing and watering before putting on their 'black' to attend church; but not for an hour or so yet.

Seven minutes' walk round the edge of the lake brought them to its far shore. At intervals in the wood along it, broad rides, which were kept clear for the pheasant shooting, came down to its edge. From one of them a turning led off to an open glade with a hillock at its far end. On it there was a small temple, or belvedere, consisting of six pillars of Verona marble on carved stone bases and supporting a dome of delicately scrolled ironwork. A dozen yards from the temple, on the edge of the flat centre of the glade, two men were standing. They were Dr. Chudleigh and Major Rawton.

Greetings were exchanged and the Doctor reported that in case one of the combatants was too seriously wounded to walk, he had left his coachman and carriage beyond the trees in the next ride, which was less than a hundred yards away.

Meanwhile, the Major, an elderly, paunchy, red-faced man who clung to the fashion of wearing a wig, was eyeing the two pikes with a puzzled frown. On being informed that they were the weapons to be used in the encounter, he almost burst with indignation declaring that he was being made a fool of, as it was unthinkable that gentlemen should resort to such unorthodox means of settling a difference of opinion.

Fortunately, at that moment the other party arrived and Sheridan, who had also brought a pair of pikes, was able to pacify him. As principals, Roger and Malderini, who was wearing a heavy cloak, stood some distance apart, and away from the others while they settled final details.

The pikes that Sheridan had brought were much lighter than those Roger had chosen, so a coin was tossed up to decide which pair should be used. Droopy lost the toss, so Roger was deprived of any advantage he might have gained from the heavier weapons. He and Malderini were then brought face to face by their seconds and asked if they could see their way to compose their differences. Roger replied that he did not regard the insult to which he had been subject as mortal; but, having been struck, he must exercise his right to strike back in accordance with the conventions of polite society.

On that the principals were marched away to prepare themselves. Roger stripped to his shirt, but Malderini, alleging the chill of the early morning air as his reason, refused to take off anything except his cloak. Roger, who now felt that, as he had to fight with a strange weapon, he would be foolish to give away too many advantages, then wondered if he had been wise. The thick cloth of Malderini's coat, and even the multiple folds of his cravat, would, to some extent, protect him from a thrust. On the other hand, they would tend to restrict swift movement, and as Roger was relying mainly on his agility to secure a quick victory, he decided to face his antagonist in shirt sleeves and open necked.

Side by side, Colonel Thursby and Major Rawton measured twelve paces in the middle of the most even stretch of turf. Droopy and Sheridan handed their principals the pikes and led them up to the markers. Stepping back to a central position on either side of the combatants, they received from the Colonel and the Major the two heavier pikes, so that they might, if necessary, intervene and with them beat down the weapons of their principals.

'Attention!' cried Sheridan. 'Lord Edward will count three; and on the word three, you will engage.'

'One!' Droopy's voice rang through the silence of the woodland glade. 'Two!' The duellists raised the points of the long pikes. 'Three!'

Next moment they were at it hammer and tongs. Roger had never before handled a pike and, as far as he could judge, neither had Malderini. Both, at first, used them much in the way they would have single-sticks, each endeavouring to knock aside the other's weapon. But, very soon, Roger realized that he dared not put his full strength into his blows; for, if he did, the wooden staff of his pike might snap and leave him at the mercy of his antagonist.

Malderini had, from the beginning, done little more than parry Roger's efforts to beat down his guard; so the tempo of the fight changed and, following each sharp clack of the wooden shafts, one of them essayed a swift thrust at the body of the other. Yet both were greatly handicapped by the fact that the pikes were ten feet long, so terribly unwieldy for anyone who had had no experience of handling them. The tassle-decorated, sharp, metal spears on their ends tended to weigh them down, and after each thrust it needed a considerable effort to make a swift recovery.

Owing to Roger's ignorance about pike fighting, it was some minutes before he realized that the Venetian was fighting an almost entirely defensive encounter. He had hardly shifted his ground at all, but was stamping back and forth over the same square yard, while his attacker circled round and round him, striving to find an opening. For every three times Roger thrust, Malderini thrust only once, conserving his strength and waiting his opportunity.

Yet Roger, as he sprang in and out and from side to side, felt confident that Malderini could not stand the pace, and must shortly weaken so that for a moment he would lower his guard. Then, one swift lunge would settle the business.

The witnesses of the encounter maintained an absolute silence. The stillness of the glade was broken only by the clack of the wooden pike shafts as they came together, and the heavy breathing of the duellists

By the time they had been at this furious slash and thrust for six or seven minutes, Roger was sweating from his exertions. During them he had been constantly switching his glance from Malderini's pike point to his face. This, again, was on account of the strangeness to him of the weapon he was using. Had it been a sword, he would have kept his gaze riveted on his enemy's eyes, it being a first principle of fencing that only by so doing can one divine's one's opponent's intentions. Now, he decided that he would be wiser to adopt deceptive tactics. He would pretend to tire, slacken off his attack and tempt the Venetian into making an all-out lunge at him. By watching his eyes he should be able to foresee the movement, sidestep the thrust and come in himself with a well-aimed stab, which would render the heavy, awkward figure confronting him *hors de combat*.

He had adopted this new policy for not more than a long half-minute before he suddenly became aware that he had thrown himself open to a deadly peril. Having stared for that time into the curious eyes of the Venetian, he could not now wrench his gaze away from them. In vain he strove to do so. Like a magnet applied to iron filings they held his own eyes fixed. Too late, he recalled the Princess Sirīsha's warning: 'Have care not to look in his eyes.' He was doing so and now he could not stop himself.

In an agony of apprehension he continued to flail this way and that with his pike. He knew now that Malderini had got the best of him. The Venetian's choice of pikes had had more to it than a reluctance to fight with swords or pistols. He had known that such a long weapon would give him the best chance of fending his enemy off until he could hold his gaze and exert hypnotic influence on him.

Sweating now with a fear greater than he had known for many years past, Roger faced the fact that within a few minutes he might be dead. Those saucer-like eyes into which he was staring were now impelling him to lower the point of his weapon. Desperately he summoned every ounce of will-power he had to resist the impulse. There was cold, calculating evil in those eyes and an undisguised hatred. He felt certain that the moment he gave up his now rapidly weakening efforts to guard himself, the point of Malderini's pike would thrust into his heart.

Gasping, and with the sweat pouring from him, so that his shirt was now sticking to his back and chest, he plunged wildly from side to side across the already brutally trampled earth. It flashed into his mind that it was madness to stay there and be slaughtered. A serious wound he would have faced rather than be branded as a coward; but this was a question of life or death. And to die in fair combat was one thing; to be rendered helpless by invisible bonds, then murdered, was quite another. Whatever the shame he would have to live down, he decided to throw away his pike and dash off into the woods.

Yet, no sooner had he taken the decision, than he realized that it was beyond his power to carry it out. Those enormous soulless eyes held him captive.

Suddenly a sharp, agonized cry pierced his half-dazed consciousness. Within seconds those huge eyes that had blotted out everything else contracted. With startling rapidity they shrank back to normal and Roger found himself able to focus the whole of his terrible antagonist's person. Malderini was standing rigid, his head thrown back, his mouth still wide open from the cry he had uttered.

With blind instinct, impelled by the imperative urge of self-preservation, Roger rushed in upon him. The point of his pike caught the Venetian on the left side of the chin and tore a long gash from it right up to his ear. Malderini screamed again, lurched sideways and thrust at Roger's face. He ducked and the pike passed harmlessly over his left shoulder. At the same instant his own pike ripped through Malderini's coat just below the armpit. Wounded again, the Venetian swung round, and with the blood now gushing from his slashed cheek, fell face forward to the ground.

Panting, Roger stared down at him. He could hardly believe his eyes. The feathered shaft of a long arrow was sticking up from Malderini's backside.

CHAPTER SIX

The Venetian Strikes Back

THE point of the arrow had buried itself in the right-hand side of Malderini's broad bottom. Major Rawton was also staring down at it. His pendulous cheeks going a deeper shade of purple and his blue eyes popping, he exclaimed:

'First pikes, now arrows! Damme, I'm mad; or mixed up with a set of madmen!'

The Doctor ran up with his black bag. The seconds, with the exception of Sheridan, crowded round. He was looking in the direction of the temple, and gave a loud shout:

'There she goes! There! The devilish jade! She should be put in the stocks for this!'

Roger followed his glance and was just in time to catch a glimpse of pale gold hair as, to the left of the knoll on which the temple stood, and some way beyond it, a running figure disappeared into the woods.

'By God, I'll see to it that she's not!' he cried. 'This carrion here had hypnotized me. I had no more fight left in me than a rabbit set before a snake. He would have butchered me by now had she not shot him in his fat arse the moment that she did.'

Although he had seen the running figure indistinctly and for only a second, he had no doubt that it was Clarissa who had saved him. In the garden of the Governor's residence in Martinique there had been three targets at which guests sometimes amused themselves by shooting. One of her beaux had persuaded her to take up the sport and, at medium range, she had become a surprisingly good bow-woman. At Stillwaters, too, there were targets at the far end of the bowling green; so she would have had no difficulty in getting hold of a bow and arrows. He wondered now if the Princess, with intent to strengthen this chance of getting rid of the husband she hated, had incited Clarissa to the act. But it was most unlikely that the two women would have exchanged confidences, or even had an opportunity of meeting during the night. It seemed more probable that Clarissa, having had personal experience of Malderini's hypnotic powers, had foreseen that he might use them during the duel, and so taken this desperate means of intervention.

Another yelp of pain from the Venetian drew Roger's attention back to him. The muscles of the buttock contract and exert a tight grip on any weapon which pierces them; so to get the arrow out, the Doctor had had to grasp it with both hands, put a foot in the small of Malderini's back, and give a sharp tug. Major Rawton then helped him turn the wounded man over so that he could examine the injury to his face. The gash was long but not deep and, after swabbing it with an astringent to check the bleeding, he said:

'There's nought dangerous about that; but there may be about the wound in his side. Look, blood is seeping through his coat. Help me to get him out of it. Perhaps, though, it would be better to cut it off him.'

'No!' cried Malderini. 'No!' Clutching the lapels of his coat, he held them fast against his chest, and went on in his indifferent English. 'I forbid! You will not cut him! I not have it. I forbid! I forbid!'

'Heaven defend me!' exclaimed the Major. 'This is the maddest meeting that ever I attended. A man who will not let a doctor staunch his blood should be in Bedlam.'

Sheridan added a swift expostulation in French. 'You must let the doctor get at your wound and plug it. What's a coat matter when your life may be in danger?'

Using the same language, Malderini gasped out, 'It is not serious! If it were I'd know it. My servant, Pietro, has salves and will do all that is needful.'

Meanwhile, unnoticed by them, Pietro had appeared on the edge of the group. Servants sometimes accompanied their masters to such encounters to act as horse-holders, but were left at some distance from the place of meeting and never permitted to witness the actual engagement. So Sheridan, catching sight of him at that moment, asked him what the devil he was doing there.

The tall, black-haired valet's bony face showed his agitation, and he replied: 'My master ordered me to follow, and to watch from the edge of the wood. He said that, should he be wounded, I was to let no one touch him and bind up his wound myself.'

'Then Major Rawton is right,' murmured Colonel Thursby. 'He ought to be in Bedlam. Were the wound serious he might, by rejecting the services of a qualified medical man, die of it before he could be moved.'

'I know what I am about,' Malderini snarled, 'and I am worried only for my face.' Breaking into English, he added, 'Will it make scar, Doctor? Tell me? Make no hidings. Will I have scar for life?'

Although his plump face was so lacking in distinction, its skin was smooth, a good colour, and of a fine texture; so there was justification for his concern at the possibility of an ugly blemish on it. All the same, they were distinctly taken aback by the vindictiveness his vanity led him to display a moment later. On the doctor's replying: 'Providing no infection sets in, the wound should heal fairly quickly; but I fear it will leave a permanent mark.' Malderini looked up at Roger, his eyes blazing with hatred, and gulped out:

'As you have spoiled my face, so I will spoil your life. Remember that! Remember! Sooner or later you shall pay for this a hundredfold.'

In normal circumstances, Roger would have offered a defeated antagonist his hand, and expressed the hope that he would soon be recovered from his wounds. Faced with such malice, there was nothing to be said. Shrugging his shoulders, he turned away and walked towards the place where he had left his coat.

Droopy Ned and the Colonel went with him. As soon as they were out of earshot of the others, the latter said, 'My boy, this is a bad business. I thought it your intention to handle matters so that the affair should have no sequel.'

'It did not lie with me,' Roger replied angrily. 'He mesmerized me, and would have killed me in another few moments. Once freed of his gaze, I struck out at him like a madman, caring not what might happen, providing I could end the encounter while I had the chance.'

'That explanation is acceptable to us, but will not prove so to others.'

'I see no reason why I should be called on to explain to anyone. That he was put off his stroke through being shot with an arrow from behind was my good fortune, but I was in no way responsible for it.'

'Such marksmanship would not have disgraced Diana herself,' remarked Droopy, laconically, 'and, in such a setting, it would have been easy to take Miss Marsham for the goddess.'

'You saw her, then?'

'Yes. My long-sight is far better than my short-sight. I glimpsed her running into the woods. It is unfortunate that Sheridan should have done so too.'

'So it was Clarissa!' the Colonel exclaimed. 'I'd not yet even formed a theory on whom it could have been. And Sheridan saw her. That may provoke a damnably worrying situation. He'll not have meant what he said about clapping her in the stocks, but it's too intriguing a story for him to keep to himself; and she has laid herself open to prosecution. She could be charged with doing grievous bodily harm—nay, even with attempted murder.'

'You're right, Sir,' Droopy nodded. 'And when Malderini learns who pipped him, his malice is such that I greatly fear he will demand the issuing of a warrant.'

Roger's face expressed his consternation. 'We must protect her at all costs,' he said quickly. 'She must leave Stillwaters before a warrant can be served on her. I'll take her down to my father's house at Lymington. She could live there for a year without anyone here or in London being the wiser. We'll set off as soon as she has had time to get her things together.'

'Steady on, my boy, steady on,' the Colonel sought to calm him. 'There is no call to rush your fences. Sheridan is too much of a gentleman to lay any information against a woman, and especially one who is a close friend of Georgina. He'll take no action, even should Malderini press him to. If the Venetian is determined to be revenged upon her he'll have to apply to the bench himself, and he'll be in no state to do so for some days to come. Better still, as soon as we can get Sheridan on his own, we'll endeavour to persuade him to hold his tongue. If we succeed and he has not yet told Malderini, there will be no need for you to take Clarissa down into Hampshire.'

While they had been talking, Sheridan had fetched the doctor's carriage, and Malderini was now being helped into it. Both Roger and Droopy agreed that the Colonel's advice was sound, and the three of them set off for the house. As the carriage would have to go round by the drive and road, and move only at a walk to avoid jolting its injured passenger, they did not expect it to arrive for some twenty minutes after themselves; but the Colonel and Droopy remained in the hall, in order to seize the first opportunity of getting hold of Sheridan, while Roger went up to Georgina.

When he came through the boudoir to her room, he found that her curtains were drawn back and she was sitting up in bed wide awake. As he
began to tell her what had taken place, she interrupted him:

'I know all, short of the final outcome. Clarissa has but this moment left
me, and she waited until she saw you strike Malderini down. Is he badly
wounded?'

'Her arrow must have made a fairish hole in his bottom; I drew blood
from his left side in the region of the ribs and laid open his cheek from
chin to ear; so at the moment he must be suffering a fine variety of pains.
But there is no cause for alarm on his account and after a week or so his
hurts should not prevent his resuming his diplomatic negotiations.'

'Then that is something. It cannot be said, though, that you kept your
promise to me of letting him off lightly. Why, in God's name, did you
have to wound him twice and thrust your pike into his face? I'd hoped that
after this meeting we might count the whole horrid business done with;
but now I fear he may seek to be revenged upon you.'

'You are right in that,' Roger admitted. 'It seems he's mighty vain of
that smooth skin of his; so he has sworn to make me pay for ruining it. But
I was fighting for my life. The swine used his power to hypnotize me, and
all but had me at his mercy.'

She nodded. 'Clarissa feared that might prove the case, and gave it as
her reason for creeping up on the meeting and shooting at him.'

'Thank God she did; or I'd not be here to tell the tale. I must go to her
now and thank her.'

'No, Roger, you must not. To prevent you doing so was her main reason
for coming to me. She displayed a fine nerve in carrying through such a
daring feat; for, had her aim been bad, she might have killed you. But
afterwards, reaction set in and, by the time she reached me, the poor child
was in a storm of tears, I gather that yesterday she asked you to marry her,
and you refused. Now, she is afraid that you might change your mind, but
only because you feel that she has placed you under an obligation to her;
and that would be more than she could bear. She implored me to do my
utmost to convince you that she would have done the same for any man she
liked, and all the thanks she asks is that the matter should never be
mentioned between you.'

'Then she has shown great sensibility as well as courage,' he said slowly.
'I appreciate the embarrassment it would cause her if I suddenly displayed
a change of heart, and equally the disappointment she might feel if I
failed to give any sign that her act had strengthened the ties of affection
that already exist between us. I will, in private, observe her wish; but
there can be no escaping references to the affair by us in her presence if,
as may occur, proceedings are taken against her for assault.'

'What say you?' Georgina exclaimed, sitting up with a jerk.

Roger told her how matters stood and when he had done, she cried, 'But this might mean prison for her—or even transportation. Oh God, Roger, the Devil himself must have been lurking at my elbow when I agreed to invite this vile Venetian to the house. Papa is right, though. We must nip in the bud this threat to her. They'll be back by now. Go down and find out what has happened. If Dick Sheridan has made the least difficulty about promising to keep silent, send him straight up to me. He shall swear on the Bible not to give Clarissa away, or it will cost him my friendship, and much more besides.'

Down in the front hall, Roger found the Colonel and Droopy still waiting. The latter had just been outside and reported that there was no sign of the carriage. They remained there uneasily for a further quarter of an hour, then decided either that it must have broken down, or that Malderini's injuries had proved more serious than expected and that, instead of bringing him to the house, Dr. Chudleigh had had him carried into a game-keeper's cottage.

Before leaving the house, the Colonel had ordered breakfast to be served early against their return; so, leaving a footman to report should the carriage make a belated appearance, they decided to go in to it. Beckford joined them shortly afterwards, all agog to hear details of the encounter. Suppressing Clarissa's part in it and all reference to the arrow, they told him what had occurred, then for the remainder of the meal observed a gloomy silence, broken only by occasional platitudes.

Roger was wondering if he should, or even could, inform the Princess of the result of the meeting. The last thing he wished was to court the possibility of becoming further involved by seeking a private interview with her, and it seemed very possible that, though she could speak English, she could not read it. It occurred to him that he might ask the Colonel or Droopy to act as his messenger, but he still felt reluctant to give away her secret; so, eventually, he decided to take a chance on her ability to read a foreign language and, when he had finished his breakfast, went to the writing room. There, knowing her French to be better than her English, he wrote in that language, and in bold clear calligraphy, a brief résumé of the present situation, and sent it up to her by a footman.

Ten o'clock came, and eleven, while they hung about wondering where Malderini was and what had happened to prevent him being brought back to the house. Then, shortly after eleven, Sheridan arrived on his own in a hired carriage. He told them that he had come to fetch the Princess and Malderini's baggage, as the Venetian had refused to return to Stillwaters. At Ripley, only a little over a mile away, there was a good coaching inn called 'The Talbot'; so they had taken him there, and Pietro had put him to bed.

Tackled at once by the Colonel, Sheridan said that, although he considered Clarissa's part in the affair most reprehensible, he had no intention of giving her away. Then he went upstairs to see the Princess and supervise the packing of his own bags. By half-past twelve all was completed. Georgina was present to see them off and, accompanied by the Princess and his pretty young wife, Sheridan drove away.

The remainder of the Sunday passed uneventfully, but the atmosphere was by no means a happy one. Clarissa took her meals up in her room and the others found it difficult to conceal their anxieties. On the Monday morning Beckford departed, but Droopy, having no important engagements in London, agreed to stay on for another few days. On Monday evening they learned from Dr. Chudleigh that Malderini had been taken with a slight fever on the Sunday afternoon, but as it had completely abated within twenty-four hours, Sheridan had decided to remove him on the following morning from the inn to the greater comfort of his house at Polesden. It was on Wednesday, while they were sitting at dinner, that a groom arrived from Polesden with a letter marked 'urgent' from Sheridan for Georgina. When it was brought to her, she glanced through it; then, having sent the servants from the room, she read it aloud. It ran:

'*Believe me, sweet friend, it is with the deepest regret that I now address myself to you upon a subject which must prove highly distasteful to us both. Having enjoyed so many hours of happiness under your hospitable roof, the last thing I would wish is to disturb the tranquillity of its inmates. But, alas, I have no choice; for, despite my most earnest representations and endeavours, the matter has gone beyond my powers of control.*

'*It has now emerged that Signor Malderini's servant, Pietro, also observed Miss Marsham, bow in hand, a few moments after she had discharged her arrow at his master. He, of course, had seen Miss Marsham about the house, and from his description of her, Malderini had no hesitation in identifying his assailant. My appeals to his chivalry have proved in vain. This forenoon he sent for the Sheriff's officers from Guildford and has since made a deposition to them.*

'*Further to this, while there are many matters upon which Mr. Brook and I most sharply disagree, I feel that, as gentleman to gentleman, I would be failing in honourable conduct did I not convey a warning to him through you that he should also look to the continued freedom of his person. Signor Malderini is so set upon being revenged upon him that, again despite my vigorous protests, he now asserts that their meeting was forced upon him and declares it to be his intention to invoke the anti-duelling laws against Mr. Brook.*

'*I am your most distressed, humble, obedient . . .*'

Breaking off, Georgina gave a little gasp of dismay, and looked in consternation round the table.

CHAPTER SEVEN

Alarms and Excursions

FOR a moment there was a grim silence, then Roger turned to Clarissa, who was seated beside him, and said: 'For reasons you will appreciate, I have so far refrained from opening this matter to you; but all of us have been dreading the possibility of such an outcome to it. Now, it would be futile to pretend that, should you remain here, you will not be exposed to grave danger. There will shortly be a warrant out for your arrest, and if we allow it to be executed I greatly doubt whether we could save you from being sent to prison.'

As Clarissa paled, he gave her a smile and went on, 'But be of good heart. Within a month or two, Malderini will have left the country, and you may be sure that the Sheriff of Guildford will not pursue the affair with vindictiveness. You have only to disappear for a while and Georgina will see to it that he conveniently forgets that the warrant was ever issued. But leave here you must and, first thing tomorrow, I propose to escort you down to my old home at Lymington. You have kinsfolk of your own across the river at Walhampton; so you should be able to spend the rest of the summer very pleasantly there while everyone outside south Hampshire, except ourselves, will remain in ignorance of your whereabouts.'

'I thank you, Roger, for your thought for me,' she said, a little breathlessly. But Colonel Thursby commented uneasily:

'When we first discussed it, I thought that plan a good one, but now I am far from certain that it is. In seeking you the Sheriff's men are hardly likely to neglect a visit to your father's house. Gossip, in so small a town as Lymington, might easily inform them that Clarissa was living there. If so, they'd nab her.'

'I agree that would be a risk, Sir, were they seeking me. But I count negligible the odds against their doing so.'

'Surely you heard Georgina read out Dick Sheridan's warning, that Malderini intends to invoke the anti-duelling laws against you?'

Roger shrugged. 'They are rarely applied in practice, except when a death has occurred as a result of a meeting, and it has not done so in this case.'

'True, but they are the law; so when this accursed Venetian applies for a warrant for your arrest, no bench of magistrates, however great their reluctance, could possibly refuse to issue one.'

'Moreover,' Droopy added, 'the law has its minimum penalty for every infringement of it. That you would be found guilty is self-evident, and even a sympathetic judge would have to inflict on you a prison sentence.'

'You paint a gloomy picture, Ned, but I'm not scared by it,' Roger smiled. 'No man can drag his opponent to a meeting and force him to fight against his will; so Malderini is as guilty as myself. You seem to have forgotten that should he set the law in motion he too will have to answer to it. When he realizes that he'll be anxious enough to let sleeping dogs lie.'

The Colonel shook his head. 'It is you, Roger, who have forgotten a salient feature of the affair. Malderini is a Plenipotentiary Extraordinary, accredited to the Court of St. James by the Serene Republic, and so immune from prosecution by diplomatic privilege.'

At that Roger frowned; and, after a few seconds, he said: 'You are right, Sir, and have caught me out. I agree now that there would be a risk in Clarissa's going to Lymington; so we must think of some other refuge for her.'

'If Miss Marsham would do me the honour,' Droopy bowed, 'I would willingly become responsible for her. One of my aunts, and her two girls, who are much of Miss Marsham's age, have been installed for some time at Normanrood. She would, I think, find them pleasant company, and our Wiltshire air hard to beat in the summer months.'

Clarissa returned his bow. 'Indeed, Lord Edward, I gladly accept your offer. It is most handsome of you to take pity on a hunted criminal, as it now seems I am.'

Their laughter lightened the atmosphere for a moment, but Georgina asked quickly, 'What of yourself, Roger? This news of Dick Sheridan's now makes it imperative that you, too, should go into hiding until Malderini has left the country. Where will you go?'

'Why not accompany Miss Marsham to Normanrood?' suggested Droopy.

Roger shook his head. 'I thank you, Ned, but I am greatly averse to being driven into hiding by this rogue. I've much of a mind to remain here and accept the summons.'

'I'll not allow you to!' cried Georgina. 'Such wanton folly could have but one end. You would find yourself shackled to a ball and chain in Guildford Prison.'

'Not necessarily, m'dear. Did I fight the issue in the courts, I'd have everyone's sympathy and . . .'

'You have no means of proving that he hypnotized you,' the Colonel cut in.

'And I'd not attempt to, Sir. But all of you, and Sheridan and Beckford, too, could bear witness to the events that led up to the duel—I mean the demonstration in the afternoon, by which he lured his fellow guests here into wagering two thousand guineas that he could not levitate his wife, and then his complete exposure as a fraud. We would brand him publicly for the swindler and charlatan he is, and so ensure that he would never again be received into decent society in this country.'

'Since he refused to pay up, I have already circulated the leading London Clubs to that effect; and though you might derive much satisfaction in giving far wider publicity to his villainy, that would not save you from being guilty of the charge, and receiving a sentence.'

'Of that I am aware. But it does not follow that I would have to serve it. Any sentence can be quashed by the King's pardon, and I hardly think that Mr. Pitt would hesitate to obtain one for me.'

'Ah, that's another matter!' said the Colonel more cheerfully. 'And I agree. After your many services to him he could not stand by and see you sent to prison for conduct which, law or no law, all persons of quality would account him justified in obtaining a pardon for you.'

Droopy Ned still looked somewhat dubious, as he remarked: 'Seeing that Mr. Pitt hopes to do business with the Venetian, I fear he will be far from pleased when he learns what has taken place here.'

'It is a private quarrel; so I see no reason why it should prejudice his negotiations. In fact, it may even be of some value in revealing to him that the Senate of the Serene Republic has, no doubt unwittingly, picked a knave to represent them. In any case, I count the Venetians a decadent worthless lot with whom he would do better to have no dealings.'

'Roger.' Georgina's voice was low and urgent. 'On one thing I insist. You must see Mr. Pitt before you embark on this dangerous course and get his assurance that he will secure you a free pardon.'

'Certainly, m'dear,' he smiled at her. 'I'm not quite such a fool as to neglect so elementary a precaution. I will accompany Droopy and Clarissa to London tomorrow morning.'

Now satisfied that he would not run his head into a noose, out of casual bravado, she tinkled the little glass bell that stood on the table before her. The servants returned, bringing in the 'remove', and the dinner proceeded without further reference to the matter that still occupied their minds.

Later that evening, as Clarissa had so much packing to do, she asked if it would be possible to postpone her departure till the following afternoon. It being considered unlikely that Malderini would be sufficiently recovered for some days actually to apply to the bench for a warrant for her arrest, the postponement was agreed to. In consequence, it was not until three o'clock on the Thursday that, accompanied by Roger and Droopy, she set out for London.

They arrived at Amesbury House, the family mansion in Arlington Street of Droopy's father, in time for a late dinner. Roger was well known to all its inmates, as he always stayed there when in London, and Clarissa was given a warm welcome. Droopy's invitation to her to stay at Normanrood for an indefinite period was at once endorsed by his father, the Marquess; and as, having been removed from Stillwaters, she was no longer in any immediate danger, it was decided that Monday would be time enough for Droopy to escort her down to Wiltshire.

Next morning, Roger strolled along to Downing Street and enquired for his master. He was informed that the Prime Minister was at his country home, Holwood House, near Bromley. It would have been easy for Roger to secure a mount from the Amesbury House stables and ride down there, but on learning that Mr. Pitt had business that would bring him to London on Saturday morning, he decided to save himself the journey and call again next day.

Twenty-four hours later he again waited on the Prime Minister. For over an hour he was kept kicking his heels in the downstairs lobby, then a footman took him up to Mr. Pitt's sanctum on the first floor. As he entered it he felt instinctively that the atmosphere was loaded with trouble but, until the storm burst, he had no premonition that it would be upon himself.

For a few minutes Mr. Pitt continued writing without looking up from his big table desk. Suddenly throwing down his quill, he lifted his glance, gave Roger a cold stare, and exclaimed; 'Mr. Brook, I am near speechless from amazement that you should have the effrontery to present yourself before me.'

Only the iron nerve that had more than once enabled Roger to keep his head attached to his shoulders enabled him to reply with a calm lift of the eyebrows. 'And I, Sir, am even more amazed at your reception of me. Pray inform me what I have done to merit your displeasure?'

'Done!' repeated the Prime Minister, coming slowly to his feet. 'Did I not charge you to exercise your charm upon the Venetian envoy? And how have you observed my wish? First you inveigle him into wagering two thousand guineas, then with the help of your unscrupulous friends at Stillwaters deprive him of a fair chance to win his bet. When he protests you and your cronies fall upon him. On his striking out in self-defence you taunt him until he reluctantly agrees to give you satisfaction by meeting you in a duel. Finally, you concert a despicable plot, as a result of which he is shot by an arrow in the back, and is thus made easier for you to half butcher without risk to yourself.'

Roger's blue eyes had gone as hard as ice and his voice was equally cold as he refuted the charge. 'Knowing me as you do, Sir, I marvel that you could for one instant believe such lies.'

'Know you!' came the irate rejoinder. 'Having employed you for so long how can I fail to do so? Your intelligence, you gift for languages, your ready wit, unscrupulous and easy charm make you the best secret agent of your

generation. But you are self-willed, and lecherous and, at the least provocation, will whip out the sword you have trained yourself to use with such
dexterity. There have been previous occasions when a woman's smile has
caused you to forget all else. And I gather there is one involved in this. I
have no doubt but that it was due to your pursuit of her that you threw my
interests to the winds.'

'Damme, Sir! You go too far. All men are not so sluggish blooded as
yourself, and . . .'

'How dare you stand there and indulge in such personalities!'

With a stiff little bow, Roger rapped back, 'I withdraw that, and will
admit that of all the joys of this world I have found none to compare with
a woman one loves beside one in a bed. Yet in the final outcome, of no
mission have you charged me with have I allowed my love for one of the
sex to interfere. In the present instance, no such predilection plays any
part at all. As a matter of simple justice I must ask from what source this
tissue of lies was poured into your ears?'

'My cousin Grenville passed the night at Holwood with me, and he was
full of it. Before he left London the Ambassador of the Serene Republic
had requested an urgent audience of him. The Venetian brought with him
a letter from his colleague, Signor Malderini, containing this account of
your scandalous treatment of him. Bearing in mind the mission with which
I had charged you, I could hardly credit your behaviour; yet chapter and
verse was given for it.'

'Be good enough to remember, Sir, that on Saturday morning last you
relieved me of my mission. The events to which Malderini's letter refer
occurred subsequently to that, and . . .'

'No matter. You knew my mind, and the importance I attached to
winning the good-will of the envoy of this powerful State.'

'Should you succeed 'twill do you no more good than securing that of
the rottenest Borough in England,' Roger replied tartly.

'How dare you! I am convinced that the Serene Republic could prove a most
powerful ally; and it is not for you to question my assessments or decisions.'

'Believe it if you like; but time will prove you wrong. That, though, is
beside the point. Such action as I took against the Venetian was fully
justified. He is a rogue, a liar and a swindler. He is a faker of occult
phenomena and . . .'

'How can you expect me to believe such charges when he has been
selected by his Senate to represent them?'

'That he is rich, powerful, cunning and ambitious would be enough to
account for that. I can prove to you that his unscrupulous greed is at the
bottom of this whole business and I have come here for the especial
purpose of requesting your protection from him.'

'My protection?'

'Yes. I have been warned that Malderini intends to invoke the anti-duelling laws against me.'

'You should need no telling that once the law is set in motion, even a Prime Minister cannot interfere with its course.'

'Nay; but a prisoner having been convicted, there is naught to prevent His Majesty granting him a free pardon.'

'I fail to grasp what you would be at?'

''Tis this. Continue to disbelieve me, if you choose. But no judge and jury will reject the evidence of such reputable persons as Colonel Thursby, Lord Edward Fitz-Deverel, Mr. William Beckford—aye, and even Sheridan, for he's too decent a man to perjure himself. I wish to stand my trial and show up this blackguard.'

Mr. Pitt sat down again. For a moment he was silent, then he said:

'Your willingness to do so shows that I have been overhasty in my judgment. For that you must blame previous occasions on which you have temporarily neglected my interests to pursue your love affairs; and you cannot deny that a young woman is involved in this.'

'True, but not in the way you think. May I take it now, Sir, that I can count on your protection? It goes without saying that I'll be found guilty and, eager as I am to expose this villain, imprisonment for myself is too high a price to pay.'

'So you wish to go into Court with the King's Pardon as good as in your pocket?'

'Exactly, Sir. And to you there is not the least possibility of His Majesty refusing it.'

'That I admit and, were this a private matter, I would obtain one for you; but it is not.' The Prime Minister shook his head. 'It has become an Affair of State. The Ambassador of a friendly power has asked that justice should be done upon you. By now, I imagine a warrant for your arrest has been issued. Should the Bow Street Runners catch you, your trial and condemnation must follow. How, after you have been found guilty, can I possibly take steps to prevent your punishment? To do so would be to inflict a deliberate insult on the Venetians, and at the very time I am most eager to draw them into an alliance.'

Roger's face expressed his consternation. 'But, Sir,' he burst out, 'consider the alternatives. To escape prison I must go into hiding, or take refuge abroad.'

'I appreciate that; but you are used to travelling, and in a few months this affair will have blown over.'

'Perhaps! But in all but having broken a law which it is common practice to ignore, I am innocent. And I resent being driven from my country.'

Mr. Pitt spread out his slim hands. 'I fear there is no help for it. The best I can do is to ensure you a clear start. I will give instructions that on some technicality the execution of the warrant should be suspended for a week. Meanwhile I will speak to my cousin Grenville and see if he can suggest some suitable employment for you while you are in exile.'

Roger, as was usual on such occasions, had been standing in front of the Prime Minister's desk, with his hat beneath his arm. Cramming it violently upon his head, he cried: 'You may save your breath, Sir! If into exile I must go, it will not be in your service.' Then he strode out of the room.

He had arranged to meet Droopy Ned at White's, to which they both belonged, and tell him there over a pint of sack the result of his interview with Mr. Pitt; so, still seething with rage, he walked across the Park and up St. James's Street.

Droopy was already in the Club and listened sympathetically while Roger poured out his disgust at his master's having sacrificed him rather than give offence to the Venetians. When he had done, Droopy said:

'I hesitated to say so the other night, but I had a feeling then that Mr. Pitt would put his interest with them before yours. What will you do? My invitation to lie low at Normanrood is naturally still open.'

'Thanks, Ned, but no.' Roger shook his head. 'For one thing, the constant presence of Clarissa might prove too great a temptation to me. I've no wish to marry again, and I'd be ashamed of myself did I make her my mistress. For another, I have never been a great lover of country pursuits and after a week, with no company but women, I'd be prodigious bored. I see nothing for it but to go abroad.'

'At least Mr. Pitt is giving you seven days in which to make your arrangements; and that is something. To what country will you go?'

'Heaven knows! If I return to Paris I'll get myself involved in political affairs, and I've no mind to start tightrope-walking again as yet. I could go to my little château near St. Raphael in the South of France. I bought it early this year so that I might tell Barras and his cronies that I'd been sojourning there for my health as cover for returning in secret to England whenever I wished; but I'd be even more lonely there than I would confined to the estate at Normanrood. I'd like to go to Italy or the Rhineland again, but the war, with its hordes of soldiery marching and countermarching, must keep both those countries in a constant turmoil. It seems that I must go further afield.'

For half an hour they discussed the attractions and drawbacks of numerous countries, then Droopy suggested, 'Why not make a voyage to India? I am told that society in Calcutta is now both civilized and gay. You could winter there in the sunshine and return here by next summer.'

At that, Roger brightened and, after a moment's thought, said, 'Strap me, Ned; I believe you've hit on it. I've always wanted to see the gorgeous East, and I'll have no better opportunity. What of a passage, though. I've an idea that most of the sailings take place during the first half of the year, and after that June there is only one more in September.'

'You are right in that, but I think with luck you might just catch the summer convoy. Only yesterday someone mentioned in my hearing that it had not yet completed mustering in the Downs. The rub is that all the best accommodation must already be bespoke.'

'Oh, I'd share a cabin if need be; though, naturally, I'd rather have one to myself.'

'You really mean, Roger, that you are set on making this voyage to the East?'

'Indeed, yes. The prospect of seeing Rajahs weighed down with diamonds, and going tiger shooting on an elephant, holds such fascination for me that I am already near inclined to forgive Mr. Pitt his churlishness.'

'Then, as I have some influence with the Company, I will do my best to get you a comfortable passage. This afternoon I have an appointment in Hatton Garden to view a ruby ring said to have been fished up from a Spanish galleon sunk at the time of the Armada. I'll go on from there to the India House in Leadenhall Street.'

When they had finished their wine they left the Club and crossed the road to Arlington Street. In the big library they spent some time hunting out books on India that had illustrations of the country and its peoples. Later, Droopy suggested that Roger should accompany him down to the City, but he had other plans for the afternoon; so he declined and, as soon as Droopy had gone, went in search of Clarissa.

She knew London very little and had spent only one night in it since her return from the West Indies; so when Roger suggested taking her for a walk round the shops she was delighted. The most fashionable ones then lay south of Piccadilly; so they made a leisurely progress along Pall Mall, up through the Opera Arcade, down the Haymarket and round by way of Cockspur Street up to Leicester Square, where the house still stood in which King George had spent most of his boyhood.

Early in this little expedition, Clarissa admired a bonnet in a bow-fronted window; so he insisted on buying it for her and, in other shops, despite her protests, he bought her a long-handled parasol, scent, gloves, hand-kerchiefs, a lace scarf, a reticule, a fan and several pounds of sweets for her to take with her to Normanrood. Then, on their way back through Piccadilly, he took her into the Egyptian Hall to see Captain Tom Thumb and his performing fleas. When they parted in the hall at Amesbury House, Roger to seek Droopy and Clarissa to go up and change for dinner, they agreed that it had been a lovely afternoon and that they had enjoyed themselves immensely.

Droopy had good news. The refitting of one of the Company's ships, the *Minerva*, Captain Finch, had been delayed; so that it had been feared that she would not be ready in time to sail with the convoy. In consequence, it was not until forty-eight hours earlier, when it had been found that great efforts could make her ready after all, that any passenger accommodation in her had been on offer. As few people had left their bookings so late, she was still half empty and Roger had been allotted a good large cabin. She had just completed taking on cargo at Gravesend, and was due to sail again the following day.

This last piece of information somewhat damped Roger's gratification, and he said, 'I am once more your debtor, Ned; and if I miss the *Minerva* at Gravesend, no doubt I can pick her up off Margate. I would, though, that I had had a day or two's grace; for I am loath to leave the country without having made my farewells to Georgina.'

'You can still do so,' Droopy replied cheerfully. 'Without *Minerva* it will be two days yet before the muster is completed; and even when a convoy is complete, almost invariably it has to wait several days for a favourable wind to set sail down Channel. Knowing that they will be cooped up in close quarters for so long a voyage, few persons of quality ever take ship from London, or even Margate. There are good inns at Deal from which an eye can be kept on the convoy riding in the Downs; so they spend the time of waiting in them, and go aboard only when the warning gun is fired to give notice that the ships are about to sail. Providing you are at Deal by Tuesday, you may be sure of not being left behind.'

Much relieved, Roger said, 'I'll go to Stillwaters again tomorrow then, and post cross-country to Deal on Monday. I pray you, though, say nothing of this yet to Clarissa, as I wish to break the news to her privately of my intended long absence.'

He took the opportunity to do so after dinner. The great mansion had a terrace behind it and a small garden that adjoined the Green Park. It was still twilight and after the long hot summer day a little oppressive, so he suggested that they should go out onto the terrace for a breath of air. She readily assented and they walked out of the candle-lit drawing-room side by side.

To their right lay Piccadilly with its long range of houses running down the slope, many of their windows brightly lit; to their left front, the dark silhouette of the upper part of Buckingham House stood out above the trees. For a moment they stood looking out across the Park in silence, then she said: 'Roger, I have not thanked you half enough for this afternoon, and all those lovely things you bought me.'

'You will, I fear, be less pleased when I tell you my reason for taking you upon our little outing,' he replied quietly. 'It was in the nature of a farewell. I have much to do tomorrow, so shall be up and gone early. After tonight we'll not be seeing one another for many months, perhaps even years.'

Her eyes grew wide and she laid a hand quickly upon a big stone vase beside her. 'But Roger! What of your determination to stay and fight it out with Malderini in the Courts? That was so typical of you and made me even more proud to be . . . to be your friend.'

'Mr. Pitt has refused me his protection if I submit to arrest; so it's a choice of flight or prison, and I prefer to retain my liberty.'

'Then I'd be the first to urge flight upon you. But where . . . where do you intend to go?'

'To India.'

'India!' she exclaimed. 'Why, India might well have been the setting for my vision—the dream I had when Malderini put me into a hypnotic sleep.'

He took her hand. 'Clarissa, I implore you to put that from your mind. It could not possibly become reality. Within a month or two Malderini will have left the country and you will be free to re-enter society. I, on the other hand, having broken with Mr. Pitt, may even decide to settle in the East. You must not waste the best years of your life hoping for my return, but throw yourself joyously into every party, ball or rout with the idea that at it you may meet the man who will become the real love of your life.'

'Roger, you are that man! Kiss me at least before we go in.'

'Very well, then.' He swung her towards him. 'But I'll kiss you only to stress the fact that this is a parting of the ways between us; a final farewell.'

For a long moment they stood close embraced, their mouths warm, avid, greedy, moist, seeking to draw something beyond the physical out of one another. As they broke both let out a gasp, then she gave a bitter laugh:

'Roger, you are a fool to reject my love for you, and you must know it.' But he already had her by the arm and was half pushing her back through the french window into the drawing-room.

That night he took his leave of Droopy's father and the other members of the family staying in the house. Next morning he was at Hoare's Bank in the Strand soon after it opened, making his financial arrangements. Going on to Leadenhall Street, he paid for his passage in the *Minerva*. On his return to Arlington Street, he found one of the Marquess's coaches already loaded with his luggage and Droopy waiting by it to say good-bye to him and wish him luck. By the late afternoon he was at Stillwaters.

Georgina and her father were distressed to learn that Roger's plan for exposing Malderini at no cost to himself had gone awry; but the Colonel was not altogether surprised at the attitude Mr. Pitt had taken up. As all three of them were philosophical by nature, they did not allow themselves to be too depressed by the turn events had taken. Georgina and Roger had already loved and parted more than once before, and both were convinced that the intangible but indestructible bond between them would, sooner or later, draw them back into one another's arms again.

On Monday morning Roger left Stillwaters. He slept the night at Maidstone, and by midday Tuesday reached Deal. The inns there were crowded with the better class of passengers awaiting the departure of the convoy, and it was only by heavy bribery that he secured an attic room.

During the next two days he made the acquaintance of a number of people who were voyaging to India, among them one couple who were to be his fellow-passengers—a Sir Curtis and Lady Beaumont. Their reason for sailing in the *Minerva* was, he learned, because at short notice Sir Curtis had been appointed a judge of the Indian High Court.

On Friday at midday they were informed that, the wind having become favourable, the convoy would sail that night. During the afternoon a score of row-boats were taking off passengers and light baggage to the eight ships making up the convoy, that still lay gently rocking at anchor in the fairway.

Having dined on shore, at about five o'clock, Roger and the Beaumonts went aboard the *Minerva*. They were received most courteously by Captain Finch, a broad-shouldered, square-faced man of about forty. After expressing his pleasure that he would have them at his table, he ordered the Purser to show them to their cabins.

Roger was a far from good sailor, so he was pleased to find that he had been given one amidships, and on the lee side, for the long run down through the Atlantic. It had two berths and ample cupboard space; his heavy luggage, which he had sent aboard soon after reaching Deal, lay still corded on its deck.

Turning to the Purser he said: 'I take it you will provide a steward to valet me, and he may as well make a start by unpacking my things.'

Looking somewhat surprised, the Purser replied:

'But you have your own servant, Sir. He came aboard off Margate and handed me a letter from Lord Edward Fitz-Deverel, stating that his Lordship had engaged him to serve you on the voyage.'

Smiling, Roger thought how typical it was of his good friend Droopy to show such concern for his comfort. Then he asked the Purser, 'Where is this man of mine?'

The Purser made a vague gesture. 'I don't rightly know, Sir. And being about to sail I've got my hands full at the moment; so you must forgive me if I don't go hunting for him. But if I do see him I'll send him to you.'

For the hour that followed, Roger watched the scene of almost indescribable confusion on deck; last minute mails arriving, tearful farewells, sailors' molls, who had been hidden below decks during the voyage from London, being bundled off into the boats, a dead drunk soldier being hauled aboard by a bowline, all amidst a din of shouted orders and counter orders.

At last, as twilight fell, the boats pulled away. With the ship's fiddler sitting crosslegged on the capstan, and the crew singing a hearty sea-chanty, the anchor was weighed. To the rattle and scream of blocks, the vast acreage of canvas aloft was unfurled and set. In company with her seven sister ships and their escorting frigate, the *Minerva* began to plough her way down Channel under a fair breeze.

In those days, tropical diseases took a high toll of Europeans in the East, and the wastage by death in the Army was as high as one man in ten per annum; so even in peace-time large numbers of reinforcements had to be sent out by every convoy. The *Minerva* was carrying a dozen officers and over a hundred other ranks; but, owing to the uncertainty of her sailing, until near the date her civilian passengers were few.

When they assembled in the saloon, Roger found that, in addition to the Beaumonts, they were a portly Mrs. Armitage and her skinny daughter, an elderly lawyer named Musgrave and a plump, middle-aged merchant named Winters. Besides these there were a number of Servants of the Company, mostly young 'writers', as civil servants were then called, going out for the first time.

Captain Finch introduced them to one another, to the Army officers, to his own officers, and to the surgeon. He then solemnly read prayers for a fortunate voyage and confided the ship and her company into the hands of God, against the perils of the ocean. The brief service over, Madeira was produced and numerous toasts drunk. It was fully dark and close on ten o'clock when the company broke up and went down to their cabins.

To Roger's annoyance he found his trunks still corded, which did not augur well for Droopy's choice of a servant for him. But he had often looked after himself for many months at a stretch; so, without giving the matter another thought, he undid the valise that he had brought aboard with him, and got out his night things.

He was only half undressed when he heard the door rattle, then a knock upon it. As he had put the catch up, he walked over and threw it open. In the dim light of the gently swinging lantern hooked to a beam in the passageway, he saw a youngster with a woollen stocking cap pulled well down over his ears.

For a moment they faced one another in silence; then in a lilting voice, bubbling with suppressed laughter, the boy spoke:

'May it please you, Sir. I am your servant.'

Only then, to his amazement and fury, did Roger realize that he was staring at Clarissa.

CHAPTER EIGHT

The Great Temptation

GRASPING Clarissa by the arm, Roger pulled her through into the cabin. With his free hand he slammed the door. With the other he gave her a violent shake, as he cried:

'How dare you spring this upon me! What's the meaning of this masquerade?'

'Roger!' she gasped. 'Let go! Please! You're hurting!'

As he released her, she stumbled back against a sea chest and sat down upon it with a bump.

'To play such a prank you must be out of your wits,' he stormed. 'And Ned, too; for it seems he must have aided you in this.'

'He did, bless his kind heart. I unbosomed myself to him, and he could not refuse my plea to help me in my plan for accompanying you to India.'

'To India, eh?' Roger gave a short harsh laugh. 'The sooner you disabuse yourself of that idea, Miss, the better. By morning we should be abreast the Isle of Wight. I shall have you put off there; or, failing that, at Poole or Weymouth.'

'Oh, Roger!' There were tears in her voice. 'And I thought you would be pleased to see me.'

'You mean you thought you'd trap me into this marriage that you desire. That, having compromised yourself so fully, I'd not have the strength of mind to refuse to make an honest woman of you. But in that you were mistaken. You must pay the price of your own folly.'

'No! No, no!' she cried in sharp protest. 'You wrong me there! I intended nothing of the kind. In Martinique, after Amanda died, I offered to become your mistress. I know that it was mainly out of chivalry that you refused; but partly, too, because you were then so grief-stricken by your loss. Now you are over that; and I would liefer be your mistress than any man's wife. It is as your mistress that I want you to take me to India with you.'

His expression softened, but he still frowned. 'How can I, even if I would? The Company's ships maintain a high standard of respectability. None of their Captains would tolerate on board a couple living openly in sin.'

'Not openly, perhaps, But they wink the eye at men of position, like yourself, taking a young woman with them on a voyage. 'Tis a common practice.'

'I am amazed to hear it. What leads you to suppose so?'

'Julia Carruthers told me of it in Martinique.'

'D'you mean the wife of Captain Carruthers, who came out, just before I left, to take over the naval dockyard?'

'Yes. He was in the service of the Company before transferring to the Royal Navy. She told me that in India young coloured girls can be had at the lifting of a finger, but, their physical attractions apart, they have nothing to offer a man of quality; and good-looking white women are near as scarce as rubies. That being the case, wealthy bachelors often take their mistresses out with them; but, of course, they have to travel in men's clothes, and in the guise of their lovers' servants.'

'So it was that which led you to this masquerade. Surely, though, the servants have their own quarters, and for the greater part of the time are expected to occupy them?'

'There is a noisome cubby-hole in which they eat by day and some sleep at night; but most of them prefer to doss down in the passageways outside their masters' cabins, and I gather that single gentlemen often allow their servants to lay a mattress on the floor inside them. In our case, it would be thought that you had shown this last consideration to me.'

'I take it then that, since coming aboard from Margate, you have slept in here.'

'Naturally. And I was much pleased to find that you had been given a two-berth cabin. I am sure you would not be happy for me to sleep upon the floor; yet, were there only one, I'd have no alternative during the spells of rough weather, for at such times it's certain you'll be seasick.'

Clarissa was an exceptionally good sailor, whereas Roger was a bad one. Her reminder of the miserable state he was likely to be in for at least a part of the long voyage was far from welcome, but it was not on that account that he replied sharply: 'You go too fast. I've not said I'd have you in my cabin, and I won't.'

'Oh, Roger,' she pleaded, 'be not hard upon yourself as well as on me. Strive as you may to conceal it, I know that you find me desirable; and, as I have already assured you, even should some people come to suspect that I am a woman, no trouble will be made for you because of it.'

'Since you are so well informed about what goes on in the Company's ships, I'll not argue that point with you. But you seem to have overlooked the situation in which you would find yourself when we reached Calcutta. 'Tis not like London, where a man can carry on a clandestine affair with an unmarried girl, or even keep her in an apartment of her own, without anyone who matters being the wiser. You have yourself pointed out that in the East attractive white women are few and far between; that fact alone would render concealment impossible.'

'It would not be necessary. The very scarcity you speak of has led to entirely different conditions. Society there has become far more tolerant than it is in England. Julia told me that in India white mistresses live openly with their lovers and by custom take their names. Providing that they know how to conduct themselves decently they are received on equal terms with married women; so that in all but the blessing of the Church, I'd be Mrs. Brook.'

'And what when we returned to England? Do you suppose that no tales ever drift back from those distant shores? You suggest that on our arriving in Calcutta I should produce you, apparently from nowhere, as Mrs. Brook. But a change to female garments will not prevent the officers, every passenger, and all the crew in this ship recognizing you as the youth who played the part of my servant on the voyage out; so there'll be no disguising the fact that we're not married. Then, within a week or two, someone will appear on the scene who knew you either in England or Martinique, and your true identity will become common property. What with your looks and the fact that you are of good family, the next ship will carry back to London the news of our liaison. Your name will be dragged in the mud and your chances of making a good marriage for ever ruined.'

'I care not!' she declared stubbornly. 'I've no close relatives who would be shamed by me, and I've a right to dispose of myself as I wish.'

'But I do care,' he rapped back, 'and I'll not have you ruining your whole life. I am honoured and touched by your love for me, but on those terms I would feel disgraced did I accept it.'

Suddenly she stood up. Her voice was low and she leaned towards him, as she said, 'Roger, kiss me. Kiss me as you did the other night.'

'No!' he exclaimed, pushing her off. 'No! I'll be damned if I will.'

'You daren't,' she taunted him. 'You dare not, because you know that if you did you would give in. You'd rather keep your stupid pride and let me break my heart.'

'I'm not the keeper of your heart, but I am of my own conscience,' he cried angrily. 'I'll have naught to do with you. Get out of here! Get out!'

In an instant her shoulders sagged pathetically, and her hands shook as she held them out to him. 'You cannot mean this, Roger. Think what you are sending me to. It was bad enough down in the servants' cubby-hole waiting to come to you until the ship was well out at sea. The men have brought aboard great flasks of gin and are drinking to a fortunate voyage. I had great difficulty in avoiding having a drink with them. It will be worse by now, and soon they'll all be roaring drunk. Anything might happen to me.'

'It would serve you right if I did send you there; but I see it to be impossible.'

For a moment he was silent and her heart leapt with hope again; but he crushed it by adding curtly, 'Very well, then. It is I who must pass a night in discomfort.'

Quickly putting on again the things he had taken off, he got into his heavy many-collared top-coat, picked up his hat, and said, 'You are to remain here until I come to you in the morning. And make up your mind to it, I am not changing mine. I mean to have you put ashore before we pass the Needles.'

Slamming the door behind him, he made his way on deck and up to the poop. There was hardly room to move on it as it was piled high with hundreds of barred crates and coops. Each was crammed to capacity with live sheep, pigs, turkeys, geese, chickens or ducks, which would be slaughtered as required to provide fresh meat at the Captain's table throughout the voyage. The stench was indescribable.

Still seething with rage, he thrust his way down one of the narrow alleys that had been left between the crates, until he reached the Chart House. On this first night of the voyage he expected that Captain Finch would be up there until at least midnight, observing the behaviour of his ship under her new rigging; but the Second Mate, whose watch it was, promptly disabused him of any hope of seeing the Captain before morning.

He learned that the Captains, or Commanders as they were called, of East Indiamen regarded themselves as considerable personages. On landing in India they were greeted with a salute of thirteen guns, and on entering or leaving a fort, guards turned out for them. While at sea they had six mates and several midshipmen; so it was beneath their dignity to take any active part in the navigation of the ship, except in such exceptional circumstances as tempest or attack by an enemy.

Roger felt it to be out of the question to confide the delicate matter of Clarissa's presence aboard to anyone other than the Commander, although this meant that, instead of quietly being put into a spare cabin for the night, he must shift for himself as well as he could.

Gloomily he began to pace the deck, but gradually his anger evaporated. He had left Clarissa in tears and he began to wonder if he had not behaved unduly harshly towards her. Grievous as was the embarrassment which her folly must cause them both when steps had to be taken to put her ashore, he was forced to recognize that only love for him had impelled her to her act. From that he passed to wondering if he was not behaving like a priggish fool.

In those days, girls were frequently married at the age of fourteen, and Clarissa was no little chit just out of the schoolroom whose head might be turned by a handsome fellow asking her to dance three times in one evening. She had had a dozen offers of marriage and men of all sorts and conditions had tried to make love to her; so hers was no case of a girl who did not know what she was doing, or even of one swept off her feet by a sudden passion.

The more he thought of the matter, the more he was tempted to go below, kiss away her tears, and hold her for the rest of the night in the warm embrace to which he knew she would be so willing to yield herself. And there was much more to it than that. Fascinating as he believed India would prove, with its rich sights and sounds, dusky potentates and fabulous palaces, the voyage to it was long and must prove incredibly tedious. Instead, with Clarissa for company, it could be turned into a honeymoon holding a thousand secret delights. Pausing at the head of the companion-way, he decided that it would be flying in the faces of the gods to reject this wonderful gift they were offering him.

Yet, with his hand upon the rail, he still hesitated. If he once took the plunge, there could be no escaping what would follow. She might be right about society in India tolerating such liaisons. If so, they could continue their honeymoon for a few more months in glamorous surround-ings. But he had no intention of remaining away from Europe for longer than the inside of a year, and when they returned to England she would have to pay the price for having thrown her shift over the moon. Georgina in her 'teens had been an heiress, so could afford to ignore rumours that her morals were no better than they should be, but Clarissa had neither family nor fortune—and in her case it would not be merely rumours. She would be ostracized by women who had young daughters, as unfitted to be seen in their company, the baser type of men would snigger behind their hands to one another as she passed, and she would be considered fair game for every sort of indecent proposal. As these thoughts raced through Roger's mind, he reverted to his former feeling, that it would be unutterably mean to bring such shame upon her.

For another hour he remained on deck, now and then going to the ship's side to watch the white foam racing along under her counter, or looking up at the ghostly sails with their intricate criss-cross of groaning rigging. At length he decided that he must try to find somewhere to sleep, so he went down to the saloon, stumbled about in the darkness there, and fumbled his way to a long settee. Wrapping his big coat more closely about him he lay down and, his mind still tormented by the allurement of Clarissa, eventually dropped into an uneasy doze.

Soon after five in the morning he was roused by the rhythmic swish and thud of scrubbers on the deck above him. As he sat up, the previous night's events became again clear in his mind and added to the wretchedness he felt owing to his almost sleepless night. Hoping that the fresh air would clear his head, he went up on deck.

During the night the weather had worsened. The sea was choppy and there was no sight of land. Roger began to wonder uneasily if seasickness was soon to be added to his other miseries, but the deck was fairly steady as, with all sail set and a stiff breeze, the great ship sped at a fine pace through the dark green water.

For a while he watched the line of seamen gradually moving backwards as they scrubbed, their long-handled brushes moving in time to the beat of a Petty Officer's turks-headed leather wanger. Then, knowing that the best precaution against seasickness was to keep the stomach busy, he went down to the 'cuddy', as the dining cabin was called. The stewards were cleaning it and he asked one of them how soon he could have breakfast.

The man replied that tea and biscuits were served for such passengers who cared to come in for them at eight o'clock, but obligingly brought Roger a plate of biscuits and a steaming hot mug of strong tea from the crew's galley. After them he felt distinctly better; so he wandered up on deck again, wondering how he could best kill the two hours which it seemed there were still to go before a chance would come for him to speak to the Commander; but one occurred much sooner than he expected.

At a quarter-past six Captain Finch emerged from under the poop. For a moment Roger failed to recognize him, as his short broad figure was swathed in Turkish towelling. Stepping forward onto the quarter-deck, he threw off this robe and a nearby seaman, without waiting for an order, so evidently by custom, turned a salt-water hose on the now naked Commander. After a thorough sousing from head to foot, he resumed his robe and, puffing and blowing, began vigorously to rub himself down with it. Then, catching sight of Roger, he wished him a cheery good morning.

Several seamen being within earshot, this was no place in which to raise the matter of Clarissa, but Roger was anxious to know by when he might hope to be done with the business; so, having returned the Commander's greeting, he asked,

'At what hour do you anticipate we'll come opposite the Isle of Wight, Sir?'

Captain Finch cast a knowledgeable eye aloft, then replied; 'Any time now. With this fine breeze behind us we should be well past the Needles by mid-morning. Why did you wish to know?'

'I'd be grateful, Sir, if when we sight St. Catherine's Point a signal could be made for a boat to come off. My old home is at Lymington, and I particularly want to send off a . . . a packet to be delivered there.'

'St. Catherine's Point!' repeated the Commander. 'Good gracious, man, we'll not pass within twenty miles of it. What is more, sorry as I am to disoblige you, Mr. Brook, with such fine sailing weather to carry us down Channel I'd not lose an hour of it to turn inshore—no, not for a thousand pounds. I hope we'll not see land again till we sight Madeira.'

With a murmur of apology, Roger turned away to hide his perturbation. Fate had taken matters out of his hands and, whether he would or no, he must now remain responsible for his lovely stowaway for some two weeks. During them he could not possibly spend every night prowling about the deck or napping fully dressed in the saloon, and, if he shared his cabin with her for so long, the damage would be done; so he might as well take her on to India.

As he paced the deck once more, he could not help feeling elated that the gods had now made it practically impossible for him to reject the prize they offered him, and two possibilities crossed his mind, both of which tended to quiet his scruples at accepting it. One was that, when he decided to leave India, Clarissa, who would by then have made many friends there, might stay on; and with her youth and beauty it was certain that she would receive in such a lax society offers of honourable marriage from a variety of rich suitors. The other was that by then he might feel like marrying her himself.

He quickly dismissed the second. In the main, his marriage to Amanda had been a happy one; but there had been periods when they had made one another desperately unhappy, partly because of her hopeless extravagance and even more so through his failure to remain faithful to her during his long absences abroad.

He was now very much better off than he had been during the first years of their marriage, and another woman might prove a better manager; but he now knew himself too well to believe that he would either be content to settle down in England, or remain faithful to any woman if separated from her for a considerable period; so the major rock remained. Had Amanda lived, now that they would have had little Susan as an additional tie, he felt that he could have been to her, even despite occasional lapses, a better husband than would have most men of his class; but since she was dead it seemed downright folly to give some other woman the right to harrow him with jealous scenes when he might lead a carefree life.

The other possibility seemed much more promising. That way he could have his cake and eat it too; and, quite apart from any selfish motive, there was much to recommend it. He was rich enough to take a good house in Calcutta, to entertain fairly lavishly, and to give Clarissa everything that a woman of fashion needed. She would become the reigning beauty of the place and her salon would soon be thronged with the most eligible bachelors and widowers in India. In six months' time the edge of their first fine hectic passion would have beome sufficiently blunted for her to look at other men with more appreciative eyes. Instead of returning to England as a penniless girl with a ruined reputation, she could make her choice and, in a few years' time, come home as the respectable wife of some wealthy Nabob.

To see her becoming interested in someone else and secretly encourage her to safeguard her future would, he knew, prove a severe strain on himself; but that was the price he must pay, and pay it ungrudgingly, for her having given herself to him.

Greatly cheered by this solution, he again turned towards the companion-way, but once more he paused on the top step, considering what he should say to her. To disclose his plan was out of the question as, in her present state of mind, she would certainly be horrified at the idea that in due course he meant to pass her on to someone else. He could only say that as it proved impossible to put her ashore in England his scruples had been overcome and that he would joyfully take her as his mistress.

At that, the practical implications of the step began, for the first time, to drift through his mind. She could spend the nights in his cabin, but what of the days? There could be no question of her eating with the passengers or joining in their amusements. It would be difficult for him even to smuggle her tit-bits now and then; so she would have to rely for food mainly on the salt-pork and weevily biscuits that were the hard tack of servants and the crew. For weeks on end she would have to take her meals in the 'noisome hole' she had described to him, with rough, uncultured men. As a 'boy' she would almost certainly be made to drudge for the others and, quite probably, be bullied unmercifully. And there would be little that he could do to ameliorate her lot.

Probably she had not realized the full horror of what the months ahead would hold for her; but she must to some extent have visualized what she was letting herself in for—and that was the measure of her love for him.

That thought gave him pause again. Women, he knew, were by nature much more faithful than men. It was two years all but three months since they had sailed together for Martinique, and she had told him later that she had fallen in love with him from the beginning of the voyage. That he had been married, and that numerous handsome suitors had since done their utmost to win her, had failed to make her turn her thoughts elsewhere. Was it, then, really to be supposed that after living with him for six months she would become interested in some other man? No, the odds were that to take her would only add fuel to the fire. To abandon her in Calcutta was unthinkable, and to bring her home would mean for her disgrace.

Once more a prey to terrible indecision, Roger again began to pace the deck. The more he thought about it now the more convinced he became that to make Clarissa his mistress must prove her ultimate ruin and that, even if he were wrong in that and Fate proved more kind to her than there was any reason to expect, he could not allow her to endure the hardships and brutalities which were certain to be her portion if she continued to pose as his servant.

By eight o'clock he had made up his mind on a course of action. Going down to the 'cuddy', he found that the portly merchant, and two of the older Army officers, were the only passengers to have so far made their appearance. He wished them a curt 'good morning', helped himself to a mug of tea from the samovar and drank it. Then he poured another, picked up a handful of biscuits and, without explanation, carried them out of the cabin.

Down in his own he found Clarissa lying in the lower bunk, but wide awake. She had scragged her pale gold hair back over her head, cut six inches off it and done the rest up in a tight, seaman's pigtail; so, covered to her chin as she was, she looked very boyish. But directly they had exchanged greetings she sat up and, as she held out her hands for the tea and biscuits, he caught a momentary glimpse of one of her breasts. Small and firm though it was, it proclaimed more certainly than wearing a petticoat would have, that she was a woman. She had on one of his shirts, which were open at the neck, and he thought it highly probable that she had made the brief revelation on purpose; but it might have been through carelessness, and he shuddered to think what could happen to her if she gave her sex away while among the men servants. The thought strengthened him in his resolution.

As he sat down on the sea chest opposite to her, the light fell on the dark shadows beneath his eyes and his unshaven chin. With a contrite smile, she said, 'My poor Roger. 'Tis clear that you have passed a horrid night. And I'm to blame; so I fear you must be more than ever angry with me.'

He shook his head. 'Some wise man said "to understand is to forgive". I've now had time to appreciate how strong the feeling must be that nerved you to face the grim commitments of the rôle you meant to play. My sole distress is that it should not have for its object a man who could return it fully, and be more worthy of it than myself.'

She started to protest, but he cut her short. 'That is the truth, and the sooner you recognize it the better. I am both too selfish to ask the Captain to marry us, and too selfish to accept the joys you offer me without that, because I rate too high the price that I would later have to pay.'

'That is not the whole truth, Roger. If you cared for me less you'd not let your conscience worry you. 'Tis that, at whatever cost to both of us, you are determined not to spoil my chances of a good marriage. Remember, you once told me that you would have no scruples were I a married woman.'

For a moment he was silent, then his blue eyes became merry and he smiled at her. 'Very well then. When we reach India you must get yourself a rich husband, and I'll become your lover.'

'What say you!' Her face flushed with delight. 'D'you really mean that you are taking me to India with you after all?'

'I have no option. The ship has a stiff breeze behind her, and two hours back the Commander told me that nothing would induce him to waste it by putting in to send ashore—well, I called it a packet.'

She laughed. 'A packet of trouble, you should have said, for that's what I've become to you.' Suddenly her smile vanished, and she added, 'But if you'll not let me share this cabin with you . . . Oh Roger, I dread to think . . .'

'Be easy, m'dear. This cabin will be yours. I'm moving to another. But tell me: have you only boys' clothes, or did you also bring aboard some feminine garments?'

'I brought two trunks of my own things, but labelled with your name; and, not expecting to require them until our arrival in India, I had them put in the hold.'

'God be praised for that! 'Twill make matters far easier. As they were late stowed there should be no difficulty in getting them up from the hold, and I'll say that you directed them to be stowed there only because you knew no better.'

Leaning forward, he went on earnestly: 'Now this is our story. In some respects it is thin, but since I did not pass the night here, and intend to report the matter to the Commander at the earliest opportunity, it stands a good chance of being given credence. That is, if you play your part convincingly.

'You must appear a nit-wit of a girl whose head is full of romantic notions of the East. It was not any attachment to myself which led you to become the next thing to a stowaway, but a moon-struck desire to see the marvels you had read about. We are by marriage cousins, and the position you filled in relation to Amanda while in Martinique might well have led you to look upon me as an honorary Uncle. So you will call me Uncle Roger. What happened was that, on learning that I was going to India, you begged me to take you with me. I refused. But being spoilt, irresponsible and strong-willed, you hatched this plot to accompany me whether I would or no.

'You would, of course, have known that, had we come face to face before the ship was well out at sea, I should have had you put ashore. So you came aboard at Margate, slept in my cabin until I joined the ship, and did not intend to reveal yourself to me until the morning. But, when it came to a pinch, you could not stomach the thought of spending last night in the servants' quarters, so you came here, and I gave up my cabin to you. Had that been the true sequence of events, you would have known that, however angry your "dear Uncle Roger" might be, he would have had no alternative but to get you a cabin for yourself as soon as possible, have your boxes brought to it and, when you had resumed your frills and furbelows, present you to the Commander, officers and passengers as his niece. And that is our programme for the forenoon.'

'Oh, Roger, what a man you are!' she laughed. 'I believe you would pull the wool over the eyes of the devil himself.'

'We'll not succeed in this without your loyal help,' he warned her seriously. 'During the whole voyage you must not give away by a word or a look that your feelings for me are anything but those a young girl should have for a normally indulgent uncle. Have I your promise on that?'

'Yes,' she said a shade reluctantly. ''Twill be hard to appear indifferent to you for so long, but I learnt to do so while Amanda was alive—at least, I thought I had. To hold to such a resolution, though, I'll need some earnest of future happiness to buoy me up; so I must have a promise from you in return.'

'M'dear, your situation is hardly one which gives you the right to demand promises about the future.'

'Oh, but it is,' she smiled up at him. 'Do I not play this game as you would have me play it, what then? I could tell the Captain that having seduced me you would have abandoned me, had I not learnt your intention in time and succeeded in getting aboard without your knowledge. Thus I could swiftly deprive you of the vast satisfaction you expect to derive from having saved me from myself, and make you appear a heartless villain into the bargain.'

Roger was not often caught out, and this was the second time that Clarissa had used her wits to get him in a cleft stick. Despite her unscrupulous methods, he admired her for it; and, although he did not believe that she would really go to such lengths, he thought it wiser at least to appear willing to consider any proposal she might make, so he said:

'I recall that you as good as blackmailed me into refraining from sending you home from the Indies; but I warn you that I will dig my heels in should you demand anything I consider it unreasonable to grant.'

She laughed. 'How cautious you are; but I ask no more than to take you at your word, and my condition is one that you should not find onerous. It is that, should I find in Calcutta some impotent old dodderer who would like a decorative wife to brighten his last years until he sinks into his grave, you will become my lover.'

After only a second's hesitation, he stood up and bowed. 'Should that happen I'd count myself the most fortunate man in India.'

Serious now, she nodded. 'You see, although I would much liefer have been free to love you openly, I am willing to accept even half a loaf rather than starve for lack of bread. Go now, if you wish, and tell your story to the Captain.'

As he left her and made his way up to the deck, he could not decide whether he was glad or sorry that, although he had triumphed over immediate temptation, he was now, in given circumstances, committed to her. He had spoken the truth when he said that if she were married he would have no scruples about becoming her lover; but it had never occurred to him that she might be prepared to tie herself to some other man in order to become his mistress. That she appeared willing to do so was yet another revelation of the profoundness of her love for him, and he found it a little frightening.

Unthinkingly, he had given her the power to call the tune. If her obsession for him continued, she had only to let it be known on reaching Calcutta that she had come out to look for a husband, and within weeks that tune would be the wedding-march. But what would be the outcome of such a desperate measure? So fierce a passion as hers, when consummated, might become a cauldron of white hot fire and, once they had plunged into it, consume them both.

CHAPTER NINE

The Trials of an Uncle

GLIBLY as Roger had told Clarissa the story he had thought up to account for her presence on board, he was by no means confident that Captain Finch would swallow it hook, line and sinker. If he did not, he might discuss the matter with his Purser, or others, and that could lead to most undesirable speculations. It might, just possibly, emerge that, although Roger claimed to be Clarissa's uncle, he was not so in fact; and, anyway, he knew himself to be too young and good-looking for it not to cause at least mild surprise that he should be the uncle of a fully grown woman. In the close confines of a ship, it needed only a rumour that it was Clarissa's eagerness not to visit the gorgeous East, but to be ith him, that had brought her among them, and his whole plan to protect her reputation would fall to the ground.

It was, therefore, of the first importance that he should play his cards in such a way that Captain Finch would believe him from the beginning and not be left with doubts which he might mention to anyone else.

Having made up his mind on the line he meant to take, he went up to the poop and asked the officer of the watch to secure him an interview with he Commander. The officer sent a midshipman down with his request and the youth disappeared through a doorway under the poop. Two minutes later he reappeared and led Roger to a handsomely furnished cabin with tall sloping windows that looked out onto the churning wake of the ship.

Captain Finch politely rose from the desk table at which he was seated but, as he was a stickler for cleanliness in the small community of which, while it was at sea, he was the absolute master, he gave a quick frown of disapproval at Roger's dishevelled appearance. Before his visitor could even speak, he said sharply: 'Mr. Brook, it is one thing for me to see a passenger on deck with unshaven chin and hair like a bird's nest at six in the morning, and quite another for him to present himself before me in that state at this hour. Kindly retire and tidy yourself.'

Roger had purposely refrained from doing so before asking for an interview because he counted on the fact of his still being ungroomed being taken as sound corroborative evidence that he had not considered himself free to use his own cabin. Standing his ground, he said:

'My most humble apologies, Sir; but when I have informed you of the trouble I am in, I feel confident I may count on your forgiveness.'

'Well, what have you to say to me?'

'It is about the packet, Sir, of which I spoke to you earlier this morning.'

'I have already told you that there is no possibility whatever of my putting in to land your packet.'

'Unfortunately, Sir, the packet is a woman.'

'What!' Captain Finch's blue eyes almost shot sparks. 'D'you mean to tell me that you had the temerity to bring aboard some trollop at Deal, for the purpose of a last-night fling before putting her off at Lymington?'

Pretending righteous wrath, Roger drew himself up and let him have it back. 'Were that the case I would count it no cause for you to make such a display of indignation. I am informed, Sir, that not infrequently men of quality bring aboard, in the guise of servants, trollops, as you term them, to provide them with amusement through the whole voyage.'

The sailor flinched a trifle, but he replied stoutly, 'Sir! Were such an irregularity brought to the knowledge of a Commander of one of the Company's ships, he would not tolerate it for an instant.'

'No doubt,' retorted Roger. 'But I'll wager some of them take good care that it is not brought to their knowledge. At all events that is so if the table talk of Mr. Secretary Dundas is to be relied upon.'

Again Captain Finch's stern glance wavered for a second and, in a slightly less belligerent tone, he asked:

'Are you, then, well acquainted with Mr. Dundas?'

'Indeed, yes; he is an old friend and I have dined at his house out at Wimbledon in company with Mr. Pitt and others many times.'

In that, Roger told no lie, although he had made a completely unscrupulous use of Dundas's name when introducing it into the conversation.

R.V.—4

Harry Dundas was the Prime Minister's most powerful colleague in the Cabinet. He was a man of great ability and boundless energy. He managed their party, ruled the Scottish members with a rod of iron, and did all the unsavoury political jobbery with which Mr. Pitt did not care to soil his hands. In addition to being Minister of War he had, two years earlier, become President of the India Board, a new creation that now gave Parliament control over the affairs of the East India Company which, under its ancient Charter, had previously enjoyed complete immunity from interference in its activities.

It was, therefore, not to be wondered at that even a stout-hearted man like Captain Finch should, in those days when nepotism and patronage were almost universal, now display a somewhat greater readiness to deserve the good opinion of a gentleman possessing such powerful friends as did the tousle-haired and unshaven Mr. Roger Brook. With an abrupt little bow, he said: 'I can only regret, Sir, that I am unable to oblige you. To land your, er, hum—packet now would be contrary to my duty to the Company. With such a stiff breeze blowing the delay might even cause us permanently to lose touch with the convoy and our escort.'

Roger had feared as much, but the sailor's change of tone told him that his tactics of first treading on his corns, then revealing himself as a man with too much political influence behind him to be offended lightly, had served their purpose. The thing which concerned him was that the Commander should accept his story without question, whether he entirely believed it or not, and give his willing co-operation to transforming Clarissa as smoothly as possible from her present state to that of a respectable passenger. Judging that he had now been manœuvred into a suitable state of mind, Roger returned his bow and said:

'Believe me, Sir, I fully understood how you were situated when we first spoke of the matter this morning; and in coming here I had no intention of endeavouring to persuade you to alter your decision. Moreover, I am happy to be able to assure you that the unauthorized presence aboard of this young woman is in no way due to moral turpitude on my part. Far from it. She is, I admit, a flighty, spoilt, adventurous-minded minx and has played upon me a most wicked prank. But she is no trollop, Sir. She is my niece.'

'God bless me!' exclaimed the stalwart sailor, his prawn-like eyebrows shooting up into his square forehead. 'This is a fine kettle of fish!'

'It is one, Sir,' rejoined Roger grimly, 'that not only causes me grave embarrassment, but is like to put me to considerable expense, and she should be punished for it.'

Captain Finch suddenly sat down, motioned Roger to a chair and said with quick sympathy. 'You imply that you did not know her to be aboard until after we had sailed. If so I can appreciate the intense annoyance you must feel. Pray disclose the whole matter to me without delay.'

At this friendly invitation Roger turned on all his charm, told the story he had made up, and put forward his proposals for dealing with the affair. When he had done, Captain Finch said:

'One must admit the young lady has shown exceptional spirit in her determination to see the East, and I trust you will not deal too harshly with her by confining her to her cabin for a while, or anything of that kind. The ladies aboard are few upon this trip, so she will make a welcome addition to our company. I would have suggested saying that on her coming aboard I showed her straight down to her cabin myself and that suffering from a malaise last night she decided against leaving it. But, unfortunately, her joining the ship at Margate and her face having since become familiar to the other servants puts that out of the question. There can be no concealing her escapade, so we must make of it the best we can. In any case, it was most wise of you to elect to spend a wretchedly un-comfortable night rather than occupy the other berth in your cabin, as many uncles would have done. Your forethought in that was most praise-worthy, as there will now be no grounds for wagging tongues. Since you wish her to retain your cabin, I'll order your luggage to be removed to another, then have hers retrieved from the hold and sent down to her. I shall look forward to your presenting her to the company when we meet for dinner.'

He coughed and added, 'It only remains now for us to arrange about her passage money.'

The officers in the Company's ships were paid only a nominal salary, but were more than amply compensated for that by being allowed, on a scale in accordance with their rank, free shipping space to conduct a private trade of their own. On outward voyages the allowance ranged from fifty-six tons for a Commander to one ton for a midshipman; and even the petty officers were allowed a certain number of cubic feet. On the home-ward voyages the allowances were reduced by roughly one third all round but, even so, sound buying could bring them very handsome profits. In addition, while the Commander was responsible for feeding the passengers, any profit he could make out of their passage money was also part of his perquisites. For the Company's Servants there were fixed rates of from £95 to £250 according to rank for the one-way trip out, but private passengers had to make their own bargain with the Commanders and in a good ship, homeward bound, for which the rates were considerably higher, they often asked as much as £1,000.

Droopy had secured for Roger a passage at a cost of £500, which included £100 for the privilege of sitting at the Commander's table, where the food served was of a far higher standard than the ordinary passengers' fare.

Now, Roger had no option but to enter into a bond for a further £500 to secure for Clarissa the same amenities as he was to enjoy himself. While making the transaction he was hard put to it to conceal his chagrin, and Captain Finch to conceal his delight. The latter was under no obligation to purchase a single extra chicken or bottle of wine; so if, on account of this extra passenger, his table had to go a little short towards the end of the voyage, he could not be blamed for it, and the £500 could be regarded as clear profit. A few minutes later he bowed Roger out of his cabin with the greatest affability and his assurances that he would give the necessary orders forthwith.

Within a quarter of an hour, Roger's trunks were transferred to another cabin, and shortly afterwards, Clarissa's were brought to her; so they were able to set about making themselves presentable. When Roger emerged clad with his usual elegance, he again looked in on her to tell her to remain below until he came to fetch her, then he went up on deck to carry out another, and he hoped less tricky, part of his programme for protecting her reputation.

As he had expected, most of the passengers were now on deck enjoying the sunshine; and near the quarter-deck, a little apart from the rest, Sir Curtis and Lady Beaumont were occupying two chairs that had been specially placed there for them. Halting before them he made his bow and with a grave face enquired how they had slept.

'Not too badly for a first night at sea,' Lady Beaumont smiled, and her hook-nosed husband added, 'Tolerably, tolerably; and I hope, Sir, you fared no worse?' Then he offered Roger snuff.

Roger accepted a pinch, flicked his lace handkerchief and replied with a sigh, 'Alas, I got not a wink of sleep, but was kept from my berth all night by the most plaguey infuriating happening that ever did befall a man.'

On their both expressing their surprise, and asking him to tell them the cause of his plight, he turned towards the judge's plump, motherly wife, and said, 'It is to you, Ma'am, that I should principally address myself; for, unless you consent to afford me your charitable assistance, I know not what I shall do.'

Then he told them the same story about Clarissa as he had told Captain Finch; and ended by saying, 'So you see, I am landed for the voyage with a wilful though, to give the chit her due, quite passably good-looking niece. Since she is unmarried it is a certainty that she will become the centre of attraction for all the young officers abroad; and, as I entirely lack experience in handling such a situation, I fear it will prove beyond my control. Would you, therefore . . . could you . . . may I beg that you will do me the honour and kindness to act as her chaperone?'

'Why, of course I will,' Lady Beaumont replied at once. 'She certainly sounds a most wayward miss and, I trust, will not prove too much of a handful for me. But your request is a most proper one. 'Tis unthinkable that an unmarried girl of good family should make so long a voyage without an older woman to act as her confidante, and protect her reputation; so I will willingly oblige.'

Roger overwhelmed her with thanks and, declaring that she had taken a great weight off his mind, became his usual gay self again. Sitting down on a nearby coil of rope he gave the Beaumonts an account of Clarissa's background and, on learning that she was an orphan, Lady Beaumont exclaimed:

'Having lacked a mother's care is some excuse, at least, for her unruly, headstrong act; it makes me all the more willing to take the poor child under my wing. I am all eagerness to meet her.'

'I doubt if she will have finished titivating herself,' Roger replied, 'so we had best give her another half-hour; then I'll go fetch and present her to you, Ma'am.'

When he did go down to the cabin, he found Clarissa fully dressed but still fiddling with her hair. It had lost its curl and she had cut off the last six inches of the golden lovelocks which she normally displayed so attractively dangling over her left breast. As she had no means of heating her curling irons she was in a great state about how best to dress it.

Roger pointed out that she would have ample time to experiment with new styles later, and that for the early part of the voyage it would be all to the good that she should wear it simply dressed, as the younger she looked the more appropriate she would appear in her rôle as his niece. As he helped her fix it finally with a big bow at the back of her neck, he told her that Lady Beaumont had agreed to chaperone her, then they went up on deck.

The whole of its forepart was now crowded with soldiers, and the remainder of it well sprinkled with officers and passengers. A moment after they emerged from the hatchway, the laughter and chatter dwindled, then it ceased completely. In dead silence and with a hundred pairs of surprised, curious eyes fixed upon them, Roger, with Clarissa on his arm and a severe expression on his face, led her to the quarter-deck.

The judge and his wife stood up as they approached. Spreading her skirts wide, Clarissa sank down in a graceful curtsey and, instead of rising at once remained there with her head bowed for a moment. Lady Beaumont stepped quickly forward, raised her by the arms and kissed her on both cheeks, exclaiming:

'You sweet, wicked child! How lovely you are, and how pleased I am that for a while you are to be my daughter.'

The stern 'Uncle' now permitted himself a smile. 'Sweet and wicked,' he was thinking, were fair enough, but 'child' hardly applicable if one knew the truth; and he wondered what the good lady would say if she learned that only a few hours ago Clarissa had been hoping to pass the night in his arms. But, after Lady Beaumont's reception of her in front of nearly the whole ship's company, there was no danger of anyone suspecting that. He had played his cards well and timed her presentation perfectly.

Half an hour later, the after-deck began to clear, as the passengers went down either to change or at least tidy themselves for dinner. At two o'clock they assembled in the 'cuddy' for the meal. Clarissa was duly presented to Captain Finch, Lady Beaumont introduced her to Mrs. and Miss Armitage, and the other officers and passengers were in turn presented to her. The only sour looks came from Mrs. Armitage and her pimply daughter Jane. Everyone else expressed themselves as enchanted that Clarissa was to make the voyage with them. Within a few minutes all the younger men were buzzing round her like bees around a honey-pot, and as the dishes were brought in had to be almost driven away to their tables.

The Commander's table consisted of the Beaumonts, Roger, Clarissa, Mr. Winters, a senior servant of the Company named Cruishank, a Colonel Jeffs, a Major Routledge, and a dashing young subaltern of Hussars, the Honourable Gerald Keeble. The last, it soon became known, belonged to a rich and influential family, but was going out to India on account of the mountain of debts he had accumulated at home. The Major was an engineer and a taciturn man who seemed to have few pleasures in life except food. Mr. Cruishank and Sir Curtis were old friends and both had the dry pleasant wit that so frequently accompanies a high degree of education, coupled with a sense of humour. The Colonel was a red-faced gouty man, but of cheerful and kindly disposition when not suffering from a bout of his infliction.

Such a well-assorted little company could provide many topics of conversation and, the majority of them being genial by nature, bade fair to make the voyage more enjoyable than was usually the case with small parties cooped up for many months together. The meal was a leisurely one and the ladies did not leave the table till nearly four o'clock; the men sat over their port for an hour, then joined them in the saloon. Tea was served at six and a light supper at nine. Ten o'clock was the ritual hour for them to retire to their cabins.

Next day was Sunday, and for the first time Roger and Clarissa were able fully to appreciate how different an East Indiaman was to any other ships in which they had sailed. The average tonnage of merchant ships trading across the Atlantic or to the Baltic was little more than 300 tons, whereas the hundred odd ships that made up the Company's fleet were incomparably larger. They were of three grades, the smallest being 500 tons, the mediums 800, and the top class over 1,100. The Minerva was an 800 tonner.

But the difference did not lie in size alone. Most merchant ships were officered by men who had worked their way up from before the mast; sometimes no more than two of them were really capable navigators, and their Captains were often drunkards; whereas the officers of the Company's ships ranked nearly as high as those of the Royal Navy. Indeed, transferences between the two Services were frequent, particularly from the Navy to the Company in peace-time, as the Commander of an Indiaman, although usually financed by City Merchants, could often show a profit of as much as £10,000 on his personal trading in a single voyage.

In addition to six mates and four midshipmen, the average Indiaman carried a purser, surgeon, surgeon's mate, boatswain, gunner, coxswain, six quartermasters, captain's steward, captain's cook, barber, armourer, sailmaker, caulker, cooper, butcher, baker, poulterer, and teams of carpenters, cooks and stewards. The crews of such ships were well-drilled in arms and they were equipped with as many as thirty-two guns; so convoys had nothing to dread from sea-rovers, and had often given a good account of themselves when attacked by enemy squadrons during the wars with France.

It was on Sunday mornings that these fine ships were seen at their best, as the officers donned their uniforms, which differed only slightly from those of the Royal Navy, all beardless seamen had to shave, the whole ship's company put on their best clothes, and everything was made spick and span for the Commander's inspection. He began by making a round of the whole ship while the men stood to attention at their various posts. When he had finished, drums beat to quarters and everyone, including the male passengers who were armed with boarding-pikes, went to their action stations. Afterwards the Commander held a service, and the rest of the day was one of leisure for the crew.

On week days, weather permitting, from eight o'clock onward, a good part of the deck was occupied by the Army officers drilling their men to keep them as fit as possible. By half-past eight the space reserved for passengers began to fill up, and they either read their books or played games such as quoits, cup and ball, darts and shuttle cock, until one o'clock, when they went down to change for dinner. In the evenings they amused themselves with music, amateur theatricals, charades, spelling bees, poetry readings and guessing games.

At table the conversation, as was to be expected, turned frequently to Indian affairs. Even those who were going out for the first time were fairly well informed upon them, as for the past quarter of a century they had been the subject of many a heated discussion in England, and Parliament had given as much time to debating them as it was later to do in the 1890's and 1900's to the affairs of Ireland.

Within living memory the whole sub-continent had been the Empire of the Great Moguls, whose capital was at Delhi. For two centuries they had ruled it through their Nizams or Nawabs, as were called the Viceroys to whom they delegated their authority over vast areas of the country. But early in the reign of King George II the Mogul Empire had begun to disintegrate.

The Persians invaded, and for a time annexed, the provinces in the north-west; the Nawabs of Oudh, Bihar and Bengal, in the north-east asserted their independence, and all central and southern India also broke away, Hyderabad, Mysore, and the Carnatic became great sovereign states in the south. The Rajput Princes formed their own confederacy, and below it the whole of central India, from Gujarat on the Arabian sea to Orissa on the Bay of Bengal, became a still more powerful confederacy under the Maratha Princes, who had their capital at Poona. The result had been that during the middle decades of the century, these many nobles, great and small, had torn the country with a score of wars, each seeking to enlarge his territories or to overrun temporarily and plunder those of his neighbours.

This long period of strife and uncertainty had had a profound effect on the affairs of the Honourable East India Company. For a hundred and fifty years the Company had adhered to the Charter granted to it by Queen Elizabeth, in the heart of which stood the noble phrase, 'for the honour of this our realm of England as for the increase of our navigation and the advancement of trade . . .' The Company had never sought conquest and had resorted little to arms, except against its competitors: the Portuguese, Dutch and French; and its monopoly of the right to trade, which included China and the whole of South-East Asia, had brought it enormous wealth. But with India divided into as many states as Europe, and a number of them ruled by treacherous warrior adventurers, the Company found itself compelled not only to wage minor wars in the protection of its interests, but, in certain cases, to protect them for the future by assuming permanent control over territories in which those interests lay.

Apart from outlying trading posts, these territories were three in number. The most important was in the most distant part of India: its extreme north-eastern province of Bengal. In the wide mouth of the Hooghly river there the Portuguese had very early established a settlement, but in 1632 Shah Jahan had exterminated it and, soon afterwards, the Dutch and English managed to get a foothold; although it was not until sixty years later the Company received permission to move its headquarters farther up the river to a little fishing village, later to become the great city of Calcutta.

In the hundred years that followed, the Company's Servants penetrated deep into the interior to the north-west, through the rich provinces of Bengal, Bihar and Oudh up to Delhi and far beyond into the Punjab and Kashmir. The river of trade that flowed back had, by Roger's day, made

Calcutta one of the great metropoli of India with its British residents and garrison already numbering several thousands.

The Company's next most important centre was at Madras, another small fishing village a thousand miles south-west of Calcutta, on the Carnatic coast, at which in 1640 they had been given permission to erect a fort. From it they traded right up the east coast of India, across its tip through Mysore to the Malabar coast on the west, and up into the great province of Hyderabad, which occupied nearly the whole of the central part of Southern India.

Lastly, more than half-way up the west coast, six hundred miles from Madras and over a thousand from Calcutta—both across country as the crow flies—lay the island of Bombay. It had come to the British Crown as part of the dowry of Catherine of Braganza, and in 1667 King Charles II had leased it to the Company for £10 per annum. It was the finest natural harbour in India, no greater distance from London than Madras and a thousand miles nearer than Calcutta; but it had not developed to anything approaching the other two, the reason being that it was too far north to handle the Malabar coast trade and was cut off by difficult mountain country from the productive regions to the north and east. Nevertheless, it had grown into a considerable city and was a most valuable naval base.

The anarchy following the dissolution of the Mogul Empire had been further aggravated by the outbreak of war between Britain and France in 1743 over the question of the Austrian Succession. By this time the French, who had come later into the field than the Portuguese, Dutch and British, had also established powerful trading centres, notably at Chandernagore on the Hooghly and at Pondicherry, about a hundred miles south of Madras.

Pondicherry was the French headquarters and its able and energetic governor, the Marquis de Dupliex, promptly attempted to bring the whole of Southern India under French influence. He captured Madras and forced the remnant of the British community there to shut themselves up in Fort St. David. He then supported the claims of two pretenders to the thrones of Hyderabad and the Carnatic and ousted the pro-British potentates who occupied them.

It was then that Robert, afterwards Lord, Clive had first made a name for himself. Originally a young writer to the Company, he had early transferred to a cadetship in its armed forces. By 1751 the British cause was in a parlous state. Mohammed Ali, whom they were supporting as the rightful ruler of the Carnatic, had been driven from his capital at Arcot and, heavily outnumbered, was beseiged in Trichinopoly. Clive's force was so meagre that he could not possibly hope to defeat the besieging army. Instead, with the intention of drawing them off, he surprised and took Arcot, the capital newly won by the pretender.

This brilliant stroke succeeded. Mohammed Ali was saved from surrender and death by the pretender's hurriedly abandoning the siege and hastening back with his army to Arcot; but he now bottled Clive up in it. With only eight young officers, two hundred Europeans and six hundred Indian troops, Clive withstood for fifty days a seige and assaults by an army twenty thousand strong. At length a Maratha Prince, out of admiration for his bravery, brought an army to his assistance. Arcot was relieved and the Carnatic preserved as a sphere of British influence.

In Hyderabad, things went the other way. Dupliex's talented second-in-command, the Comte de Bussy, secured this vast central territory for the French and became, in effect, for several years, its ruler.

In 1754, peace in Europe brought peace in India. Dupliex was recalled and Clive went home. But the peace was only a very temporary one. In '56 the general war broke out again, and it was in that year that the young, dissolute and avaricious Nawab of Bengal, Surajah Dowlah, inspired by the French, made a treacherous surprise attack on Calcutta. The fortress was in an ill state of repair and the garrison below strength, but that hardly excuses the cowardly conduct of the governor who fled with his council to the ships in the harbour, leaving 146 Europeans to the mercy of the enemy. They were jammed into an old prison known as the Black Hole, and only 23 of them were still alive next morning.

In the meantime, Clive was on his way out again, now with full powers as the Company's General. The following January he took the field. With nine hundred British soldiers and fifteen hundred 'sepoys', as the European-trained Indian troops were called, he recaptured Calcutta and repulsed the forty thousand-strong army of Surajah Dowlah. In the spring, the French settlement of Chandernagore was captured and, in June, Clive again faced Surajah Dowlah's army at Plassey. The young Prince's contemptuous treatment of his nobles had made him many enemies at his own court, and his principal General, Mīr Jafer, treacherously advised retreat. Clive then fell upon and routed Surajah Dowlah's army; he was murdered and Mīr Jafer placed on his throne.

That was the end of French influence in Northern India and they were soon to lose their hold in the south. In January 1760, they were decisively defeated at Waniwash and a year later had to surrender Pondicherry. Meanwhile, a year earlier, Clive had defeated a powerful Dutch expedition, and when he left India no European power remained there capable of challenging British interests.

The Indian States were, however, far from permanently pacified, and in 1765 Clive was sent back for a further term of office. With a diplomacy equalling his military renown, he entered into treaties with numerous potentates, including the titular Emperor in Delhi, which gave the

Company control of the state revenues in Bengal and Bihar, made it the virtual master of Oudh and the Carnatic, and gave it the trading rights in the Northern Circas, which had previously been enjoyed by the French.

There followed the events which for the whole of Roger's lifetime had caused an almost constant succession of heated debates in the British Parliament.

The struggle with France and Clive's activities had changed the Company from a great organization concerned only with trade to one also responsible for the administration of vast territories. The Company had not sought, and was actually averse to assuming, such responsibilities, and the majority of its Servants were unsuited, by habits they had already acquired, to be trusted with such work.

Those habits arose from the fact that the Company paid its Servants hopelessly inadequate salaries, compensating them with the right to trade on their own account, and that in the East, immemorial custom decreed that anyone who benefited from a transaction should give the other party to it a present. Mir Jafer, for example, on being placed by the British on the throne of Bengal, had distributed among Clive and his officers half a million pounds. Later Clive had been called to account by Parliament. His reaction had been to protest that he stood astonished that he had been content with such a modest sum, and Parliament, knowing the circumstances, unanimously acquitted him of having used his power to enrich himself unreasonably. But, now that the Servants of the Company, great and small, had become officials with such wide powers of patronage, they proceeded to use them most unscrupulously.

Stories came home to England of Indian merchants and landowners being blackmailed and otherwise oppressed. Such tales were soon followed by an influx of middle-class and often vulgar Servants of the Company who had brought home fortunes, were termed in no friendly spirit 'Nabobs', and whose ostentation gave considerable offence in the country areas where they bought properties from the worse-off of the old landowning class. The misery of the Indian people had been further increased in 1770 by the most terrible famine on record, and hundreds of influential people in Britain were agitating for their interests to be protected.

This national outcry led to the Regulating Act of 1773, by which the Company's nominee for Governor-General had to be approved by Government and, although given authority over Madras and Bombay as well as Calcutta, his every act had to receive the sanction of a Council, a majority of whom could, if they disagreed with his policy, obstruct it with a veto. The Act also created a High Court of Justice to which Indians could appeal without fear that it would favour the Company, since its Judges were responsible only to the Home Government.

This was the first shackle put upon the complete independence of the
Company, and it fell heaviest on Warren Hastings, whom they had
appointed as Governor of Bengal the previous year. Hastings was a man of
integrity, vision and vigour, but he was faced with the still unsettled state
of India and the competing ambitions of its many Princes.

The Marathas, who had combined under the Peshwa at Poona, were
again in control in the north at Delhi. To the east of it an Afghan chief
had usurped the throne of Rohilkhand and was threatening Oudh. In the
west, owing to a trade-route dispute, the Marathas were threatening
Bombay. In the south Hyderabad had become hostile to the Company and
the throne of Mysore had been seized by a Mohammedan adventurer named
Hyder Ali, who threatened to, and later did, overrun the Carnatic.

The new Council consisted of five members, Hastings: who was its
chairman, Barwell, a senior Servant who understood the problems of the
Company and so loyally supported Hastings, and three nominees of
Parliament whose ignorance of India was such that, on landing in Calcutta,
they thought that because the natives had bare feet it was because the
Company had inflicted taxes so crushing upon them that they could no
longer afford boots. Led by Philip Francis, the newcomers at once adopted
a line of violent opposition to Hastings, and by their majority in Council
consistently thwarted his attempts to bring order out of chaos.

For two years his position was made intolerable, then one of Francis's
supporters died, giving Hastings control through his casting vote as chairman. But the bitter struggle continued for another four years until Francis,
after having been wounded in a duel by Hastings, went home.

During those years Britain had become involved in war with her American
Colonists, France, Holland and Spain, and once more events in Europe had
their repercussions in India. Although Britain's enemies could no longer
put an army in the field there, they could still stimulate avaricious Princes
to take up arms against the Company, and Hastings had to wage wars against
the Marathas who menaced Bombay, the Rohillas in support of Britain's
ally Oudh, and Hyder Ali the bold usurper of the throne of Mysore. With
the aid of three fine soldiers, General Sir Eyre Coote and Colonels Goddard
and Popham, all three wars were won, and by brilliant diplomacy Hastings
secured the paramountcy of the Company over vast areas of India.

But the wars had to be paid for. The Company grudged every penny
spent on military operations and, owing to many years of rapacity and mis-
management by its Servants, its funds had dwindled alarmingly. The war
in America and Europe had strained the resources of the Government at
home to such a point that it could not afford to give help. So Hastings had
to find the money himself. He found it in the only way possible for him:
by withholding subsidies the Company had contracted to pay to certain

potentates whose friendship was now doubtful, and by extracting great sums from the Indian allies whose territories he was protecting.

In 1773 a general peace was agreed by the Powers. The following year young Mr. Pitt, who had recently become Prime Minister, put through Parliament his India Act. Its object was to put to an end corrupt and arbitrary administration by the Company's Servants. In effect, Parliament took over the responsibility for ruling all areas that were, or should come, under British control. An India Board was created with Dundas as its President, and for the future the Company was required to frame its policy, and nominate its senior Servants, in consultation with the Board. Thus after two hundred years the Company finally lost all power in India other than its trading monopoly.

In the teeth of extraordinary difficulties, Hastings had already introduced many of the reforms which were the object of Pitt's Bill. He was the best friend that the people of India ever had, and he laid the foundations for the just and honourable administration of the Indian Civil Service which, in the following century, did so much to develop the country and bring western civilization to it.

But in 1784 he returned home to be met with ingratitude and obloquy. With almost unbelievable venom his old enemy Francis stirred up Parliament against him. He was made the scapegoat for his corrupt predecessors and colleagues, and impeached. Burke, the most brilliant orator of the day, had taken up the cause of the oppressed people of India and hurled invective at him. Fox and Sheridan resorted to every mean trick their excellent intelligences could devise to pull him down.

The trial dragged on for seven years. Every act of Hastings during his fourteen years of administration was gone into minutely in the hope of finding evidence of his corruption. The main charges concerned his conduct in connection with the Rohilla war, and the way in which he had raised money for that and other wars, particularly his extraction of a large sum from Chait Singh, the Rajah of Benares, and his attempts to secure from the Begums of Oudh a million pounds that these two Princesses had been left by the late Nawab of that country. At last he was acquitted on all charges and, although his defence had cost him his fortune, the Company supported him in his old age. In 1813, at the age of 81, he was called on to give evidence before Parliament on a matter concerning India. The House then did him the honour of receiving him standing and bareheaded.

Hastings was succeeded by Lord Cornwallis, another honourable and intelligent Governor, who was also a fine soldier. He did much to strengthen and improve upon Hastings's wise measures for the administration of the British-controlled territories; but, like his predecessor, he was not left to do so in peace. Hyder Ali's son, Tipoo Sahib, launched his warrior hordes from Mysore, first against his neighbours to the north, then against Travancore, a small state in the south-west which was in alliance with Britain. Cornwallis came to the rescue, Tipoo Sahib was defeated and compelled to surrender a great part of his territories.

In 1793 Cornwallis was succeeded by Sir John Shore, an able civilian who had been in the Company's service for a quarter of a century. Wars were still going on in the north and west. An Afghan adventurer seized the throne in Delhi, the Maratha Princes were fighting among themselves, and the Maharajah of Sindhia was involved in a long conflict with the Rajputs. But Sir John Shore was a man of peace and, as British territory was not actually threatened, he refused to allow himself to be drawn into any of these struggles.

That was still the situation in July 1796, so the company aboard the *Minerva* had every reason to hope that when they landed in Calcutta they would not be met with the news of any fresh alarms and excursions.

Clarissa played well the part assigned to her by Roger. Although, like everyone else, she knew the main trend that events in India had taken, she lost no suitable opportunity when they met at meals of asking questions about Clive and Hastings, its more recent wars, Calcutta, and Madras its Princes and peoples, religions, jungles, animals and flowers.

Her principal informant was Mr. Sidney Winters. He was a big, paunchy man just on the right side of fifty. Most of his life had been spent in India and he was the senior partner of a Calcutta firm which, under the Company's licence, had grown and prospered with the years. His hair was grey, his face florid, and he carried his large stomach on two absurdly short legs; but he had a pleasant disposition and, while not an educated man in the same sense as Sir Curtis Beaumont or Mr. Cruishank, there was nothing about India that he did not know. He delighted in drawing on this bottomless fund of knowledge for Clarissa and, as she was genuinely interested, at times she even made him come and sit with her up on deck, to the annoyance of the little group of beaux who constantly pursued her.

Of these, the Honourable Gerald Keeble had a big advantage, as he also sat at the Commander's table; but Clarissa was inclined to prefer Robert McIvor, a young Scot who by patronage of Dundas was being sent out to fill an administrative post—because he had more brains—and Mr. Fenton, of the 61st Foot—because he had a readier sense of humour. A heavy-featured Captain of Dragoons and a wiry little Lt.-Colonel from the Ordnance Department made up her regular court, but a number of others were geneally hovering in the offing.

With regard to Roger himself, she also played her part well—almost too well he was inclined to think as the voyage progressed. It was one thing that she should never permit her glance to linger on him with any hint of more than a niece's affection, but another that she hardly spoke to him unless he first addressed her. It was not that she was deliberately rude to him, but she was so fully occupied talking to other men; and his situation made it impossible for him to appear a competitor for her interest or company.

As a means of keeping his mind off her, he determined to learn Persian. That was then the diplomatic language of India and spoken at all its Courts; so, even during the brief stay he contemplated, he thought it might come in useful if he visited any of them. Warren Hastings, himself a fine Persian scholar, had initiated and encouraged the study, by Servants of the Company, of languages used in India; so Roger had no difficulty in finding among those aboard the *Minerva* one who could speak Persian fluently. He was a middle-aged man named James Griffin and under his tuition Roger, having a flair for languages, was soon making good progress.

As far as the weather was concerned, they were remarkably fortunate. After they had been at sea a week, they met with one bad patch which, for a few days, caused them a certain amount of discomfort and resulted in a sharp decline in the variety of the dishes served at dinner; but it was not anything approaching a tempest, and Roger succeeded in stalling off his dreaded seasickness. After calling at Madeira, they picked up the South-West Trades, to be wafted by them right across the Atlantic and over the Equator till they sighted Cape St. Roque, the westernmost point of Brazil.

When they crossed the Line, several sailors disguised as King Neptune and his Court clambered up over the ship's side and the usual ceremonies, followed by much rough horseplay, were performed. As similar rites were customary in ships sailing to the West Indies on crossing the Tropic of Cancer, Roger had already 'met' Neptune; so he was not expected either to participate or to exercise his privilege as a first-class passenger of paying a forfeit to be excused a ducking. All the same, he made the Sea King a handsome present, and was given a front-row seat to watch the fun.

As was almost always the case with East India convoys, when they reached the neighbourhood of Cape St. Roque they lay for some days almost completely becalmed. It was intolerably hot; so much so that the pitch became soft in the caulking of the upper decks and their planks so roasting that even the sailors with their hardened feet, could not bear to walk about them for any length of time without shoes. Normally the crew and the troops slept in hammocks, slung head to tail, and so close together that they resembled sardines in a tin; so, even at the best of times, their quarters were terribly overcrowded. Now, the greater part of them slept nearly naked on deck and the passengers, in their stifling cabins, envied them.

As long as the *Minerva* was becalmed, her boats were kept lowered, tow ropes were attached to all of them and relays of the crew laboured at their oars, dragging the heavy ship a mile or so an hour while her sails hung slack but still set to catch the faintest puff of breeze. For ten days, with the sweat running from them at every movement, the passengers and crew endured this inferno; then at last the South-East Trades picked up the ship and life aboard once more became livable.

Cape Town was their next scheduled port of call, but again, by custom dictated by the prevailing winds, the convoy did not head straight for it. Instead, it let the Trades carry it in a great sweep far to the south of the tip of Africa and some way round the corner, until it reached the 'roaring forties'; only then did it turn north-west in the direction of the port.

It was now early September and so on the verge of spring in the Southern Hemisphere. This saved them from the winter gales they might otherwise have encountered; although the climate had become chilly compared with that to which for so many weeks they had been accustomed. But it was still warm enough to spend long hours sitting about the deck, and the competition for a place near Clarissa showed no signs of lessening.

Lady Beaumont had long proclaimed her to be the 'dearest girl' and she certainly gave no trouble to her chaperone by being discovered with chosen admirers on deck after lights out at night, or being found in other such compromising situations. For that Roger had little doubt about the reason, and now and then he felt a cynical satisfaction in the knowledge that he had only to say the word for her to brush aside all her beaux and come running to his arms.

Yet that was a poor compensation for the fact that, except at table, he hardly had a word with her. Her face, now tanned by the sun and framed in her pale gold hair, which had grown again, was more than ever lovely to look at, and he knew her to be an intelligent and charming companion. Through the long weeks of his automatic exclusion from her playtime circle, he had gradually developed a sub-conscious jealousy of the men she favoured with her smiles, and he even envied old Sidney Winters the *tête-à-têtes* she still accorded him now and then to natter to her about India.

The Cape was barely half-way to Calcutta; so there were at least another two months to go before there could be any change in their relationship and, even then, the final result of any such change provoked speculations about which he did not care to think. He only knew that being within sight of her nearly all of every day, yet debarred from the friendly intimacy they had previously enjoyed, made him see her differently and had immensely increased his desire for her.

At dinner on the 10th September, Captain Finch told them that he estimated the *Minerva* now to be no more than forty-eight hours out of Cape Town. That evening, about nine o'clock, the portly Mr. Winters came up to Roger in the saloon and asked him if he would favour him with a short conversation up on deck. Somewhat surprised, but by no means averse to a breath of fresh air, Roger agreed; so the two men collected their cloaks and met again at the top of the hatchway.

After they had covered a few paces side by side, Winters said: 'I understand that we shall reach Cape Town the day after tomorrow; and I owe you a sincere apology, Mr. Brook, for not having addressed you before this on the subject of which I am now about to speak.'

Roger had not the faintest idea what the subject could be, but he replied politely, 'No matter, Sir. Be kind enough to inform me of it.'

'It is'—Winters coughed, then went on suddenly—'a formal request that you will permit me to pay my addresses to your niece.'

The idea seemed so preposterous that Roger did not take it seriously. Swiftly suppressing a desire to laugh, and wishing to let the elderly merchant down lightly, he said: 'Your proposal being an honourable one, I feel sure Miss Marsham will be flattered by it; but before replying to your request, I must speak to her on the matter.'

Winters coughed again, then said hurriedly, 'You must be aware, Sir, that during the voyage, I have spent many hours in conversation with Miss Marsham. I had no intention of marrying again, but I have found her such a paragon of virtue, sensibility and charm that I can now think of no greater bliss than to make her Mrs. Winters. I should add that I am in a position to support her even to the extent of providing her with every reasonable luxury.'

'Yes, yes.' Roger now spoke a shade testily. 'But you must forgive me for pointing out, Sir, that attentions of the kind you have in mind from a gentleman so much her senior might prove unwelcome to her.'

'It was with reference to that, Sir, that I made you an apology. As Miss Marsham and I conversed we became ever more fully aware of the similarity of our feelings upon a great variety of subjects. Almost with . . .'

'I pray you do not build false hopes on that,' Roger cut in.

Ignoring his remark, Winters continued, 'Almost unrealized by me, a point was reached at which, without awaiting your consent, I laid my heart and fortune at her feet.'

Roger halted in his tracks. Only the darkness hid his expression of swift apprehension. After a moment he regained sufficient control over himself to ask in a normal voice, 'What reply did she make to your proposal?'

'Why, Sir!' exclaimed the merchant rapturously, 'to my eternal joy she has accepted me.'

A dozen different emotions, none of them pleasant, simultaneously whirled and fought for first place in Roger's mind. It was obvious that Clarissa had determined to adopt the course she had implied she might on the first night of the voyage and that she had ensnared the poor fool who stood before him in order to achieve her object more quickly as, with him already engaged to her, she could get married within a week of their arrival in Calcutta. But Winters was far from being the sort of man Roger had had in mind when he had so thoughtlessly put the idea into her head. The merchant was neither old enough to be impotent, nor of a fitting station in life to make a suitable *parti* for her. Roger could only thank his stars that there were at least two months yet to go before the *Minerva* reached Calcutta. The time should be ample for him to dissuade her from the folly of taking such a husband, even for the purpose she had in mind. After a moment he said:

'It seems then that I have little option but to sanction this engagement, Sir; but I would ask you to keep it secret for a while, in case Miss Marsham should change her mind before we arrive in India.'

Winters gave a sudden laugh. 'There is no fear of that, Sir. I gather that revictualling at Cape Town will require the *Minerva* to lie in the port for some ten days; and it is Miss Marsham's own wish that we should be married there.'

CHAPTER TEN

Clarissa makes her Bed

ROGER's life had hung too often on his ability to absorb an unpleasant shock without giving himself away for him to be stampeded into showing his surprise and fury on this occasion. Instead, he said in a not unfriendly voice:

'Then I must offer you my congratulations, Sir.'

Winters thanked him effusively and began to babble about his good fortune, but Roger cut him short by saying, 'I think, Sir, this conversation had fulfilled its purpose. We will speak further on the matter when I have discussed it with my niece.'

Taking quick alarm, Winters stammered, 'I . . . I trust, Mr. Brook, you . . . you do not intend to use your influence with your niece in an attempt to make her change her mind?'

'I have so far to meet the woman who has a stronger mind than Miss Marsham,' declared Roger, with cynical truth, 'and without consulting me she has already made her intentions clear to you. Let us go below.'

Down in the saloon, Clarissa was playing a game of backgammon against Robert McIvor, while three officers stood behind her chair, giving her good advice and endeavouring to make witty remarks that would discomfit her opponent. Roger's bow to her included the whole group, and he said in the authoritative voice that he occasionally used to her in his guise of uncle:

'Gentlemen, perhaps one of you would take over my niece's hand. I regret to break up her game; but we shall shortly be in Cape Town and I wish to discuss with her how we can best employ our time there.'

Demure as ever, Clarissa rose, made her apologies to McIvor, and laid a hand on the arm that Roger offered her. As soon as they were out of earshot of the group, she whispered:

'So Sidney has told you?'

'Sidney, forsooth!' he hissed back. 'Clarissa, how could you? But this is no place to discuss it. Get your cloak and meet me up on deck near the main mast.'

Five minutes later he saw the pale blur of her face above the outline of her long grey cloak as she came towards him in the semi-darkness. Stepping forward, he took her by the arm and drew her into the still deeper shadow behind the bollards with their masses of rope and tackle.

'Well, dear Uncle?' He could guess at her wicked smile from her tone as she asked, 'Was it really necessary to get me up here in order to congratulate me?'

'Clarissa!' he said earnestly. 'This is no laughing matter. You are proposing to do a great wrong to a very decent man and also make a mess of your whole life.'

She shrugged. 'He's mad about me, but knows that I am not drawn to him by passion. How could I be? I do him no wrong, but on the contrary bring him great happiness. Think of the pride he will feel on producing me in Calcutta as his wife, and the joy he will get from seeing the amazement and envy of his friends.'

'Maybe; but their envy will turn to derision the moment it gets out that you have provided him with a pair of horns. Besides, he is utterly unsuited for the rôle that I most foolishly put into your head.'

'Why so?'

'To start with he is only in his late forties and has already been married once, so there is no reason whatever to suppose him impotent.'

'I have dealt with that.' Clarissa gave a low laugh. 'I told him that, as first pregnancies were often difficult, I considered it a great unkindness to get a new-made bride with child, and that doing so had ruined many a marriage. I asked a year to enjoy myself before starting to provide him with a family; and it is part of our agreement that our marriage should not be consummated for twelve months.'

'For cleverness I vow you beat the Devil!' Roger exclaimed in grudging admiration. 'But what when the twelve months are up? And that's not all! He is not, as a I suggested, an old fellow with one foot in the grave whose last hours you could make happy in exchange for the fortune he would leave you.'

She shrugged again, 'Let the future take care of itself.'

'Futures do not take care of themselves. You will have saddled yourself with this man. And who is he? A nobody! A tradesman! Even if you can continue to deny him his rights indefinitely he will be your husband. From his talk at table on several occasions, he has made it plain that in a few years he intends to retire from business and settle down in England. To be married to a rich merchant in Calcutta is one thing, but do you return home with him your marriage will be regarded as an appalling *mésalliance*. Neither men nor women of breeding can defy custom in such a matter. No doubt Georgina would receive him for your sake but, decent fellow though he is, he would be a constant source of shame and embarrassment to you; and in the main you would find yourself ostracized by the sort of society you were brought up to mix with.'

'Roger, dear Roger,' she shook her head. 'Your concern for me is needless. No doubt had I waited till we reached Calcutta, I would have found a man to whom there would not have been these objections. But Sidney was ready to hand and he will serve my purpose well enough. In fact he has proved a godsend for I'll be able to hold you to your promises so much sooner.'

'But it's the future, girl! You must think of the future!'

'I'll not be thwarted by consideration for it. In the last event I can always leave him.'

'You'd still be his wife, and he'd have every reason to refuse to support you.'

'Then I'd support myself.'

'How? By returning to Europe and becoming a kept woman? No, I'll not have it. I'll not allow you to marry Sidney Winters.'

'How do you propose to prevent me?'

'You are not yet twenty-one.'

'You've no proof of that and, if need be, I'll take an oath that I am. You've no proof even that you are my Uncle. It will be said that you are trying to prevent my marrying him on snobbish grounds. They are no legal objection, and there are no others.'

'There is one way I can stop you,' he said suddenly. 'That is by marrying you myself.'

'Roger! D'you mean that?'

'Yes. Why not? This voyage has been hell for me. Day after day I've had to watch you flirting with those nincompoops, while having got myself into a situation where I could hardly exchange a word alone with you. Although I know I have no right to be, and that you have given me no cause, there have been nights when I have been driven half insane with jealousy and longing for you.'

'Then you do love me!'

'Did I ever say that I did not?' Throwing his arm round her waist, he made to draw her to him, but she swiftly put a hand on his chest and pushed him back.

'Wait!' she gasped. 'One moment! Don't kiss me yet or I too shall lose my head.'

Both their hearts were hammering wildly. He refrained from tightening his hold and, when her breathing eased, she said:

'It's no good, Roger. Everyone believes you to be my Uncle.'

'Hell!' he muttered. 'I had forgotten that. But we'll get round it somehow. I'll swear an affidavit that we agreed to call one another "niece" and "uncle" only to make our association appear more conventional while travelling and that you are, in fact, only my deceased wife's cousin.'

She gave a sob. 'It . . . it's not only that! I cannot take you at the price.'

'Price!' he repeated frowning. 'What price?'

'Why, at the price of knowing that you are doing this only to save me from myself again. You made it abundant plain how much it meant to you to keep your freedom. We'd be deliriously happy for a time, I know. But later you'd come to hate me for the restraint I put upon you. I came aboard the *Minerva* to be your mistress, not to trap you into taking me as your wife; and I'll not do it.'

For a quarter of an hour they argued about it, but she remained firm in her determination. All she would agree to was that if, after she had been his mistress for six months, he then wished to marry her she would, by hook or by crook, make Winters secure an annulment of their union on the grounds of non-consummation.

Even then Roger still strove to persuade her at least to postpone her marriage to Winters until they reached Calcutta, hoping that during the two or three months the voyage had yet to run something might occur to make her change her mind about going through with it. At length he wrung a reluctant promise from her that for the next twenty-four hours she would consider the question of a postponement, and that she would tell Winters that in the meantime he was not to mention their engagement to anyone else.

Still intensely worried, Roger accompanied her across the deck then down the companionway. At the bottom they separated to take their cloaks back to their cabins. As he hung his up his natural buoyancy of spirit came to his aid. He had before now countered in much less than twenty-four hours worse blows of Fate.

Having secured a night to think in and a day to work in, he felt that he would have lost his touch if he could not prevent Clarissa marrying Winters in Cape Town. There must be some way of sabotaging the old fool's joyful expectations; and in the long run that would be for his own good, however much Clarissa might have persuaded herself to the contrary. If there were no other way, Roger decided, he could always force a duel on him; although it would be hateful to have to do so. The odds were all against the merchant's daring to fight and, if he refused, Clarissa, who admired bravery above all things, would never marry him after he had displayed cowardice.

But wouldn't she? There was no question of her admiring, or not admiring Sidney Winters. She was simply making use of him for her own ends. She would probably marry him all the same and all he, Roger, would have done would be to earn the frigid disapproval of the whole ship's Company for having challenged a man who was so obviously unable to meet him on equal terms. He would be sent to Coventry and Winters would have everyone's sympathy. No, that would not do. But there must be a way and he was determined to find it.

He met Clarissa again at the entrance of the saloon and they went in together. On their appearance there fell a sudden hush. The various games that had been in progress twenty minutes earlier had all broken up; the passengers had congregated in a little crowd at the far end of the saloon, and in their centre stood Sidney Winters. Lady Beaumont broke from it and came hurrying towards Clarissa.

'My dear!' she exclaimed, fluttering her plump hands, uncertainly. 'My dear; can this really be true? If so, I'm sure I wish you happiness.'

Winters, a seraphic grin on his face, came forward just behind her. Clarissa, frowning at him over her chaperone's shoulder, said quickly: 'It seems, Sir, you have deprived me of the pleasure of informing our friends of our intentions.'

'My love,' he replied, with a smile of contrition. 'Having obtained your uncle's consent to our engagement, how could you expect me to wait one moment longer before publicly declaring myself to be the happiest man in the world?'

At that Roger really was hard put to it to restrain an impulse to stride forward and smack the ecstatic smile from the merchant's face. He felt certain that Winters, having seen him take Clarissa up on deck, had feared that he would persuade her to change her mind; so to make it more difficult for her to do so he had deliberately made the announcement while they were still absent. And he had played an ace. Clarissa had been loath to postpone the announcement for twenty-four hours; so she would not now retract. Winters had, too, been justified in saying that Roger had 'sanctioned the engagement'. That was another ace; for, although Roger had actually prefixed the words with 'it seems I have little option but to . . .', he could not now flatly deny that he had done so. Seething with concealed fury, he was compelled to admit to himself that, for the time being at least, Winters had got the better of him.

Everyone was now crowding round Clarissa offering congratulations. Even the sour Mrs. Armitage and her pimply Jane politely hid their surprise by gushing and simpering. Winters sent a steward for champagne and, as it was now getting on for ten o'clock, asked the Second Mate, who happened to be present, to use his good offices with the Commander to secure an hour's extension of 'lights out', and to request his presence at the celebration.

Captain Finch and the champagne arrived together. The engaged couple's health was drunk, their plan for marrying in Cape Town was discussed, and Clarissa, all smiles, graciously asked Jane to be her bridesmaid. The ladies retired soon after eleven, but the Commander did not insist on the extra time being limited to an hour; so it was near one o'clock before the party broke up and most of the men, having taken full advantage of Winters's liberal supplies of champagne, staggered tipsy to their bunks.

Next day a more sober atmosphere prevailed. Winters proudly paraded Clarissa about the deck but whenever they paused to talk with some of her young men conversation proved slow and awkward. None of her ex-court now attempted to laugh and jest with her; they seemed to regard her with different eyes, as though she were some strange bright-plumaged bird that might without the least warning either lay a golden egg or suddenly peck at them.

Roger went into private conference with the Beaumonts. He told them that the engagement had been sprung upon him, that he had been more or less trapped into giving his consent and most strongly disapproved of the match. He then admitted that Clarissa called him 'uncle' only as a courtesy and because his late wife, being considerably older than herself, had been looked on by her as an aunt.

The Beaumonts also regarded Clarissa's choice as most unsuitable, but her conduct in the matter tallied with the way in which she was supposed to have smuggled herself aboard from a wilful determination to see the gorgeous East. As Roger unburdened himself to them, they received his confidences with the deepest sympathy; but the judge ruled that since Roger was, in fact, only a kinsman of Clarissa's by marriage, and had been vested with no powers as her guardian, although she was under twenty-one, there was no legal step that he could take to stop her marriage.

Roger then detached Winters from Clarissa on the plea of discussing business with him. As soon as they had found a quiet corner, the merchant said, 'From your manner last night and your abruptness this morning,

Mr. Brook, I very much fear that you do not approve of me as a husband for Miss Marsham.'

'Frankly, I do not,' Roger replied crisply. 'I have nothing against you personally, Sir, but I consider you far too old for my niece; and, without offence, I have no reason to believe that your family is one with whom mine would ordinarily seek an alliance.'

Winters made a slight bow. 'I will not argue with you on either point. I can only say that no man could be prepared to do more to make her happy.'

'Whatever you may do it will not be enough,' Roger retorted brutally. 'Within three months she'll have a gallant in your bed.'

'Sir!' Winters's heavy face went as red as a turkey cock's. 'You have no right . . .'

'Right be damned!' Roger cut him short. 'Although I am twenty years your junior, I'll vow that I have forgotten more about women than you have ever learned. Once Clarissa's natural passions are aroused you'll never be able to satisfy her. She will swiftly come to desire young, handsome men, and soon take one or more as lovers. If you truly love her, your life will become a misery and you will become the laughing stock of all your friends. Have some sense, man! Relinquish her before it is too late. I'll deal with any tantrum she may throw, while you save your face by leaving this ship at Cape Town and transferring to another.'

Drawing himself up to the limited height that his absurdly short legs would allow, Winters replied with dignity: 'You insult me, Sir; and I count your conduct in traducing the virtue of your own niece infamous.'

Roger bared his teeth for a second in an ugly grin.

'So far, I have prophesied only what any reasonable man would agree with me is most likely to come about. Now I intend to insult you. But before giving open vent to any umbrage you may take, be good enough to get it clearly into your mind that with my sword I could spit you in thirty seconds like a turkey cock, and that with a pistol I could shoot you dead at a hundred yards. All your life you have been a man of business. Act like one now. Accept the substance and reject the shadow. If you will repudiate your engagement to Miss Marsham, I will enter into a bond to pay you the sum of ten thousand pounds.'

'No, Sir!' came the swift retort. 'I'd not do it if you paid me a hundred thousand.'

'Then you must be richer than I thought,' Roger sneered. 'I'll wager, though, that you could not yourself produce the hundred thousand that you so glibly speak about.'

'I could, Sir, and fifty thousand more!'

Roger had now extracted the information the obtaining of which had been his object should his offer be rejected. With a shrug, he said, 'Very

well, then. Since you will not see sense, your blood be upon your own head.
It remains only for me to safeguard my niece's interests. How much do you
propose to settle on her?'

After a moment's hesitation, Winters replied, 'I have a son, Sir, and too
great a withdrawal of capital would handicap him in the business. I would
suggest fifty thousand pounds.'

With a slightly contemptuous look, Roger said, 'At home Miss Marsham would have had only to lift her finger to get an Earl, or a quarter of
a million pounds. As your son is already established in trade, I am sure he
will be able to look after himself well enough. I would prefer to spare her
any part in discussions on such a sordid subject; but, in the circumstances,
I feel she would have grave reasons to doubt your regard for her do you
settle on her less than a hundred thousand.'

Before the implied threat, Winters wilted. 'So be it, then,' he murmured.
'I will make it a hundred thousand.'

'Good,' Roger nodded. 'That would be in the event of your death, of
course. And now, should you part company for any reason? Shall we say
twenty-five thousand?'

'But . . . but . . .' Winters stammered, 'such a possibility is not normally
envisaged in a marriage contract.'

'Your experience appears to be limited, Sir,' Roger said stiffly. 'In good
families it is far from unusual. If I am to leave my niece in India, many
thousand miles from home, the least I can do is to protect her against the
possibility of your turning her out of house and home. I am her uncle,
remember and, whatever she may say, I will ask the Court in Cape Town
to forbid her marriage on the grounds that she is not yet twenty-one unless
you agree to my very reasonable requirements.'

For a moment Winters hesitated, then he asked, 'May I take it that if I
do agree you will raise no further objection to the marriage?'

'Yes,' Roger nodded rather grudgingly. 'My niece has made it plain that
it is her wish; and I've no desire to quarrel with her, or yourself. But I've
a duty to fulfil. Do you agree my terms and I'll say no more.'

'It is a bargain, then.' The merchant held out his hand and Roger took
it. Each gave the other a formal smile, then they separated.

As Roger turned away he could not remember a time when he had felt
so awful. It gave him no satisfaction at all to know that, though Winters
had got the best of him overnight, he had been made to pay for it by
mortgaging a large part of his fortune in the morning. Now, if Clarissa
could put up with him until he died, she would come into a hundred
thousand pounds. That was fair enough. But if she chose to leave him at
any time, he would have to pay her twenty-five thousand. And she intended
to refuse him his marital rights while deceiving him with someone else.

He would find out, they would quarrel, she would leave, and he, poor wretch, would have to pay up.

Roger felt that if he had been a professional swindler and Clarissa his moll they could not have devised a better plan for robbing an honest man of his money. As she was unaware of the arrangements he had made on her behalf, she was not quite as guilty as himself; but nearly so, as she was entering on the marriage with the deliberate intent to cheat. Yet, since he no longer had any hope of preventing the marriage, he had felt impelled to do what he could while he could to insure her against the future which she refused to contemplate for herself.

Only one thought came to console him for the part he had played, and it lightened his shame a little. His object, at least in part, had been to provide Clarissa with a lever that she could use should Winters prove obdurate when, in due course, she asked him to procure an annulment. But now he realized that that would work both ways. Unless she decided to take the money rather than secure her freedom to marry again, it put Winters in a position to bargain with her. He could refuse to apply to the Court for an annulment unless she was prepared to forgo the twenty-five thousand.

Still sick at heart, Roger sought out Mr. Musgrove, the dried-up old stick of a lawyer who had been one of their companions throughout the voyage and asked him to draw up a marriage contract on the lines agreed.

That evening he again took Clarissa up on deck and, in the shadows, pleaded with her to exercise a woman's privilege of changing her mind. He told her plainly that, greatly as he longed to have her in his arms, he would not even so much as kiss her until she was established in Calcutta; and urged her once more to postpone her marriage until their arrival there.

Angrily she took him to task for adhering to the letter of their agreement rather than observing its spirit. Calmly he countered her attack by pointing out that she would no longer be free to come and go as she chose, but sharing a cabin with her husband, and that, in the close confines of a ship packed with several hundred passengers and crew, it would be impossible to carry on an intrigue for more than a week without it being discovered. He added that the scandal of a bride betraying her husband on her honeymoon would be bad enough, but she must remember that everyone still believed him to be her uncle, so if they were caught it would be regarded as incest, into the bargain; and that being a criminal offence, the Commander might order him to be put in irons for the rest of the voyage.

These arguments swiftly brought Clarissa to reason, but she would not alter her decision to be married in Cape Town, as that would the sooner give them a more open field to become lovers on reaching India.

The next day passed in a bustle of activity as everyone was excited at the prospect of being on land again after so many weeks at sea. Before they went down to dinner, the vague blur of Table Mountain had already been sighted on the horizon. By five o'clock it reared high above Table Bay, a blanket of white cloud standing out against the blue sky on its flat top. The *Minerva* dropped anchor in the roads just as darkness fell.

Until the previous year, the Cape had been a Dutch possession, the Netherlands East India Company having used it as a naval base since 1652. From 1685 they had colonized it, but very few Dutch families of good standing had been persuaded to go out; so the first colonists had mainly been ne'er-do-wells, and batches of poor orphan girls sent out by order of the Government. Among the first settlers, too, there had been 150 French Protestants, driven from France by the Edict of Nantes. They were greatly superior in culture to the Dutch, but their numbers were insufficient to raise to any marked extent the general level of poverty, idleness and illiteracy. So great was the latter that after the colony had been shamefully neglected by its Home Government for a hundred years, the majority of its inhabitants could not speak their parent language, but were using a meagre *patois*, called Taal, which consisted of only a few hundred words.

After the conquest of Holland in 1795 by the French Republican armies, Admiral Elphinstone had taken over the Cape, which was now held by Britain in the name of their ally in exile, the Prince of Orange; but few British families had as yet settled there, and the little town was still a poor ramshackle place.

When they all went ashore the following morning, Clarissa was bitterly disappointed to find so few shops and in them such a limited choice of materials for her trousseau. But Roger bought for her everything suitable they could find, and the Governor, who had received them most cordially, later procured half a dozen needle-women who set to work on garments that she had to design for herself.

The Governor had sent messages to the Captains of all ships in the convoy inviting them to dine that afternoon, and to bring with them a few of their principal passengers. Captain Finch selected the Beaumonts, Roger, Clarissa and, on account of her engagement, Winters, whom he would not normally have included. This big party, including a dozen of the leading colonists whom the Governor had also asked, numbered nearly seventy people; so the meal provided was a cold buffet, but such a gathering provided a delightful change.

Among the colonists were a couple named Marais. Both were descended from old French families through Huguenot settlers who had come out to the Cape a hundred years earlier, and they owned one of the best estates in the Colony. Clarissa was introduced to them and when the topic of her marriage came up, both the Governor and Marais agreed that it was quite

out of the question for her to be married from, or spend the first days of
her honeymoon at, one of the inns in the town, as even the best of them was
hopelessly primitive. Everyone was anxious to be helpful to such a lovely
bride; so it was decided that she should be married from the Residence by
the Governor's Chaplain, and that afterwards the newly-weds should
occupy the guest wing of the Marais's comfortable home until the *Minerva*
was ready to sail again.

Captain Finch had already given them to understand that watering and
re-provisioning the ship would take about ten days, and Clarissa had
secretly made up her mind to make her stay on land with her bridegroom
as brief as possible; so, in spite of Sidney Winters's pressing, she insisted
that her trousseau would not be finished for a week, and the day of the
wedding was fixed accordingly. Clarissa then asked the Governor's pretty
daughter to act as a second bridesmaid; after which the ladies withdrew to
further elaborate plans for the wedding.

As the men circulated the wine, the talk turned as usual to affairs in
Europe and the progress of the war. A frigate that had left Portsmouth
ten days after the *Minerva* sailed had reached Cape Town two days earlier;
so it was the Governor who gave them the latest news instead of receiving it.

In June, the armies of Generals Moreau and Jourdan had launched a new
campaign against the Austrians and crossed the Rhine, threatening to
overrun Swabia. In Italy their colleague, General Buonaparte, was laying
siege to Mantua, but it was said that the Emperor Francis had mustered
a great army of Austrians, Hungarians and Tyrolese to send to the relief of
this all-important fortress.

Before Roger left England, he had heard only vague rumours of an
abortive conspiracy in Paris led by a man named Babeuf; since then a fairly
full account of it had come to hand. After the fall of Robespierre a strong
reaction against the extremists of the Revolution had set in. Only a handful of the most notorious had been sent to the guillotine; a few, such as
Tallien and Fréron, who had taken an active part in pulling the 'Incorrup-
tible' down, had by so doing saved their own skins and positions as
leaders; but all over France the smaller ex-terrorists had been deprived of
their offices and were being proscribed and hunted by the people of the
middle-classes who had suffered at their hands.

In Paris these blood-stained criminals congregated regularly at the Pan-
theon Club to discuss measures for their mutual protection, and their
numbers had been swollen to over four thousand by other ex-Jacobins
being driven from the Provinces seeking refuge in the capital.

As Roger had known, since it was his business to do so, there existed a
secret club within the club, which was known as the *Société des Ègaux*.
Among its most prominent members were 'Gracchus' Babeuf, the editor

of the *Tribune du Peuple*, Antonelle, an ex-juryman of the Revolutionary Tribunal, and Jean-Antoine Rossignol who, as a General of the Convention, had ordered whole villages in La Vendée to be burnt with their inhabitants in them. These, and others of their kidney, had planned yet another revolution, in which the Directors and the *Corps Législatif* were to be murdered and a Government of Anarchists set up.

They had endeavoured to win over the six-thousand-strong Legion of Police which was stationed at Grenelle, and was also largely composed of ex-terrorists. In May, owing to its semi-mutinous condition, the Legion had been broken up and one of the agents employed to corrupt it informed Carnot of the conspiracy. The Directory had acted promptly and on the eve of the insurrection had arrested Babeuf and his friends; so temporarily, at least, the capital had been saved from further bloodshed, and the Whites were still in the ascendant.

While listening to the rather garbled account of this conspiracy, Roger felt as though he was being told of events in another world. He had known both Antonelle and Rossignol and, little more than six months ago, had been on intimate terms with Barras, Carnot, Dubois-Crancé and a dozen others of the 'moderates' who had now taken over the leadership of the Revolution; but during the long voyage he had hardly given them a thought. General Buonaparte's Italian campaign and Mr. Pitt's idea of securing the Serene Republic as an ally had, too, soon lost interest for him, simply because he had no possible chance of learning how matters were progressing.

During the next few days the company made up excursions to see the sights in the vicinity, riding through wooded country in which there were many trees and plants strange to them, to the vineyards at Constantia and to False Bay, and making the ascent of Table Mountain in basket chairs borne by native bearers.

On September 14th Clarissa was duly married to Sidney Winters. Roger, with a reluctance which he found it difficult to conceal, gave her away and, with a genuine good-will inspired by secret pity, did his utmost now to show friendliness to the bridegroom. A guard of honour was formed by Clarissa's officer admirers, Roger paid for the reception at the Residence, to which all the *Minerva*'s passengers were invited, and stood free beer to the troops and crew. Half the town also turned out, so as the newly wed couple drove away they were cheered by over a thousand people, and by six o'clock in the evening the greater part of them, both inside as well as outside the Residence, were well on their way to getting drunk. Except for Roger, and a few more thoughtful people, like the Beaumonts, who feared that a union between parties so divergent in age and circumstances could bring no lasting happiness, the whole affair was a roaring success.

On the evening of the 16th the *Minerva* sailed again. That afternoon, on coming aboard, Clarissa had greeted everyone with a good display of cheerfulness, but her face was pale and behind her smile Roger saw signs of strain in her blue eyes. She went straight to the double cabin that she was now to share with Winters, and it was not until the ship had sailed that Roger managed to get her a little apart from the other passengers for a few moments.

As they stood side by side watching the little town beneath the great mountain gradually becoming more indistinct in the evening light, he asked in a low voice:

'Is all well with you? For the past forty-eight hours I have been consumed with anxiety on your account. Though I could not stop you, short of making us both notorious for the rest of our lives by creating some frightful scene, I've cursed myself a thousand times for letting you carry out your plan.'

'I hated every moment of it,' she replied in an equally low tone. 'He is uncouth beyond anything I had imagined. But I have no right to complain. I brought it on myself.'

'What happened?' Roger snapped out the question. 'Did he go back on his agreement with you? If so, I'll wring his neck and throw him overboard.'

'Be careful!' she whispered. 'Keep your voice low or someone will overhear us. No; he did not attempt to break his word. On the first night he could not have, even if he had had a mind to. After we had dined with the Marais he became drunk as a hog and was incapable even of undressing himself.'

'You must blame me for that,' Roger murmured. 'I feared that the excitement of having you to himself in a bedroom for the first time might prove too much for him; so I laced his drink at the reception. After that it was odds on that, unless he stuck to water with his dinner, more wine would bowl him over.'

'Then I'm grateful to you. It saved me during the first night from anything more unpleasant than his being sick on the floor, then snoring till morning like a grampus!'

'But what of the second?'

'I have survived it, so I beg you not to worry; but it was a hideous experience. He maintained, fairly I suppose, that my bargain with him that we should not consummate our marriage for a year did not debar him from kissing me, and taking other liberties. I submitted for a while with the best grace that I could, then evaded his further unpleasant attentions by pretending I had the vapours. But it is his habits I find so repulsive. He slobbers, belches and conceals nothing of himself, maintaining that a husband and wife when alone should be natural with one another.'

'Clarissa! This cannot be allowed to continue.' Roger's blue eyes had gone a shade darker than usual, and his finger-nails were digging into the palms of his hands. 'I feel such shame for this business as I have never felt before in my whole life. How we ever allowed ourselves to get into such a ghastly tangle, I cannot think.'

'It is my fault. I should never have pursued you onto the *Minerva*.'

'In the first place, yes. But I am the man of the party, and am supposed to have some brains. I should never have let matters come to this.'

'You could not help it. You offered to marry me before we landed in Cape Town. You could not have done more.'

'I could have disclosed the truth to Winters, then sworn to cut his gizzard out if he breathed one word of it. Had he known your reason for accepting him he would have backed out of his engagement. I would to God I'd thought of that.'

'Well, as you didn't, I've made my bed and must lie on it.'

'No! There's a way out yet. It's not too late for us to land again in Cape Town. I'll see Captain Finch and pay him whatever he asks to have a boat lowered to take us back there.'

'Roger, no! That would indeed be madness. I am Mrs. Winters now. The scandal you have so long sought to avoid would be ten times as great as if we had been discovered as lovers before my marriage. It would stink to high heaven, and we'd never live it down. Should you do as you suggest, I'll refuse to come with you. For me the worst is already over. I'll not have to share a double bed with him again. Things will be easier for me now we'll occupy a cabin and sleep in separate bunks. I warn you, I won't come. I swear it.'

At that moment Winters came waddling up to them, bringing an abrupt end to their private conversation.

After a few days, life on shipboard settled down to normal. Clarissa's old admirers soon got over the shock they had sustained by their divinity's strange choice of a husband, and once more clustered around, discreetly flirting with her as they would have with any other pretty young married woman. Winters looked on, beaming with self-satisfaction and the pride of ownership. Roger, too, frequently joined the group. Previously he had been ultra cautious from fear that an unguarded word or glance might arouse suspicions that he and Clarissa had some secret understanding; but now she was just married such an idea would have been so preposterous that he felt it safe to spend much more time in her company.

Having rounded the Cape, the *Minerva* spent close on a fortnight beating up the east coast of Africa and through the Mozambique Channel. After clearing the northern tip of Madagascar she altered course to north-east, in order to pick up the favourable south-west winds that would carry her in the direction of Ceylon; but now, for the first time during the voyage, she met with really rough weather.

For two days she battled against a heavy cross-sea. The buffet of each
great wave made her shudder from stem to stern, and she rolled atrociously
so that any article left unsecured, even for a few moments, fell and
smashed, or was flung across the cabins. At times there were downpours of
torrential rain, which blotted out from view the other heaving ships in the
convoy. Captain Finch took charge himself and was almost permanently up
on the poop. The food at his table deteriorated sadly to snacks of cold meat
and ship's biscuits, for those who could still keep food down.

Roger was not among them. Quite early in the storm, seasickness over-
came him and for the next few days he lay wretchedly ill in his bunk. On
the second day most of the passengers, including Winters, who had stuck
out the first night also succumbed. Clarissa was one of the few who remained
unaffected. She was something more than a splendid sailor; she actually
enjoyed a storm at sea. During a hurricane on the way to the West Indies,
she had had herself lashed to a stanchion on deck, so that she could feel
the wind tearing at her hair and the rain driving into her face. Now, she
staggered from cabin to cabin, doing what she could to look after her
husband, Roger, the Beaumonts, the Armitages and one of the sailors who
had missed his footing on a ladder, fallen and broken his leg.

It was on the third day that tragedy overtook them. In mid-morning a
sudden squall, more violent than any they had yet encountered, snapped
off the main top-gallant and it came crashing down on the poop. By the
most evil chance it smashed in the left side of the Wheel House, demolish-
ing the wheel, injuring a Quartermaster and killing Captain Finch. Thus,
at one stroke, the ship was put temporarily out of control and deprived of
her most capable officer.

Immediately, she began to veer round sideways on to the great white-
crested waves. It was the watch of the First Mate, Mr. Evans. In a gallant
attempt to save the situation he ran towards the emergency steering wheel
at the stern of the vessel. For many hours no one had been able to move about
the deck without using a succession of hand-holds. Evans paid the penalty
of his rashness. He was flung off his feet and fractured his skull against a
chicken coop.

The Third Mate then took charge. Having sent another Quartermaster
to the stern, he had all hands piped on deck and ordered the taking in of
the remaining sails with which the ship had been fighting the storm. But
by now the *Minerva* had swung right round; the sails went slack then
suddenly billowed out again with reports like cannon. Two of them were
rent from top to bottom and their canvas flapped wildly on either side like
streaming banners in the howling wind.

A moment later there came an awful rending sound. The foremast had
snapped off low down. It fell across the fo'c's'le, its yards, spars and rigging

forming an incredible tangle, and killing or injuring another half-dozen sailors.

A part of the crew managed to haul in the mainsail, while the rest strove to clear the fallen mast. Its upper part dragged in the water, giving the ship a terrifying list to port; but the troops were called up to help. Under the direction of the Second Mate, Mr. Garner, who had now come on deck, and the boatswain, a hundred desperate hands wielding axes, cutlasses and knives managed to hack through scores of ropes. The huge broken column of timber slid overboard and the ship righted herself.

She was now running before the storm under bare, broken masts, and soon all the other ships in the convoy were lost to view. Her emergency wheel in the stern was manned, but no use could be made of it until the storm lessened and it was safe to attempt to turn her back onto her course by hoisting sail again. There were now a dozen casualties in the sick-bay and wreckage still littered all the fore part of the deck. During the afternoon it was gradually cleared, but the tempest showed no sign of abating and the weighty foretop had stove in the port side of the fo'c's'le. From time to time waves broke over the bow and the water rushed down the gaping hole, rendering the crew's quarters untenable, and necessitating the manning of the pumps.

That night Mr. Garner, who was now acting Commander, told the Army officers and the few civilian passengers who were not helpless in their cabins from seasickness, that the position was dangerous but not desperate. The ship was being driven at great speed north-westwards, back towards the coast of Africa, but it was still several hundred miles distant, so there was no risk of her being driven ashore. Efforts to get a sail over the wrecked section of the fo'c's'le had failed, so water was gaining in the fore hold, but not to an alarming degree. He had hopes that the storm would have blown itself out by morning, and, if so, all would be well.

But as the hours wore on, it increased in fury. All through the night the helpless ship was rushed up mountainous waves to crash through their tops and come slithering down into seemingly bottomless gulfs. Each time she breasted one its spume hissed through her rigging, and now and then a following sea curled right up over her poop to come cascading down into her well, filling it for some moments waist high with water. Her timbers groaned, her rigging screamed, the hundreds of tons of water hit her decks with a boom like thunder. It seemed to all the passengers, and the wretched troops crowded vomiting on the lower deck, that every time the ship plunged downward would be the last, and that she could not possibly survive till morning.

Yet, when morning came, she was still afloat and the tempest had perceptibly moderated. The waves were no longer white-crested; a heavy swell now made them look like vast rolling downs, with a blue-green glassy surface; the wind had ceased to tear wildly at severed ropes and the remnants of torn sails. But things were far from well with the *Minerva*.

During the night she had shipped a great deal of water, three of her boats had been stove in and some of her cargo had shifted. She was much lower in the water than she should have been, again had a list to port, and was down at the head. All through the forenoon, relays of men worked frantically at the pumps while others laboured feverishly lashing together ratings and spars to form rafts. Despite all efforts, the level of the water in the holds rose steadily.

The officers came to the conclusion that the cargo which had come adrift must have struck the ship's side with such force that she had sprung a leak, but the water had now risen in the holds to a height that made it impossible for the carpenters to get at the seat of the trouble.

It was shortly after one o'clock that the *Minerva* gave a sudden lurch. More of the cargo had shifted, and increased her list to port by several degrees. Mr. Garner realized that the position was now critical and that with little warning she might dive bows first to the bottom. Calling his officers together, he told them to pass the word that he intended shortly to give the order to abandon ship.

When Clarissa heard the news, she was with the Captain's cook collecting packets of cold meat and biscuits to take down to her invalids who, with the abating of the tempest, were beginning to show signs of recovery. Stuffing all the packets of food into the capacious pockets of her cape, she ran along to Roger's cabin. Throwing open the door, she cried:

'Get up! Get your clothes on! The ship may go down at any moment!'

Roger tumbled from his bunk, staggered slightly owing to weakness from his three days of sickness, then pulled himself together and muttered: 'So it's come to that, eh? Last night I would have been pleased rather than otherwise at the idea of being swiftly carried down to Davy Jones's Locker. But now I feel better, I've no mind for a watery grave. How is Winters showing in this emergency?'

'He's been near as ill as you,' she replied quickly. 'I haven't told him yet, and I've no need to. The stewards are knocking on every cabin door warning people to get ready. Whatever may betide, I'll not risk being separated from you for a moment.'

'I'll not let you be until I've got you into a boat. With Captain Finch gone there may be panic and fighting up on deck. Mr. Cruishank told me that with troops aboard there are never enough boats to take off everybody. The ships haven't the space to carry them.'

'Three have been smashed by the waves last night; but the men have been making rafts this morning.'

'It takes a lot of rafts to make up for a boat. Unless the discipline proves better than one can expect, there will be a horrible scrimmage for a chance of survival. As a woman you are entitled to a first place in a boat; but if there is a panic the rush may deprive you of it.'

'In any case, I'd not take it unless you could come with me.'

Roger shrugged. 'There are few women aboard; so I'd have as much right to a place beside you as any other man. But in such circumstances, boats are liable to become dangerously overcrowded. I believe we'd stand a better chance on a raft, especially if we could get one to ourselves.'

'I'll do whatever you think best; but hurry! Hurry!'

He had been swiftly pulling his clothes on. Having buckled on his sword, he snatched his pistols from a drawer and thrust them into the pockets of his coat. As he did so he muttered, 'At least, being in tropical waters we'll be in no danger from the cold.' But, all the same, he swung his heavy cloak round his shoulders. Quickly he collected all his papers, put them into a large waterproof wallet made of fish-skin, with which he travelled in case of emergencies, and strapped it round his waist. Lastly he grabbed a flask of cognac, and another of powder for his pistols; then they ran from the cabin and up to the upper deck.

Already, although no panic showed, it was a seething mass of people, many of whom were working on rafts with desperate haste, while others, whose faces showed them to be half-stunned with fear, stood staring in horrified silence at the fo'c's'le, which was now awash with water.

A boat towards the stern on the port side was being lowered. Lady Beaumont was in it. Catching sight of Clarissa she shouted and beckoned, but her voice was drowned by the din; next moment the falls were let go and the boatload of people disappeared from view.

Another boat on the starboard side was being manned. A midshipman ran up to Clarissa, seized her by the arm and tried to drag her towards it. She shook him off and refused to go. It was as well. A few minutes later, as the boat, now crammed with people, was lowered, the after fall jammed; its bow went down with a rush, precipitating everyone in it into the heaving sea.

Some rafts, heavily loaded, mostly with soldiers, were already floating off from the half-submerged fo'c's'le. Groups of men, odd passengers and officers, either squatted on, or stood near, all the others. Desperately Roger looked round for something buoyant which would support Clarissa and himself. Suddenly his eye lit on a stack of deck chairs which had already been firmly lashed together to prevent their being swept overboard.

Pieces of torn sail and lengths of severed rope littered the deck about them. Snatching up one of the pieces of rope, Roger set frantically to work. With Clarissa's help he threaded it twice through the chairs and twice right round the stack. Next he tied one end of the rope round Clarissa's waist and the other end round his own. Then he cut the cords that held the stack of chairs to the deck.

They had hardly done, and climbed on to the stack, when the squat figure of Winters came blundering through the crowd towards them.

'Clarissa!' he cried. 'Clarissa! I have been searching for you everywhere! Why did you not seek a place in one of the boats?'

'Because they are too heavy laden,' Roger replied tersely for her. 'If the wind gets up again the water will wash over their gunwales; they'll be swamped and everyone in them drowned.'

'Then . . . then . . .' Winters stammered, 'you'll be safer using these chairs as a raft. Make room for me, I implore you.'

In this crisis, which might so soon lead to their deaths, the last thing that either Roger or Clarissa wanted was to have Winters with them; yet they could hardly refuse. The whole of the front half of the ship was now under water. A wavelet lapped at the chairs on which they were sitting. Although there was barely room Winters, without waiting for a reply, scrambled up beside Clarissa.

A moment later the deck suddenly tilted, launching the stack of chairs onto the water. Above them the tip of the main mast seemed to sweep forward. The stern of the ship rose up against the sky. There were shrieks, cries and imprecations. As the sea surged across the deck, the rafts were thrown one against another; many of the occupants were pitched into the water. Shouts, prayers and a great roar of rushing waters filled the air.

Through the bubbling water, Roger caught a glimpse of the deck, now sliding swiftly away twelve feet below them. A wave swept several of the rafts, and the stack of chairs, just clear of the bulwark. The *Minerva*, only a few feet from them, was now standing on end, her bowsprit ten fathoms down, her poop reared up towards the sky. A cluster of men dived from it; without a sound it slid swiftly downwards. With the rush of waters, the windows of the stern cabin shattered and through them fountains of foam spurted into the air. In a matter of moments, it was all over. The fine ship had totally disappeared.

Some of the crowded rafts had already overturned and the men from them were fighting in the water. The men on the others were awed into silence. Suddenly there was a shout:

'The whirlpool! The whirlpool!'

The cluster of rafts began to circle. A hideous conical pit had formed at the spot where the *Minerva* had gone down. Raft after raft was drawn into it and sucked under. The chairs, in turn, raced round it for a moment then the stack tilted and was engulfed. Roger threw an arm round Clarissa. Next second they were plunged beneath the surface; blinded, their mouths full of water, they felt themselves rushing downwards to die with the ship from which they thought they had escaped.

CHAPTER ELEVEN

Death Reaches Out

ALTHOUGH they were within a few degrees of the equator the water had struck chill as it surged over them. But in a moment all sensation was forgotten, except the pain and terror of suffocation. They had been drawn into the whirlpool so swiftly that they had not even had time to gulp in a deep breath. The sea had slapped into their partly open mouths, blinded their eyes and rushed up their nostrils.

The *Minerva*, plunging to the depths, dragged them after her—down, down, down. It seemed that, like stones cast into a pond, they would never stop until they reached bottom. With every instant, greater pressure upon their chests and backs threatened to force out the air remaining in their lungs. The blood throbbed madly in their temples and their eyes started from their sockets.

Suddenly the water below them seemed to open. They shot down at still greater speed, were flung head over heels, whirled round, then felt themselves being carried swiftly upwards. Another few awful moments and they were catapulted several feet above the surface of the sea. Then they splashed into and under it. Temporarily, they had been saved from drowning by the final death throe of the *Minerva*. The increasing pressure on the air caught in her between-decks had caused it to burst out in a great bubble; like rocks caught up in a volcanic eruption, they had been hurled by it right out of the water.

Flailing his arms wildly, Roger came to the surface again. He was still tied by the rope's end to the stack of chairs, and it bobbed up beside him. Gasping in breath and dashing the water from his eyes, he looked round for Clarissa, but could not see her. The chairs were riding some three feet out of the water, so the level of the uppermost one was well above his head. The rope by which he was tied to them was too short to allow of his swimming round the chairs, so he grasped the top one and strove to haul himself up onto the top of the stack.

Under his weight the stack tipped sharply but did not turn over, as he feared it would. When he had struggled onto it he saw the reason. To his immense relief Clarissa was on its far side and it was her weight which had kept the stack steady enough for him to get up on it.

An instant later his relief at seeing her was submerged in a wave of fury.

The tipping of the stack had brought her up, but as it rolled back her head went under water. At the first glance he had taken in only the fact that Winters was beside and just below her. Now he realized that her husband, not being roped to the stack, had evidently been swept from it as it went down, and had saved himself by clinging to her.

Winters's upturned face showed that he was half mad from terror. With his right hand he was striving frantically but unsuccessfully to grab the nearest chair strut; his left was clasped firmly on the collar of Clarissa's cape. But for the rope round her waist they would both have gone under. As it was, the rope was taut, and his pull on her had dragged her backwards. Each time he heaved himself up in an attempt to get a hold on the chairs, his weight forced her head below the water. She writhed and struggled, but as he was behind her she could do nothing to free herself.

'Let go!' snarled Roger, his eyes blazing. 'Let go, God damn you!'

'Help!' Winters gasped. 'Help!'

At that moment, by a great effort, Clarissa managed to get her head right round. Baring her teeth she bit savagely into the hand that threatened to drown her. With a yelp of pain Winters let go his hold, but at once he made another grab at her. Kicking out she eluded his clutch, then struck him in the face with her clenched fist. His hands shot up, clawing at the air, then he sank from sight.

Roger, sprawled on top of the stack of chairs, and encumbered by his heavy saturated clothing, had, in these few brief moments, been unable to aid Clarissa, but he had managed to wriggle his sword out of its sheath. As Winters came struggling back to the surface, he brandished it and cried:

'You miserable coward! Lay hand on her again and I'll kill you!'

'Mercy!' Winters croaked, spluttering out a mouthful of water. 'Give me a hand! I can't swim! I'll drown if you don't help me!'

At that despairing cry Roger's heart softened. There were reasons enough why he would have liked to see Winters drown. His death would free Clarissa from her entanglement; but, more important at the moment, on the surface of the chair-stack there was barely room for two people to lie down. Three would mean acute discomfort and seriously reduce the chances of any of them surviving. Yet the fact that Winters had clutched at Clarissa was at least palliated by his being unable to swim and, before his mind had become temporarily deranged by fear of death, he had shown himself to be a generous and honourable man.

Seeing that Clarissa was now supporting herself without difficulty, Roger flattened himself again and stretched out a hand to Winters. He grasped it with a grateful sob of thanks and was drawn near enough to the stack to get a hold upon it. Turning back to Clarissa, Roger drew her up onto its narrow surface. With her feet still dangling in the water, she collapsed upon it. She had not fainted, but the ordeal she had just been through had left her near exhaustion. Roger began to chafe her hands, and while doing so, had his first chance to look about him.

Now that the raft of chairs was supporting three people it was very low in the water, and while crouching on it Roger's field of view was confined to an area of a few hundred yards. The oily post-storm swell now rose and fell rhythmically, the wave crests no longer breaking but just flecked with foam. On one of them a longboat stood out for a minute or two against the still sullen sky. It was packed with people but the distance was too great for him to identify any of them. Round it in the water there bobbed a cluster of heads, from which came faint cries as the swimmers pleaded to be taken into the already overloaded boat, and struggled for places at which to cling to the cords along its sides.

Within sight there was at least a score of rafts. Some were crowded and some, having been drawn under by the whirlpool and since returned to the surface, were empty. The great air buble had thrown up from the depths fifty or sixty men, and each of them was now striving to reach the raft nearest to him. A group of four soldiers, two swimming strongly and a third supporting the fourth, were heading for the chairs and only a dozen yards away. Roger pointed to an empty raft some sixty feet distant and shouted.

'Over there! Over there! These chairs can carry no more weight. You'll only sink us.' But, ignoring him, the swimmers continued to come on.

A few more strokes and the two strongest reached Winters. Wrenching him from his hold, they thrust him back and attempted to clamber up on the chairs. Roger, now kneeling, and sword in hand again, cursed and threatened them. Panting, they cursed back at him. Under their combined weight the chairs dipped dangerously. Seeing no alternative but death for Clarissa and himself, Roger slashed swiftly with his blade at the soldiers' clutching hands. Wailing and groaning they snatched their bleeding fingers away, and struck out for the empty raft. Their two struggling companions turned and followed.

Brief as the encounter was, Roger had temporarily lost sight of Winters. Now he realized that the near-exhausted merchant, robbed of his support, had again gone under. The patch of sea where he had been remained empty. Roger stared at it and round about for some while, but Winters did not reappear. There could be little doubt that he had gone down for good.

Within the next ten minutes, Fate swiftly dealt out death or a new chance of life for many people. A score of men who endeavoured to get onto already full rafts were thrust off to drown; the others hauled themselves up onto the empty rafts and squatted bemused upon them. After a babble of shouts, prayers, and curses, a brooding silence descended on the scene.

Roger, meanwhile, had lifted Clarissa's legs from the water and laid her down at full length. She smiled up at him, showing that she was still both conscious and in good heart; but it was only with difficulty that he returned her smile, for he felt that their chances of being picked up before they were driven mad by thirst and hunger were extremely slender.

During the long afternoon, governed by their wind-resistance, or lack of it, some of the rafts dispersed over a wider area while others drew together and, a little before sundown, one with a single occupant drifted to within thirty feet of them. It consisted of a nine-foot square hatchway, so its surface, strength and buoyancy were all greater than the precariously lashed-together float of chairs on which Roger and Clarissa were so uncomfortably perched.

Roger hailed the man on it and he proved to be one of the *Minerva's* Quartermasters. He said that all his mates had been washed from the raft when it had been sucked under, and that he would welcome company; so Roger slipped into the water and, with the rope still round his waist, towed the chairs alongside the hatchway. As the latter was so much more stable, Roger and Clarissa were able, as soon as they were on it, to dispense with the rope's ends round their waists and, at the suggestion of the occupant of the raft, the rope was used, with his help, to secure one half of the chairs on each side of it to give it still greater buoyancy.

The Quartermaster's name was Bill Bodkin and, after they had talked to him for a while, they felt they were lucky to have chanced on such a companion. He was a big, brown-bearded man of about forty, with an open face and cheerful disposition. From boyhood all his life had been spent at sea and, while he admitted that their situation was about as bad as it could be, having twice before been wrecked and picked up in the ocean, he was optimistic enough to believe that he would escape death a third time.

He backed his opinion that God meant him to live with the facts that, of the dozen men who had been with him on the raft when it went under, he alone had come up still clinging to it; that, although most of the gear they had lashed onto it had been torn away by the force of the whirlpool, the one essential to life—a six-gallon keg of water—had been held fast by its moorings; and that although their box of food had been swept away, Clarissa had brought a good quantity of meat and biscuits in the pockets of her cloak, of which he might now expect a share in return for a share of his water.

While they had been talking, the swift darkness of the tropics had fallen; so, considerably cheered by Bodkin's conviction that the Almighty had them under his special protection, they settled down for the night. It was warm enough for them to use their sodden cloaks as pillows, but there was little else they could do for their comfort, and for a good part of the long hours that followed they lay gazing up at the brightly twinkling stars in the dark vault overhead, wondering unhappily if there really was much chance of being rescued within the next few days.

When dawn at last came, although the swell had gone down and so much increased their field of vision none of the other rafts was to be seen. The only trace of the *Minerva*, other than themselves, was a broken hen-coop bobbing up and down some dozen yards away. Bill Bodkin was most anxious to secure it, but he could not swim; so Roger took off his outer garments, which had dried during the night, went in and brought it alongside.

The coop contained ten chickens. Waves breaking over the stern of the *Minerva* had drowned all the live-stock on her poop; so the birds must have been dead for at least two days and, during their immersion in the sea, small fish, having got between their feathers, had, in places, nibbled their flesh away to the bone; so Roger thought their find useless. But Bodkin said that if the birds were gutted, salt water would preserve their meat for a while, and if it did turn their stomachs it could anyway be used as bait for fish; then he promptly set about dealing with this windfall.

During the day the big, bearded Quartermaster busied himself in a dozen other ways. He counted the chairs a great blessing, as the worst enemy of the people adrift on a raft in the tropics was the power of the sun. The wood and canvas of the chairs could be used to make a shelter and, perhaps, even a squat mast with a sail. While he worked away with his sharp jack-knife, Roger unravelled the strands of rope and Clarissa unpicked the stitching of some of the canvas chair seats.

By midday they had rigged up a temporary structure that would give them some protection from the searing rays which by then threatened them with severe sunburn, and after lying for two hours sweating under it they again set to work further to improve their situation.

Next day, from the twine binding that Clarissa had unpicked, Bodkin made a fishing line and baited it with the entrails of one of the chickens. The result was most unwelcome. Within a few minutes the bait was taken and the line snapped. Peering over the side of the raft down through the clear water they caught the flash of a white belly. As they watched, it turned over, merging into a long grey shape that shot upwards. A moment later an eight-foot shark broke the surface within a few feet of the raft.

Roger remarked that he had been surprised that sharks had not arrived on the scene to attack the many men swimming in the sea shortly after the *Minerva* went down. Bodkin told him that, during rough weather, sharks kept well under water, but he added that, now it was calm and they had attracted one, the brute would never leave them till they were either dead or rescued. And so it proved. A more gentle wind was still wafting them north-westward towards the distant coast of Africa and hour after hour the triangular fin of the great fish now cut through the water, like a small sail, as it followed in their wake. It was still there when they roused up to face their third day on the raft.

That day they completed and rigged a low sail. With their very limited resources there was then no more that they could do, except try to keep cheerful and prevent their thoughts dwelling on how long they had to wait until they were due for the next meagre ration of water and food, which was all they allowed themselves thrice daily.

As an aid to keeping their minds occupied, they started sing-songs, but soon gave up because in the great heat singing parched their throats and made them crave more than ever for a drink. Instead, they took turns to tell stories, and played guessing games; but Bodkin was not much good at either, and having no education except in seamanship was often at a loss to understand what his companions were talking about.

Yet he fared better than they did physically, for he was much tougher. In spite of every precaution to keep in the shade, it proved impossible to protect more than their heads for any length of time; so from their first full day on the raft both Clarissa and Roger suffered a great deal from sunburn on the backs of their hands, ankles and insteps.

From dawn to dusk each day they took hourly turns at the duty of keeping a constant watch for a ship on the horizon, and from a strip of Clarissa's petticoat they had made a flag to wave as a signal should they see one. But they watched in vain; the weather remained calm, the sky a brassy blue and the ocean empty.

Bill Bodkin remained optimistic about their chances of being picked up, but Roger had all he could do to hide his growing fears from Clarissa. They still had water enough to last them for another week, but they had had to finish the meat up on the third day because the heat was beginning to turn it bad; it was futile to fish because the shark would have snapped up anything they caught before they could pull it in and, although they had been allowing themselves only one thick ship's biscuit each a day, their sixth night on the raft would find them foodless. Already they were suffering pangs of hunger and conjuring up visions of their favourite dishes, so he dreaded to think of the state to which they would be reduced when they had not even a morsel of stale baked flour and water with which, every few hours, to still their cravings.

By the fifth day they had almost given up talking and lay for long periods silent and unmoving, trying to keep their thoughts off such heavenly delights as fresh juicy fruits, chilled white wine, cold lobsters and iced *parfaits*. All through the day they sweltered, protected only by the thin canvas of the chairs from the direct rays of the blazing sun. At last it set and with darkness they dropped off into a fitful doze.

It was Clarissa who roused them. A little after midnight she shook

Roger by the shoulder, and said in a husky voice: 'Have I been dreaming, or is the air different? It has become . . . well, balmy describes it; and it smells scented . . . like apple pie.'

Bodkin had woken on the instant. He sniffed loudly, then exclaimed: 'You're right, Missey! Praise be to God! I believe we're hard by the Isle of Cloves!'

Hurriedly they wriggled out from under the flimsy shelter and stood up. Clearly defined against the starlit sky a jagged frieze of blackness rose from the horizon towards which the raft was drifting. There could be no doubt about its being a coast-line. It seemed to them an interminable time before they came any closer to it, but actually within an hour they could make out groups of tall palms standing out from a solid mass along a low shore, and the white line of foam as curling waves broke upon it.

There followed twenty minutes of agonized waiting. From fear that their dread companion, the shark, was still lurking somewhere nearby in the darkness, they dared not attempt to swim ashore. They could only pray that the tide would not turn and carry the raft out to sea again before it was cast up on the beach.

At last it was caught in the boiling surf, whirled round and turned over. As they were dashed from it a wave broke over them, but their hands and knees met slithering pebbles. They staggered to their feet. Roger and Bodkin each seized Clarissa by an arm. But they could not advance; the undertow was too strong for them. Another wave hit them and flung them forward. Again they were on their knees, but this time in shallower water. Once more they strove to get a firm foothold on the treacherous shingle. Step by step they fought the backwash. One final effort and the three of them, drenched and breathless but triumphant, lurched clear of the water and threw themselves down on the pebbly strand.

For some minutes they lay where they had fallen, spitting out water and getting back their breath. As soon as they had recovered, they moved farther up the steeply shelving shore to the dark line of trees, but found beneath them thick jungle; so they settled down on its fringe and, wearied out, dozed there for the rest of the night.

When dawn came they saw that they were near one extremity of a long bay. Towards its centre there were sandy stretches, but from end to end jungle, topped by tall palm trees, enclosed it, and it held no habitation or sign of life.

While they were on the raft, anxiety to be saved from death upon it had dominated their minds; now they felt they were in little better case, for they knew only that they had been cast up somewhere upon the immensely long, unexplored coast of East Africa, so must face many perils before they could hope to reach a place of safety.

But their empty stomachs were rumbling with hunger, so their first thought was to find food. The jungle was thick but not impenetrable, and quite near in from its edge they came upon several kinds of trees bearing fruit. All of them were strange so they feared that some might be poisonous, but they were so hungry that they had to take that risk. They minimized it by each eating only of one sort and only enough to still their immediate craving.

Fearing that they might get lost if they went deeper in, they returned to the beach and made their way round the point of the bay, hoping that on its far side they might find a native village, but they were disappointed; another long stretch of desolate shore lay before them.

The scent of cloves was again strong in the balmy air, and Bodkin said he had heard tell that the Portuguese had a settlement on the Isle of Cloves, for collecting the clove crop and shipping it to Europe; so if this was the island, a few hours' walk should bring them to a plantation and the means of getting back to civilization.

Cheered by this thought, they set off along the shore, but they had not gone far before Clarissa complained of pains in her stomach, and there could be little doubt that the particular fruit she had eaten had poisoned her. Halting, they sat her down in the shade of a palm and Roger told her that she must make herself sick. But she could not, so Bodkin fetched sea-water in a large leaf and they kept pouring it down her throat until she vomited.

Still racked with pain she rolled from side to side; her skin was hot and large red blotches appeared upon it. Bodkin stood by, murmuring from time to time, 'Poor Missey! Oh, the poor Missey, and she so brave too,' while Roger, distraught with fear that she was about to die, alternatively pressed her hands and soothed her burning forehead.

For over an hour she writhed and groaned; but then her pains gradually eased, and it was clear that having made her sick as soon as possible had saved her. Her ordeal had left her much too exhausted to walk for some time to come; so they decided to stay where they were through the rest of the morning and until the midday heat was well past.

Bodkin suggested that by noon the stones on the beach would be so hot that it should be possible to par-cook slices of meat with them; so Roger got out his pistols and powder flask with the intention of shooting a bird, or one of the small animals of which they had seen several rooting about in the fringe of the jungle.

Their sadly tattered clothes had dried on them, but the powder was still damp; so Roger spread it out on his handkerchief to dry in the sun. As soon as it was ready he began to prime his pistols, and he was still working on the second when Bodkin gave a sudden joyous shout:

'Sail ahoy! Sail ahoy!'

Unnoticed by them until then, a boat with a single triangular sail had come round the promontory and was now crossing the bay. Bodkin ran down to the edge of the sea, shouting and waving. There were half a dozen men in the boat; they waved back, then altered course and brought their craft close in. As it approached, Roger could see that the men in it were coal-black, fuzzy haired, and naked except for loin-cloths, and had pieces of bone stuck through their noses.

As he watched he wondered uneasily if it would be wise to trust themselves to these savages. Apart from a few trading centres, mostly separated by many hundreds of miles, Africa, south of its Mediterranean shore, was totally unknown, and tales came back to Europe that its black inhabitants included races of ape-men, dwarfs and cannibals.

To have escaped drowning, starvation and the shark would be no comfort if they were to be killed with fiendish rites as food for a tribe of man-eaters. Yet their only hope of ever getting back to civilization lay in reaching a port and their prospects of doing so, without guides and help, were infinitesimal; so he could only be thankful that, for the moment at least, the natives in the boat showed no signs of hostility. All the same, he felt sure that at best they would not be able to keep their hands off his jewellery; so he swiftly transferred his beautiful diamond brooch from his cravat, and his ring from his finger, to the fob pocket of his breeches.

With great dexterity the natives manœuvred the boat in, lowered its sail and, judging the big rollers to a nicety, ran it ashore, Jumping out, they dragged it clear of the surf, then formed an excited, jabbering group about the castaways. By pointing at the jungle, Clarissa, her mouth, and then rubbing his own tummy, Roger indicated that she had eaten some poisonous fruit and their grimaces showed that they understood him. The oldest among them, a tall lean man with a lined face and a fringe of grizzled curls round an otherwise bald pate, made strange clicking noises with his mouth and tongue, upon which two of the others picked up Clarissa as though she weighed no more than a sack of feathers and ran with her down to the boat.

Roger followed promptly on their heels and saw them deposit her upon a pile of newly caught fish. This living, slimy, silver couch was hardly one a European invalid would have chosen, yet it was dictated by common sense, since the boat was a most primitive affair with neither thwarts, stern seats nor bottom boards. Roger and Bodkin climbed in, the old man took the tiller, his crew of brawny negroes ran the boat back into the pounding surf, then like a team of acrobats leapt into her.

For the best part of two hours the boat tacked along the coast, while her crew displayed a mixture of shyness, friendliness and curiosity. The whites of their eyes showing up vividly in their coal-black faces, they chattered away in their strange clicking language, their gaze riveted on their passengers and, now and then, hesitantly put out a hand to feel the texture of their garments.

At length the boat rounded another promontory and entered the mouth of a small river. Half a mile up it they arrived at a clearing in which stood one great conical-roofed hut and half a hundred smaller ones grouped about it. The midday sun was now blazing down from almost immediately overhead, and apart from a few tethered goats and some naked children playing in the dust, the native village appeared deserted. But the old man at the tiller blew loudly on a conch shell and almost immediately the place came to life.

Tall warriors armed with hastily snatched up spears, knobkerries and hide shields, women of all ages, with their pierced ear lobes stretched six or eight inches by the insertion of brass ornaments, and innumerable children, came streaming out of the huts. Pushing and jostling they formed an excited jabbering concourse at the riverside as the boat drew in and her three passengers were landed.

After a few moments the crowd fell back and made a space for an old, old, wizened man. He addressed the strangers, but they could not understand him. All Roger could do was to lift his right hand open and with its palm outward, in the knights' gesture from which the salute originated, indicating that it held no weapon and that they came in peace.

Several other elderly men joined the wizened one. They held a swift palaver, then the three Europeans were beckoned forward and led to an empty hut. Presently women brought them bowls of stew, fruit and a fermented liquor that tasted rather like sour beer; but they signed to Clarissa that she should take none of these and, instead, gave her a half-coconut filled with a strong, but not unpleasant smelling, porridge, In spite of these attentions, Roger noted with some misgivings that a big negro with a tufted spear had been placed on guard outside the hut.

After the meal, in spite of their anxieties, they all fell asleep in the close hot darkness. They were woken by the rhythmic beating of drums, and soon afterwards their guard shouted to them to come out of the hut. Clarissa was now recovered and, as the three of them emerged from the low doorway, they saw that night had come. A group of a dozen warriors, some holding torches and others spears, were waiting for them outside and closed round them immediately they appeared. Emitting high piercing cries and doing a dance-march of two steps forward, stamp, one back, this formidable escort conducted them to an open space in front of the great hut where the whole tribe had now assembled and was squatting cross-legged on the ground.

There, too, enthroned upon a pile of bleached skulls, and surrounded by a score of wives, the Chief was sitting. He was a huge man with a broad fleshy face and an enormous stomach. On his head he wore a fan-shaped crown of ostrich-feathers, round his neck were half a dozen necklaces of beaten gold, and his loin-cloth was of leopard skin. Otherwise he was naked and his ebony stomach, knees and bulging arms glistened from the oil with which they had been massaged.

Beside him was an even more terrifying figure, and Roger had little doubt but that it was the old, old, wizened man who had met them at the landing place, now dressed in his ceremonial trappings. His feet were in shoes each made from the head of a baby alligator, the jaws with their long rows of teeth pointing forward and wide open. His skinny calfs disappeared under a grass skirt, above which he was girdled by a large living snake that flickered its tongue and slowly waved its head to and fro. His naked chest was painted with white and ochre markings, the most prominent of which were two ovals on his nipples, and with lighter strokes below, obviously intended to represent two huge eyes. His wrists and elbows were tufted with monkey fur and from his shoulders there arose a huge and hideous mask surmounted by a pair of bull's horns.

A hush fell on the assembly; the Witch Doctor sprang forward. With clicking tongue and falsetto voice echoing strangely from inside his great hollow mask, he addressed the Chief, but from time to time swung round towards the people as though appealing for their support. From the way in which he pointed to the three prisoners, stamped his alligator-shod feet, and frequently waved a short glittering knife threateningly in front of their faces, it was inescapably clear that he was demanding their deaths. And Roger, grimly eyeing two great cauldrons with fires ready lit below them, a little distance away outside the great hut, decided that the tales of cannibalism he had heard must be true and that, if they were slaughtered, they would afterwards be eaten.

While the hideously apparelled priest raved and ranted, the Chief remained impassive. Seated cross-legged on his throne of skulls he might have been an obese ebony idol, but for the fact that he now and then stretched out a hand to one of his women, who handed him a calabash from which he swilled down a gulp or two of some whitish liquid.

At first the people, too, while watching the proceedings intently, remained silent; but, after a little, appreciative murmurs began to run through them. Soon these increased until each of the Witch Doctor's violent outpourings met with a great shout of endorsement. Suddenly he ceased, stopped dead in front of the Chief and flung wide his arms, clearly asking that the prisoners should be given to him to kill.

CHAPTER TWELVE

The Will of Allah

ROGER, Clarissa and Bill Bodkin stood before the throne of skulls in their tattered rags, just as they had been washed ashore. Nothing had been taken from them and Bodkin was wondering how many of the warriors he could kill with his cutlass before he was killed himself. He doubted if it would be more than one, as all of them had spears in their hands. In two swift moves, he reckoned, he could draw and nearly decapitate a painted brave who stood within a yard of him, but it seemed unlikely that he would have time to raise his blade again before a shower of spears pierced him and forced him to the ground. He was not afraid of death, but the thought of the spears piercing his body made him break out into a sweat. His lips moved in a prayer that it would be over quickly, for he had no doubt at all that his last hour had come.

Clarissa was standing between the two men. Although she was a little above the average height for a woman, with the heels of her shoes broken down and her hair scragged back flat on her head, she looked small and frail. She had never been given to deceiving herself, and like Bodkin, felt that there was no hope for them. Only one thought comforted her a little. When they had first been brought before the Chief she had seen his eyes run over her, openly appraising her as if she were a head of cattle. Too many men had looked at her with desire for her to mistake the expression in his eyes. It was not desire, but contempt. His reaction to her pale slim beauty had been exactly the same as would have been a fastidious white man's to an enormously fat coal-black negress. That being so, she had only death to fear, and if Roger was to die she had no wish to live. Her heart was pounding heavily, but she was clasping his left hand with her right hand which her will was strong enough to prevent from trembling.

Almost from the beginning of the Witch Doctor's oration, Roger had felt sure that his worst fears were to be realized. Whether or not the tribe were cannibals and intended later to feast upon their flesh was immaterial. The croaking and gestures of the hideously masked old man made it clear beyond all doubt that he was demanding to be allowed to butcher them as a sacrifice to some obscene jungle god; and, since the whole tribe were obviously in favour of his demand, there seemed no reason whatever why the Chief should refuse it.

Like Bodkin, Roger meant to go down fighting—if he had time; for, unlike Clarissa, he had not taken in the Chief's appraisal of her, so he meant to kill her first. He would have time for that, but it seemed doubtful if he would afterwards be able to make another move before a spear was thrust through his back or a knobkerrie smashed in his head.

That, of course, was if he waited for the Chief to give the Witch Doctor the signal to proceed with their butchery. He could act first and, although there was no possible hope of cutting their way to safety, it meant that before killing Clarissa he would have dealt the whole tribe a blow that they would not soon forget. It was, too, a blow that his shrewdness told him might just possibly lead to saving their lives.

As the grotesquely masked old man stood with arms outspread before the Chief, Roger drew his pistol and shot him in the back.

The result of his act was beyond his wildest hopes or expectations. The pistol flashed, its loud report shattered the tense silence that had fallen on the assembly. The Witch Doctor gave a screech, threw up his clawlike hands and collapsed at the foot of the pile of skulls. He gave one convulsive jerk that threw his mask off and sent him rolling over on his back. Then he lay still, his wizened face contorted in a grin of death.

Next moment pandemonium broke loose. The Chief's wives sprang to their feet; screaming and fighting, they tumbled over one another to get back inside the great hut. The warriors, the whites of their eyes rolling with terror in their painted faces, leapt away from the captives, turned and mingled with the crowd of women, older men and youths who were already stampeding away between the huts. With wails of fear and lamentation, as though expecting their village was about to be destroyed by a succession of thunderbolts, they fled helter-skelter into the jungle.

Within two minutes there was not a soul to be seen except the Chief and five of a group of elders who had been squatting near him. They were now all on their feet and, although too brave to run, huddled round him eyeing Roger with mingled fear and amazement.

Roger had thought that if he killed the Witch Doctor there was a chance in a hundred that instead of being slaughtered immediately they might gain a night of grace while another Witch Doctor was installed and, perhaps, in the early hours while the tribe was sleeping, kill any sentries that had been set to guard them and escape into the jungle. But the moment panic seized the tribe, it flashed upon him that they could never have seen a fire-arm; so, to them, he had worked a greater magic than any ever accomplished by his victim.

As the terror-stricken natives fled, his mind became a whirlpool of jostling thoughts. This heaven-sent reprieve could be only temporary, unless he used it rightly. On that the saving of their lives still hung. And he must act quickly. If he showed hesitation or weakness now, the ascendancy that had been so miraculously thrust upon him would be lost, and lost for good.

They had a free field for escape. No one would dare to stop them if they walked quickly off. But what then? They would be no better off in the jungle than they had been on the shore that morning when the fisherman had found them. He had his second pistol and that too was loaded. He could threaten the Chief with it. But to what useful purpose could he threaten him? And for how long could he keep up the threat? Soon, some of the braver warriors might recover from their panic and come creeping back. It needed only one well-aimed spear, thrown from the cover of the huts, and he would be as dead as the Witch Doctor.

With sudden resolution he took a few steps forward. Reversing the empty pistol he went down on one knee, smiled at the Chief and, holding the weapon by the barrel, offered it to him.

Astonishment, suspicion, pleasure chased one another over the big negro's bloated features. Smiling he stepped forward to accept the proffered gift. But Roger stood up, waved him back, returned the pistol to his belt then, still smiling, drew his sword.

With its sharp point he began to rip a series of furrows in the hard trampled dirt of the ground. First he drew a tall gateway with towers on either side of it, then long lines on either side to represent walls, and above one of them the dome and minaret of a mosque, such as he had seen in pictures of Eastern cities.

The Chief and his elders looked on with puzzled expressions, but as soon as Roger had done he resheathed his sword and proceeded to explain in a series of gestures. With a sweep of the hand he included Clarissa, Bodkin and himself, then he pointed first at his picture of a town, then up river. Next he tapped the pistol and pointed at the Chief. Even a child could not have mistaken his meaning. 'Send us to a town and the magic weapon is yours.'

The thick red lips of the Chief parted in a grin. Three times he brought his head forward in a slow nod and the spreading crown of ostrich feathers upon it waved gently to and fro. Pointing to himself he said 'Kobo' several times, and Roger in turn pointed to himself saying 'Brook'. Then Chief Kobo issued a sharp command to one of his elders. The old man blew upon a conch shell that was slung from his waist and, within a few minutes, the members of the tribe, still showing much nervous apprehension, began to trickle back into the clearing.

As soon as a good part of the tribe were reassembled, the Chief began to bellow at them, evidently reproving them for their cowardice, but a few moments later he said something that was greeted with a great shout of laughter. In an instant, the whole atmosphere had changed and, their fright forgotten, they were chattering away like happy children.

The Witch Doctor's body was carried away and Kobo, now treating Roger, Clarissa and Bodkin as honoured guests, made them sit beside him while cooking pots and calabashes were brought from the huts.

The feast that followed lasted far into the night. All the cooked food was very highly spiced and, from fear of offending their host, the guests had to eat something from each pot offered to them; but they made their main meal off fruit. At intervals there were dances, first by the stamping warriors, then by the young women, and finally one in which a long line of each sex swayed, postured and stamped facing each other. During the dances the white liquid was passed round and Roger warned his two companions to drink sparingly of it. That was just as well, for it was palm spirit beaten up with ground cereal and highly intoxicating.

At length Kobo, now decidedly drunk, called a halt to the festivities. With a rolling gait he escorted his guests to their hut, then staggered away among his equally tipsy warriors. Even so, Roger feared that they might yet lose their lives through treachery, or by some relative of the Witch Doctor's seeking to revenge him while they slept; so he arranged to share watches for the rest of the night with Bodkin, and took the first himself.

As silence gradually settled over the village, he told himself that they were very lucky to be alive, but he could not help wondering a little grimly what other perils Fate had in store for them, and reflecting on their very small chance of ever again setting foot in England.

His fears of a treacherous attack proved groundless. Next morning the village slept late but, soon after rousing, a group of shy, frightened women brought them fruit, drink and flowers. When they had eaten, a tall warrior with a headband and a single ostrich plume rising from it took them again to Kobo, who was once more seated on his throne of skulls.

The Chief pointed in turn at the drawing on the ground that Roger had made the night before, at the tall warrior, and at Roger's pistol. But Roger had no intention of giving up the pistol yet. Shaking his head, he pointed in turn at the drawing, the pistol and the warrior, conveying that he would give the weapon to the man only when they reached the town.

For some minutes, Kobo scowled and kept repeating his gestures, but each time Roger shook his head; so at length the hulking negro gave in and beckoned up a group of his people who were standing some way off. The group consisted of six more warriors and four women. Each of the women held the end of one of a pair of poles, between the middle sections of which were plaited rushes forming the seat of a backless carrying chair.

Kobo signed to Roger to take the seat, but he, greatly relieved that Clarissa would not have to make the journey on foot, gave her his hand and settled her in it. His act called forth looks of puzzled disapproval, but ignoring them he indicated that they were now ready to start. For a moment the Chief rested his heavy hand on Roger's shoulder. He did the same to that warrior with the single ostrich plume, and repeated the word 'Immu' three times; so they took that to be the man's name. Then he nodded his befeathered head, and 'Immu', raising his spear aloft, led the way by a main path through the huts out of the village.

For four days they trekked through jungles and across wide stretches of open ground covered with coarse scrub. The going was hard, for the jungle paths were tortuous, and at times obstructed by fallen trees, steep gullies and small rivers. Their progress was difficult to estimate but Roger judged it to be from twelve to fifteen miles a day, and he could tell from the sun that they were moving roughly in a north-westerly direction.

From time to time Immu sent one of his warriors as a runner to inform the Chief of the next village of their approach; so that when they arrived in it they were provided with a meal and huts in which to sleep either for the night or during the hottest hours of the day. At every village they entered, the entire population turned out to crowd round them, eyes goggling with curiosity, and, as they always arrived semi-exhausted from a long trudge in the damp heat, this proved particularly trying; but Immu generally managed to drive the people off after a while, presumably by telling them that Roger was a powerful Witch Doctor, and they were then able to relax in the grateful shade of one of the huts.

On the morning of the fifth day, they came out of a belt of forest on high ground to see a magnificent panorama spread before them. A gentle slope some six miles long led down to the sea. The slope, which formed a deep belt right along the coast, was almost entirely covered by plantations from which came more strongly than ever the spicy smell of cloves. Beyond them the sun sparkled on an azure sea dotted with small coral atolls, and in the hazy distance another coast-line could be seen. As they were facing west, Roger had no doubt that the far shore was the coast of Africa, and that Bill Bodkin had been right in his belief that it was upon the fabulous Isle of Cloves that they had been cast ashore.

But it was not upon the coast that their eyes were riveted. In the very centre of it there stood a town. It had battlemented walls above which rose several large buildings with domes and turrets, and beyond them a big ship with all sail set was tacking out across the bay.

Immu made it clear that he and his party would go no farther; so Roger carried out his part of the bargain. First he showed him how the pistol worked, then gave it to him with half the powder, two flints, and six of the dozen bullets, which were all that he had with him. The farewells could be only by smiles and gestures. Five minutes later the negro warriors and carrier women had disappeared along the jungle track. Then, although the hottest hours of the day were approaching, Roger, Clarissa and Bodkin were so eager to reach the town that they at once set off down hill towards it.

The sun's rays were so intense that they were forced to rest every half-mile or so in the shade of palms and, even then, the six-mile walk proved most fatiguing. But they derived one benefit from making the journey in the midday hours: no one was working in the plantations, so it was not until they were covering the last mile that they attracted the attention of the natives.

Once that happened, a crowd quickly gathered, but it was of a very different type from those which had surrounded them in the villages. These people were considerably lighter in colour, most of them had straight hair, good noses and better-formed features and, except for the children, they all wore some form of loose garment. Yet they showed nearly as much excitement and curiosity as had the negroes, as they pranced along beside the three strangers, calling to one another, and pointing at Clarissa's pale gold hair.

Dusty, perspiring and footsore, they at last reached a great gate set between two towers in the wall of the town. The sight of the approaching crowd had brought out from it a guard with spears. Their officer wore a round brass helmet which rose to a sharp spike on top and had pieces of chain-mail dangling from its rim on either side to protect his ears and cheeks.

He spoke to them in what they took to be Arabic, and Roger tried out his Persian on him, but neither understood the other. Roger then tried Latin, and the smatterings he had of Greek and Spanish, but all proved equally useless. With a shrug the officer ordered his men to put them in the gate-house and, as soon as they were inside it, the door was slammed upon them.

It was a stone apartment in the base of one of the towers that flanked the gate; its floor was a little below ground-level and it was unfurnished except for a rough wooden table. After the heat and glare of the sun they were glad of the cool semi-darkness, and sank wearily down on a stone bench that ran along one wall; but this was not the sort of reception they had hoped for and, as soon as they had recovered a little from their fatigue, they began to speculate on how long it would be until they were taken before the Portuguese Governor.

Over two hours elapsed and they started up from a fitful doze when the door opened and the officer came in. He was followed by a short, very fat, man, but fat in quite a different way from Kobo, for the negro Chief's bulk had been largely due to huge muscles, whereas this man gave the impression, even though he was wearing flowing robes, of being soft, and when he spoke it was in a high falsetto. Although Roger had never met a eunuch, he felt sure the fat man was one; but all that concerned him was that he had spoken in Persian. Thanking God for the hours he had spent learning that language while in the *Minerva*, he introduced himself and the others. In response, the eunuch said he was called Khunsa Bajazet.

Roger then gave a brief account of their misadventures and asked to be taken to the European quarter of the town.

Bajazet replied that there was no such quarter; upon which Roger said, 'Am I not right in supposing this to be the Isle of Cloves, and that on the island there is a Portuguese trading station?'

At that the eunuch began to laugh, and his several chins quivered like a jelly. When he had done laughing, he piped: 'Indeed it is the Isle of Cloves, and this is the city of Zanzibar, but there are no Portuguese here. We drove them out over sixty years ago.'

Endeavouring to conceal his sudden alarm at this news, Roger asked, 'Then who rules here now?'

'His Highness the Vali Abdul ben Mazuri,' came the response. 'He is Viceroy for the Sultan of Muscat, who by Allah's grace is the Sovereign Lord of all this part of the world.' As the eunuch pronounced the name of Allah, he bowed; then he added, 'Come to the light, all of you, so that I can see you better.'

A gesture with which he accompanied his words conveyed their meaning to Clarissa and Bodkin; so all three of them accompanied him to the door. There he turned and, with little pig's eyes encased in rolls of fat, surveyed each of them critically in turn. Pointing to Roger's sword, and the gold embroidered belt from which it hung, he said:

'It seems that in spite of your rags you are a rich man; so you may be of some value to us.' Then stretching out a fat hand he took Clarissa by the arm, half turned her and taking the ends of her fair hair between his fingers gently fluffed it out.

As she drew swiftly away, Roger said in a carefully controlled voice, 'Doubtless, Sir, you mean no harm; but in our country to touch a lady so is considered an act of rudeness.'

Bajazet shrugged his sloping shoulders and replied with a sneer, 'But this, Infidel, is not your country. It is the Isle of Cloves; and cloves are not the only thing we export from it. The greater part of out wealth comes from the sale of slaves. But I'll have no need to export you. For you three Roumis I'll get a fine price here.'

Turning to the officer he put into his hand a small canvas bag from which there came the clink of coin, then he waddled out into the street. The officer signed to the others to follow and shouted an order to his men. As Roger and Bodkin emerged into the daylight, the guards fell upon them. Taken by surprise they had no chance to resist, even if there had been anything to gain by doing so. Their weapons were taken from them and their wrists were bound.

Meanwhile the eunuch had been helped into a litter. Clarissa was swiftly lifted into it beside him and its curtains were drawn. Roger and Bodkin were attached to it by the cords that tied their wrists and, when it moved off, two of the armed guards followed with spears at the ready to prick them should they try to break away or dally.

The little procession wound its way through narrow, cobbled streets thronged with people of every shade from coal-black to pale coffee. The negroes were mostly naked to the waist, but many of the lighter-skinned Arabs, Indians and Persians were clad in handsome robes of striped cotton, wool and silk. There were many donkeys, mostly heavy-laden with goods, others carrying men and women. All the women were in shapeless garments and wore the veil. Nearly everyone paused to stare at the prisoners, some shouted abuse and now and then an urchin threw a piece of garbage at them before darting off into an alley.

After a slow progress of a quarter of an hour, they turned up a steep slope and at its top went through a tall gateway where more guards, all wearing the pointed brass helmets, stood aside to let them pass. Entering a wide court, they crossed it and, from the doorway of a building on its far side, several servants ran out. Some of them helped the eunuch to alight; others, on his orders, took charge of the prisoners. They were hurried down a short passage and locked into a small empty cell-like room.

As soon as they were alone, Clarissa asked what the eunuch had said, and what was to become of them. Roger was so distressed that he had not the heart to tell her outright but, after a while, he decided that it would be no kindness to allow their harsh fate to be sprung upon her as a surprise; so he broke it to her and Bodkin as gently as he could that the town was a Mohammedan stronghold, and that they were to be sold into slavery.

The eunuch's rough treatment of them had to some extent prepared Clarissa for ill-tidings, but when she grasped to the full the awful implications of what Roger was saying she burst into tears, and there was no way in which he could comfort her.

Presently some of the eunuch's servants returned, untied their hands and set before them bowls of water to wash in and of fruits to stay their hunger and thirst. Silently they cleaned themselves up as well as they could and ate a few of the fruits; then, in tongue-tied misery, they settled down again on the floor with their backs against the wall, to await further developments.

In vain Roger racked his brain for a way out of this situation which, faced frankly, held grimmer prospects for them than a sudden death; for they were threatened not only with temporary degradation and hardship but with a life sentence. Had they been captured by Barbary pirates from Morocco, Algeria or Tunis, they might, sooner or later, have escaped across the Mediterranean; but here, thousands of miles from any Christian country, they were as far removed from sanctuary as though they had been transported to another planet. Month after month, and for as many years as they escaped fatal accident or disease, they must labour under the blistering equatorial sun upon such tasks as were set them, and submit to beatings and all other shames that might be put upon them.

All he could do was to strive to recall everything that Droopy Ned had told him about the Mohammedan religion, and what he had learned of Eastern customs while studying Persian on the voyage out; so that should an opportunity arise he could use them to win the good-will of the master to whom he could only hope the eunuch would sell all three of them together.

Darkness fell and about an hour afterwards, Bajazet came to the cell with servants carrying torches. The eunuch was in a most evil temper and did not disguise the reason for it. Roughly ordering them to get up he said to Roger:

'My unlucky star must be in the ascendant today. The arrival of three Roumis in the city has come to the ears of His Highness, and learning that I had you here he has ordered me to bring you before him. This is a misfortune for both of us. It is certain that he will regard you as his property, and state slaves, are far more harshly treated then those who are owned privately.' Glancing at Clarissa, he added, with a heavy sigh, 'And to think that I could have sold her to a merchant of my acquaintance for at least five thousand *dinars*, whereas now she'll go to the Vali's harem and I'll get nothing.'

Pleasing as it was to know that the eunuch was to be deprived of the handsome sum he had hoped to make out of their misfortune, Roger felt that he was right in his assertion that they would have fared better in his hands than in those of the Vali, particularly as far as Clarissa was concerned. Either way there was no escape for her from becoming the concubine of an Arab and perhaps one whose approaches would make her shudder with repulsion, but a rich merchant might later have raised her to the status of wife and given her all the amenities that went with such a position; whereas as one of a large harem all the chances were that, after her lord had enjoyed her for a while, she would remain for ever a prisoner, wasting her life in the company of a score or more of other jealous neglected women.

Naturally he kept these gloomy thoughts to himself; but he told Clarissa and Bodkin that they were to be taken before the Vali, and the three of them obeyed the eunuch's order to follow him. He led them out across the court, down a long arcade, then through a beautifully carved doorway, at which two guards were standing, and into another, smaller court.

Its four sides were colonnades each of a dozen arches formed by slender pillars of various coloured marbles. The walls beyond them were covered shoulder high with brightly painted tiles, and between and above the arches stonework fretted like lace gave the whole a delightfully light and airy appearance. From the centre of each arch hung a brass lantern with many little panes of different coloured glass, diffusing a warm, gentle light. In the middle of the court a fountain played into a sunken marble basin, and the floor was a mosaic of black-and-white marble squares.

At its far end, opposite the doorway, there was a group of people. In the centre Abdul ben Mazuri sat cross-legged on a broad divan with many cushions. Below him on his left, half lying on more cushions and leaning on the side of the divan, there reposed a young woman. She was wearing voluminous trousers caught in at the ankles, and a bright red sleeveless Turkish jacket. On her bare arms there were several jewelled bangles and, although her face was veiled, she was, judging by its upper half, very beautiful. A little to the right of the divan an elderly grey-bearded man was seated on a leather pouf. In the background stood two more men. One, wearing a brass corselet and plumed helmet, was obviously the Captain of the Guard; the other, who wore only a leopard-skin about his middle and held resting against his shoulder a gleaming scimitar, was a huge negro.

As they advanced, Roger's gaze was riveted on the Vali. He was a well-made man, probably in his early forties. He had a black beard and moustache, a full red mouth, a hooked nose and piercing black eyes. Upon his head he wore a green turban, showing that he had made the pilgrimage to Mecca; in its centre there was a splendid diamond, and rising from it an aigrette. He was dressed in a loose silk robe, from which protruded the hilt of a dagger heavily damascened with gold. Round his neck there were four ropes of pearls.

'Down on your knees!' piped the eunuch in his high falsetto.

Clarissa and Bodkin did not understand the order, so the one made a low curtsey and the other an awkward bob. Roger ignored it, and made his most graceful bow. Then, before anyone else could speak, he got out the few sentences of Persian that he had been preparing on their way there.

'Noble Vali, may the peace and blessing of Allah—praised be his name and that of his Prophet—be upon you. I too am a lord in my own country but, as it says in the Holy Koran, "the fate of every man is bound about his brow". It was decreed that I should come before you in rags and craving your protection. Yet Allah is the Merciful, the Compassionate. By His will I have been spared this unworthy trinket; so that on arriving at your court I may not be found lacking in politeness.'

With his last sentence he produced from his fob pocket the diamond brooch that he usually wore in his cravat. It was a beautiful jewel worth

several hundred pounds, and had been given to him by Georgina; so he was
loath to part with it, but he knew that now was the time to do so, for if
he did not it would certainly be taken from him later.

Holding it in the palm of his hand, he flashed it for a moment so that it
sparkled in the light of the lanterns; then taking a swift step forward, he
laid it on the divan beside Abdul ben Mazuri's left knee and within easy
each of his lovely houri's hand.

At the first sight of it she had smiled, and he had seen her big doe-like
eyes light up with excitement. As he was desperately hoping she would,
she reached out for it. The Vali made a quick gesture to stop her, but he
was too late. Her slender brown fingers had closed upon the jewel.

With an angry mutter, the Vali gave her a sharp slap on her bare shoulder
with his ivory fan. Her thinly pencilled brows creased in swift dismay and
uncertainty. Throwing herself forward she kissed his slipper, but she still
held on to her prize. Frowning, Abdul ben Mazuri looked over her head
at Roger. Upon Roger's face there was a broad smile. The eagle features
of the Arab relaxed, and a moment later he too was smiling.

Without a word said both men knew the implications of the little scene
that had just taken place. Had the girl not touched the brooch, the Vali
could have refused the gift and sent Roger to the slaves' quarters, then
ordered the jewel to be brought to him. But by picking up the brooch the
girl had accepted it on her lord's behalf; and honour would not permit a
noble Arab to make a slave of a man who had just made him a present.

Suddenly Abdul ben Mazuri began to laugh. With a heavily beringed
hand he turned his favourite's lovely face up towards his own, pinched her
ear and caressed her cheek. Her eyes, which had begun to brim with tears,
smiled again and chattering in Arabic her delighted thanks that she might
keep the brooch, she pinned it in her dark hair.

Turning back to Roger, the Vali pointed at Bill Bodkin and asked in
Persian, 'Who is that man?'

'He is my servant, Illustrious One,' Roger replied, 'and I crave your
gracious permission to keep him with me.'

Abdul ben Mazuri nodded, 'So be it,' and Roger breathed a sigh of
relief. Not only had his trick to save himself worked, but everything was
going magnificently. Yet, next moment, he knew that he had counted his
chickens before they were hatched. The Vali's dark eyes were resting on
Clarissa, and he said:

'The woman you have brought is in an ill state from your journey; but
scratches and sunburns soon heal and beneath them I discern a haughty
beauty which pleases me. I have, too, never owned a woman of such
astonishing fairness. Owing to that you no doubt had to pay a high price
for her, and I do not wish to rob you. But I can provide you with a good

choice of darker beauties, and I would have this one for my harem. How much will you take for her?'

For a moment Roger was silent. His heart seemed to have stopped beating; but it started again with a violent thump. His lips had suddenly gone dry and he moistened them with the tip of his tongue. Then he made the only reply that he could think of; and, even in that tense moment, it struck him as a bitter mockery by Fate that it had needed their being brought to such a desperate pass for him to claim a thing that he might never now enjoy.

'Illustrious One,' he said, a little hoarsely, 'Allah, who is witness to the good deeds and the bad deeds of every man—praise be on His name and that of His Prophet—has placed us in your power. Should you demand it of me, I must give her to you. But I cannot sell her; for that would bring upon me eternal shame. She is my wife.'

CHAPTER THIRTEEN

A Bolt from the Blue

CLARISSA lay upon a broad low divan. She was waiting for her lover to come to her, and she gave a heavy sigh.

Her long slim legs were easily discernible through the filmy muslin of the balloon-like trousers worn by Mohammedan ladies; above, she had on a short sleeveless jacket of a blue to match her eyes, heavily worked with an intricate pattern in gold thread. Her only other garment was a diaphanous veil, caught by a jewel to her left ear, and having a clip by which she could hook it to a jewel in the other; but now it hung down beside her leaving her fair face fully revealed. The skin of her stomach, arms, hands and feet were an even deeper shade of golden brown than they had been when the *Minerva* went down, and by contrast her hair seemed an even paler glory of fine-spun golden-tinted silk. Upon her skin, too, there was not a single blemish; for perfumed unguents had soon charmed away the bruises, burns and scratches that she had come by on the raft and during her journey through the jungle.

The divan on which she lay, propped up on cushions, was situated in a one-storeyed pavilion. Its front wall was composed only of lattice wood-work over which curtains of silk could be drawn for privacy, or at night. Centrally opposite the divan was an open archway through which she could look out onto a small court. In its centre a fountain tinkled into a circular basin that held brightly coloured fish. At intervals round the sides of the court were set tubs containing flowering shrubs or planted with exotic blossoms. They gave off a heady scent which mingled with that from the perfume burner beside the divan, and the all-pervading spicy odour wafted from the clove plantations.

The heat of the day was past and soon now she would know if she was to be allowed to remain there like a Princess in an Eastern fairy-tale, or if she was to be cast out of this earthly paradise. Lazily stretching out a hand to a silver filigree dish on a nearby table inlaid with mother-of-pearl, she picked up a piece of Rahat Lacoum. The sugar-powdered jelly had pistachio nuts in it, and as she munched them she wondered how much longer Roger would be. At that moment she heard on the marble flags outside the swift padding of the soft leather boots he now always wore.

He, too, was dressed in Eastern fashion, and his face was now so bronzed that in his rich robe, with its crimson cummerbund and the dagger inlaid with gold thrust through it, any casual observer would have taken him for a Moorish nobleman. Coming quickly through the archway to the divan he bent and kissed Clarissa on the half-open mouth she held up to him.

Her arm curled round his neck and she closed her eyes, but she was too anxious to hear his news to wish to be made love to now; so, after a moment, she pulled her mouth away and asked:

'Well? Has His Highness agreed?'

He nodded. 'Yes. We leave tomorrow morning.'

She sighed. 'Oh, Roger! Why did you have to do this? We have been so deliriously happy here.'

That was true. Roger's ready wit had enabled him to make the best possible use of all he could recall of his talks with Droopy Ned about Mohammedan customs. Abdul ben Mazuri had admired his spirit and been favourably impressed by the way in which, although an Infidel, he spoke with knowledge and respect of the 'true' religion. For so powerful a Prince there could be no middle course; this Roumi who claimed to be a lord in his own distant land and, despite his rags, had the bearing of one, must either be accounted an enemy and enslaved, or treated as an honoured guest. The gift of the diamond brooch had made it impossible to enslave him, and his invocation of Allah as a witness to all that passed between them would have made it a flagrant sin to rob him of his wife. Refreshments had been brought; they had ceremoniously broken bread and eaten salt together. His Highness had then ordered the old grey-bearded man, who was his Vizier, to see to it that his guests lacked for nothing. Roger and Clarissa had been installed in the pavilion, where they now were, that night, and the following day they had been provided with slaves and every sort of lovely raiment.

During the three weeks that had since elapsed their existence had been idyllic. It would have been impossible to find more delightful surroundings in which to give full expression to those feelings for one another that they had so long repressed and, during the warm starlit nights in the pavilion that they shared, their caresses had been mingled with a thousand murmured endearments coming truly from the hearts of both. Yet there was no danger of their becoming cloyed with a surfeit of passionate embraces from having no other thoughts to occupy their minds.

Every day Roger spent several hours with Abdul ben Mazuri, discussing military matters, geography, and the innumerable differences between their two civilizations; and Roger was fascinated to find that in many respects the Mohammedan culture was in advance of the European, particularly where cleanliness, medicine and knowledge of ancient civilizations were concerned.

Clarissa spent those hours in the Vali's harem. His beautiful favourite, Dár-el-Naim—Dwelling of Delight—had shown the greatest friendliness, introduced her to all the other inmates of the harem, and soon taught her a few score words in Arabic which, eked out with gestures, were enough for simple conversation. The whole life of an Eastern beauty being love, Dár-el-Naim had also taught Clarissa certain things about love-making that she would never have dreamed of for herself, and several secrets of the toilette by which she might make herself even more beautiful and desirable. Then in the evenings they attended the Vali's court to dine off fabulous delicacies and witness entertainments by jugglers, dancing-girls and conjurers.

It was, therefore, not to be wondered at that Clarissa was most reluctant to have this lotus-eating existence brought to an end. Yet Roger, on learning that an Arab merchant was shortly leaving in his ship for India, had insisted on asking Abdul ben Mazuri's permission for them to sail in it. Smiling down at her, he said:

'My sweet, I truly grieve that my decision should be so displeasing to you; but we have discussed the matter *ad nauseam* already, and you know my reasons for it.'

'But I don't agree with them,' she protested. 'His Highness dotes upon you, and would never allow anyone to harm a hair of our heads.'

'He does at present. I had the greatest difficulty in persuading him to let us go. And, believe me, I too am most distressed to have to make this break. I have become greatly attached to him; and, as far as we are concerned, you have made this pavilion heaven for me.'

'Then why leave it? Why allow your morbid suspicions to play the part of a serpent in our Eden? I'll vow they are unfounded.'

He sat down on the edge of the divan, took her hand, kissed it, ran his lips up her bare arm and kissed her again below the ear. Then he replied. 'Alas, they are not. Khunsa Bajazet has never forgiven us that for having concealed our arrival Abdul ben Mazuri had him given ten strokes on the soles of his feet with the bastinado, and the old Vizier has become bitterly jealous of me. The Imam, too, protests as much as he dares at His Highness's showing favour to an Infidel. These and others are intriguing against us, and Eastern potentates are said to be fickle in their affections. Should these enemies of ours bring against us some trumped-up charge and produce enough bribed witnesses to support it, we might well find ourselves dragged from this scene of our delights to rot in separate dungeons. And I'll not risk that. Loving you as I do, I'd be mad did I not insist on sacrificing our present comfort in order to secure our future safety.'

Unhappy as his decision made Clarissa, she knew that he would not have taken it had he not had good grounds for his fears; so she argued no further. Together they went into the tiled bathroom next door, in which they were in turn massaged by expert slaves each morning. Stripping off their clothes they both clambered into the great stone bath fed from a marble lion's head with constantly flowing water and, having refreshed themselves, banged the little gong that brought their slaves hurrying to help them with their toilettes for the evening.

Early the following morning, porters came for the hampers of clothes and many other presents they had been given, then they took a sad farewell of Abdul ben Mazuri, of the beautiful Dár-el-Naim and of the other friends that they had made during their stay in the palace. As a last courtesy the Vali ordered his Captain of the Guard to escort them and Bill Bodkin—who was as loath as Clarissa to give up the life of ease and plenty he had been leading—down to the harbour. There the Arab merchant, Selim Zamurrud, welcomed them most politely and took them aboard his ship.

She was very different from the *Minerva* and, like most Arab ships of the period, built upon the two-hundred-year-old pattern of a Spanish galleon; but they were the only passengers and were given both clean and ample accommodation in her stern-castle.

For an hour the Arab sailors sweated at long sweeps, rowing the ship northward till she passed the promontory that sheltered the harbour. Once round the point, her sails caught the breeze and she started on her tricky passage south through the many coral atolls in the channel. By mid-afternoon they were rounding the southern end of the fifty-mile-long island where, nearly a month before, they had been washed ashore. A mile or more out, in a line running parallel with the coast for as far as the eye could see, huge waves were breaking in cascades of white foam. Zamurrud told them that the line marked the barrier reef, which almost encircled the island, and that when their raft was swept through a gap in it they had been extraordinarily lucky, as otherwise they would certainly have been dashed to pieces on the coral. As night fell they were heading north-east out in the open ocean.

The Arab trader was bound for Goa, the Portuguese settlement on the west coast of India some two hundred and sixty miles south of Bombay. The direct run to it from Zanzibar was well over two thousand miles and, as they had to make the best use of the winds, the actual mileage covered was far greater. But they were lucky with the weather and had a following wind for a good part of the voyage; so they made the passage in eighteen days, which was highly satisfactory. They had lost touch with the Christian calendar and now learned on landing that it was November 21st.

Zamurrud went ashore with them and introduced Roger to an Indian banker who gave him a fair rate in sicca rupees for one of the Bills of Exchange on London that his fish-skin wallet had preserved from serious damage by sea-water. After paying the Arab the passage money agreed on, they set about finding another ship, but those of the Company called at Goa only in exceptional circumstances and no large ship was due to sail from the port in the near future other than one bound for Europe.

She was expected to reach Lisbon towards the middle of March and they toyed with the idea of returning in her, then spending the spring in Portugal; but, having actually arrived in India, it seemed foolish to forgo seeing the most interesting part of that country just because to reach Calcutta would entail a month or so spent mainly in small, not very comfortable, vessels. Later Roger was most bitterly to regret the decision to go on there, but no sense of foreboding suggested to either of them at the time that they might be heading towards tragedy, and on the 23rd they set out on the first part of their new journey in a Portuguese coaster that was trading down to Colombo.

Although the accommodation and food left much to be desired, the ten days that followed were the most pleasant of any they had spent at sea. The weather was still good, and the little ship did the six hundred miles in leisurely fashion, calling at Mangalore, Calicut on the Malabar coast, Cochin, and Trivandrum, the capital of Travancore; so they saw much beautiful tropical scenery, several different Indian races, a number of splendid oriental palaces and four fascinating bazaars.

They reached Colombo on December 3rd, and would have liked to stay there for a while to see something of Ceylon; but on the afternoon of their landing they met a Captain Jarvis of the frigate *Amazon* who, it transpired, had served under Roger's father, Rear-Admiral Sir Christopher Brook. The *Amazon* had met with bad weather and put into Colombo for repairs. She was sailing again the following day for Madras and when Captain Jarvis offered them a passage in her they felt it too good a chance proceeding with a maximum of speed and safety to be refused.

As *Amazon* had come out direct from England, Captain Jarvis was able to give them news of the principal happenings in Europe during the late summer and early autumn. In the last days of July the Austrian General, Würmser, had in turn defeated the best French troops in the Army of Italy, under Masséna and Augereau, and very nearly succeeded in cutting its communications. But its Commander-in-Chief, General Buonaparte, had shown great resolution in this crisis. Ruthlessly abandoning all but essentials, he had raised the siege of Mantua and ordered Serurier to throw his siege artillery into the river Mincio rather than allow it to be captured. He had then succeeded in manœuvring himself into a position between the two main bodies of the Austrians and a week later heavily defeated them at Solferino.

In a further series of smaller battles, things had gone badly for the Austrians, and these had culminated in mid-September in a further heavy defeat. Würmser's original army of 41,000 men had been whittled down to a fragment. To save that, he had been forced to throw it into Mantua, and the French had resumed the siege of that key fortress.

Despite these many Austrian reverses, Roger felt that the campaign might have gone far worse. Although Moreau and Jourdan had crossed the Rhine, the Archduke Charles had prevented their making any serious advance; so there was no question of their coming south to Buonaparte's assistance, and he was still bogged down before Mantua. Owing to a lagoon and much marshy ground outside its walls, the fortress was in any case a very difficult one to take. Würmser had at least succeeded in revictualling and reinforcing it, and the Corsican had lost his siege train; so there was every prospect that he would be held up there for the rest of the year's serious fighting. In any case, he had been thwarted in his grand design of joining up with the Army of the Rhine and advancing through the Tyrol on Vienna; and it was that which really mattered.

On the other hand, Roger learned with a cynicism that gave him no satisfaction that his predictions to Mr. Pitt about Buonaparte treating Italy as the Treasure Chest of Europe, to be robbed at will, had duly come to pass. While keeping his eagle eye on the main conflict, Buonaparte had detached an expedition to strike south which had crossed the Po and seized Bologna in the Papal States. The terrified Cardinals had at once signed an armistice, closing their territories to the English, agreeing to yield up one hundred classic works of Art, to accept a French garrison in the important port of Ancona, and to pay in specie and kind an indemnity amounting to many millions of francs. Further, on the excuse that by allowing English ships to use Leghorn the Grand Duke of Tuscany was not observing strict neutrality, Buonaparte had sent another expedition to seize the port, and had himself gone down to the Tuscan capital. Although technically on a visit, he had entered Florence like a conqueror, browbeaten the Senate into accepting his orders regarding their future foreign policy, and extorted from them many works of art and a huge indemnity in 'compensation' for having 'had to' occupy Leghorn.

The worst news that Captain Jarvis gave them was that Spain had gone over to the enemy. On August 19th she had signed the treaty of San Idlefonso, allying herself with France and, when calling to deliver mails at Gibraltar, he had learned that Spain had declared war on England on October 5th.

From Colombo, *Amazon* made a swift passage round to Madras, arriving off the Company's headquarters in the Carnatic on December 8th. Next morning, Roger and Clarissa went ashore with Captain Jarvis in a Masulah boat. These were a type of long, very broad punt, the flat boards of which were held together only by coconut fibre. They had been evolved as the best means of passing the three distinct barriers of surf, each separated by over a hundred yards, which made landing on this coast a matter of no small danger. So dangerous, in fact, was it considered that each Masulah boat was accompanied by several hollowed-out tree trunks, called Catamarans, to act as life-boats should the larger craft capsize. The natives who manned the Masulah and Catamarans were all naked, except for a small piece of rag attached to a string round their middles, and so violent was the sea that those in the Catamarans were frequently thrown into it; but they swam like fish and soon clambered back into their tree trunks. Captain Jarvis's party reached the shore safely but, as was usual, they had all been soaked to the skin by the blinding sheets of spray, and poor Clarissa presented a sadly bedraggled sight.

They had left Bill Bodkin aboard the *Amazon*, and before going ashore said good-bye to him with mixed feelings. Like all ships in the Royal Navy, the *Amazon* was always short of hands; so, although protected from being 'pressed' by travelling as Roger's servant, Bodkin had, during the short voyage from Colombo, volunteered to serve in a watch. Finding him a first-class seaman, Captain Jarvis had offered to make him a petty-officer if he would sign on permanently instead of returning to the service of the Company. Bodkin had agreed, so Roger had made him a handsome present of money and, after having wished him luck, that was the last they saw of him.

In spite of their liking for the honest seaman they were, owing to their unorthodox relationship, far from sorry to be freed from his company. He had known them in the *Minerva* as uncle and niece, and that at Cape Town Clarissa had become Mrs. Winters. The fact that in Zanzibar they had declared themselves to be husband and wife had, Roger had explained to him, been the only means of saving Clarissa from being taken into the Vali's harem as a concubine; so the lovers had fair reason to suppose that

R.V.—6

although they shared a pavilion while there, the simple sailor would assume that they were doing so only as close relatives. In the circumstances, they could not have avoided leaving Zanzibar as Mr. and Mrs. Brook, and having arrived in Goa as a married couple it would obviously have been embarrassing to reveal there that they were not so in fact. The same applied, although with less force, on their arrival in Colombo, and by then Bodkin must have been beginning to wonder when they did mean to resume their proper relationship in public.

But that was now the last thing that either of them wished to do. They had gone quite mad about one another. The idea of their having once again to disguise their feelings and resort to clandestine meetings in order to give free rein to their passion, was intolerable to them. They were both set upon getting properly married as soon as a situation arose in which they could conveniently do so; and, in the meantime, they were determined to continue to enjoy to the full the status of marriage which Fate had thrust upon them. On arriving in Calcutta, they meant to set up house together, and to have done so with Bodkin at length forced to the conclusion that they were committing incest would have proved extremely awkward; so they were greatly relieved that he had signed on in *Amazon*, which was to remain on the Madras Station.

On Captain Jarvis's introduction Lord Hobart, the vigorous Governor of Madras, received them most kindly. For four days they enjoyed his hospitality and made several very pleasant excursions into the country round about the settlement. Then on December 12th they went aboard one of the Company's ships that was sailing for Calcutta. She made an average passage for that time of year, entered the broad mouth of the Hooghly early on the morning of the 22nd and dropped anchor in Diamond Harbour. A pilot schooner took them up the river, past the wealthy suburb of Garden Reach, to the city, and by evening they were installed at its leading hotel.

Regarding himself as still upon a honeymoon, Roger spared no expense and took the best suite available. It was on the ground floor on the garden side, and had a wide private veranda. They had supper in their private sitting-room and, after seven weeks, during nearly all of which they had had to spend their nights in the narrow confines of cabins, they derived a special joy from being able to sleep together in a great mosquito-curtained double bed.

Next morning, Roger sent for mercers, haberdashers, tailors, dressmakers, bootmakers, milliners and hatters, so that they might again fit themselves out with fashionable European wardrobes. At a little before midday Clarissa went into their bedroom with an attendant little crowd of women to be measured for various garments. Roger remained out on the veranda looking at silks and satins for his own clothes.

He had just settled on a rich cherry colour for a coat when one of the hotel's English-speaking servants came up to him, put the tips of his fingers to his forehead, salaamed almost to the ground, and said:

'Sahib, a gentleman is outside. He asks urgently that you receive him. He is the merchant Mr. Winters.'

CHAPTER FOURTEEN

A Lie Comes Home to Roost

ROGER dropped the piece of cherry-coloured silk he was fingering. Had the Archangel Gabriel been announced he could not have been more astonished and confounded. In fact he was, for once, as shocked out of his wits as would have been a revivalist preacher, exhorting his flock to prepare for Judgment, had the Last Trump suddenly sounded.

The last he had seen of Winters was as the red-coat pulled him from his hold on the stack of chairs. For some minutes afterwards he had been fully engaged driving off the two soldiers, so he had not actually seen Winters go down. At the time, in the immediate vicinity there had been scores of men splashing about in the sea and endeavouring to clamber onto rafts from which they had been swept when the *Minerva* sucked them under. At a distance of more than a few yards, one bobbing head looked very like another; so it was possible that, unnoticed by Roger or Clarissa while they were striving to keep the stack of chairs from turning over, Winters had succeeded in getting onto one of the rafts, and later been rescued. That, indeed, seemed the only explanation for his reappearance in Calcutta.

The implications of his survival made Roger go white to the lips. Far from familiarity having bred contempt, he was now as desperately in love with Clarissa as she was with him. But she was Mrs. Winters. Without a doubt, her husband would reclaim her. What would he say, though, when he learned that she had arrived in Calcutta as Mrs. Brook? There could be no concealing that. Yet, worse, for her to have taken Roger's name as a protection from being forced to become a concubine in an Arab's harem was justifiable; for her to have shared a cabin with her 'uncle' in a ship might, at a pinch, be excused on the grounds that it was the only accommodation available; but the whole hotel staff knew that they had spent the previous night in a double bed together, and to explain that away was beyond even Roger's ingenuity.

On one point he was determined. Nothing would now induce him to give up Clarissa. In any case, a frightful scandal was inevitable and Winters would, no doubt, sue him for enticement. But that must be faced, and they would leave Calcutta as soon as possible. If Winters started legal proceedings, though, would they be allowed to?

His mind teeming with a dozen unpleasant possibilities, Roger dismissed the mercer and the tailor till the afternoon, and told the servant to show Mr. Winters in.

Two minutes later a stocky young man of about twenty-three entered the sitting-room. Roger gave him one glance, gasped and, instead of returning his bow, suddenly began to laugh. Those rather close-set eyes under sandy eyebrows were a family resemblance too clear to be mistaken; this could only be Sidney Winters's son by his first marriage. That it might be had never occurred to Roger because, as far as he knew, Winters's son had never even heard of him, and how he had done so was still a mystery.

Drawing himself up, the young man said stiffly; 'I am at a loss, Sir, to understand your mirth.'

'Forgive me!' Roger spluttered. 'I was laughing at a joke against myself.' That, in a sense was true; as he had rarely been taken in by such groundless fears. With unutterable relief he swiftly proceeded to do the courtesies for his visitor, bowing him to a chair and offering him a glass of claret from a bottle that stood open on the table.

Winters shook his head. 'I thank you, no. I come, Sir, as you will have guessed, to speak of my father. I am informed that you were seen with him when the *Minerva* went down. Your arrival in Calcutta gave me the hope—although I admit a slender hope—that he too may have been saved and that you can give me news of him.'

'Alas, I cannot,' Roger replied gravely. 'We went under together holding to a float of chairs; but he lost his hold while I was engaged in helping another person. As you may be aware, your father could not swim and, when I turned to see what had become of him, he had disappeared. I fear there can be no doubt at all that he was drowned.'

'You tell me only what I expected,' Winters nodded. 'In fact, for some weeks past I have resigned myself to the loss of my excellent parent.'

'From what you say, it seemed that other survivors from the *Minerva* arrived here some time ago, and informed you of her sinking.'

'Yes, six weeks back.'

Roger was surprised at that. He had assumed, with some reason, that anyone else saved from the wreck would also have been washed up on the east coast of Africa and that, not having heard of any such parties while in Zanzibar, either there were none or that later they had died in the jungle or fallen victims to the savages. Having expressed his pleasure at this news, he added, 'I wonder that no one in Madras was informed of this when I described to the Governor and others there the sad fate which had befallen the *Minerva*.'

With a shrug, Winters said, 'A month or more sometimes goes by without an exchange of news between the two Presidencies. If a favourable wind was carrying the convoy up the Carnatic coast, it would not have put in to Madras; so there is nothing strange about people there not having heard details of the tragedy.'

'It was then the other ships of the convoy that picked up the survivors?'

'Yes. Some of them heard the *Minerva*'s distress signals and, as soon as the tempest abated, turned back to search for her. They picked up nearly a hundred people, mostly soldiers; but among those saved was the fourth mate, Mr. Bellamy. It was he who told me of my father's marriage in Cape Town to your Miss Marsham.'

Roger noted the inelegant way in which the young merchant referred to Clarissa as *your* Miss Marsham. That it had a vague flavour of accusation could for the moment be overlooked; but the thing that could not was that it spelled the death-knell of Clarissa's reputation. His sudden elation at finding it was only Sidney Winters's son with whom he had to deal collapsed like a pricked bubble.

With so many people who knew the facts now in Calcutta he could not deny that she had married Winters or that here and now she was living as his mistress. And although social conventions in Calcutta might be lax, those people saved from the *Minerva* had known Clarissa as his niece. That meant that, instead of the pleasant time to which they had been looking forward, they would certainly be ostracized and, perhaps, hounded out of the city. They might well be asked to leave the hotel, yet have difficulty in finding a Captain who would provide them with accommodation in a ship to take them elsewhere.

As these intensely worrying thoughts rushed through Roger's mind, Winters was going on in a suavely offensive tone that showed he had sized up the situation: 'I gather, Sir, that you arrived in Calcutta yesterday with a strikingly beautiful young woman, who is occupying this apartment with you as your wife. Her description fits that given to me of the young lady who in Cape Town became Mrs. Winters; and at that time, I understand, you were unmarried. You will appreciate that I have a right to enquire what has become of my step-mother. Was she also drowned or—or can it be that the two are one and the same?'

'They are the same, Sir,' Roger replied and, having hesitated only for a second, he added, 'After your father's death the one-time Miss Marsham did me the honour to become my wife.'

Winters raised his sandy eyebrows in feigned surprise. 'Indeed. I am glad to hear it, Sir. It may make the object of my visit easier for us to agree upon. Since my father did not arrive here in company with you, I had small hope that he had been saved. I came mainly, therefore, to discuss with you the matter of a marriage settlement entered into by him in favour of your niece. Mr. Musgrove, the lawyer who drew it up, was also one of the survivors from the *Minerva*. He told me of its provisions and, I must confess, I was greatly shocked to learn that my poor father, owing to his infatuation, had shown in it such neglect of my interests.'

'Pray proceed, Sir,' said Roger quietly.

'Since the young lady is now married to yourself and so, no doubt, handsomely provided for, I hope I may take it that she will not put forward any claim to this settlement made upon her as Mrs. Winters.'

'You go a little fast, Sir. I cannot speak for her, and we have not even discussed the matter since the settlement was entered into. But the fact that she has since become my wife has no bearing on the matter. She is still entitled . . .'

Roger got no further. Jumping to his feet, Winters pointed an accusing finger and cried, 'Oh, yes it does! It sets the seal on what I suspected the moment Mr. Musgrove told me of this iniquitous settlement. I guessed then that it was my father's fortune that led your hussy to exercise her wiles upon him. Now, 'tis clear, you set her on. Otherwise you would not since have married her. Why should you have if not to make certain of getting your own hands on the money? You feared that if you didn't she might run off with some other rogue. But neither of you shall have a penny of it! I'll show you up in the courts for the pair of villainous adventurers that you are!'

With difficulty Roger kept his temper, but his blue eyes had gone dangerously hard. Pointing at his sword, which hung from a hook on the wall, he said, 'Mr. Winters, for what you have said I could call you out; and, believe me, I am accounted no mean swordsman. But your father was a very decent man and, although you are labouring under a series of misapprehensions, I can appreciate how these matters must appear to you. Fortunately, there have been no witnesses to the unjust aspersions you have cast upon myself and the lady who now bears my name; so I can afford to ignore them. Be pleased, though, to heed this warning. Should you repeat them in public, I will make you pay dearly for it, both in your pocket and your person.'

'You may bluster as you will, Sir,' Winters retorted. 'Your threats shall not stop me exposing the cheat you put upon my father and defending the fortune which is now rightly mine. You thought, did you not, that you and your woman were the only survivors of the *Minerva*; so that you could come here and rob me with impunity? In that you were mistaken, and it will prove your undoing. Mr. Musgrove and the others all knew her as your niece. By marrying her before you had made certain they were dead, you have over-reached yourself. By having had the effrontery to continue your incestuous intercourse here in this hotel, you have played into my hands. Incest is a crime! A crime, Sir, and a most serious one! For having been parties to it, I mean to send you both to rot in prison.'

With those last words young Winters flung out of the room and, as the door slammed behind him, Roger gave a heavy sigh. To act the bully was most repugnant to him, yet he had been forced into doing so with both father and son; and with the latter it had not succeeded.

At that moment Clarissa came running in from the bedroom, exclaiming anxiously, 'Who was that, Roger? I heard raised voices; so I packed off my dressmaking woman. You were quarrelling with someone. Who was it?'

He gave her a rueful smile. 'It was young Winters. When he was first announced I had a most awful fright. I thought it was your late husband, saved from Davy Jones's Locker to confound us. Thank God it was not; but near a hundred others who were with us in the *Minerva* have been saved.'

'That is wonderful news.'

'It is, except as it affects ourselves. This young man has learned from Mr. Musgrove, and others among them, about your ensnaring his papa and the marriage settlement. Finding us ensconced here like a pair of turtle doves, he not unnaturally jumped to the conclusion that from the beginning you had been my moll and that we deliberately plotted to rob his papa.'

'How dare he!' Clarissa's eyes flashed. 'And out of the kindness of my heart, I had meant to let him off with a payment of fifty thousand. Now he shall pay every penny of the hundred thousand.'

Roger stared at her. 'My pet, it amazes me to hear that you meant to claim any part of this money. I told him that we had not discussed it, and I was actually on the point of saying that, although you are legally entitled to it, I felt confident you would take no action in the matter, when the young fool cut me short and began to make his accusations against us.'

'What is the point of having a marriage settlement if one does not benefit from it?' she asked innocently.

He shrugged. 'In normal circumstances a woman has every right to do so. In this case, I exacted the maximum terms I could get for you from Winters for two reasons. First, so that you might use them as a powerful bargaining weapon at any time you wished to leave him. Second, so that should you decide to remain on and run his house until he died, you would be compensated for your lost years with a fine fortune. But neither of these cases now applies. You are already free of him and I consider it would be morally wrong to take from his son a big sum which you have done nothing to deserve.'

'But, Roger, I want this money. The thought that by coming to Calcutta I could obtain it quickly has been my great consolation for leaving the paradise in which we lived while at Zanzibar.'

'My love; as you have always been a poor relation and dependent on others' generosity, I can well understand that this chance to achieve financial security weighs more with you than it would with most women. But I pray you to remember that you need no longer have any fears for your future, because you are now my responsibility. If you wish it, without waiting until we can marry I will willingly settle a good round sum upon you.'

Her mouth twitching in a smile, she asked, 'Pray what is the size of your fortune, Mr. Brook?'

'Between thirty and forty thousand pounds; and I'll settle ten thousand of it on you tomorrow if you wish.'

Jumping onto his lap, she threw her arms round his neck and cried in delight, 'Oh, my own darling one, how I do love you! Yet there are times when you are the most foolish of men. I do not want this money for myself. I know now that as long as you live you will provide for me and, should you die, then I'll die, too, of a broken heart. But here is a chance for me to become a fine *parti*; and being a woman, I'll have no scruples in taking it. Can you not realize the intense joy it will be to me, instead of coming to you empty handed, to bring you a dowry of fifty, nay, a hundred, thousand pounds?'

'My sweet! My sweet!' Clasping her to him so that her cheek was against his, he shut his eyes and gently shook his head. 'You overwhelm me, and I am more than ever shamed that for so long I rejected the wondrous gift of your love. What you decide about the settlement is your affair, and it is not for me to seek to deprive you of the pleasure of giving. Yet I pray you to remember that you did ensnare Winters—not for money, it is true, but for your own ends; so it would be ungenerous to deprive his son of a portion of his fortune sufficiently large to prejudice his future.'

'So be it then,' she laughed. 'We will enquire into his affairs, and find out how much he can afford without crippling his business.'

Roger remained silent for a moment, then he said, 'I only hope we'll be given an opportunity to do so. He has declared war against us, and I'll not disguise from you, my pet, that our situation at the moment is uncommon black.'

'Why so, my love?'

'Our trouble springs from the false relationship I thrust upon you on our first morning at sea in the *Minerva*. At the time it went a long way to establishing the respectability of our association; but now, it has recoiled upon us in a most dangerous manner. Our travelling companions in the *Minerva* will all be prepared to swear that we are uncle and niece; yet here we are living as husband and wife. That our union has not yet actually been blessed makes no difference in such a case. It is the fact that we are cohabiting. All who know us in this city will regard us as guilty of incest. 'Tis a crime for which there are most grievous penalties, and Winters intends to charge us with it.'

Clarissa's face showed her alarm, and she slipped from Roger's knees. 'Surely,' she said after a moment, 'there is some way in which we can prove that we are only cousins by marriage.'

'I know of none,' he replied gloomily, 'save having sworn affidavits regarding ourselves sent out from England. To write home and receive a reply would take nine months at the least, and it is what is to befall us in the meantime that worries me. Were we in Europe we'd be to horse in the next half-hour and be over a frontier before a charge could be preferred against us; but that's not possible here. I'm at my wits' end what to do.'

'Could we not bribe Winters into taking no action by offering to forgo the settlement?'

'Unfortunately that could prove only a temporary expedient. Shutting his mouth would not shut those of others. As two additional survivors from the *Minerva*, the news of our arrival must by now be all over the city, and with it the news that you are now living with me as Mrs. Brook. 'Twill be matter for righteous condemnation of us in every *salon*, and either the Church or the Law will feel called on to see that such sinners are made an example of.'

'What can they do to us? Tell me the worst, Roger. I pray you hide nothing from me.'

'I hardly know, my love. I think it unlikely that a court would condemn us in the face of our oath that the charge is brought under a misapprehension; so it would have to postpone a verdict until evidence of our true relationship could be procured from home. But the court would certainly order that during the interim we must not live together. It might even prohibit us from meeting, under pain of being sent to prison should we be caught doing so.'

'What say you? Oh, Roger, no! For us not to be able to even see one another for the best part of a year would be utterly intolerable.'

CHAPTER FIFTEEN

The Golden Age in Bengal

IT was as Clarissa gave this anguished cry, and tears sprang to her blue eyes, that the Bengali servant again appeared at the door, salaamed and addressed Roger:

'More people to see you, Sahib. The Sir Curtis Beaumont Sahib, and his Lady. They request receiving.'

At the unexpected news that these good friends too had been rescued, Roger and Clarissa's faces lit up with joy; but after a second, Clarissa's fell, and she exclaimed in consternation:

'Oh, Roger! How can we now receive them? They cannot yet know . . . but, oh, I'll sink through the floor from shame.'

To her amazement he was still smiling. Suddenly he leapt to his feet, seized her round the waist, threw her up in the air, caught her in a bearlike hug as she came down and cried, 'Praise be to God! We're saved! Saved, saved, saved, my dearest dear!' Then, turning to the servant, 'Show them in, no one was ever more welcome.'

Before the Beaumonts were half through the doorway, Roger had Sir Curtis by the hand and was wringing it like a pump handle. Lady Beaumont gave Clarissa a somewhat uncertain look; but Clarissa's face showed no trace of embarrassment, only transparent joy, as she ran towards the older woman, and next moment they were kissing one another most affectionately.

Drawing Sir Curtis into the room, Roger exclaimed, 'Sir, your arrival could not be more opportune. No one could be more delighted than Clarissa and myself to learn that you and your lady survived the *Minerva* disaster, but we'll talk of that anon. At the very moment of your being announced we were in the depths of despair about a matter that concerns us most closely. Should your memory not have deteriorated since we last met, you have it in your power to relieve us of all anxiety. Do you recall the conversation you and I had the morning after Clarissa became engaged to Sidney Winters?'

'Why, yes,' the judge smiled. 'You were greatly opposed to the match, and consulted me on the feasability of applying to the Court when we reached Cape Town for an injunction restraining the marriage on the grounds that she was not yet twenty-one.'

'And your reply, Sir, your reply?'

'It was to the effect that you lacked the legal status necessary to make such an application, because you were not her guardian; or, as you had led us to suppose, her uncle, but only a cousin of hers by marriage.'

'That's right!' Roger exclaimed joyfully. 'That's right! Thank God, Sir, that your memory is clear upon the point, for we are like to be charged with having committed incest.'

Lady Beaumont's face showed how shocked she was, and she said with swift disapproval, ''Tis true, then, that you are living together? I could not believe it. Had I done so I would never have come here.'

'Oh, please, please!' Clarissa seized her hands. 'You don't understand. Roger had to pretend I was his wife to save me from an Arab who would have taken me for his harem, and . . .'

'And we were later married by a Protestant Missionary in Goa,' put in Roger swiftly.

'Yes . . . yes!' Clarissa endorsed the lie. Then, her face radiant, she cried, 'And it was the happiest day of my life; because I've been desperately in love with Roger for years.'

'Tut, tut!' murmured Sir Curtis. 'That's a strange statement, young lady, seeing that barely three months back, without the least pressure from anyone, you married Mr. Winters.'

Clarissa blushed scarlet as she recalled her real reason for marrying Winters, but covered her confusion with a bold white lie. 'I became engaged to him, Sir, with the intent of making Roger jealous. I hoped up to the last moment to bring him up to scratch. Then, in despair and finding myself so deeply committed, I felt that I must go through with it.'

'The fault was mine,' Roger declared, putting an arm round her waist. 'I knew she loved me, and I loved her; but most selfishly I had set my mind against marrying again. It is I who am to blame for all our troubles from the very beginning.'

Sir Curtis gave him a quizzical look. 'Are we to take it, then, that Miss Marsham's presence in the *Minerva* was not due to any headstrong determination to see the gorgeous East, but that she smuggled herself aboard in pursuit of you?'

'Yes,' laughed Clarissa. ''Twas a monstrously unmaidenly act. But I confess it; you have hit upon the truth.'

'We owe you both a deep apology,' Roger added, 'for the deception we practised upon you; but at the time it seemed the only way in which I could preserve Clarissa's reputation.'

Lady Beaumont was smiling now, and said, 'For that I would be the last to blame you; and it seems that I am to be called on to save her reputation yet again.'

'Oh, dear Lady Beaumont!' Clarissa cried, throwing her arms round her ex-chaperone. 'You are, indeed, our fairy godmother. It needs only that you and Sir Curtis should clear us of this terrible imputation for us to reach the seventh heaven; for I vow that Roger has already made me the happiest woman in the world.'

'And you, my love,' smiled Roger, 'although I don't deserve it, have made me the happiest man.'

Champagne was sent for and an hour went swiftly while the four of them told of their adventures since they had parted in sight of the *Minerva* going down. They also discussed the matter of young Winters and the marriage settlement. Roger produced the document from his big fish-skin wallet, and Sir Curtis said there could be no question about Clarissa's legal title to the money. He added that Winters's firm was a very rich one, so he would not be jeopardized if called on to pay out a sum running into five figures. On that assurance Clarissa stuck to her intention of making her claim and the judge said that after Christmas he would introduce them to a good lawyer who would handle the matter for her. The following day was Christmas Eve, and on it Lady Beaumont was giving a reception; so it was agreed that no better opportunity could be found for her to present Mr. and Mrs. Roger Brook to Calcutta society.

After the Beaumonts had left, Roger and Clarissa, now almost intoxicated with joy at this most fortunate outcome to their affairs, sent for the clothiers again, who, with the willingness of Orientals to work all night, promised that they should have at least one set of European garments apiece by the following day.

On Christmas Eve, lolling side by side on the cushions of a hired palanquin, which was borne by a team of sweating natives, they had their first proper sight of central Calcutta, and were much surprised to find that its principal streets and open spaces differed little from those of a large English town. For the past half-century the architects had copied faithfully the prevailing fashion in London, and some of the larger private mansions might have been lifted bodily from Grosvenor Square. By contrast with the adjacent streets of native houses made from wood and bamboo, they looked all the stranger, and the more so as their gardens had nothing in common with those at home, their most striking features being tall palms, deodars, baobabs and other tropical trees. But the people in the streets and the new bazaar—which against strenuous opposition by property-owners had been erected in the middle of the town—they found fascinating, for the crowds were larger, and displayed a far greater variety of colourful costume, turbans, hats made from leaves, and strange weapons, than in any other place in India that they had so far visited.

In those days every city displayed evidence of great wealth side by side with the direst poverty, but such contrasts were far more evident in this eastern metropolis than in the capitals of Europe. Most of the well-dressed Europeans and many richly robed Bengalis were escorted in their palanquins by a dozen or more servants dressed in colourful liveries; yet half the native population wore only a single ragged garment, and at the mouth of every alleyway crouched cripples and beggars who appeared to be in the last stage of destitution.

The mixture of smells was indescribable, as the better off of both sexes, white and brown alike, soused themselves with perfumes, many of the women wore garlands of flowers, and from market and warehouses there frequently came a fragrant whiff of aromatic herbs; but these pleasant scents were never strong enough to overcome for more than a moment the all-pervading odour of stale sweat and rotting garbage, which at times was

augmented to a revolting stench coming from some dead pariah dog or
the corners at which men and women were often to be seen relieving themselves in public without shame.

On the waterfront, hundreds of coolies wearing only a loin-cloth were
humping the rich cargoes that scores of lighters and small schooners had
brought up from the ships at anchor in Diamond Harbour at the mouth
of the Hooghly. Bills of Exchange and canvas bags of gold running into
many thousand pounds a day were being chaffered over between merchants,
ships' captains, agents and the Parsee bankers; yet in the ghats that led
down to the river there huddled scores of emaciated figures picking the
lice from one another's hair and bathing their sores in the dirty water.

Every boat that drew alongside holding a passenger was met by a bevy
of young girls, many of whom were obviously not yet in their teens,
offering themselves for prostitution; and, from the upper windows of the
houses in all the streets outside the European quarter, more prosperous
houris with gold buttons in their nostrils, ignoring Clarissa, called down
invitations to Roger to return and visit them.

Yet wealth was far from being confined to the Europeans. In the better
part of the city, there were scores of shops—jewellers, silk-merchants,
saddlers, silversmiths, sword-makers, confectioners and wine merchants—
which rivalled those of London, and the great majority of them were
native owned.

At the Beaumonts' reception that evening, they were presented to Sir
John Shore, the Governor-General. He had succeeded Lord Cornwallis in
'93 and was a very different type from that handsome, much-beloved
soldier. Sir John had spent a lifetime in the Company's service and risen
to its highest post by his industry, honesty and capability as a civil administrator; but he was an ugly ungracious man, incapable of inspiring affection,
and of a deeply religious bent which did nothing to add to his popularity
in a society which, though outwardly elegant, found its principal distrac-
tions in drunkenness and lechery.

Sir Robert Abercrombie, the Commander-in-Chief, Admiral Elphinstone, Commanding the Bengal Squadron and General Brisco, the Commander of the Company's Troops, were also there. The first, who was
purblind and looked like a Skye terrier, but was at that date Britain's most
brilliant soldier, Roger had already met in the West Indies. The second,
who had recently been conducting a drive against French pirates along
the Assam coast, was an old friend of Roger's father. The third he found
a pleasant but unusually stupid man.

Among the legal lights were Sir Robert Chambers, Sir William Dunkin,
a Mr. Macnaghten and a Mr. Hickey. The two first were Sir Curtis's
colleagues on the Supreme Court, the third the High Sheriff and the fourth

a lawyer whom Sir Curtis introduced as the gentleman he had had in mind to act for Clarissa in the matter of the settlement.

The ladies were by no means so numerous, but under Lady Beaumont's wing Clarissa was most kindly received by them, and they were all agog to hear about her narrow escape from becoming a permanent inmate of the harem of the Vali of Zanzibar. Men as well as women were soon clustering round her, and it gave her a secret thrill to be able, for the first time, to reply to the many invitations that were pressed upon her that she 'was mightily obliged but left all such arrangements to her husband'.

Roger noted with interest that many of the men still wore powder and that their clothes were much gayer than had in recent years become the prevailing mode in London. In fact, but for the difference in the language spoken, he felt as though he had gone back a decade in time and was once more attending a *soirée* in Paris in the days before the Revolution. Being an exquisite by nature, nothing could have pleased him better, and he promptly made up his mind to order some more suits for himself of brighter silks, with wide skirts, deep cuffs and plenty of gold galloon.

He was, however, much surprised, when the party had been under way for some time, to see in the distance young Winters scowling at him. Etiquette in England was still most strict upon such matters as precedence on going in to dinner, who should be admitted to social functions at the Assembly Rooms in County Towns, and who should be permitted to sit in the presence of their betters. The higher grades of professional men were becoming more and more admitted to the friendship of the quality, but tradesmen never, with the one exception of wine merchants, who had always been accepted into county society.

But Roger soon learned that in India matters were very different. In the early days of the settlements the number of Europeans had been so small that, for the sake of company, the very few gentry among them had been forced to ignore such arbitrary considerations as birth and breeding.

In consequence, matters had continued that way, and now the only qualifications needed for the entrée to Government House circles were passable manners, coupled with enough money to keep a good establishment and return hospitality.

During the weeks that followed, Roger and Clarissa had ample evidence of what was meant by hospitality in India. Bengal particularly was a land of 'easy come, easy go'. By judicious bribery, skilful speculation, or even astute honest trading, fortunes could be made in a matter of months, and they were generally spent just as quickly.

Everybody who was anybody at all lived in a house with at the least twenty rooms, kept a score of servants, riding horses, a carriage and palanquins. All the wealthier ones kept open house, had guests staying for months at a stretch, and never knew until the meal was served if they would sit down twelve or thirty to dinner.

Only the cooler hours of the morning were devoted to work. At half-past three they sat down to an enormous meal, slept after it, and in the evenings amused themselves either with dancing, gambling, music, amateur theatricals, or bachelor suppers from which they were generally carried away by their servants, dead drunk, in the small hours of the morning. It was an uproarious, hectic life, to which only men with iron constitutions could stand up for more than a few seasons, and it was not to be wondered at that the Calcutta grave-yard contained more stones erected to men who had died in their thirties than to stalwarts who had stuck it out till their fifties.

Christmas in strong sunshine was a new experience for Roger and Clarissa, and they were enabled to enjoy it to the full as, at the Beaumont reception, Sir Curtis and his Lady had, once and for all, scotched the scandalous rumour that they were uncle and niece. They now had not a care in the world except for the swarms of mosquitoes that plagued them nightly and compelled them to sleep under stuffy curtains. To escape this pest, as far as was possible, and the smell of unwashed humanity which pervaded every quarter of the city, they rented a small furnished house on higher ground, some distance from the river, and moved in there early in the New Year of '97.

Mr. William Hickey found it for them and helped install them in it. A few days after Christmas they had had a conference with him about Clarissa's settlement and he proved all in favour of her proceeding with her claim.

He told them that Winters's was one of the richest merchant-houses in Calcutta, and that the late Sidney Winters's estate must be worth near a quarter of a million; so his son, Gideon, would still be a very lucky young man if he came into the greater part of that sum. He then went on to reason that, in the normal course of events, had the elder Winters married again it would have been to a middle-aged woman who, on his death, would have been unlikely to find another husband, so would certainly have claimed her legal due; therefore why should not Clarissa do so? He was also firmly of the opinion that to claim less than the full sum would show a lack of conviction in the justice of the claim and, moreover, by demanding the full hundred thousand they would protect themselves against a disappointing final settlement should the judges decide to cut down the award to Clarissa.

'Let us get the maximum award we can,' said Mr. Hickey. 'Then, afterwards, if Mrs. Brook cares to overlook young Gideon's rash and offensive behaviour towards you both, and forgo a moiety of the money, that will be her affair.'

Clarissa shook her head. 'Please, Mr. Hickey, I'd much prefer to have naught to do with it. I wish you to draw up a deed, upon the signing of which I will have made over to Mr. Brook my entire interest in the settlement; then it will be for him to decide how much we should return of whatever sum you succeed in obtaining for us.'

Roger at once saw the way her mind was working. Her one desire was to make him this gift, and by the deed she would have given him whatever the court awarded her. If he chose to return part or all of it to Winters, or give the money to charity for that matter, she could still feel that she had brought him a handsome dowry.

Hickey, however, demurred on the grounds that life in Bengal was a most uncertain asset. Young people as well as old, he told them, were quite frequently taken off overnight by a bloody flux, or a galloping consumption. Tactfully he intimated that should Roger be stricken down and Clarissa find herself unable to produce her marriage lines, apart from the money he could raise for her on this claim she might find herself destitute.

However, after some discussion, Roger suggested a way out. Mr. Hickey should draw up for Clarissa the deed of gift in accordance with her wishes, and for him a will by which he left half his estate to her and the other half to his daughter, Susan; and that was agreed upon.

They found the lawyer a most genial man, and he soon became a close friend of theirs. He was an Irishman, although born in a street off Pall Mall, and the son of a lawyer of the first standing, who had many rich connections. It was, no doubt, mixing with youngsters much better supplied with money than himself that had got him early into trouble, as he was the type of man who could not resist the lure of good company, yet would rather have died than not pay his way. Over their wine one night he confided to Roger that in his youth he had been 'a rare pickle'.

While still a schoolboy, sleeping with his sister's pretty nursemaid had given him a taste for women, and equally early he had developed a liking for strong liquor. These drains upon a slender purse, freely indulged in during many a hectic night out with dissolute young companions, had got him so deeply into debt that no sooner was he apprenticed to the law than he had given way to the temptation to embezzle his master's funds.

His kindly father had paid up for him again and again, and at last sent him with good introductions to the West Indies. But he had failed to make good there and returned to London, where he had again plunged into every sort of excess. Having made the capital too hot for him, he had decided to try India and, although almost without funds, had carried off a rich man's beautiful mistress, who had later lived with him in Calcutta as Mrs. Hickey. To his life-long distress, this beautiful creature soon met her death from being stricken with a sudden chill; but in other matters her lover had proved more fortunate.

In spite of his heavy drinking, he was shrewd and capable, and his conviviality had proved an asset in the raffish society of Calcutta. Within a few years he had built up a practice that brought him many thousands, and he continued to spend them almost as quickly as he made them; for, although he was now within a year or two of fifty, he was still 'a rare pickle'.

He now had two houses, one in the city and another, which he had had built for himself, farther up the river at the old Dutch settlement of Chinsurah. His cellars were said to contain the finest champagnes, hock and claret in Bengal; he maintained over sixty servants and two pretty concubines. The death of a third, named Jemdanee, in the previous summer was still causing him great sadness. She had been his favourite, and all who had known her spoke of her as quite an exceptional girl, as she spoke English fluently and had been greatly liked by his friends. But her loss did not prevent him continuing to entertain with his accustomed lavishness.

Before moving into their own house, Roger and Clarissa spent a weekend with him at Chinsurah, and they were amazed to find it another 'Grosvenor Square mansion' set down in the middle of the country. But it was equipped with every facility for enjoyment among them a great gilded barge with a crew of uniformed oarsmen and a private band of instrumentalists. It was through Hickey's having sent them out alone in this luxurious water-carriage that Clarissa, in great excitement somewhat tinged with awe, suddenly recognized a stretch of the river and realized that she was now actually living the vision she had seen while under Rinaldo Malderini's hypnotic influence.

Hickey engaged for them a head bearer named Chudda Gya, a trust-worthy man who spoke quite good English, and it was he who hired most of the other servants. What with jemadar, durwan, chubdars, consumahs, hurcarrahs, peons, a kitchen staff, and women to serve Clarissa, they seemed a positive horde, and Roger became considerably alarmed at the thought of what their keep and wages would run him into. But Chudda Gya explained a trifle stiffly that it was not enough for a gentleman to have six men carrying him in his palanquin, he must have at least three more to run ahead shouting aloud his name and quality; and so on, through-out the establishment. The duties of many of them seemed to overlap and often they appeared idle, but the house seemed to run itself with smooth efficiency, the sort of food they ate cost very little and, as Chudda Gya allowed no one except himself to rob his master, Roger found that, after all, his expenses were not unduly excessive.

They soon acquired a small farmyard at a ridiculously low outlay—

hens a penny apiece, sheep for one and eightpence, cows for about six shillings, and ducks, geese, calves and deer in proportion—but the natives who reared the poor creatures fed them so ill that they all had to be fattened up before they were fit to serve at a European table.

As it was still the cool season, they were not greatly troubled by the heat, although for the hottest hours of the day they always undressed and lay down to doze in the gentle twilight provided by roller blinds made from hundreds of thin green bamboos. Every morning early they went for a long ride, and later in the day they often went shooting. The country outside the city abounded in game, and the usual practice was to shoot it from the back of an elephant. Clarissa greatly enjoyed accompanying Roger on these expeditions but, when he now and again joined a party to hunt wild boar on horse-back, he would not let her come with him, as he counted her too precious to expose her to the slightest danger. In the evenings there was always some party at which they were welcome, a subscription dance or a play put on by the amateur dramatic society, and Clarissa was wise enough never to seek to restrain Roger when, at times, he felt like accepting an invitation to one of the bachelor evenings at which everyone drank deep and roared out bawdy songs at the tops of their voices.

In mid-January there came one ripple to mar the surface of this delectable existence, which for them had become an indefinitely prolonged honeymoon. Colonel George Gunston of the Dragoons, having been transferred from Madras, arrived in Calcutta. Gunston, a heavily handsome, florid red-headed man a few years older than Roger, had been at Sherborne with him and, as the bully of the school, had made his life a misery.

Since then they had come into collision on several occasions. Each had wounded the other in a duel with pistols. Roger, who was by far the finer swordsman, had humiliated Gunston in a fencing display held before a number of ladies, for the favour of one of whom they had been rivals. More recently, they had met in Martinique, and after a violent quarrel Roger, who was Governor, had ordered Gunston, who was the Garrison Commander, to leave the island.

They were, therefore, like oil and water. But in the restricted society of Calcutta, they could not avoid meeting frequently as guests under the same roof; so they resigned themselves to exchanging chilly civilities, while Gunston, who had hotly pursued Clarissa during the short time that he had been with her in Martinique, blandly ignored Roger's scowls and renewed his attentions to her as Mrs. Brook.

Although Gunston was a typical product of the fox-hunting, cock-fighting landed-gentry of the day, he was by no means a fool. He had, too, a healthy zest for life which made him good company with either men or women, and this, together with his high-coloured good looks, soon made him much sought after by the belles of Calcutta. In consequence, Clarissa would not have been human had she not shown her appreciation of his obvious preference for herself. At the receptions and dances where they met, Roger would have made himself a laughing-stock if he had played the part of a jealous husband by remaining beside her the whole evening, and he naturally resented his old enemy's seizing on any opportunity to carry her off for a *tête-à-tête*; so after a while he asked her to discourage Gunston's attentions.

But Clarissa only laughed and shrugged her slim shoulders, declaring that she was quite capable of keeping George in his place, that he was an amusing fellow and really not at all a bad sort, and that she thought it foolish of Roger not to patch up their old quarrel.

Being fully convinced that he had no real grounds for jealousy, Roger said no more; but the situation continued to irritate him until, early in February, he was unexpectedly relieved of it by Gunston's sudden disappearance from the scene. In due course he learned that his enemy had been temporarily lent to the Company, and had been sent up-country with a detachment of troops to remonstrate with the young Rajah of Bahna, who had the previous year succeeded his father and was making difficulties about the payment of twelve lakhs of rupees which were due to the Company.

Half-way through February another Colonel appeared in Calcutta and one to flutter the hearts of its belles. This was the Honourable Arthur Wesley, commanding the Thirty-third Foot. He arrived with his regiment having caught it up at Cape Town, but he had sailed from England several months later than his men, and his elder brother, Lord Mornington, being a junior member of the Government, had given him a number of official letters for delivery in Bengal. One of these was for Roger, and the Colonel naturally called to hand it over in person.

Colonel Wesley was a very different type from Gunston. He was tall and spare, thin faced, blue eyed, with a thin mouth that suggested an ironical sense of humour, and an aggressively conky nose. Seeing that the letter bore the cypher of 10 Downing Street, Roger waved the Colonel to a chair and asked leave to read it at once. It was from Mr. Pitt, and ran:

My dear Mr. Brook,

I learn from Lord Edward Fitz-Deverel that your dudgeon carried you off to India, and I trust this will find you in Calcutta. Even your annoyance with me scarcely justifies your having gone so far afield when you know very well that you are better fitted than any other man to render your country and myself certain particular services.

Lord Grenville failed to reach an understanding with Signor R.M., but that was in no way due to your unfortunate rencontre with him, and he has now left this country. His departure relieves those concerned of the necessity of taking steps against you; so I am in hopes that your friends here may have the pleasure of welcoming you home before many months are past.

May I add that, despite our occasional differences of opinion, I have long regarded myself as among them and, trusting the same sentiments may animate yourself, I shall be happy to find you fresh employment whenever you have a mind to it.

There was a postscript to the letter which read:

Henry Dundas is at my elbow as I write. He asks to be remembered cordially to you, and says that, from your past appreciations of affairs in foreign lands, he judges that no one could give him a shrewder report of conditions in India than yourself; so he also awaits your return with some impatience.

From a man so cold and unbending by nature as William Pitt, the missive could be regarded as both warm and as near to an apology as he would ever get. Seeing Roger's smile of gratification, Colonel Wesley said:

'It seems, Sir, that I have brought you good news.'

Roger's smile deepened. 'Indeed you have, Sir. I came to India because, on account of a duel, I was forced to leave England, and this is my permit to return home.'

'Then you are lucky, Sir,' came the prompt reply. 'My period of exile has but just begun, and God alone knows when it will end.'

Having clapped his hands, and sent his consumah for wine, Roger remarked, 'If I am right in supposing you to be a brother of the Earl of Mornington, and you were averse to serving in India, I wonder that his Lordship, now being Junior Lord of the Treasury, was unable to secure for you an appointment more to your liking.'

The Colonel gave a wry smile. 'It would ill-become me to complain of my brother. He has, I am sure, done his best for me, but Dublin Castle remained deaf to his appeals. I should explain, perhaps, that as an Anglo-Irish family it is to the Castle that we look for patronage, and on and off I have been kicking my heels as an A.D.C. there for years; but the Viceroy could never be got up to scratch to do anything substantial for me. He even refused me a seat on the Revenue Board and, meanwhile, as a younger son without fortune, my debts became so plaguey worrying that there was nothing for it but to escape my creditors by seeking service abroad.'

'You even thought of leaving the army, then?'

'Only from desperation and because I saw small prospect of advancement in it. As I am considered the fool of the family, it is probably best that I should continue to make soldiering my career.'

Roger laughed. 'You are mighty frank, Sir. But permit me to say that you do not strike me at all as the type of pin-head that I have met with only too often among army men.'

'Thanks for your good opinion, Mr. Brook; but I must confess that my education leaves much to be desired. I never could abide Latin or Greek, so my brother removed me early from Eton. In fairness to him, I should say that lack of money was the main cause. As you may, perhaps, have heard, my father, the first Earl, was a musician of considerable talent. He was, indeed, Professor of Music at Trinity College, Dublin; but he expended so great a sum on supporting amateur societies that he dissipated his fortune, and we have since been driven even to selling our family seat. As I took so ill to the classics, my brother decided to spend what he could afford on sending one of my younger brothers to Eton in my place.'

'You interest me greatly. What happened to you, then, after you left Eton?'

'To economize, my mother went to live abroad, and I spent a year with her in Brussels. My tutoring there was most sketchy and, as far as learning was concerned, I benefited hardly more from a year at the Academy of M. de Pignerolle in Angers. Though there, at least, I acquired a good seat on a horse and some little polish. At eighteen I was gazetted an Ensign in the Seventy-third. As the regiment was here in India at the time, I was under no necessity to join it. Two exchanges in the following year got me two steps in promotion without my even setting foot on a barrack square. I then became an A.D.C. at the Castle and sat for our family borough in the Irish Parliament. In the summer of '94, as a Lt.-Colonel, I took the Thirty-third to Ostend, where we acted as rearguard in the evacuation of that town. With the disastrous winter campaign in the Low Countries that followed, I'll not trouble you. It was bloody, Sir, positively bloody; and I lost more men from frost-bite than from bullets. Only a remnant of us got back to Ireland in the spring of '95. Since then I have done little but dance futile attendance on the Viceroy and avoid the duns; and there, Mr. Brook, you have my undistinguished story.'

Pouring him another glass of wine, Roger said; 'You will find society here most mixed, but extraordinarily hospitable. Admittedly there is no war being waged at the moment by which you might advance your career; but if you enjoy dancing, music and good company, you might be stationed in far worse places than Calcutta.'

'That's true enough,' agreed the Colonel. 'When I first made up my mind that I must take to serving with my regiment it had just been ordered to the West Indies. Two starts were made. The first met with complete disaster: seven transports wrecked on Chesil Beach and the rest only getting back to English ports in tatters. The second met another gale so severe that the whole convoy was dispersed and thirty ships, mine among them, after weeks of desperate hazard were at length driven back into the Solent. Soon after there was a change of plan and we were ordered to India. But for that, I'd now be in the Caribbean, and like as not dead from Yellow Fever.'

Roger nodded. 'The toll it has taken of our troops out there is utterly appalling. I found two ways, though, of checking the scourge considerably. On the recommendation of a learned friend, I had the men drink a tizane made from chinquona bark each morning, and as frequently as possible sent batches of them to cruise off shore for a few days in local ships; so that they might get some good sea air into their lungs.'

'Mr. Brook, you interest me mightily,' the Colonel exclaimed. 'I have ever maintained that the health of his men should be the first concern of every commander. Good food, and plenty of it, warm clothing, frequent baths and compulsory attention to feet, will do more to win a campaign than knowing the contents of all the text books on tactics and strategy ever written. But I had no idea that you had been a soldier.'

'I have not had that honour, Sir,' Roger replied politely. 'The measures I spoke of were initiated by me when I was for a while Governor of Martinique. You have just spoken, though, of the trade of arms with an enthusiasm which belies the luke-warmness you appeared to show a while ago.'

'I gave you first a wrong impression then. The man is a fool indeed who, having adopted a profession, does not make it the major interest of his life. I pray you, too, do not let me lead you to suppose that I despise books. I have brought out from England well over a hundred and they are mostly about India, its people and its wars. I am, too, learning Persian. Since I must serve here I'll neglect nothing which may make me proficient in doing so; I meant only to imply that, had I had my choice, I would have done my soldiering in Europe, as 'tis there that our struggles with the French must be decided.'

For a while they talked about the last season's campaigns on the Rhine and in Italy. When it emerged that Roger knew General Buonaparte, Colonel Wesley begged to be given the fullest possible account of this new star which had so suddenly arisen on the military horizon.

Roger sent for another bottle of claret and in the cool shade of the veranda they talked on for a further hour. He found that the Colonel knew far more than he did about the involved operations which had given the Army of Italy victory after victory, as he had studied every detail obtainable about them, but he could not hear enough concerning the French Army, its generals, officers, men, commissariat and development since the Revolution. Having been well acquainted with Dumouriez, Carnot, Dubois-Crancé, Barras, Pichegreu, and many other men who had played a part in making France's new army, Roger was able to supply him with a mass of information.

As the Colonel at length rose to go, they were speaking again of General Buonaparte, and Roger said with a laugh, 'He once offered me a Colonelcy on his staff. Should I return to my old work, maybe the day will come when I'll ask it of him.'

'You lucky fellow,' Colonel Wesley smiled. 'Could I but change my identity for a while, it's the sort of chance I'd give my right hand for. This sallow-faced little Corsican has, I am certain, a real sureness of touch where the handling of an army is concerned. To think, too, that he was born in the same year as you and I, yet here are we still almost unknown to the world, and I am by far the worse off of us two, since I'm condemned to garrison duty here, perhaps for years to come; whereas he has already made himself France's most spectacular and successful General.'

Arthur Wesley need not have worried. During the course of that year Lord Mornington was to replace Sir John Shore as Governor-General. By his desire, Arthur and the rest of the family were to change their name to the more aristocratic-sounding form of Wellesley; and Arthur was to play a leading part in the final defeat of Tipoo Sahib. He was to leave India as Major-General Sir Arthur, C.B. Ten years later, as Commander-in-Chief in Portugal, he was raised to the peerage, and, although his Latin remained poor to the end of his life, he was in due course to surpass by far his clever elder brother; for he became His Grace the Duke of Wellington, Knight of the Garter, and Prime Minister of Great Britain.

During the next few weeks, Roger and Arthur Wesley saw a lot of one another and became firm friends. At Hickey's invitation, the Colonel took the chair at the St. Patrick's Day dinner, which proved a most hilarious occasion, and the party did not break up till past three in the morning.

In March, two distinguished Generals arrived from England: Sir Alured Clarke, who was to take over as Commander-in-Chief, and Major-General John St. Ledger who, from having for a long period been a boon companion of the Prince of Wales, had so depleted his fortune that, like Colonel Wesley, he had come to India to escape the unwelcome attention of his creditors.

For these two gentlemen a whole succession of bachelor evenings were given by the leading residents of Calcutta and, in consequence, Roger found himself staggering to bed at dawn several times a week. In such a society there was nothing reprehensible about that, as it was common practice; but Clarissa now and then reproached him mildly and he did begin to feel somewhat guilty about his neglect of her.

After the arrival of Mr. Pitt's letter, they had talked of taking a passage home before the monsoon set in, and it was fully understood between them that as soon as they reached England they would give out that they had been married by a Christian missionary in Zanzibar, then have the actual ceremony performed in some quiet village where they were known to no one.

But Roger had taken no steps about securing a passage, because they were both to be called as witnesses when the case of Clarissa's marriage settlement came before the Court. After Lady Beaumont's Christmas Eve reception, young Winters had wisely refrained from making any slanderous statements regarding their relationship, but he had instructed his lawyers to contest the validity of the settlement. Hickey was confident that the Court would give a verdict in Clarissa's favour, but the law could not be hurried, and no definite date could yet be given on which the case would be heard.

Meanwhile, the morning hours now frequently found Roger in a heavy sleep, which deprived Clarissa of their ride together. With the household Chudda Gya would, in accordance with Indian custom, allow her nothing whatever to do. She had only to express a wish for it to be carried out, but even her one attempt to feed the chickens was swiftly and reproachfully prevented. The bachelor parties Roger attended entailed her spending more and more evenings at home alone, and she found a pet monkey and a parrot she had acquired poor substitutes for his company.

They still made love with fervour and lavished endearments on one another, but she could not help showing some resentment that he so often now seemed to prefer his friends' society to hers; and, while this was far from being the fact, he found great difficulty in persuading her of it, because he had got himself caught up in a round of engagements which he could not break without giving offence.

This was the case with a bachelor weekend that William Hickey had planned to have up at Chinsurah. He had General St. Ledger, Colonel Wesley, Sir Alexander Seton, Captain de Lancy and several others coming, had arranged some horse-racing and secured a turtle with a special chef to cook it for the main course of their Saturday dinner, and he positively refused to let Roger back out.

It proved one of the best parties of its kind that Roger had ever attended. For three nights in succession they drank, laughed, sang and played the fool from dusk to dawn, pulling themselves round at about eleven each morning by the time-honoured remedy of 'a hair of the dog that had bitten them'—sufficiently at least to engage in erratic games of snooker, career wildly about on their horses, and disport themselves on the river.

In the cool of Monday evening, decidedly part-worn and very bleary-eyed, Roger returned home. He was still so bemused by the enormous quantities of champagne, claret, hock and Madeira he had consumed that, on riding up the drive to his house, he failed to notice that on seeing him the usual cluster of squatting servants swiftly made themselves scarce. It was not until no one appeared to take his horse that he realized something must be wrong.

Stamping into the house, he shouted for Chudda Gya, for his jemadar, and finally for Clarissa. There was no reply. Alarmed now, he ran upstairs and into Clarissa's apartments. He was in time to see one of her native women run from the room out onto the covered balcony, scramble over its rail and shin down one of its supporting posts to the ground, but she ignored his calls to stop as she scurried head down to the servants' quarters. Taking the stairs three at a time, he plunged back down into the hall, seized a drum stick and beat upon the big gong until the house was quivering with the sound.

After a few minutes Chudda Gya appeared from the back of the house. Putting the tips of his fingers to his forehead, he bent almost double in a deep salaam; then he went down on his knees with the resigned look of a man who expects to be beheaded.

'What is the meaning of this?' Roger roared. 'Where has everybody got to? What has happened? Where is the Memsahib?'

Displaying the calm of an Oriental reared to accept the gifts the gods may send one day and death the next, without revealing his feelings, Chudda Gya replied:

'She has left you, Sahib. On Friday evening a Sahib came here. An hour later the Memsahib ordered her bags to be packed and at dusk she went away with him.'

CHAPTER SIXTEEN

The Mysterious Elopement

FOR a moment Roger was too stunned to answer. It was true that during the past few weeks Clarissa had become distinctly petulant about his neglect of her, and the more or less drunken state in which he rolled home from bachelor parties. But for gentlemen to return from such sprees far gone in liquor was the rule rather than the exception in London as well as in Calcutta. The Prince of Wales and his brothers were frequently carried drunk to bed, and in every city it was no uncommon sight at night to see a man lying dead drunk in a gutter. Women of all classes accepted such excesses as a normal feature of male conduct; so why Clarissa should resent it more than other ladies Roger could not think.

His neglect of her, too, had not been of an extent to justify serious complaint, as there were few husbands in Calcutta society who did not leave their wives one or two nights a week to go out to gamble, drink or be unfaithful—and at least he had not been guilty of the last. Admittedly, since the arrival of Colonel Wesley and General St. Ledger, there had been a special spate of bachelor evenings, but never before had Roger left Clarissa for a whole weekend, and before setting out for Chinsurah he had promised her he would accept no more such invitations.

Yet on the very evening of the day he had gone up-river, she had eloped. That surely meant that she must for some time have been having a secret love-affair with someone, and had already made her plans to desert him. He could not believe it; yet the fact stared him in the face. The thing that made it so inexplicable was that they had had no open quarrel. Far from it. Even her complaints had been made more as gentle reproaches than in anger. Between his nights out, the delight they derived from one another's companionship had not lessened. On the Thursday night they had made love with mutual zest, and on the Friday morning she had seen him off with a smiling injunction to give her love to dear Mr. Hickey and to enjoy himself.

Roger's wide experience of women had made him cynical about them. He knew that even the most stupid were capable of laying plans to ensnare a man better than most generals could plan a battle, and that their natural ability for acting was a thing to marvel at. Memories flashed into his mind of lovely, seemingly innocent faces listening, apparently with eager interest, to a husband's wearisome discourse, while their owners were, in fact, counting the minutes until they could give themselves to a lover—and most people present, except the husbands, had known it. There were times when, being the lover, he had watched such little comedies with special amusement. Now, it seemed for some weeks past, he must have been the victim of just such a pretty deception, and the odds were that Calcutta society had been laughing at him behind his back.

The shock had cleared the last fumes of wine from his brain. Just as when surprised by some sudden danger, it had become cold, swift, calculating. He wasted no time in mawkish self-pity, or senselessly berating Chudda Gya; instead he questioned the still-kneeling servant quickly and to the point. But Chudda Gya's replies threw little fresh light on the situation.

He did not know the Sahib with whom the Memsahib had gone away; had never seen him before. The stranger sahib had arrived in a handsome palanquin; he was richly dressed but not young, of medium height, with broad shoulders and a commanding manner. He had given no name but said only that he was a friend of the Memsahib and she would be pleased to see him. That was soon after the siesta hour. He had been asked to wait, and the Memsahib had come downstairs to him. She had taken him through to the veranda-lounge and sent for drinks. About an hour later she had gone upstairs and ordered her woman to pack for her. Meanwhile, her visitor had sent one of his people down the road out of sight, but the man had not gone far as he shortly returned with others leading pack-horses. Onto these the Memsahib's baggage had been loaded. Then, without a word to Chudda Gya or any of the other servants, who had watched these proceedings with considerable surprise. she had allowed herself to be helped into the palanquin and carried away.

Roger had Chudda Gya bring all the other servants and questioned them in turn, but got little further. It emerged that the visitor spoke Urdu fluently, had been wearing a number of valuable jewels, and that his servants had given the impression that they went in fear of him. Clarissa had appeared calm and collected. She had not been seen or heard to laugh with her visitor; but, on the other hand, she had not cried, or shown the least sign of distress when leaving. Strangest of all, as it seemed to Roger, she had left no farewell note for him or even a message with one of her women.

It occurred to him that they might have been bribed to give him the minimum of information, and so make it more difficult for him to get on her track. Promptly, he offered any or all of them a year's wages if they would help him to solve the mystery of her disappearance; but they only shook their heads and protested that they knew nothing more. Chudda Gya even assured him that, as he had proved a kind master and the Memsahib a kind mistress, they would have risked their lives in her defence, had it appeared to them that she was being taken away against her will; but her departure had been as unforced and deliberate as if she had been setting out with him, her lord, to spend a weekend with friends in the country.

Clearly, no more could be learnt from them, so Roger strode out of the house, remounted his horse and set off at a canter for the city. With Hickey and the others he had come down river that afternoon by barge as far as Barangar on the outskirts of Calcutta, and only then collected the mount that he had left stabled there over the weekend. So the horse was fairly fresh, and carried him to Hickey's town residence within a quarter of an hour. The lawyer was engaged with his chief clerk, running through the major cases being handled by the firm during the current week, but at Roger's urgent request he postponed further business and had him shown in.

As soon as they were alone, Roger asked, 'Will, am I right in counting you a friend who would not lie to me?'

'Why, yes, my dear Roger,' replied the astonished lawyer. 'But, Heavens alive, man, what's come over you? You're as white as if you'd seen a ghost.'

'Maybe! No matter! You know more of what goes on in Calcutta than any man. No beating about the bush now! I want the name of the man who has been pursuing Clarissa these past three weeks or more.'

Hickey would have smiled, had not Roger's face been so black and threatening. As it was, he shrugged and replied quietly, 'My dear fellow, would you have me name half the bucks of the town. Mrs. Brook is the loveliest woman in it, and 'twould be against nature did not every gallant who sets eyes on her try his luck to intrigue her while you are engaged with others in more serious conversation.'

'To the devil with that!' exclaimed Roger. 'I mean some man of parts and wealth who has been making the running with her in such a way that could not have escaped your notice.'

'No, no.' Hickey shook his head. 'Many have tried and their endeavours have been evident enough; but all have been shortly chilled into desisting. Your sweet Clarissa does not seek to disguise the fact that your smile has the power to make her warmly human; but for all other men she is an icicle.'

'You're wrong in that!' Roger burst out. 'Utterly wrong! On my return home I found her gone. And gone bag and baggage with some other man who came to fetch her on Friday evening.'

Hickey came to his feet, staring at Roger in astonishment. 'You say she's left you? Damne I'd never have believed it!'

'It's true enough. She eloped with some wealthy nabob within a few hours of my setting out for Chinsurah; and she'd never have done that unless they had had some previous understanding. Surely you must at least have heard by rumour the name of some man with whom she has been carrying on an intrigue?'

'I have not. That I swear to you. But why should she do this? Had you quarrelled?'

'No; at least, no more than that she had complained somewhat of late that I've spent so many evenings away from home. Maybe I am to blame for that; though not overmuch, unless you grant a woman the right to become plaguey dictatorial.'

'Did she not leave a letter giving her reasons for leaving you?'

'Nay, not a thing.'

'Then all is not lost. It may be that she is only giving you a fright to punish you for your neglect of her. When you get home again you may find her there, and learn that she spent the weekend quite innocently with friends.'

'I would I could think it; but I can't. In such a case she would never have removed all her belongings from the house—even to her pets. No, no; some soft-tongued schemer has taken advantage of her temporary disgruntlement and persuaded her to leave me for him. And once her mind's made up about a thing, nothing will turn her from it. But I'll be even with him. By the time I've done with him his body will be as full of holes as a garden sieve.'

'Of course. Quite right,' declared the tactful Hickey, seeking to pacify his scowling visitor. 'But first we must find him. Sit down, my dear friend, and tell me all you can about this unfortunate affair.'

With an effort Roger controlled the anger that was shaking him, sat down and gave a detailed account of all that had happened when he arrived home. As he finished Hickey said:

"Twould add to your distress to return there tonight; so you had best sleep here. After our weekend I had planned a quiet evening; but if you'd prefer it, and it would take your mind off this trouble, I'll get a few cronies in to sup with us.'

Roger shook his head. 'I'm in no mood for company; but I'll gladly accept your offer of a bed, and I'd like to go to it early. There will be much to do tomorrow, and after a long sleep—if sleep will come to me—I'll be a better man to do it.'

'That is sound sense,' Hickey agreed. 'Make yourself comfortable in the library while I see some of my people. They shall start enquiries at once and I'll be much surprised if by morning they cannot tell us the name of the man who has enticed Clarissa from you and where he has taken her.'

In that Hickey proved over-optimistic. That night, after several wretched hours of soul-searching and self-reproach, Roger had fallen into a heavy sleep. From it he woke refreshed, and came downstairs filled with impatience to set off in pursuit of Clarissa and her seducer; but to his chagrin he learned that Hickey had no definite news to give him.

Over breakfast the lawyer made his report. His agents confirmed that Clarissa's companion was a man of wealth and evidently of some importance, as an escort of half a dozen mounted men, a second palanquin and two extra teams of bearers had been waiting not far from the house to join his palanquin and pack-horses. He was a bulky man wearing a grey wig and, instead of riding alongside her, as a younger man would have done, had had himself carried with her in the palanquin. Only Roger's servants had seen him and, from their somewhat conflicting descriptions, Hickey could not identify anyone he knew; moreover, the trappings of the palanquin were unlike those of any belonging to a resident of Calcutta. This, and his having been accompanied by armed retainers, suggested that he had come from up-country; a theory that was strengthened from the party's having crossed the Hooghly by the ferry to Ghoosery, which they would not normally have done unless they were heading away from the city. Yet this slender clue served only to deepen the mystery for, if Clarissa had had any wealthy acquaintances living up-country, Roger felt sure he would have known of them, and he was positive that she had none.

They were still puzzling over the problem when word was brought in that another of Hickey's agents was asking to see him. He went out to the man, then rejoined Roger a few minutes later with a few items of more definite information. The agent had traced the palanquin to the village of Andul, about seven miles west of Calcutta. It had passed through the village at about half-past seven on the Friday evening, and the horse of one of the escort had cast a shoe; so he had remained behind there while it was being re-shod. The village smith had taken no particular interest in the man, but he stated that the escort had been composed of Bahnas, and that, on leaving, the warrior had galloped off after the palanquin along the road that led to his own country.

'Bahna,' Roger frowned. 'The name is vaguely familiar to me, but no more. Where is it?'

'It is a small state sandwiched between the two great ones of Bihar and Orissa, and some hundred and sixty miles from here.'

'Is it controlled by the Company?'

'Yes and no,' Hickey hesitated. 'That is to say, the Company has a treaty with its Rajah by which he gave them certain trading and revenue rights in return for an alliance and our protection against the aggressive Maratha Princes. But that was in Mr. Hastings's time; today, I would not count the treaty worth the paper it is written on.'

'Why so? Do you imply that, the present Governor's policy being peace at any price, he would not honour it?'

'Precisely. Look what happened in the case of the Deccan. We had a similar treaty with the Rajah of Travancore. When he was attacked by Tipoo Sahib, Lord Cornwallis, who was Governor-General at that time, went to his assistance. Tipoo was defeated. My Lord Cornwallis took his two sons as hostages, then pacified the whole of south and central India by guaranteeing the Nizam of Hyderabad also against attack. Two years ago Tipoo's sons were returned to him. By way of thanks, he promptly threatened to invade the Deccan. The Nizam at once appealed to Sir John Shore for assistance. Our lily-livered Governor refused it and left him to his fate. Tipoo then sent his hordes against the Nizam, defeated him and annexed a great part of his territories. Thereafter, the Nizam put the training of his own army into the hands of Frenchmen, and in every state in India, the British name became mud. Since Sir John would not lift a finger to honour our bond with the Prince who rules over more subjects than any other in India, you may be sure that he would not involve himself in a war on behalf of a little state like Bahna.'

'You mean, then, that the Company no longer has any influence with its Rajah?'

'I do; even though it be on the very border of Bengal. I tell you, Roger, should the Company maintain this Bible-punching fellow Shore in office for another five years, we are like to lose all India. Only a strong policy can keep these turbulent native Princes down. Even this youngster who is now Rajah of Bahna regards us with contempt. The old Rajah, his father, died something over a year ago. There was owing to the Company twelve lakhs of rupees on account of revenue collection and administrative services. The young Prince refused to pay and sent the Company's officials packing. Instead of taking instant action, Sir John havered for months, and it was no more than six weeks ago that he brought himself to send a regiment of sepoys up to Bahna; but, even then, their commander had orders only to remonstrate, so nothing has come of it.'

'By God, I have it!' Roger sprang to his feet. 'I remember now the connection in which I heard of Bahna. The commander of the regiment was a man named Gunston—Colonel George Gunston. He and I have been enemies all our lives. He would go to any length to spite me; and he knew Clarissa in Martinique. He made a set at her there and as I was married at the time I was in no situation to spike his guns. She told me that she rated him crude in his amorous advances and liked him only for his high spirits. But who can say if she was speaking the truth? He is just the type of virile fresh-faced bounder that appeals to many women. And you know how they'll lie about one man to please another. Perhaps matters may have gone further between them than I supposed in the short time before I had sound official reasons for ordering him out of the island. Perhaps the truth is that she regretted seeing him go. She was young and impressionable then, and must have come to think of the love she had for me as hopeless. Perforce we resumed our acquaintance with him when he arrived recently in Calcutta, and it may be that before going up-country he saw her a number of times unknown to me. Perhaps they have been carrying on a secret correspondence. She could have let him know in advance that I meant to spend the weekend with you at Chinsurah. He is a heavy thickset man and, no doubt, wore a grey wig over his red hair so that I should not recognize him from the servants' description. It must have been him; it must! Clarissa would never have gone off with some man she hardly knew.'

As Roger ceased his furious tirade, Hickey nodded. 'I think you have hit upon it. I'll vow that had she been having an affaire with anyone in Calcutta it would have come to my ears. But the reappearance on the scene of a former lover, and one who has not been in the city for the past month or more, provides a logical explanation to our riddle. The fact that Colonel Gunston has been stationed up in Bahna, and that Bahna warriors were used as an escort in carrying her away, seems to clinch the matter.'

Roger put his face in his hands and groaned. 'I would have wagered my whole fortune against Clarissa's deceiving me. That she should have done so with an oaf like Gunston fills my cup to overflowing.'

Suddenly he looked up, and went on, with a menacing scowl. 'But he shall not enjoy his triumph for long. I'll see to that. Did he love her there might be some justification for his act. But I'll vow that's not the case. I know the man. He'll treat her no better than a light-o'-love, and has pursued this scheme mainly to have the laugh of me. He'll laugh no more, though, when I confront him. By wrecking Clarissa's happiness and mine, he has signed his own death warrant.'

'You imply that you intend to go in pursuit of them,' Hickey said. 'If so you'll need an escort. To my regret my age, and the accursed attacks which sometimes suddenly prostrate me as a result of the stone, debar me from riding with you; but I'll have one of my people enrol a troop of good fighting men and a guide who is conversant with the road to Bahna.'

'Thanks, Will, for your offer,' Roger smiled bleakly. 'Of course, I mean to hunt them down. But it is now Tuesday morning, and they left on Friday night. From their having a palanquin apiece and relief teams of bearers, it's clear that they mean to travel fast; it is as good as certain they will be back in Bahna before I can catch up with them. Nothing would have pleased me better than the chance to attack them on the road; but it would be suicide for me to attempt to pluck Clarissa from Gunston with only a dozen or so men against his regiment. I must rely on calling him personally to account; and at least he is no coward. Besides, did he refuse my challenge, he would be shamed before Clarissa. He must fight or lose her. So all I'll need is a guide and a couple of good men with led horses.'

As soon as they had finished breakfast, Hickey went off to make the arrangements, and knowing Roger's impatience to set out he made certain that his orders should be executed without the lethargic delays so usual in the East. By ten o'clock a reliable guide named Tej Mewár was at the door with two well-armed companions, and led horses on which were packed a tent, stores, and other equipment which might be needed on the journey. Roger, meanwhile, had ridden out to his house to change into travelling clothes and collect a small portmanteau with his belongings. At a quarter-past, Hickey wished him good luck, and he rode away wretchedly miserable but fully confident in his ability to bring Gunston to book before the week was out.

The little cavalcade first crossed the river to Howrah, then took the road south-west to Ulubaria, as that was the direct route to Bahna; but Roger did not halt to make enquiries there, as the party he was pursuing had passed through Andul, so would not have struck the main road to Bahna until considerably farther west.

Ten miles farther on, at the town of Bagnan, he did get Tej Mewár to enquire, while his party rested their horses for an hour and had a meal, but none of the inn people had seen the palanquins. As they would have passed through after dark, that was not surprising, and the same applied at Panskura which they reached late in the evening. By then they had covered forty miles; so although he would have liked to push on, he knew that he would regret it later if he did not give the horses a good night's rest. The town caravanserai, would, he felt sure, be riddled by bugs; so he put up his men and stabled the horses there, but had the tent erected for himself in the garden, and spent another miserable night.

Next morning they were off soon after dawn and reached Debra by eight o'clock. There again, no one could be found who had seen the palanquins, and Roger began to fear that he was on the wrong track; for it was quite possible that, as Gunston's regiment was not on active service, he had not returned to Bahna, but had taken Clarissa to some other place up-country in a totally different direction. But by half-past ten they reached the considerable town of Midnapore and, to his great relief, learned at the principal inn that Gunston's party had had a meal there on Sunday evening.

Knowing the pace at which a double team of bearers, each eight strong, could travel with a palanquin, and the staying powers of such specially trained natives, Roger was not surprised that they had got so far in some forty-eight hours; and it confirmed his belief that Gunston would reach Bahna at least a day ahead of him, as both parties would have to stop now and then for a few hours' sleep. Nevertheless, to reduce the time of agonized waiting until he could confront Gunston, he pressed on hard all day, halting only at Jhargram and Chakulia to rest the horses and snatch meals.

At both places they picked up news of Gunston, and again at Raghunath-pur, where his party had arrived late on Monday night. Roger reached the latter township on Wednesday evening, but after their arduous day both his men and horses were done up; so, as he had to halt there for the night, when he set off again at dawn on Thursday, Gunston was still two days ahead of him.

From Raghunathpur they took a road that led south and in a few miles came to the village of Kokpada, which lay on the east bank of the broad Subarnarekha. Its waters were not yet in flood, so there was no difficulty about their being ferried across it; but on the far side of the river they entered very different country.

Ever since leaving Calcutta they had been riding across the western part of the great plains of Bengal, with its fertile soil and teeming population. The roads had been dusty but only slightly undulating and, for the most part, straight. As long as daylight lasted, they had never been out of sight of a hamlet or group of rickety farm buildings; while the ryots working in the fields, naked but for a loin-cloth and turban, women with water-jars or bundles on their heads, shouting children and strangely humped oxen, which they had passed, could be numbered by the thousands. But at the river the plain ended. Beyond it there were low foothills, then more rugged country with stony crags and precipitous gorges. Only patches here and there on the less steep hill-sides were cultivated, few bullock-wagons were to be met with on the sharply curving roads, and a solitary goatherd was usually the only figure to be seen in this much harsher landscape.

By midday they reached Paruli and by evening Bahalda, having covered little more than half the distance that they had on the previous day. At neither place could they find anyone who had seen Gunston's party go through, which disquieted Roger somewhat; but Tej Mewár assured him that they were taking the quickest road to Bahna and should reach the city by the following night.

On the Friday they came down through the mountains to Boalda, and Roger's fears that Gunston might have taken some other direction were stilled by learning that his party had breakfasted there the day before; so they had doubtless arrived in the city of Bahna the previous evening. Soon after leaving Boalda, Roger and his three companions crossed another river, the Kharkai. By mid-morning they were on its far side up in another range of mountains and making their way through a pass that led into the little state of Bahna. Late in the afternoon, they came to a forked gorge with a small stream running through it, and dismounted to water their horses. It was there that swift and unexpected disaster fell upon them.

From somewhere up in the crags a single long-drawn note sounded on a horn. Instantly it was followed by the thunder of horses' hooves, wild shouting, and confused echoes from the surrounding rocky defiles. Down both forks of the gorge ahead, and from behind as well, groups of white-clad, turbaned horsemen converged upon Roger's little party.

They had no time to mount; hardly time to draw their weapons. Before they could even get back to back, the three troops of native warriors had met and formed a swirling cloud about them so dense that it shut out the sight of the hills and gorges. Close beside Roger one of his men went down with a shriek, pierced through the chest with a lance that, from the force of the thrust, protruded nearly a foot behind his back. Of the others Roger temporarily lost sight while striving to defend himself. He shot at one warrior with a pistol he had snatched from his holster, and had the brief satisfaction of seeing him roll from his saddle. Throwing the empty pistol in the face of another he whipped out his sword. As he lunged upward with it, the weapon was nearly struck from his hand by the fierce sweep of a weighty scimitar. At the same instant, a hand from behind seized him by the hair. With a violent jerk of his head, he freed himself, ducked under his horse's belly and came up the other side. As he did so he nearly tripped over Tej Mewár's body. He caught a glimpse of the guide's head; it was almost unrecognizable, having been cloven in two halves from crown to chin. Again Roger lunged with his sword at the nearest of the yelling mob of dark-faced horsemen, but again his slender blade was beaten down. Next moment he received a blow on the back of his head that sent him reeling. He fell to his knees. Before he could get back on his feet, two natives had flung themselves off their horses and seized him from behind. His wrist was twisted until he was forced to let go his sword and his arms were swiftly bound behind his back.

In another few minutes the din, and the cloud of dust kicked up by the mêlée, had subsided. Still dazed by the blow on the back of the head, Roger looked about him. His other escort had survived the fray, but was held between two of the attackers. A tall man mounted on a fine black charger, and wearing a bright red sash, who seemed to be their leader grunted an order. To Roger's horror one of the men who was holding the prisoner promptly drew a curved dagger and slit the poor fellow's throat from ear to ear.

For an awful moment Roger's anger and disgust were mingled with fear that a similar fate was about to overtake himself. But swiftly his reason told him that he was the prize that the ambush had been set to catch. That explained why care had been taken during the scrimmage not to do him serious injury; these fierce-looking hill men were a band of robbers and meant to hold him to ransom.

Within the next five minutes he had abandoned that idea and come to quite a different conclusion. During that time, with his arms still bound behind him, he had been lifted into his saddle and one of his captors had taken the bridle of his horse; the led horses and the mounts of his dead escort had been rounded up, and the man wearing the red sash had shouted a number of staccato orders. As a result, the thirty-odd horsemen had formed up with military precision, two abreast in a long column, having Roger about half-way down it. The butts of their lances were now stalled so that they stood upright, their bright pennants fluttering in the gentle breeze above the men's heads as they moved off after their leader up the wider of the two gorges. Roger saw now, too, that the flowing white habits of the men, their turbans and accoutrements had a definite similarity, which was as near to uniform as native cavalry ever came. Suddenly it flashed upon him that he had been captured not by brigands but by troops.

For that there could be only one explanation. Gunston must have realized that the golden-haired Clarissa would be easy to trace, and that on Tuesday Roger might set out in pursuit of them. He had known that by driving his bearers hard he could easily get back to Bahna before Roger could catch him; but on arrival he had taken precautions against Roger's coming upon him unexpectedly there, perhaps by night. To make certain of not being surprised at a disadvantage, he had sent out a troop of cavalry to lay an ambush and, if his old enemy did appear, capture him before he reached the city.

At these thoughts Roger positively seethed with rage; not so much on account of the humiliation that had now been put upon himself, although that was infuriating enough, but at the utter unscrupulousness of Gunston's latest move. He had not the faintest justification for using the Company's troops for his private ends, and as a result of his orders three innocent men had been brutally slaughtered. In the circumstances, Roger felt his own situation to be distinctly precarious; but, even so, he could not believe that Gunston would go to the length of having him killed too. He thought it more likely that Gunston meant to hold him prisoner for a time, while pursuing his amour with Clarissa and unknown to her. Grimly Roger decided that somehow he would manage to escape, and when he did it should no longer be a matter of a duel. He would see to it that Gunston was court-martialled, cashiered and hanged for the murder of his escort.

Meanwhile the cavalcade wended its way, mostly at a trot, along the winding road through the mountains. As dusk fell, the way began to lead downwards and, after a sharp turn round a great head of rock, Roger saw in the evening light a valley below from which, a few miles distant, there arose the turrets and domes of a walled city. Another hour and they were riding along the flat with farm buildings at intervals at the sides of the road, and the dark silhouette of the city, not far ahead, standing out starkly against the pinkish-gold of a sunset sky.

At length they entered a belt of shadow thrown by a lofty wall, and pulled up before a great arched gateway in it. A horn was blown, a pair of huge wooden gates were dragged open and the cavalcade rode into the city. The horses' hooves ringing on the cobbles, it clattered through several dimly seen streets, then through another archway into a courtyard. Roger was lifted down from his horse and led by the arms by two of his captors through a low doorway. It gave onto a corridor; some way along it another door was opened and he was thrust through it, the door was slammed and bolted behind him.

Left in the dark, and with his arms still bound, he went forward cautiously, feeling his way a footstep at a time. After he had taken a few steps, his eyes grew accustomed to the darkness, as enough light was percolating in from the cracks round the door for him to see that he was in a small, unfurnished room. But along one wall there was a stone bench, so he sat down upon it.

He had only a vague idea how long he sat there, but it was in fact just on an hour. Then two armed men in costumes made rich with much gold braid came in for him. They pushed him along through several passages and courts then finally through an ornate doorway into a lofty pillared hall hung with many lamps.

At the far end of it a young native was seated on a throne made from a score of elephant tusks that had been carved, gilded and inlaid with semi-precious stones. At his right on a low stool sat an older military-looking man with a grey upturned moustache. Behind them, rigid but watchful, stood a score or more richly dressed courtiers, guards, and servants bearing peacock-feather fans on long handles.

Roger's escort hurried him forward across the highly polished floor; then, when he had come to within two yards of the throne, they suddenly jerked him back, thrust a foot apiece in front of his, and flung him forward. He fell flat on his face, his forehead landing with a bump on the lowest step up to the throne.

Slowly he struggled to his knees, then to his feet. Meanwhile the young Rajah smiled with amusement. Roger put him down as about nineteen. His eyes were black, narrow and cruel; he had a big hooked nose, and a fleshy sensual mouth. Suddenly he spoke, in excellent Persian, but with a slight lisp.

'I take it there has been no mistake. You are Mr. Brook, are you not?'

'I am,' replied Roger tersely. 'And I take it that you are the Rajah of Bahna. May I ask if it was by your Highness's orders that my escort has been killed and myself brought here as a prisoner?'

'You are quite right,' smiled the young man. 'We thought it best to arrange matters in that way.'

'Arrange matters!' Roger burst out. 'You have been guilty of murder and the illegal arrest of a British subject. I'll have you know that no man within the Company's sphere of influence can commit such crimes with impunity. Unless you intend to murder me, too, the Governor shall hear of this and . . .'

'Oh, but we do.' The Rajah cut him short. 'Even if Sir John Shore should learn that your death was no accident, he is far too cowardly a man to attempt to call me to account. But there is little likelihood of his ever hearing anything except that you and your men were set upon by robbers up in the mountains and slain there.'

Faced with this callous sentence of death, Roger felt the sweat break out on his forehead. He had never imagined for a moment that Gunston would go to such lengths to have him murdered. In desperation, he cried out:

'Your Highness cannot mean this! Why should you desire my death? You have no quarrel with me.'

'No, none,' the young man replied still smiling. 'But you must die all the same. I have done what I have done, and shall do that which there is to do, to pleasure one whom I honour and admire. He is, I know, waiting impatiently to see you.'

As he finished speaking, he made a sign to one of the men behind him, who struck three times on a small gong.

For two long minutes nothing happened. While the Rajah and his court remained regarding Roger in calm silence he breathed again. The gong could have been rung only to summon Gunston. Blackguard as he might be, he was a British officer. It was impossible that he really intended to go through with this ghastly business. Roger felt certain now that the whole affair had been staged to scare him and, perhaps, because Gunston expected to enjoy the spectacle of seeing him plead for his life.

The thought filled him with new resolution. He would not plead. Instead he would make Gunston look a fool in front of his friend the Rajah by refusing to do so; Gunston might threaten and bluster, but he would never dare to order the cold-blooded murder of a fellow countryman.

A door at the side of the hall swung open. Roger turned towards it with a smile of contempt. The smile froze on his lips. It was not Gunston who was advancing towards him but Signor Rinaldo Malderini.

CHAPTER SEVENTEEN

In Desperate Straits

AT the sight of the Venetian Roger's heart missed a beat. For a second the blood hammered in his ears and he thought he was about to choke. All his new-found resolution and optimism ebbed from him. Since this was the friend that the Rajah had 'pleasured' by having his men murdered and himself captured, his hope of life was now even less than it had been when he was dragged down by the whirlpool of the sinking *Minerva*. As he looked again at the pasty pudding-like face with the abnormally compelling eyes, he read his death sentence in it.

Like a large grey cat, Malderini padded up to within a few feet of him, smiled and said in French, 'Welcome to Bahna, Mr. Brook. When I set out for India I little thought that we should meet here. But I had not forgotten you, Mr. Brook. Oh, dear me no. I owe you far too much. And did I not promise that sooner or later I would find an opportunity to repay you all I owe with interest? When I learnt by chance in a conversation with Colonel Gunston that . . .'

'Gunston!' The word burst from Roger's lips. For the past four days he had been praying for a speedy chance to plunge his rapier through the gallant Colonel's heart; now he would have opened his arms to him as to a long-lost brother. His eyes lighting up with the sudden new hope that if Gunston was in the city he might play the rôle of a guardian angel, Roger hurried on: 'Gunston! Colonel Gunston. Where is he? I demand to see him!'

'You are no longer in a position to demand anything—not even satisfaction, should I again knock you down,' Malderini replied with a sneer. 'As for Colonel Gunston, when His Highness learned that troops were advancing in this direction from Orissa he sent heralds forbidding them to cross his border; but later he graciously consented to receive their Commander. So Colonel Gunston came here for only three nights as a visitor. The lack of success which he met with in his mission was, I think, more than made up for by the happy time he had with the dancing girls that His Highness provided for his entertainment. He left here with obvious regret and many expressions of friendship, to return, presumably, to the encampment he had established across the mountains in Orissa.'

Having rendered Roger's new hope still-born, the Venetian went on, 'But, as I was about to say, when describing to us the present state of society in Calcutta, among other names the Colonel mentioned yours. That you should chance to be in India at the same time as myself seemed to me an unmistakable indication by the Fates that they had arranged matters to facilitate my paying my debt to you. I at once put in hand the necessary measures and my faith in the Fates was justified. Like a lamb to the slaughter you walked into my little trap. I felt confident you would have wit enough to pick up the clue of my using Bahna warriors as an escort and, once you were directed to the road we had taken, our gaudy palanquins must have proved as good confirmation as paper scattered by the hare in a paper chase that Bahna was our goal. The Fates were kind to me, too, in having made you so obsessed with Miss Marsham's charms as to marry her. That was guarantee enough that, did I bait my trap with her, you would be certain to come after her in hot pursuit.'

'Where is she?' Roger croaked. 'What have you done with her?'

'She is here in the palace; in good health and being well cared for. Tomorrow I propose to provide her with a little sport. She is, as you know, a fine shot with a bow and arrow. I intend to provide her with a special target. We shall make a package of you so that you have no resemblance to a man, and your vital parts will be well protected, as I do not mean you to be killed—as yet. We shall gag you, then tie you firmly in position, with only your behind unprotected, and that we shall cover with a paper target, painted in circles of red, white and blue. Miss Marsham—or rather Mrs. Brook—will I am sure greatly enjoy practising her skill upon you.'

Roger's tongue seemed to be stuck to the roof of his mouth. Malderini's hypnotic eyes held his so that he was forced to listen, while unable even to curse him. The Venetian touched the still-livid scar that ran from his ear down to his chin, and went on:

'There is then this. I think to make you a just return for it I had best rip your face open with a piece of glass; but you may rest assured that I shall exercise great care that I cut no vein which might cause you to bleed to death. I do not mean you to die for a long time yet. But we must also consider the question of interest on the debt. Since you will never again be in a position to enjoy your wife, your manhood will be useless to you. I shall therefore deprive you of it and watch you grow fat, as is the case with eunuchs.'

With a supreme effort Roger had managed to force his eyes away from the Venetian's and down to the floor. Sweating with horror at the thought of these tortures from which there could be no escape, he gasped out:

'Go on! Go on! Then, no doubt, you'll have my nails torn out, my bones broken and my flesh burnt with hot irons till I die a mangled travesty of a man. Helpless as I am, I can rely only on God to punish you in the long hereafter. And in that I'll not be disappointed. But what of her? What of Clarissa? You cannot keep her indefinitely under the vile spell you have cast upon her.'

Malderini shrugged his drooping shoulders. 'I can for long enough to serve my purpose. Because I substituted a trick for a genuine attempt to levitate the Princess Sirīsha, you must not assume that I have had no success in practising the Secret Art. I have long needed a fair woman born under the sign of Leo, and with Jupiter in the ascendant, for a ritual which I mean soon to attempt. She fulfils these conditions, so her body shall serve as an altar on which to make sacrifice to the Indian form of Bahomet, the giver of all power on this earth. After that I'll have no use for her, but there are others here who will have.'

His eyes still downcast, and with his arms bound behind him, but distraught with rage, Roger suddenly ran at his tormentor, swung back his right foot encased in its heavy riding boot, and kicked him in the stomach.

With a scream, Malderini went over backwards. There came a shout from the young Rajah, a sudden rush of trampling feet and the guards seized Roger, dragging him back from the squirming Venetian.

For a minute or more the silence was broken only by Malderini's groans. Then, having been helped to his feet, still sweating and panting for breath, he gasped out at Roger:

'A new debt. . . . A new debt! It shall be paid . . . paid in full. When . . . when I have done with your . . . your wife, we'll give her to Alāuddin . . . His Highness's pet baboon. Alāuddin likes women. It is good sport to see what he does with them. You shall see too. Yes, I'll have your eyes held open so that you'll not miss a thing.'

Driven near mad by the hellish picture Malderini had conjured up, Roger exerted every ounce of his strength in an attempt to break away from his guards and get at him again. It was useless. They had him firmly by the arms and kicked his feet from under him. As he lay between them, half sprawled upon the floor, the Venetian glowered over him and wheezed:

'You hoped to provoke me into making a quick finish of you, did you not? But I have learned to control anger and to prevent myself from giving way to impulses which I should later regret. Tonight you may sleep in peace— if you can. It is said, though, that anticipation is the greater part of pleasure. That it may harrow the mind with the thought of pain to come is equally true. I think that you will get little sleep while through the dark hours you contemplate the promises I have made you.'

From French he broke into fluent Urdu and, after making a jerky bow to the young Rajah, ordered the guards to take Roger away.

Still struggling, he was dragged from the lofty hall, along several corridors and down a dark stairway. At its bottom there was a narrow chamber dimly lit by a smoky oil lamp. Along one side of it were a row of stout wooden doors, and a burly man was sitting there on a stool eating a mess out of a brass bowl. As the man stood up, a bunch of keys jangled at his girdle. Selecting one he unlocked one of the doors, and Roger was pitched through it, down a short flight of steps into a lightless dungeon.

How long he lay where he had fallen, his body a mass of pains and aches from the kicks and cuffs he had received, and his brain half numbed by shock and hopeless misery, he never knew. Scratchings, squeaks and scamperings came to his ears without meaning; it was not until a rat actually ran across his face that he jerked himself up and made a conscious endeavour to think coherently. Wriggling along the floor he reached a wall, turned over, sat up with his back to it, and tried to sort out the nightmare through which he had lived since being brought before the Rajah of Bahna.

Bemused as his mind still was, one clear thought dominated it. He had done Clarissa a terrible injustice. On the flimsy grounds that she had encouraged Gunston's attentions during the latter half of January, he had allowed himself to believe that she had eloped with him. For four days he had been obsessed with that thought, yet now it seemed positively farcical. Worse, it was an insult to her honest and fearless character. The depth and tenacity of the love with which she had pursued him for so long should have been guarantee enough that she would never abandon him lightly, and that even if they had tired of one another to the extent of quarrelling most bitterly, she would have had the courage to tell him her intention before finally committing herself with another lover. Tears of shame welled up into his eyes and he mentally squirmed at the memory of having thought so meanly of her.

About what had actually taken place, he now had no doubts at all. As he had warned Clarissa at Stillwaters, no hypnotist could obtain power over a person unless that person willingly submitted to being hypnotized. But once they had surrendered their will to the hypnotist, he could without their consent hypnotize them again. The tragedy was that his warning had been given too late. In her eagerness to catch a glimpse of the future, Clarissa had asked Malderini to hypnotize her that afternoon, and all she could promise afterwards was to keep away from him, so that he should have no opportunity of throwing her into a trance again.

Evidently, on learning from Gunston that they were in Calcutta, Malderini had set off there and, probably, stayed for some days at a place outside the city while he sent spies into it. All native servants were born gossips, and delighted in talking boastfully about their masters' and mistresses' affairs; so it would have been easy for a spy to learn from one of Roger's household that he intended to spend the weekend up at Chinsurah.

After that all Malderini would have had to do was to come face to face with Clarissa so that he could stare at her for a few moments with those compelling eyes of his. To enforce silence on her temporarily and the suggestion that she must hear what he had to say in private would have been his first move. No doubt to break her will to a degree at which she would consent to have all her things packed and go away, apparently quite willingly, with him had required far greater effort and prolonged concentration, as it was certain that in her subconscious mind she would have fought desperately against such a command; but that explained why they had remained for over an hour together out on the veranda before she had begun to make her preparations for departure.

Roger could only hope now that Malderini had kept her in a state of trance right up to the present; for, if so, it seemed possible that she was still unaware that she had really been abducted, and thought herself only the victim of a horrid dream, so was at least not a prey to an agony of apprehension about her future.

He had got only so far in his unhappy speculations when the big key grated in the lock, the door swung open and the powerful-looking jailer came down the three steps into the dungeon. The light percolating in from outside was just sufficient for Roger to see that he was carrying a calabash in one hand and a bowl in the other. Setting these down on the floor the man produced from his tunic a hammer, then fumbled about until he found the loose end of a chain that had its other end fixed to the wall.

With the deft movements of long practice he put an iron shackle round Roger's left ankle and hammered home some rivets which secured it to the chain. Next he drew a knife, and cut the cords that bound Roger's arms, then, turning away, he left the dungeon, locking the door behind him.

As Roger's arms had been bound for several hours, he at first found it very painful to move them, but after a few minutes he was able to stretch out for the food and water left for him by the jailer. The bowl contained a cold curry which was so fierce that normally he would have refused it, but he had not eaten since midday and felt that he ought to keep up his strength; so he gulped down the mess bit by bit, then drank more than half the water in the calabash in an attempt to allay the burning of his throat.

The meal did him good and after it he began to wonder if there was any conceivable means by which he might escape. Now that his arms were free, next time the jailer came in to bring him a meal he might seize and attempt to overpower him. But the man was bigger than he was, so the chance of succeeding was poor. Perhaps, though, he could even up the odds by first snatching the jailer's knife. One swift ruthless stab, and to silence him after that would be easy. But did he carry his hammer on him? Roger had already examined the chain that held him by the leg and found it impossible to shift with his fingers the bolts fastening the ankle clamp. Without the hammer he would be unable to free himself—unless. Yes, he should be able to work the staple, that secured the chain to the wall, out from between the stones with the point of the jailer's knife. But that might take hours. And what then?

He had been hustled through a maze of courts and corridors, vague memories of which now confused him rather than helped him to form any idea of the geography of the palace. When he reached the top of the stairs, he would not even know which way to turn with the best chance of getting out. He could disguise himself in the jailer's clothes; but he could not conceal his blue eyes and fair-skinned face. They would betray him at one glance from any of the Rajah's people; and it was a certainty that he could not for long seek a way to freedom without coming upon some of them. Then, should he have the luck to reach a gate, during the night it would be locked and, since he was a foreigner, he could not hope to bluff the guards into letting him through. Even if by some miracle he escaped all these hazards and found a wall over which he could climb into the street, he would be little better off. As a single European in a native city his recapture within a few hours was certain.

Roger was an optimist by nature and, however desperate his situation, his resolution had never failed him; but he was forced to admit to himself now that to escape from Bahna, without help from outside, was beyond his capabilities. If he attempted to kill his jailer and failed, he could expect a frightful beating. If he managed to get up into the palace, to the gate, or even out into the city, his eventual recapture, wherever it might take place, would certainly be accompanied by kicks and blows. Apart from a few bruises he was still in good shape, and he decided that it was better that he should remain so rather than expose himself to serious injury in attempting a forlorn hope. As long as he continued sound in wind and limb there was at least a chance that an opportunity would occur for him to spring upon and kill Malderini. If he could do that, whatever the Rajah's people might do to him afterwards, he would have the consolation of knowing that he had saved his sweet Clarissa from being made use of in some abominable Black Magic ceremony.

What sort of ceremony Malderini intended to perform, Roger could only guess at. But the Venetian had spoken of using Clarissa's body as an altar; so it sounded like a form of the Black Mass. Roger recalled a book he had read while in France which described the Marquise de Montespan's efforts to recapture the love of King Louis XIV. Apparently the discarded favourite had secured the infamous Abbé Gibourg to perform a number of Black Masses dedicated to that intent. There had followed a description of the Abbé saying the Mass backwards over the naked body of the beautiful Marquise, then cutting the throat of a kidnapped infant; after which both had drunk of the blood of the sacrifice and finished up blood-spattered and mouthing obscenities in a violent sexual embrace.

From the mental picture of Malderini and Clarissa, under hypnotic domination, engaged in such a scene, Roger's mind revolted. He felt that if he allowed himself to think of it for any length of time he would go mad; so he sought desperately for some other matter upon which he could concentrate his thoughts.

The possibility of their being rescued seemed terribly remote; but at least it was a subject he could speculate upon. As he realized now, the three men of his escort had been deliberately murdered to ensure that no news of what had happened to him should get back to Calcutta. There, only Hickey knew that he had set out for Bahna; but Hickey believed that it was Gunston who had carried off Clarissa. He would therefore expect that Roger would regain possession of her and return with her towards the middle of the coming week or, should he fail to do so, presume that Gunston had proved the better man and that Roger had either been killed or seriously wounded by him in a duel. Either way, as far as he was concerned, it was a private quarrel between two young men over the possession of a pretty young woman and, whether or not he learned the outcome of it, no matter about which to go to the Governor.

If, after several weeks, Roger did not return, and when Gunston did but without Clarissa, Hickey's curiosity would naturally be aroused. Then, because he was representing Mr. and Mrs. Brook in the case against Winters, if for no other reason, he would set active enquiries on foot; but by that time Roger had good reason to suppose he, and probably Clarissa as well, would be beyond human aid.

That left only Gunston who, presumably, was still encamped with his miniature army some twenty or thirty miles to the south, in Orissa. By this time he would have reported to Sir John Shore his failure to extract the twelve lakhs of rupees from the Rajah of Bahna; and Sir John might have sent him fresh instructions. Being so well aware of the Governor's pacifist policy, Roger could pin no hope of these being an order to attack the city. At best, Gunston might be ordered to request the Rajah to receive him again so that they might discuss matters further. And if he did arrive on a second visit, that would be of no help, because it was quite certain that no one would tell him that two English people were being held prisoners there.

Thinking about Gunston caused Roger to feel a little guilty about the intense, and quite unjustified, hatred he had been stoking up against his old enemy during the past few days. It was abundantly clear now that Gunston was in no way responsible for Clarissa's abduction. All the same, Roger was inclined to excuse his injustice on the grounds that Gunston *had* pursued Clarissa and a firm belief that, had he had the wit and opportunity, and had she been a weaker, vainer woman than she was, he would have carried her off, if only to score for once off her husband, who had so often got the better of him.

Time drifted by while a series of ghastly images chased one another through Roger's tired brain. Clarissa innocently shooting at a paper target forming the centre of an apparently solid six feet square of covered straw in which, after being gagged, he had been embedded; the arrows penetrating the taut muscles of his behind; Clarissa naked on a stone slab in some heathen temple; the blood streaming from his torn face as Malderini ripped it with a piece of jagged glass; Clarissa screaming and struggling vainly in the grip of a great gibbering baboon; the young, hook-nosed, sensual-mouthed Rajah looking on with gloating pleasure at these sadistic acts conjured up by the evil mind of the Venetian.

These tormenting pictures flickered in turn like the steps of a treadmill, each of which kept coming to the surface in swift rotation, across his distraught imagination. So obsessed, in fact, had his mind become with these threatened horrors that the sounds of a struggle outside the dungeon did not consciously penetrate it. Not until the door was flung open and two men ran down the steps towards him did he rouse up with a sudden start.

One held a lamp. He was a smallish man and wore a red jacket with gilt buttons. His teeth gleamed very white under a thin moustache that had long drooping ends. Evidently he was the leader as he stood by while the other, who was robed in plain white, used the jailer's hammer to knock out the bolts that secured the shackle round Roger's ankle.

The moment he was free, the man in the red jacket grabbed him by the arm, pulled him to his feet and hurried him towards the door. Outside it a ghoulish scene was taking place. The big jailer lay sprawled on his back, his own knife protruding from his chest. He was near naked, as he had already been stripped of his robe, and a third man knelt above him swiftly unwinding the turban from his head. Snatching up the jailer's blood-stained robe, the leader of the party thrust it at Roger, signing to him to put it on over his clothes.

Roger needed no second bidding. The sight of the dead jailer had told him only a moment before that he was not being fetched to provide fiendish sport for Malderini, but was being rescued. Almost choking with excitement, he bent his head so that the greasy turban could be bound about it. Out of the corner of his eyes he glimpsed the jailer's body being thrown down the steps into the dungeon, and suppressed a semi-hysterical laugh. By using the man's own knife to kill him, taking his clothes and leaving his body within a few feet of where his prisoner had been chained to the wall, it was being made to appear as though Roger had actually carried out the plan that he had contemplated, and had abandoned only because he could see no hope of getting away from the city unaided.

The man in the red jacket sent one of his minions up the steep stairs, evidently to see that the coast was clear, as it was not until a low whistle sounded from above that he followed with Roger; the third man brought up the rear. On reaching the ground floor of the palace, they followed their advance guard at about twenty paces down a dim corridor, then through a doorway that gave onto a starlit court. The man who had gone ahead was waiting there and signed to them to halt. For two tense minutes they crouched in the shadow of the arched doorway, holding their breath, as they listened to the heavy treads of guards making a round some fifty paces distant.

When the sound had ceased, they went on again in the same order as before, slipping swiftly along one wall of the court, then half-way down another and in through another door. They were now in a pillared hall and, having crossed it, turned right into a broad passage. Next moment a door in it opened and a man came out. He paused to stare at them. Without a second's hesitation, all three of Roger's companions flung themselves upon him. Before he had time to shout, a hand was clapped over his mouth and he was borne to the ground. With swift, terrifying efficiency they strangled him.

The ruthless act confirmed Roger's belief that, whatever the cost, his rescuers meant to cover their tracks and leave it to be supposed that he had managed to escape unaided.

Leaving the body where it lay, they hurried on, and went through another doorway that led into a large walled garden. From somewhere in the distance there came the sound of plaintive Eastern music, then of a woman's laughter. High above the walls the fronds of tall palm trees whispered in a gentle breeze. But as they crossed the garden Roger saw that its lily ponds were sheltered, so that their waters remained unruffled and mirrored the bright stars above. A heady scent filled the air from big banks of moon-flowers, and from one of these against the far wall a hugely fat figure silently emerged. In a little piping voice that proclaimed him to be a eunuch, he said something to the man in the red jacket. There came the clink of coin as a small bag changed hands, then the eunuch turned and led the way to a low door in the wall. Its well-oiled bolts were pulled back and a moment later Roger and his rescuers were out in a dark street.

Quickly they made their way along it, and through others, some of which were so narrow that the jutting balconies of the houses in them were not much more than a yard apart, and almost shut out the stars. Occasionally a figure shuffled past or, vaguely seen, stirred in the shadow of a doorway. Now and then a dog barked, and once they had to step aside into the mouth of an alley to let a closely curtained palanquin pass. Here and there chinks of light gleamed between shutters or threw up the criss-cross woodwork fencing in the balconies overhead so that, although there was so little movement to be seen, there was a mysterious sense of wakeful life still pulsing behind the dark façades of many of the houses.

It was this which told Roger that it could not be as late as he had thought. He knew that it must have been about nine o'clock when he had been brought before the Rajah, but after that he had lost all sense of time. Although the agony he had endured in the dungeon had seemed interminable, he thought now that he had probably not been down there for much more than two hours; and as his rescue had obviously been carefully planned, it seemed probable that it would have been timed for the hour at which most of the inmates of the palace were settling down for the night, rather than later when any sound of movement would have attracted attention from the guards.

After ten minutes' walk the party pulled up half-way along a high wall, above which the tops of trees could be vaguely seen. The leader rapped in a pattern of knocks on a door in it, and at this signal the door was opened. They crossed a small garden and entered the house by a fretwork swing gate, which gave directly onto a room with silk-covered walls. In it an elderly woman was seated behind a low table, sorting out a quantity of seed-pearls and beads of different shapes and colours. The sari she wore was quite plain but of dark rich material. She had a hook nose and fine eyes which showed that when younger she must have been very handsome; age had given her a downy moustache.

The man in the red jacket went down on his knees before her and touched the ground with his forehead. Roger had already realized that she must be someone of importance and made her a low bow. His other two rescuers had disappeared. The old lady stood up and said something to their leader that caused him to open his mouth in a laugh, which suddenly revealed that he was a tongueless mute. With a wave of her hand she then dismissed him and, turning to Roger, said in Persian:

'Leave that blood-stained garment on the floor and come with me.'

Already agog with curiosity to learn who these people were, and why they should have gone to such lengths to save him, Roger threw off the jailer's robe and followed her through a curtained doorway into a larger and more richly furnished room. At one side of it a man was sitting cross-legged on a divan. He had on a pale blue robe patterned with gold thread, and a very large flat turban, and was smoking a hookah. It was not until Roger had bowed and looked up again that he recognized him, by his fine grey upturned moustache, as the nobleman who had been seated on a stool in front of the young Rajah's throne. At these much closer quarters it was also apparent that he was afflicted with an appalling squint.

Speaking as quickly as his Persian permitted, Roger at once began to express his unbounded gratitude, but his saviour cut him short by holding up his hand, waving him to be seated on a big leather pouf, and saying in the same language:

'Know Brook Sahib that I am the Wazier Rai-ul-daula, and that I have saved your life because I have hopes that you can save mine. But time is precious. Tell me what you know of Bahna and the wizard, Malderini, who bears you so great a hatred?'

'Of Bahna I know little, Excellency,' Roger replied; 'only that the old Rajah died about a year ago, and that the young one defies the Company. The Venetian I met while he was in England on a mission for his Government, and I inflicted serious injury on him in a duel. He was married to an Indian Princess, but I had not the remotest idea that he was in India or what had brought him here.'

'You know no more of him than that?'

'No; except that, although he wields hypnotic power through his eyes, he is not a true magician. My duel with him was owing to his being caught out as a fraud.'

'Yet, through his eyes his power is great. I am one of the very few immune from it; and only because of this.' The Wazier made a gesture towards his own eyes, and Roger realized that, on account of their terrible squint. Malderini would not be able to focus his directly on them.

'I must, then, tell you of Bahna,' Rai-ul-daula went on. 'The late Rajah was my brother and, at the time of which I shall first speak, I was his ambassador to the court of Delhi; so of these events I was not a witness, but I received entirely reliable accounts of them afterwards. It was fourteen years ago that the Malderinis came to India. While they traded for jewels they studied the arts of the fakirs, and by the time they reached Bahna they had mastered many of the hidden mysteries.'

'They?' Roger repeated. 'Does your Excellency mean that Malderini had with him a wife?'

'No, no; the woman was his sister—a twin sister. They are said to have been so remarkably alike that but for their clothes they could hardly be told apart, and both of them possessed the power to mesmerize. Very soon the woman had gained a great influence over the ladies of the harem, and she used it to get them to persuade my brother to give the man for a wife the little Princess Sirīsha. She was my brother's only child by his first wife; so a fine marriage portion went with her, and she was heiress on my brother's death to a far greater sum.

'Naturally, he was averse to such a match. For one thing he did not wish to see her fortune going to a foreigner instead of to a Prince of some other reigning house, an alliance with which would have been of value to Bahna. For another, the Princess was only nine years old; so over young to marry. But the ladies were set upon it and made his life a misery; the man Malderini promised by secret arts both to increase his wealth and restore his failing virility, and the question of the child's age was overcome by an undertaking that she should remain in the charge of the women until she was thirteen.

'At length my poor brother gave way and the ceremony of marriage was performed. By mesmerizing him Malderini did, for a time, increase his potency, but said that he could obtain riches for him only by making a journey to the far mountains of the north, and that he must take his young wife and sister with him. In due course, with numerous attendants, they set off. What happened later we can only guess from hearsay—the garbled versions of some of the bearers who returned weeks later.

'The sister was much the stronger personality of the two; and it may be that her brother had for long secretly resented her dominance over him. Be that as it may, after a night when the cavalcade had camped in desolate country, he suddenly announced that she was ill of fever. For two days he would allow no one except himself to tend her or enter her tent in which she lay. Two mornings later he declared her dead and that, the fever having been a form of plague, her body must be disposed of at once. He had himself already sewn it up in a sheet, and he had it thrown over a precipice.'

The Wazier paused, then went on impressively. 'Yet the bearers who returned say that the body in the sheet had already the stench of decay. And more, more; on the first morning the vultures gathered overhead. Carrion birds have an awareness of death which brings them from afar. She must have been dead then, and Malderini's pretence that she was ill of a fever a cloak to conceal that he had murdered her.'

'How long was it, Excellency,' Roger asked, 'before he again appeared in Bahna?'

'Not until six weeks ago. He had learned of my brother's death, and returned to claim his wife's inheritance.'

'Ah, now I understand. Did he bring the Princess with him?'

'No. He told us that her health would not permit her to travel.'

'She was well enough when I saw her with him in England nine months ago. But there is a very different explanation. He has almost complete control over her; yet she escaped from it the night before my duel with him long enough to beg me to kill him. She regards him as the personification of evil, and he is doubtless aware of that. If so, he would not dare to bring her back here, from fear that once she was among her own people she would find means to rid herself of him.'

Rai-ul-daula nodded. 'Poor woman. Yes; no doubt you are right. I come now to what followed my brother's death. I had for some ten years been his Wazier. It was his wish that I should retain that office. Given normal circumstances, with the exercise of tact, I foresaw no great difficulty in doing so. He chose his heir without consulting me; but my authority was sufficient to make any of his sons hold me in respect for some years at least, and during them I expected to inculcate into whichever was chosen sound principles for the government of Bahna.

'The present Rajah, Jawahir-ul-daula, is a vain and vicious youth. As is not unusual at such successions, within a week he had his two most gifted half-brothers strangled. I made no protest, for to do so would not only have been futile, but also make him distrustful of me. I gave him his head, too, when he wished to play the peacock before his court by refusing to accede to the Company's demands. Why not? The weakness and vacillation your Sir John Shore showed in the affairs of Oudh, when he had to settle the succession to our cousin the Nawab Asaf-ul-daula, made it clear to me that he would take no steps against us until positively driven to it and, in the meantime, we would have the use of the money.'

Roger could not help smiling as the squint-eyed Wazier went on. 'That was well enough; but I am not so great a fool as to expect to get the better of the Company for always. Bahna is too small a State and too near to Bengal to pick a quarrel of gravity with the English. This Sir John Shore will in time go home. There will come another. Not as great, perhaps, as your Lord Clive, or as wise and strong as your Mr. Hastings; but a true representative of your race, like the Lord Cornwallis or the Sir Eyre Coote. Then there would come war. Indian troops make brave warriors when led by their Princes one state against another, but they are no match for your redcoats, or the sepoy troops you train so cleverly. Bahna would be swiftly conquered, a huge fine imposed upon us, and the throne perhaps lost for good to my family. Am I not right?'

'Indeed, Excellency,' Roger bowed. 'Your words are full of wisdom.'

'Good! Then it will not surprise you to know that when we learned of the approach of Colonel Gunston's force I was prepared to compromise. My advice to His Highness was to pay half and to continue to argue about paying the other half for as long as possible. But the accursed Malderini had already been here for some weeks. By then he had succeeded in making himself the master not only of the mind of our young Rajah's but, apart from myself, of those of the principal men of the court.

'I believe him to be in the pay of the French; but of that I am not certain. It is clear only that he is set on making trouble for us with the English. My advice was overruled, the Company's troops were refused entrance to Bahna and the Colonel Gunston told that we would pay no part of the debt. But worse has followed. Malderini set off for Calcutta and kidnapped this English lady, your wife. Using her . . .'

At that Roger could no longer contain his impatience to speak of Clarissa, and he broke in, 'Forgive me, Excellency; but I am consumed with anxiety about her. Malderini said that she was in the palace and in good health. Was he telling the truth?'

'Yes,' the Wazier nodded. Then waving a hand towards the old lady who, since she had brought Roger into the room, had been sitting quietly in a corner listening to them, he added: 'My honoured mother, the Begum Gunavatī, saw her only this morning. She will confirm that your wife has suffered neither hardship nor injury.'

Springing up, Roger turned with a bow to the Begum and cried: 'I beg your Highness to tell me of her.'

The old lady gave him a kindly smile, and said: 'You have no cause for anxiety about her bodily state, and she seems sad rather than unhappy. She eats well but speaks little, and that is not because she lacks enough words of Urdu to make her meaning understood. For hours she sits doing nothing, as though she were living in a dream. That, I fear, is because this evil man has cast a spell upon her. The remedy is an ancient one and may prove difficult of accomplishment. To restore her to herself you must bring about his death, then burn his heart and cause her to eat some of its ashes in a stew of garlic.'

'I pray only for the chance to kill him,' Roger exclaimed, then he swung back to the Wazier. 'I implore your Excellency's help in this. Please have me taken back by your men, into the palace and led to the room he occupies.'

Rai-ul-daula shook his head. 'That is not possible. The door by which you left the palace will have been bolted after you. I have no means of communicating with the eunuch who let you out, or any other way in which I could secure your entrance.'

'Tomorrow then!' Roger urged. 'You could arrange for the eunuch to let me in tomorrow night; and if I had a man to guide me . . .'

'No, no; no! Even if I could do this without risk of it being discovered that it was I who had aided you, I would not. It could lead only to your death. Had it been possible to have him strangled, he would be dead by now. I would have seen to that. But he is too alert, too well guarded. And did he learn that I had sponsored your attempt, his influence with His Highness is enough to bring about my death also.'

'But the thought of my wife in the clutches of that devil is driving me insane. If you will not give me the chance to kill him, then I beg you to rescue her. Your people succeeded in getting me out of a dungeon, so surely . . .'

'You ask the impossible!' The Wazier cut him short with an impatient gesture. 'To rescue you without an alarm being raised, it was necessary first only to surprise and kill the keeper of the dungeon. Your wife's case is quite otherwise. She is an inmate of His Highness's seraglio. To order my people to break in there would be against all principle; neither would I ask it of them.'

'I ask only, Excellency, that they should lead me to it. I will do the rest.'

'You think so, eh? Then I will describe what would come to pass. Within five minutes a hundred screaming women would have aroused the whole palace; within ten the eunuchs would have seized, blinded and castrated you. Only a man whose mind is bemused by love would propose such wild schemes. Your wife is in no immediate danger. I pray you calm yourself. Be seated again and take heed of what I am about to say.'

With a sigh, Roger sank down on the pouf. The Wazier began to tick points off on his long fingers. 'Jawahir-ul-daula defies the Company. The Colonel Gunston is sent away empty handed. Malderini kidnaps an English lady. He uses her to lure here her husband. Both disappear in Bahna. At that the aristocrat English of Calcutta become greatly angry. They say to the weak Sir Shore: You shall shilly-shally no longer but must make an example of this small state. The force of Gunston's is ordered to advance, and it is Malderini who has the ear of His Highness. He will puff the vain youth up with pride and counsel him to fight. If I protest, that will provide the excuse Malderini is already seeking. Because my eyes are afflicted his evil glance cannot dominate me; so he bears me great hatred. He is eager for the chance to destroy me. Yet, say that I do not give it to him; what then?'

As the Wazier paused, evidently expecting an answer, Roger said: 'Your fate will be sealed just the same, because the British will defeat the Bahna army. If His Highness and yourself do not die in battle you, as his Wazier, will be held responsible with him for the policy which brought the war about, and have to pay the penalty.'

'Your thoughts are as mine. Because the evil Malderini has the power to make Jawahir-ul-daula his catspaw against the English many of our people must die, our treasury be emptied, the city perhaps sacked, and my family lose the throne. How shall we prevent this?'

Without, this time, waiting for a reply, Rai-ul-daula continued: 'We must invite attack before the English in Calcutta become really angry and force Sir Shore to order our destruction. The Colonel Gunston must march his troops swiftly through the mountains. His Highness will order his army to take the field; but it will not fight. I and its other principal commanders will so arrange that it does not. Jawahir-ul-daula has had his opportunity to reign. He has proved himself a weak and bad Prince. He will be deposed. Malderini will be seized and executed. Your wife will be freed. The Colonel Gunston will be entertained by many dancing girls and given rich presents. When he leaves he will take back with him the twelve lakhs of rupees owed to the Company. All will be well.'

'You give me new hope!' Roger exclaimed eagerly. 'But how, Excellency, are we to get Gunston to act?'

'That should not be difficult!' the Wazier shrugged, 'if you go to him, tell him how things are here, and inform him of our conversation.'

Again Roger jumped to his feet. 'Of course! He might distrust a written message, fearing it to be a trap; whereas if I tell him personally all that has occurred it cannot fail to convince him. But can you get me out of the city? I'd need a horse, too; and a guide.'

Rai-ul-daula rose from the divan. His squint was most disconcerting, but he smiled. 'I am happy that you find my plan good; for my life hangs on it, as well as the safety of your wife. All is provided for. Come with me.'

The Begum Gunavatī had also risen to her feet. Going to a cabinet she produced a flat package and, handing it to Roger, said: 'Hospitality has been outraged by our failure to offer you food and drink. That time is precious must be our poor excuse; but this may help to support you on your journey.'

Having thanked her he followed the Wazier out into a square hall. A tall hawk-featured native whose skin was paler than that of most Indians was waiting there and salaamed to him. Acknowledging the salutation with a wave of his hand, he said to Roger; 'This is Mahmud Ali Kajar, an Afghan of the far north. I brought him with me from Delhi and trust him as I would a brother. He speaks a little Persian and will take you safely through the mountains.' Then he turned and led the way up several flights of stairs.

When they reached the second floor Rai-ul-daula crossed the landing and entered a room in which a single lamp was burning. Its light was enough to show a stout rope coiled up on the floor beneath a latticed window. Mahmud Ali opened the window and threw out the unsecured end of the rope, smiled at Roger, then climbed over the sill and shinned down it.

The Wazier laid a hand on Roger's shoulder, and said, 'Follow him and have no fear. The camp is twenty miles distant and the road to it winds through the mountains making half as much again; but the moon will soon be up and prove your friend. You should be with the Colonel Gunston before the heat of morning. May the Gods protect you and bring you back swiftly.'

Roger was very conscious that, although their interests were mutual, he owed both his life and this chance to save Clarissa to the Wazier; so he thanked him most earnestly. Then, loath to lose an unnecessary moment, he slid over the window-sill and, hand-over-hand, lowered himself quickly to the ground.

The house from which he had come was built into the great wall, so he was now outside the city; and the starlight was sufficient for him to recognize, only a hundred yards away, the outline of the tower-flanked gate by which he had been brought into it soon after dusk had fallen. The rope's end danced before him as Rai-ul-daula began to draw it up, then Mahmud Ali twitched him by the sleeve, drawing him towards the open country.

For a few minutes they stumbled over rough ground, then they struck the road. A half-mile walk along it brought them to a farm house. Leaving Roger outside, Mahmud Ali went into its yard; evidently arrangements had already been made, for he emerged again almost at once leading two horses.

At a steady trot they set off, keeping to the main road for about two miles, then turning off it onto one that led southward. Half an hour later the moon had risen, silvering the tops of a low range of mountains they were approaching. Roger had met with no serious injury either while being captured or during the time he had spent as a prisoner, and although it was many hours since he had slept he was not conscious of any feeling of fatigue. The fact that, by a miracle, he was free again was sufficient to renew his vigour, and the thought that Clarissa's rescue depended on his exertions spurred him to fresh efforts.

Halting only from time to time to rest the horses, they rode hour after hour along twisting stony tracks, down steep hills, through boulder-strewn rivulets, and up again through dark gorges. The moon had set and the sky was paling in the east when Mahmud Ali reined in his mount at the farther end of a pass, and pointing southward said in his stilted Persian:

'I come no further, Sahib. From here, were it light, you could see town of Bamanghati. It lies in plain; five miles, six perhaps. To right of it lies camp. Allah be with you!'

As Roger rode on alone he suddenly felt hungry, so he took from his pocket the flat packet that the Begum had given him. To his delight he found it to be a slab of nougat, for few things could have been better suited to sustain him than the rich mixture of honey and almonds. By the time he had disposed of a dozen mouthfuls he was half-way down the winding track and, at intervals, could now see plainly both the town and camp. Another half-hour and, with his mount in a lather from having cantered the last mile, he reached the entrance to the lines.

He had made the arduous journey in about five hours, so it was not yet seven o'clock; but the camp was already stirring. The sepoys were milking their goats and lighting fires to cook their chupatties; havildars were shouting orders at fatigue squads and orderlies taking officers' chargers down to water at a stream that flowed through the camp.

A guard was being relieved at the roadside as he passed, but as he was a European no attempt was made to stop him. On slightly higher ground, a quarter of a mile away, stood a row of larger tents and two big marquees, which were obviously the officers' quarters. Riding straight up to them, he threw himself off his horse. For the first time he was conscious of a terrible fatigue and stiffness of his limbs, but the knowledge that he was now certain of securing help to rescue Clarissa kept his mind buoyant.

In front of one of the tents, a young officer, in his shirt-sleeves, was just about to wash in a canvas bucket, and Roger called to him urgently:

'Colonel Gunston! Where is he? I must see him at once.'

Pointing to one of the marquees, the young man called back, 'He is in there. But he'll still be asleep, and he is apt to resent being woken early.'

'I can't help that,' Roger croaked, his voice gone suddenly hoarse. 'Anyway, he'll not resent it on this occasion. I come on a matter of life or death.'

The young man promptly put down the bowl he was holding, ordered his servant to take Roger's mount and hurried with him over to the marquee. The sentry in front of it came to attention and stood rigid as they passed through the flap. Inside it was divided into two sections, the larger comfortably furnished as a reception room, and behind it a curtained-off sleeping quarter. In the first a native servant was seated cross-legged on the floor pipe-claying his master's equipment. With a look of surprised apprehension he quickly came to his feet and put a finger to his lips; but the officer told him sharply to wake the Colonel Sahib.

With evident reluctance the man went over to the curtain and called several times, softly, through it. After a moment there came the sound of hearty cursing, then low muttering and a pause.

Roger could hardly contain his impatience. He knew that by this time his escape must have been discovered. When it became evident that he had got clean away Malderini would expect him to return with troops. That meant that the Venetian would expedite his plan for using Clarissa in some horrible occult ceremony; or he might disappear from Bahna with her. But he could not know that Roger had been aided in his escape and supplied with a horse and guide; so he would probably count himself safe for several days at least. There was therefore still a good chance to take him by surprise before he could harm Clarissa. But only if Gunston broke camp at once, for it would take two days to march the troops through the hills; so every moment counted.

Suddenly the curtain was wrenched aside, and Gunston appeared, wrapped in a chamber-robe, his red hair tousled and his beefy face flushed with anger. Beyond him Roger caught a glimpse of a wide-eyed young native girl with small firm breasts sitting up among the rumpled coverings of a divan.

'What the hell's the meaning of this?' Gunston shouted. Then, recognizing his visitor, he exclaimed, 'Why, damn'e if it isn't Roger Brook! And what a state you're in, man! You look as if you'd been beset by robbers and barely got away. But what the devil brings you here?'

'I come from Bahna,' Roger cried. 'You were there recently. You met a Venetian, a man named Malderini, and told him that Clarissa and I were in Calcutta.'

'Did I! Why, yes; perhaps I made mention of you to him. But what of it?'

'He bears me a deadly grudge. He came down to Calcutta, and while I was up at Chinsurah kidnapped Clarissa.'

Gunston's sandy eyebrows shot up. 'Good God! The swine! D'you mean he's holding her prisoner in Bahna?'

'Yes. I followed; but he guessed I would and laid an ambush for me. He meant to kill me by slow torture; but by the grace of God I escaped, and have been riding hell-for-leather through the hills all night.'

'Well done! I will say you never lacked for guts, Brook. But what of Clarissa?'

'To arrange her escape was impossible. That fiend has her prisoner still, and threatens all sorts of abominations for her.'

'Poor girl! What a hellish business! I don't wonder at the state you're in! But what's to be done?'

'Done!' cried Roger. 'Why, sound the alarm! Parade your troops! Break camp!'

'What's this you say?'

'Give orders for an immediate march. Every moment is precious. We can start in an hour. We'll be through the mountains in two days. Two nights hence we'll take the city by surprise, and have her out of his clutches.'

Gunston's full mouth fell open; then he shook his head. 'I'm sorry for you, Brook. Indeed I am. And I've never concealed from you that I've a soft spot for Clarissa. But this trouble must have driven you out of your mind. What you suggest is impossible.'

'Impossible!' Roger gasped. 'You cannot mean . . .'

'I mean that, were you my dearest friend, or Clarissa my own wife, I could not use the Company's troops in a private quarrel. And I have my orders. They are in no circumstances to start a war with the Rajah of Bahna.'

CHAPTER EIGHTEEN

A Tough Nut to Crack

ROGER swore, argued, cursed, reasoned and pleaded; but all in vain. He explained that the Wazier intended to bring the Rajah's army over to them; so there would be no fighting. Gunston replied that he would not trust the word of any native, let alone a cross-eyed one. Roger implored him to at least make a demonstration in force. Gunston countered that it would need only one fool on either side to let off a musket for the demonstration to become a bloody battle. Roger begged for one company of infantry with which to make the attempt himself. Gunston refused on the grounds that they were his troops, his orders were positive and, if even a score of them were used in an act of war, he would be held responsible. Roger called him a coward. Gunston, with commendable restraint, declared that he would not accept a challenge from a man who was out of his mind. Finally, driven to a frenzy by the thought of Clarissa, and that Gunston had the means to save her but would not use them, Roger rushed upon him and attempted to strike him in the face.

Thoroughly worn out, as Roger was, his assault failed dismally. Gunston was fresh from a night's sleep and, in any case, the stronger physically. He seized Roger's wrists and held him off; then bellowed an order that he should be put in irons and taken to a tent. Five minutes later Roger was dragged away, manacled and pushed into a tent, the flap of which was laced up and a guard put on duty outside it.

The tent was a spare officer's quarter with a mat on the floor and a low divan. Choking with rage at having been put in irons, wracked with anguish by fears for Clarissa, and utterly distraught at the thought that there was now no hope of rescuing her, he flung himself down. Nature, too, had chosen this moment to exact from him the price of his exertions and ordeals. He ached in every limb, he could hardly see out of his eyes, his head seemed on fire and his brain was bemused.

For Roger to lose his temper was a very rare thing. Vaguely he realized that he had been a fool to do so, and that he would not have had he been thwarted by anyone other than Gunston; but, from his school-days, the sight of that ruddy, coarsely handsome face had been to him as a red rag to a bull. His mind went back to Sherborne and Gunston's bullying him there—snatching and spoiling his small precious belongings, and taunting him into fights he could not hope to win.

It was now more than twenty-four hours since he had closed his eyes. During them he had ridden nearly eighty miles, and had been harrowed by every sort of exhausting emotion. With tenuous memories of his school-days still drifting through his mind, he fell into a profound sleep.

When he awoke it was night. For a moment he could not think where he was; then, as he moved, the clank of the irons that confined his wrists and ankles brought everything back to him. He had been roused by the entrance of a tall figure holding a lantern, who now stood beside the divan. With a groan he stared up into the shadow above the light and made out the face of the officer who had taken him to Gunston's marquee. The young man said:

'The Colonel sends his compliments, Sir; and says that if you are prepared to conduct yourself in a reasonable manner he would be pleased to see you.'

Roger sat up. He had slept the clock round. Owing to the resilience from strain and exertion which came from a naturally vigorous mentality, the habit of facing up to difficult situations, and excellent health, his mind was clear and his body no longer feeling the effects of fatigue. He managed to raise a rather strained laugh, and replied:

'I fear I behaved very badly yesterday—or was it this morning? Anyway, if you'll have me relieved of these irons I'll promise not to repeat the performance.'

The officer called into the tent a farrier corporal and, with a twisted smile, Roger watched while, for the second time in twenty-four hours, fetters were knocked from his limbs; then he accompanied the youngster who had been sent to fetch him to the Colonel's marquee.

Gunston was sitting in an easy chair behind a table that had on it a decanter of Madeira and two glasses. As Roger was shown in, he gave him a sharp glance, dismissed the officer, and said:

'You were not yourself this morning, Brook; but in the circumstances I can hardly blame you. I'd have you, though, remember two things: firstly that I am not a free agent to do as I wish; secondly that, although we have never had any love for one another, this is no time to quarrel. Sit down now, and join me in a glass of wine. There will be a meal for you presently. I thought you would prefer to feed on your own rather than sup with the rest of us in mess.'

'That was considerate of you,' Roger replied. 'I am in no state to support trivial conversation with strangers. As for this morning, I apologize. You were right about my being out of my mind; but the horrors that threaten Clarissa . . .'

'I know. I would to God my hands had not been tied by our poltroon of a Governor; but we'll get nowhere by going again into that.' As Gunston spoke he was pouring the Madeira. Setting down the decanter, he added: 'I've despatched a Captain with a troop as escort to inform the Rajah that should one hair of Mrs. Brook's head be harmed we'll hang him from his own gate. But more than that I could not do. I could not demand the surrender of her person, since to do so would have amounted to an ultimatum.'

Roger's throat was parched, so he drank off the first glass of wine in three long swallows. While doing so he considered the possible results of Gunston's move. He feared the probability was that the young Rajah, being under Malderini's influence, would ignore the threat. It was certain, too, that the Captain would mention Roger's arrival at the British camp, and that might incite the Venetian to hasten in his designs against Clarissa.

However, it was clear that Gunston had acted with the best intentions, so Roger tactfully refrained from voicing his thoughts, and said, 'We can only pray that Jawahir-ul-daula heeds your warning. You will appreciate, though, that unlike yourself I am not bound by any orders, and cannot possibly sit here with folded hands awaiting events.'

'I would not expect you to; but you can do nothing without help. Your best plan would be to return to Calcutta and induce Sir John Shore to send me fresh instructions, empowering me to demand her release and, if need be, march on Bahna.'

'That seems the only course open to me,' Roger agreed. 'May I take it you would provide me with a guide and escort?'

'Certainly.' Gunston refilled their glasses, and went on after a moment, 'I must warn you of one thing, though. As the old Bible-puncher never intended me to fight, he did not provide me with a force adequate to do so. My information is that Jawahir-ul-daula can put into the field an army of some four thousand men. I have only some eight hundred: a battalion of sepoys much under strength, a single battery, and some details of scouts and sappers. Apart from the officers and a troop of horse, none of them are Europeans.'

Roger shrugged. 'As I told you this morning, the Wazier, Rai-ul-daula, will bring the Bahna army over to us.'

'If you prove right in that, well and good. But I'd not trust to it. These native gentry are tricky customers. Should things go wrong, I'd find myself with a battle on my hands that I'd not care to have to fight.'

'I see,' said Roger uneasily. 'Still, in the worst event, we might take the city by surprise in a night attack.'

'That's easier said than done. Once we have shown our hand you may be sure they'll keep the walls well manned. They might even sally out and, having so great an advantage in numbers, overwhelm us. No; the remedy lies in your bringing me reinforcements. A good stiffening of British troops is what I need—and preferably cavalry. Were he able to send me my own regiment of Dragoons, I'd make mincemeat of the whole Bahna army. But they are not available, so you must take what you can get. At a minimum it should be two hundred sabres, two companies of redcoats and another battery of artillery. With less, if your man plays the traitor to us, it could be only a desperate gamble.'

'Very well,' Roger agreed. 'You may be sure I shall secure as large a force as possible. When can I set off?'

'As early as you wish tomorrow morning.'

'Why not tonight?'

Gunston gave a sudden laugh. 'You have only yourself to blame that my hospitality up till now has been so lacking. But you should see yourself in a mirror. You are as haggard as a corpse, and look as though you had been dug up from a grave after being buried in your clothes. You need a bath, a barber, a good night's sleep and a fresh rig-out before you'll be in a fit state to travel.'

'I've slept all day,' Roger informed him, 'and I've no wounds to plague me. But I'd be grateful for the other things; and the sooner I set out the sooner I'll be back.'

'As you will.' Gunston finished his wine and stood up. 'I'll send my servant. He'll help you to get yourself clean and find you fresh linen; then he'll bring you a meal. Meanwhile, I'll arrange about an escort for you.'

After a good wash down in a canvas camp bath, a change of under-clothes, and with his hair freshly combed out, Roger felt fully equal to starting on his journey. While he ate, Gunston had had packed up for him in a haversack some emergency rations, and provided him with a sword and pistols. Then they went out to the guide, who was holding the horse on which Roger had ridden from Bahna, and two troopers who were to act as escort.

Before mounting, Roger held out his hand to his old enemy. Whether or not while in Calcutta Gunston would, if given the chance, have seduced Clarissa, Roger had had no grounds whatever for the murderous thoughts he had entertained against him in connection with her disappearance; so he now felt distinctly guilty about them. More, when in Martinique there had been an occasion when he had used his authority to force Gunston to give up his command as an alternative to being shot; so after the episode of the morning, Gunston might well have used his authority to revenge himself by much harsher measures—perhaps keeping him a prisoner in irons for a month. Whereas he had behaved very decently, and was doing his best to be helpful.

Gunston took the proffered hand, pressed it firmly, and said: 'Despite our past differences, Brook, we're on the same side of the fence this time. Get me a few hundred good British troops and another battery of guns and I'll get Clarissa for you in no time. Good luck to you!'

Ten minutes later the glow of the camp fires was fading behind Roger and his companions as they rode eastwards into the darkness. The route they took did not lead up into the mountains, but skirted them through low hills to the south of the range, so the going was comparatively easy. After twenty-odd miles, they reached the Subarnarekha, roused the ferry-men from their hut, and crossed it in bright moonlight. By ten o'clock in the morning they entered Midnapore. At the good inn there Roger rested his men and horses, lying up through the heat of the day. About six o'clock they set off again, now along the road that Roger had travelled on his outward journey. All through the night they alternately jogged along and rested. Two hours after dawn they reached Ulubaria, on the broad Hooghly, and there Roger was forced to admit that neither his horses nor men were fit to go any farther.

The fact that Calcutta lay only twenty miles up the river made the fact more infuriating. For a moment he contemplated leaving his escort, securing a fresh mount and going on alone. But he knew that he could not. In the past five days and nights he had ridden nearly three hundred and fifty miles. His muscles felt as though he had been put to the torture on a rack, his thighs were raw, and when he dismounted he could hardly stagger to the inn.

Yet his agony of mind for Clarissa was greater than his agony of body, and he would not give up. While he had been a prisoner he had not been searched and robbed, so he still had a considerable sum in gold in his money belt. After making a handsome present to his escort, he paid the landlord of the inn lavishly to make fresh arrangements for him. They were to have him carried to a boat and put aboard the first passing schooner that was making her way up-river to Calcutta.

As it was a Sunday, commercial traffic was at a standstill, but they found for him a native craft and, within a few minutes of being helped into her he was sleeping the sleep of the dead on a pile of matting in her stern. Slowly she tacked up the river past Budge-Budge and Garden Reach. It was three o'clock in the afternoon before she pulled in beside a wharf, and even then the turbanned master of the craft had difficulty in rousing him from his trance-like slumber.

Stiff as a board, and with every limb complaining, he beckoned up a sedan chair and had himself carried in the sweltering heat to William Hickey's. On the way he was a prey to fears that, as it was the weekend, this good friend upon whom he relied so much for advice and help would be up at his house at Chinsurah. But his fears proved groundless. Hickey's head boy said that his master had stayed in town to attend a party the previous night, and had gone out only half an hour before to dine with Sir William Dunkin. Roger asked that a message should be sent to inform him that he had returned from Bahna, and wished to see him urgently. Then he subsided on a sofa in Hickey's library and instantly fell asleep again.

The lawyer excused himself from sitting over the wine after dinner, and returned at six o'clock. Although physically still in poor shape, Roger, having slept for the greater part of the day, had recovered mentally sufficiently to pour out to him an account of all that had happened.

It entailed a long story as, until then, Hickey had never even heard of Malderini. When, after numerous explanatory digressions, it was done and Hickey had expressed his deep concern for Clarissa, he said:

'It looks as if Rai-ul-daula is toying with the idea of playing the part that Mīr Jafer did here in '57, when he was Wazier of Bengal. If he does, that would suit your book; but it is certain that Sir John Shore will see the parallel and, recalling that Mīr Jafer afterwards gave great trouble to the Company, he may well hesitate before agreeing to any attempt to assist Rai-ul-daula in supplanting his nephew.'

'Such finer policies can play no part in this,' Roger replied angrily. 'The honour and safety of an English lady are at stake, and he must set matters to rights or be shamed before the whole community.'

'That, certainly, is your strong suit. Much as it may go against the grain with him, I think it unlikely that he will refuse you orders for Colonel Gunston that he should demand the handing over of Clarissa. I count Gunston sound, though, in his contention that you should not rely too much on Rai-ul-daula's help. However great his good-will, when it comes to the point he may be in no situation to influence events. It would, too, be typical of such court intriguers did he let a battle start but held his hand until he saw which way it was going. You'll not find it easy to persuade our craven-hearted Governor to throw down the gauntlet, but if you succeed you'd be wise to make as certain of the outcome as you can by pressing him to let you have the maximum possible number of reinforcements.'

'I intend to. And I mean to ask him to let me have Colonel Wesley. Gunston does not lack for bravery, but he is better at chasing the fox than playing the fox. If the odds are against us shrewd handling of the situation will be half the battle; and Arthur strikes me as a man who combines caution with courage. His counsel could constrain Gunston from any head-long folly, and aid him in selecting the right moment if we have no alternative but to attack.'

Hickey shook his head. 'In that I fear you must resign yourself to dis-appointment. As you must know, my Lord Hobart, while Governor of Madras, has played a part that puts Sir John to shame. Lacking the authority to stop the rot that is undermining British influence among the Indian Princes, he has concentrated his energies against the settlements in the East of the European powers with which we are at war. He has already brought all the old Dutch settlements in Ceylon and Malacca under our flag and seized from them the valuable islands of Banda and Amboyna. This is in confidence, of course, but I had it from one who knows his Lordship's mind that he is now engaged in fitting out an expedition for the capture of the Spanish settlement in Manila, and has asked for Colonel Wesley to command it. In any case, Arthur sailed for Madras two days ago.'

'For me, that is ill news,' Roger remarked glumly. 'I had been counting on his help, if only in a private capacity. Out of respect for a brother officer having distinguished connections, Gunston would have deferred to his advice, whereas 'tis certain he'll have nought but contempt for mine. Still, I have faith in Rai-ul-daula, and doubt if it will come to a fight if only we show sufficient firmness of purpose.'

They had an early supper, then Roger lay for a long time in a hot bath and afterwards, his limbs much eased, flopped into bed, at last making up a good part of his lost sleep.

Next morning he was up early and rode out to his own house on one of Hickey's horses. Having changed his clothes, he collected certain of his private papers, then returned to the city to wait upon the Governor. To avoid working in the heat of the day, most Europeans began to transact their business at seven o'clock, and at a little before eight Sir John Shore had Roger shown in to him.

The Company's ugly, unpopular Chief Representative did not lack politeness, and he rose from behind his desk to return Roger's bow. Then he said: 'I was sorry to learn, Mr. Brook, that you have been having trouble with your wife.'

'Not with her, Sir,' Roger corrected him quickly, 'but on her account.'

Sir John raised a grey eyebrow. 'I was given to understand that some ten days ago she eloped with an admirer, and that you had gone up-country in pursuit of them.'

'Far from it. She was abducted with the connivance and assistance of a native Prince; and I am come to require your Excellency's assistance in regaining possession of her.'

'Indeed! Such a charge raises a serious issue. Pray take a chair, and give me full particulars.'

Roger had both an orderly mind and the gift of clear expression but, even so, it took him over twenty minutes to present a lucid account of his entanglement with Malderini in England, then of all that had occurred as a result of following Clarissa to Bahna.

When he had done, the Governor said: 'Mr. Brook, I pray you do not assume that I question your veracity. I would, though, suggest that you have been misled. All of us have heard of mesmerism, but few people can have seen it practised with even moderate success; and I cannot believe that anyone could apply it with sufficient potency to make a happily married young lady abandon her husband and her home against her will.'

From what Hickey had said, Roger had been prepared to find Sir John difficult; but he had not expected to be challenged on what he had come to regard as the accepted facts of his case. Switching his mind swiftly to supernatural matters, he said:

'I was unaware, Sir, that you were an atheist. Since that is so, it would be pointless for me to argue with you about spiritual forces.'

'An atheist!' Sir John exclaimed indignantly. 'I'd have you know, Sir, that I am as firm a believer in the Christian Faith as any man in this country.'

'You surprise me,' came the calm reply. 'How, pray, do you reconcile your Faith with a denial in the power of God to answer prayer?'

'I have done no such thing!'

'Your Excellency has done what amounts to that, by implying that the Devil is incapable of responding to the supplications of his worshippers.'

'That is a very different matter!'

'Permit me to disagree. Both God and the Devil are fundamental concepts of the Christian Religion. You cannot believe in the power of the one without also granting power to the other.'

'I grant your point; but where does this lead us?'

'To the fact that you have no grounds for thinking it more unlikely that a Satanist, like Malderini, should receive help and strength from his god than that we should do so from ours. In view of that, are you prepared to maintain that the Devil would never grant one of his disciples exceptionally strong mesmeric powers to enable him to dominate another person's mind for the purposes of Evil?'

The Governor gave a wry smile. 'It seems, Mr. Brook, that you have missed your vocation. You should have gone into the Church and made a name for yourself as a theologian. However, your argument when applied to the present case breaks down. You have asked me to believe that this man Malderini is a powerful magician, and that he intends to make use of Mrs. Brook in some abominable ceremony; yet you admit that in Lady St. Ermins's house you saw him unmasked as a charlatan.'

'That is true,' Roger admitted, 'but not grounds enough for supposing that Malderini is altogether incapable of securing help from the Devil. You, Sir, if inflicted with some dread disease, might pray for fortitude to support your pains, and have it granted; but if one night you prayed for wings, I greatly doubt if Our Lord would oblige you.'

'I fear I am far from being near enough a Saint to expect such a miracle.'

'And, no doubt, if Malderini has not yet qualified for the inner circle of Hell, that would explain why he had to resort to a trick, rather than rely on his Infernal Master, in his attempt to levitate the Princess Sirīsha. But of his hypnotic powers I have personal experience. During the duel I told you of . . .'

Sir John held up his hand. 'That might be accounted for by your having been in low health at the time. But there is no reason to suppose that Mrs. Brook was. Naturally, her departure has been the talk of Calcutta for this past week. Native servants always give a full account of such matters to anyone who will listen to them, so the facts are well known. After an hour's conversation with this man, she personally directed the packing of all her belongings; then, wide awake, without the least indication that she was either ill or unhappy, she mounted into his palanquin and left with him. I cannot credit that any healthy young woman could be arbitrarily hypnotized into taking such a course. No, Mr. Brook. You have my sympathy; but I fear you must accept it that your wife has deceived and deliberately left you.'

Roger fought down a rising sense of alarm. He had not yet even reached the point of endeavouring to persuade Sir John that an ultimatum to the Rajah of Bahna would not necessarily be followed by war, let alone tackled him on the subject of reinforcements for Gunston. Yet in inducing the Governor to adopt an aggressive policy lay his only hope of saving Clarissa. Clearing his throat, he said:

'Nothing can now convince me, Sir, that Mrs. Brook left me of her own free will. But there is a sure way to find out if it is you or I who are in the right of the matter. It is that the Rajah of Bahna should be required to produce her, and that, after an interval sufficient to free her from Malderini's malign influence, she should be asked to speak for herself.'

'The Rajah might well refuse to comply, maintaining that this is a private issue, and no concern of his. What then?'

'Colonel Gunston would then act upon the further instructions that your Excellency would have given him—namely to recover her by force.'

The Governor raised his long knobbly hands and gently tapped the tips of his fingers together. 'Come, come, Mr. Brook. We are no longer living in the age when Troy was besieged on account of Helen. You cannot seriously expect me to involve the Company in a war on your behalf because your beautiful wife has run away with another man.'

Angered by his assumption of Clarissa's guilt, Roger went slightly pale, but he kept his voice level as he replied, 'This is no question of personalities, but one of principle. The honour and safety of an English woman are involved.'

'You have not yet convinced me that she is in any danger. And, if she is, she has brought it on herself. There can be no justification for calling on men to fight in such a cause; and I have no intention of placing the lives of perhaps several hundred people in jeopardy on account of a truant wife.'

Roger saw now that patient argument would get him nowhere; so he replied with sudden acidity, 'Such righteous sentiments would no doubt be mightily applauded at a meeting of Puritans; but the parable of the strayed lamb would make them difficult for any true follower of Christ to justify.'

' Sir! Do you presume to lecture me on my religion?'

'No. Your Excellency's religion holds no interest for me.' Roger's tone had again become mild, but the way in which he steadily returned the Governor's angry stare through half-closed eyes showed that he was now in a highly dangerous mood. He went on quietly. 'I am concerned only with justice, and the prestige of my King and country. As regards the first, you are guilty of a gross injustice in condemning my wife unheard. With regard to the second, am I not right in believing that your real reason for refusing me your assistance is because you are anxious not to give offence to the Rajah of Bahna?'

'I am under no obligation to reply to such a question,' Sir John replied stiffly. 'But as I know myself to have been much criticized on that head, I will do so. I am the Servant of the Company. The instructions of their Honours the Directors are that I should avoid all cause for war with the native Princes, and resort to arms only should it be necessary to defend the Company's vital interests. It is my task to carry out those instructions to the best of my ability; not to question them.'

'I disagree. You are ignoring the revolutionary change that has recently taken place in the Government of India. The setting up of the India Board by Parliament has given you two masters. You are now responsible not only to the Company but also to the Crown. And it is your duty to put the interests of the Crown before those of the Company. I propose to show you a certain paper, and then . . .'

His ugly face twitching spasmodically, the Governor jumped to his feet and cried: 'How dare you attempt to teach me my business!'

'I pray your Excellency to be seated. When you have seen this paper, I think you will alter your tone.'

'Mr. Brook, you go too far. I'll not read your paper, nor will I discuss these matters with you one moment longer. This interview is ended.'

'On the contrary,' Roger retorted angrily, 'we are but just come to the essentials of it. I too have held His Majesty's Commission as a Governor; and, since you clearly need it, I intend to give you the benefit of my experience.'

'You . . . you! Your insolence is beyond bounds!' Sir John pointed with a trembling hand towards the door. 'Leave the room instantly!'

'I shall leave it when you have written and signed the instructions came here to get from you—not before.'

'You force me to extreme measures. I see that I must ring for my people and have you arrested.'

Roger made no move to rise. He knew that if he once left the room he would never be given another chance to see Sir John Shore alone. He was fighting for Clarissa's sanity and, perhaps, her life. If he failed now to wring from the Governor authority for the help he needed, all hope of saving her would be gone. He had hoped to prevail by argument, but had come prepared to stake everything for her sake. By the step he was now about to take he would, unless he succeeded in breaking the Governor's will, find himself hauled before a court and given a long prison sentence. But it was the only way in which he could force Sir John to listen to him. Without batting an eyelid, he took the plunge, and said sharply:

'In my pocket I have a small pistol. It is loaded and, if your Excellency's hand moves an inch nearer that bell, the Company will be under the necessity of appointing a new Governor.'

Sir John's hand remained poised in mid-air; then he cried, 'This . . . this is an outrage!'

'It will not be unless you force me to make it one.'

'You are mad, Sir! Mad! The loss of your wife has driven you out of your mind.'

'No, I am in full possession of my reason. But it happens that my own nterests coincide with those of His Majesty's Government. And, since you are neglectful of the latter, I regard it as my duty to see those interests safeguarded.' As he spoke, Roger put his hand into an inner pocket, and Sir John exclaimed with a sudden show of courage:

'I'll sign nothing; nothing! Not even at the pistol point!'

'I'd be a fool to force you to,' Roger replied, taking out a folded parchment, 'for if you did, you could issue an order for its cancellation within five minutes of my leaving you. I wish only to convince you that, where affairs of State are concerned, there are times when some people put a certain value on my opinion.'

'I should be much surprised ever to find myself among them.'

'That we shall see. You will recall that half an hour back I told you that it was owing to my duel with Malderini that I had to leave England. This letter was brought out by Colonel Wesley, and it is the clearance for my return.' As Roger laid the letter on the desk, he added casually, 'No doubt you are acquainted with the handwriting of the Prime Minister?'

'The Prime Minister!' echoed Sir John, his mouth dropping slightly open.

'Why, yes, Mr. Pitt has been my master for many years; and as you will see from that he looks upon me as a trusted friend.'

Sir John adjusted his steel-rimmed spectacles and his glance ran swiftly down the parchment. After a moment, Roger said, 'Permit me to direct your Excellency's special attention to the postscript.'

'I have read it.' The Governor's voice was sharp and querulous. 'May God give me patience. To think that Mr. Secretary Dundas should intend to ask you for a report on the state of things in India. What can you know of this vast country? You who have been in it less than a week for every year I have spent here!'

'Three months in a country is more than enough for anyone to learn if its government is strong or weak.'

'You can have formed your judgment only from malicious tittle-tattle, and that is no proper basis to go upon. Even if you were better qualified, that a Minister of the Crown should seek information behind the Company's back in this way is positively scandalous.'

'Your Excellency appears to forget that, as Chairman of the India Board, Mr. Dundas is responsible to His Majesty for the security of British interests in India. From having been a servant of the Company for so many years, your loyalty to it is understandable. But you must not expect me to share it; and it does not excuse British prestige having fallen so low during your stewardship. You talk of tittle-tattle, but it is far more than that when over their wine every night of the week men damn you for policies that bring shame upon our nation. Your betrayal of the Nizam of Hyderabad destroyed throughout India all faith in the British word, and but three nights ago a petty princeling, only a score of miles beyond the frontier of Bengal, treated your name with derision, declaring to me that you would not dare to lift a finger against him.'

'Enough! Enough!' cried the tortured Governor. 'I have followed the instructions of my masters. I have brought in many excellent reforms. I work far longer hours than any of my staff. I have near wrecked my health in service to the people of this country. And what is my reward? To have you, who are ignorant of all this, hold me up at pistol point in order that you can fling these terrible accusations at me.'

Roger shrugged. 'I have no pistol. I pretended that I had one as the only means of preventing you from having me thrown out. I endeavoured to show you that letter earlier, but you would not let me. Your seeing it was my only hope of bringing you to reason.'

'And now that I have,' the Governor gave a bitter laugh, 'I am faced with not a pistol but a cannon. Clearly you are offering me the choice of doing as you wish or, should I refuse, returning to England and doing your utmost to hound me out of office.'

'Say rather that, as in the case of Mr. Warren Hastings and with far better reason, I will have you impeached for treason.'

'This is no less than blackmail.'

'It could be, but it happens that I have scruples.' Roger told the glib lie because he wished to save the wretched man's face. 'I'll put no pressure on you, and give you my word that when I make my report to Harry Dundas it shall be a fair one, untinged by malice. I ask only that your Excellency should consider the advice which I propose to offer you.'

Sir John looked at him in astonishment and, after a moment, replied: 'In view of what has passed between us, you are now acting with considerable generosity, Mr. Brook. Having read this letter, too, I must concede that you are a man of much more consequence than I thought. I would that I had let you show it to me earlier, for it is a clear testimony that the highest personages set value on your opinions.'

Now that the tension was relaxed, both men again sat down, and Roger said: 'It may on first thought seem an impertinence for one who has been Governor only of a West Indian island to air his views to a man of your Excellency's exalted station and far greater experience; yet I am convinced that the art of government remains the same whatever the size of the state.

'When I arrived in Martinique, it had recently been taken from the French, and nine-tenths of its white population are of that nation. The island was in a state of acute unrest, and a revolt aimed at turning us out could be anticipated at any time. My predecessor had resorted to fiercely repressive measures, but that had led only to further antagonizing the inhabitants and paralysing the trade of the island.

'I reversed that policy and, like yourself, initiated one of appeasement. In every issue I went as far as I could to meet the wishes of the French. I revoked many restrictions that irritated them, bettered the lot of the workers, stimulated commerce. In fact, I ruled with a velvet glove. But I kept a hand of steel inside it. The least infringement of my orders and the offender got no second chance. Those who were caught talking sedition against the British rule I treated without mercy. It may well be that I had hanged a score of innocent men; but by that I stopped revolts which might have led to the deaths of many hundred.

'May I suggest, Sir John, that you have been ruling with the velvet glove, but without the steel hand inside it?'

The tired man on the other side of the desk nodded slowly. 'There is much in what you say. But my instructions from the Company . . .'

'Let us forget the Company,' Roger cut him short, 'and think only of what British rule should be. Justice, the freeing of the people from oppression by the native rulers, the introduction of better methods of agriculture, the stabilization of currency, and encouragement of the exchange of goods between provinces; all this, but also death for those who foment discontent or, through personal ambition, threaten the progress of peace and prosperity.

'In the matter of Bahna, you have to your hand a situation which, if you handle it rightly, can rehabilitate you in the eyes both of your fellow countrymen and the native potentates. This vicious young Rajah owes the Company twelve lakhs of rupees. He has refused to pay it and is confident that you will not dare to use force to collect it. I suggest that you should order Colonel Gunston to advance on Bahna and demand both the money and my wife. I go further. I suggest that you should entrust me with an order to depose Jawahir-ul-daula and appoint a suitable successor. For him to pay at this late date is not enough. Only by occupying his capital and making an example of him will you receive the full credit for having acted, however belatedly, with real resolution to restore your lost authority. Do this and the news of it will run round India in a week. From Kashmir to Travancore it will be realized that you are not, after all, a man to be trifled with.'

They argued the matter for another half-hour, but in the end Roger got his way. Sir John Shore penned a despatch giving fresh instructions to Gunston, and signed and sealed for Roger a commission as an agent of the Company authorizing him to make such changes in the government of Bahna as he saw fit. Apart from policy, the question of reinforcements for Gunston was outside his province, but he gave Roger a letter to the Commander-in-Chief, informing him of his decision to reduce Bahna to obedience, and requesting that British troops should be despatched as soon as possible to strengthen the force that Gunston was commanding on behalf of the Company.

Mentally stimulated by his triumph after this long battle, Roger took leave of the Governor and had himself carried in a chair through the noisy, crowded, smelly streets to the Red Fort, in which General Sir Alured Clarke had his headquarters.

The General kept him waiting for half an hour but then, having met him at numerous bachelor evening parties, greeted him as an old friend. Having read Sir John Shore's letter he exclaimed, 'Drat me! What can have come over that moribund cuss that, for once, he's willin' to let us chastise one of these insolent coffee-coloured gentry?'

Tactfully, Sir Alured refrained from enquiring about Clarissa, so Roger did not use her situation to urge the necessity for acting with speed. Instead, feeling that he had let the Governor down lightly, he did not scruple to imply that if matters were delayed Sir John might change his mind; as he knew very well that the soldier would go to any lengths rather than lose this unexpected chance to re-establish British prestige. He learned, though, to his dismay, that this question of speed raised a new and tricky problem.

Sir Alured had far fewer troops than he really needed to 'show the flag' and, if need be, help to defend the Indian States on which, since Clive's day, the Company had imposed a vague overlordship embodied in some form of alliance. Most of these, too, were stationed up in Oudh, or in the distant Carnatic, and recently he had had to scrape the bottom of the barrel for troops to make up Colonel Wesley's force that was mustering at Madras for the expedition to Manila. The only unit he could offer, which could be on the way in forty-eight hours, was a squadron of hussars from the Headquarter's garrison. Neither artillery nor British infantry could be made available under a fortnight, as both would have to be composite units formed from details got together in the depots.

Roger's choice, therefore, lay in either taking the cavalry only, with which he could rejoin Gunston in a week, or waiting for at least a fortnight, then making a slower march at the pace of the infantry, which meant that the best part of a month must elapse before he could hope to rescue Clarissa. As cavalry was the arm Gunston had said he needed above all else, and Roger still had faith in Rai-ul-daula bringing the greater part of the Bahna army over to them as soon as the British appeared in front of the city, he hesitated hardly a moment before deciding to make do with the hussars.

Knowing that Calcutta must by now be humming with the news of his return and a fresh wave of speculation about Clarissa's disappearance, he felt it would be highly embarrassing to meet their acquaintances; so he made only one visit, which was to his old friends the Beaumonts, and poured his woes into their sympathetic ears. Moreover, the idea of returning for two nights to his own house, where he had known so much joy with

Clarissa, was intolerable to him; so he rode out there only to give Chudda Gya a month's wages for the servants, then went to cover for the rest of the time in the mansion of the ever-hospitable Hickey.

Early on the Wednesday, still a prey to great anxiety about Clarissa, but physically again in good shape after his two days of recuperation, he set off with the squadron of hussars. They were commanded by a Captain of near his own age, named Philip Laker; a short, dark, good-looking young man, with the typical, slightly bow-legged, swagger of a cavalry officer. From the start they took a liking to one another and, as Roger trotted once more across the long dusty plain, with its endless vistas of ryots cultivating their fields, humped oxen drawing high-wheeled carts and women with bundles on their heads, he told Laker the whole story of his involvement with the abominable Malderini.

As the pace had to be kept down to one which would not tire unduly the least good mounts of the squadron, instead of making the journey, as Roger had, in little over two days it took four; so it was in the mid-morning of Sunday that they came in sight of the camp outside Bamanghati. Much to Roger's surprise, he saw that only a remnant of it remained, and it was obvious that the greater part of Gunston's force had vacated it. A quarter of an hour later, an Ensign, who had been left in charge of sick and stores, told him that the Colonel had received an urgent despatch on Thursday evening and set off in the direction of Bahna early on Friday morning.

Roger had known that Gunston would receive his new orders from Sir John Shore several days before he could rejoin him, but had not expected him to move off before he had received his reinforcements. However, that he had done so now appeared all to the good, as Laker's hussars could make the march through the hills much faster than Gunston's sepoys and artillery; so, by the latter having moved up to an advance base, a day would be gained.

As the midday heats were now increasing with the advance of spring, the track through the mountains would from ten o'clock onwards be sizzling with heat, and the glare on the bare rocks most tiring to the men; so Roger and Laker decided to rest the squadron at Gunston's old camp that afternoon, then break the back of the thirty miles they had to go by a night march. By dawn on Monday they reached the lower slopes on the far side of the range, but were much surprised to find no signs of Gunston's advance base there.

After a two-hour halt for the men to have a meal they moved on down into the plain. Three miles farther on they got their first distant sight of the city; but they had to ride another two before they came upon one of Gunston's pickets. A sepoy then led them along a track through a wood to a great sprawling collection of buildings the size of a hamlet, but in one irregular mass, instead of being dotted about. It was a typical dwelling under the Indian patriarchal system, by which one family, often of as many as a hundred people, all lived and farmed together.

The sound of hoof-beats brought Gunston out from the doorway of one of the larger buildings and, with a wave to Roger, he cried, 'Well, I never expected to see you back so soon; but I suppose you were too impatient to wait for infantry and guns.'

'That's so,' Roger replied, dismounting; and, after he had introduced Laker, he went on, 'For my part I never expected to find that you had left your camp; much less that you would have advanced so near the city. They can't possibly fail to know you are here, and that will have given them time to prepare to resist us.'

Gunston shrugged. 'Of course they know. Old man Shore's despatch was perfectly clear. I was ordered to demand payment of the money and the return of Mrs. Brook, coupled with the threat that in the event of a refusal I would come and get them. As the Rajah had already refused to pay up when I sent to demand the money three weeks or more ago, the only chance of making him change his mind was by a display of force. It has not come off, though. I sent Captain Jeckles in yesterday morning. All he got was a flat refusal, and not long after his return the Rajah's army began to pour out of the city in battle array. Naturally I made no move to attack, and nor did they. But they have come out again this morning. Come up to the roof and have a look at them.'

Much perturbed, Roger followed Gunston inside, up a rickety stairway and out onto the flat roof. The sight that met his eyes shook him badly. On the far side of a shallow stream, not much more than a mile away, the Bahna army had taken up its battle positions. Gunston had placed its strength at four thousand, and it certainly could not have been less. Great groups of white-clad figures, their spears and scimitars glinting in the sun, sat cross-legged on the ground. In the centre were a score of elephants, the howdahs on them full of men with long-barrelled muskets. On each wing there were bodies of several hundred horsemen, and with them were war chariots mounting pennants that fluttered in the breeze.

'Fine spectacle, isn't it?' remarked Gunston. 'And one can't doubt that the Rajah is spoiling for a fight.'

'It certainly looks like it,' Roger agreed glumly. 'However, I have faith in Rai-ul-daula. I am certain he means to bring the bulk of the army over to us.'

Gunston shook his head. 'No; there's now no hope of that. I sent him a letter by Jeckles; and it seems the result was unfortunate.'

'What's that you say?' Roger exclaimed. 'D'you mean you compromised him?'

'Well, perhaps. I don't really know. My letter may have had nothing to do with it. But last night we captured a merchant who was leaving the city. On questioning him we learned that, soon after Jeckles had left, the Wazier was relieved of his office and Malderini appointed in his place.'

'Oh why, in God's name, did you . . .' Roger broke off with a groan. 'Still, it's no good crying over spilt milk. Our best plan now, then, is an attempt to surprise them by a night attack.'

'That's it,' Gunston agreed. 'When do you expect your infantry and the guns to come up?'

Roger turned to stare at him. 'I . . . I thought . . . surely I made it clear that the squadron was the only reinforcement immediately available, and you said you needed cavalry above all else. To wait while other troops were mustered in the depots would have meant that we could do nothing for the best part of a month.'

Gunston returned his stare with an angry frown. 'Then you've made a mess of things. You've lost us three or four days while I send back to the General asking him to put the muster in hand after all.'

'D'you mean that you'll not attack without more troops.'

'Have some sense, man!' Gunston snapped, pointing at the Bahna host. 'I'll not see my men massacred, and I've no mind to commit suicide myself. All we can do now is to retire on the camp at Bamanghati and wait there till Sir Alured has sent up the guns and men for which I asked.'

CHAPTER NINETEEN

To Cheat the Moon

ROGER felt a sudden wave of physical sickness rising in him. It was as though he had received a blow in the stomach; hot saliva welled up in his mouth. He turned his face away to hide the shattering effect that Gunston's words had had upon him. 'A month,' he was thinking. 'A month. By the end of it either Clarissa will be dead or her mind unhinged.'

He had never dabbled in magic, but he knew enough of it from hearsay to be aware that magicians regarded certain phases of the moon as more favourable than others for their conjurations, and particularly the full moon. It was eleven nights since he had escaped from Bahna, and the moon had then been in her last quarter. The dark period was now over and the light of the new sickle had silvered the rocky track during part of his ride the previous night; so there was at least a week to go before it would reach full. He tried to force from his mind the sickening possibility that Malderini might consider the dark period more suitable for his dark ceremony, and so have already performed it. The dreadful fact with which he was now faced was that in the next twenty-eight days the moon would have passed through all her phases; so by refusing to act for a month Gunston was, in effect, declaring that Clarissa must be sacrificed.

For a moment he considered accusing Gunston of cowardice and calling him out. But Gunston, as the commander of a force in the field, could quite properly refuse to fight a duel until the campaign was over. If he waived that right, did fight and was killed, that would bring the rescue of Clarissa no nearer. Besides, it was not cowardice to refuse to pit his troops against such greatly superior forces now that there was no longer any possibility of Rai-ul-daula's bringing over a great part of the enemy.

It was on that, above all, that Roger had been counting. Fighting down his sick anger and striving to keep his voice steady, he asked: 'What on earth possessed you to send a letter to the Wazier?'

Gunston looked at him in surprise. 'You told me he was for us; so I was hoping to get speech with him. If he had slipped out of the city and come here last night, we could have concocted a plan. Given a definite assurance of his help, I would have attacked this morning, and . . .'

'But damn it, man! When I implored you ten days ago to bring your force up to Bahna, you said you'd not undertake an attack without rein-forcements.'

'You forget that I was then under orders not to attack in any circum-stances. Old Shore's new instructions created a very different situation. If, having talked with the Wazier personally, I'd felt I could trust him, I'd have gone ahead, and might by this morning be in Bahna.'

'What did you put in your letter to him?'

'Seeing that he is your friend, I made use of your name. I said only that you were in a great state of anxiety about Mrs. Brook and, should His Highness not see his way to handing her over immediately, I'd count it a civil act if he'd send someone here to report on her state of health to you personally—hoping, of course, that he'd take the hint and come himself.'

'And he was given this at the same time as the Rajah was handed your ultimatum?'

'Why, yes. Jeckles had no opportunity of seeing him alone. His sudden downfall may have been from some quite other cause. I only suspect the letter because Jeckles told me later that no sooner had he given it to him than the Venetian demanded a sight of it; then two of them began to yammer at one another in some heathen tongue. Yet there was nought in it that could fairly be said to compromise him.'

'Not in so many words, perhaps; but Malderini possesses psychic qualities that render him doubly dangerous. I would to God you had left well alone and awaited my return.'

Gunston gave an abrupt, unpleasant laugh. 'I see now how the land lies. You'd rather have your wife left longer than need be in the clutches of these devils than be deprived of the credit of rescuing her yourself.'

'Longer than need be!' Roger took him up with sudden fury. 'That comes well from you, who declare that she must be left to her fate for another month.'

'Had you brought me the redcoats and the guns . . .'

'Had you not bungled our present chances . . .'

'I acted for the best!'

'You acted like a fool!'

'By God, I've a mind to call you out for that!'

'At your service! Any time you wish!'

All memory that they had buried the hatchet only ten days before now gone from their minds, the two old enemies stood glaring at one another. But, after a moment, Roger gave a weary shrug.

'I spoke in haste. That is no apology. I'll meet you at some future time which is more convenient to us both. But for us to fight while you are in command here might jeopardize your career; and, as long as Clarissa is a prisoner, I owe it to her to risk a wound only on her account.'

'That suits me,' Gunston agreed. 'I doubt, though, that either of our tempers will support a month in each other's company; so you must excuse me if, while we are waiting for Sir Alured to send up more troops, I do not invite you to join my Headquarters' mess. Captain Laker and his officers will form their own mess when we get back to Bamanghati, and the cavalry always do themselves well, so you'll lose nothing by feeding with them.'

'Thank you for the thought,' replied Roger, acidly. 'But your concern for me is needless. I am not going back to Bamanghati.'

'You mean to return to Calcutta and attempt to hasten matters?'

'No; I mean to stay here.'

'Then you should be put in irons again. Staring at the turrets of Bahna will not free your lady; and do you remain lurking in these woods 'tis a certainty that you will find yourself a prisoner within twenty-four hours of my drawing off my troops.'

'My escort will prove quite adequate to protect me. Even under Malderini's malign influence the Rajah, unless first attacked, is hardly likely to send his troops against a squadron of British horse.'

'Your escort!' Gunston's pale blue eyes began to bulge. 'Captain Laker's squadron was sent up as a reinforcement. It has now come under my orders. If you elect to stay here, you stay alone. I intend that the squadron shall retire tonight on Bamanghati with the rest of my force.'

Roger's glance was cold and hard. 'In that you are quite mistaken. Had you been willing to fight a battle, the squadron would have come under your command. That, I could not prevent. But at least I was successful in persuading Sir John Shore that I am a more suitable person than yourself to order matters for the best in Bahna once the Rajah has been brought to heel. He has appointed me the Company's political agent in Bahna. The Company's political agents are entitled to adequate protection in the course of their duties. I might demand more of you; but I will content myself with Captain Laker's squadron.'

Taking his commission from his pocket, Roger showed it to Gunston, who glanced down it, then said: 'So be it. As the price of parting company with you, I count the temporary loss of the squadron cheap. But it is getting plaguey hot up here. Now that you have seen for yourself the impossibility of taking Bahna with the forces I have available, we had best go downstairs and at least attempt to be civil to one another for the next few hours.'

With the advance of the morning it had become intensely hot up on the flat roof, and both of them were already sweating profusely; so Roger was by no means loath to follow Gunston below. There, the latter sent for his principal officers and gave them their order of march in a retirement which was to begin two hours before sundown; it was also agreed that Laker should then take over the sprawling group of buildings, that the headquarters now occupied, as quarters for his squadron. Then, except for the sentries they all slept through the heat of the day.

Dinner, with the habitual disregard of the British for unusual circumstances, was served according to custom at half-past three. Despite the fact that four thousand Indians, all of whom would have taken joy in cutting their throats if a battle had started, were still concentrated within a mile and a half of them, the assembled officers cheerfully gorged themselves with roast meats, and washed their food down with liberal potations of claret and Madeira. Either belching freely or partially concealing their digestive processes with varying degrees of politeness, they then made their way back to their men, who had also been feeding to capacity, and an hour later the retreat began.

While Gunston's force was marching off, Roger again went up to the roof, and he saw that the Bahna army was also beating a retreat. Evidently the Rajah had now come to the conclusion that there would be no battle that day, and was withdrawing his troops into the city for the night.

After half an hour spent studying the walls of the city through a spyglass, Roger discussed the situation very fully with Philip Laker. He then disclosed his intention of attempting a forlorn hope if the Captain would support him in it with his squadron. At first Laker was distinctly dubious about committing his officers and men to such a desperate venture, but he felt that Gunston had behaved very ill towards Roger, which made him the more anxious to help him; and, after some discussion, he agreed that, if his subordinates proved willing to risk their lives in such an affair, he would take the responsibility for leading them.

The Lieutenants and Cornets were summoned and Roger explained his plan to them. They were mainly young men, mostly eager for a scrap; and, their Squadron Commander having clearly stated that this was a chance in a thousand for them to earn glory for their regiment, they were swiftly caught up in a wave of enthusiasm.

The hundred and eighty-odd non-commissioned officers and men were then paraded, and Roger addressed them. He said that within a few hours they might be ordered into action. If they were, it would be a desperate business and many of them might be dead before morning. But they would not be ordered to attack unless there was a fair chance of victory. Should the action prove successful, they would be hailed as heroes throughout the whole British army, and to enable them to celebrate he meant to distribute a thousand guineas amongst them. Any man who had no stomach for such a fight might take one pace to the rear, and he would be left to do a woman's task of getting breakfast ready for those who had survived the fray.

It was as wicked a blackmail as he had put on Sir John Shore; but the troops did not regard it in that light. As with British soldiers of every generation, from Agincourt to Plassey, they liked the idea of a scrap that had an element of the unusual about it, and provided they were given good leadership, were not afraid to enter one knowing that the odds would be against them. Not a man stepped back.

Roger then called for a dozen men willing to come with him on the specially hazardous first stage of the night's work. There was no lack of volunteers; so he had the officers pick him three men from each of the four troops, and placed them under a Cornet named Angus McCloud—a gaily impudent young blade of whom he had formed a particularly good opinion on the march up from Calcutta.

Soon after darkness had fallen, the final arrangements were made; then there ensued a nerve-wracking period of waiting. The young moon was due to rise soon after midnight; so the initial stage of the operation had to be completed before that, otherwise the sentries who were certain to be posted on the walls might detect an approach to it, however cautiously made. On the other hand, the longer that could be allowed for the inhabitants of the city to settle down for the night, the better.

At half-past ten Roger and McCloud set off on foot with their squad, avoiding the road but making across country for the great gate. A quarter of a mile from it they left the men lying in a ditch and went forward on their own. Through his spy-glass earlier in the evening, Roger had located the house from which he had been let down by a rope, and made a careful estimate of its distance from the gate. The towers at either side of the gate now stood out as stark black masses against the star-lit sky, so he had no difficulty in identifying the house. The windows in it that looked out over the country-side were thirty feet from the ground and there were five of them in a single row. There was a light in only one, and was not the one from which Roger had descended; but he felt that he was lucky to find even one which was apparently occupied.

McCloud, in accordance with their plan, went right up to the wall and took up a position with his back against it so that he could not be seen from above. Roger remained about twenty feet away from it and, taking a handful of pebbles from his pocket, began to throw them up at the lighted window. His fourth shot struck the wooden lattice-work with a clatter that sounded abnormally loud in the stillness of the night.

After a moment the lattice swung back and the dark silhouette of what he felt sure was a woman's head appeared. Softly he called up to her in Urdu, 'I would have speech with the Begum Gunavatī.'

She did not reply and the head disappeared. With his pulses racing, he waited. He had decided against disguising himself in one of the native robes left in the big farm-house, as its whiteness would have made him much more conspicuous when approaching the city, so the starlight might be sufficient for the woman to have seen that he was wearing European clothes. In any case, his accent must have told her that he was a foreigner and he thought it certain that she would have guessed him to be an Englishman from Gunston's force. If, after the Wazier's fall, his house had been taken over by the Rajah's people, within a few minutes men might be poking long-barrelled guns out of the window.

Roger, standing there with his pale face upturned, knew that he would then provide a perfect sitting target. He could only hope that, if his fears were realized, the first shots would miss him. By dropping at once he meant to sham death, then, even if he were wounded, the men would after an interval, leave the window, and McCloud have a fair chance of getting him away before the guard on the gate came out to collect his body.

The minutes seemed endless, but at length another head appeared at the window. No long muzzle was thrust out so he called up again. For a second time there was no reply and the head was withdrawn. Another wait ensued, but he was more hopeful now, which made it a shade less agonizing. Five more minutes passed, then the same head reappeared and another wearing a turban. A voice came to him from above and with immense relief he recognized it as that of Mahmud Ali Kajar.

A quick stumbling exchange in Persian followed. Mahmud Ali left the window and reappeared at another farther along the row. Down came the rope and Roger hauled himself up it. On clambering into the room, he found that Mahmud Ali's companion was the mute in the red jacket who had rescued him from the dungeon. The latter grinned at him and, leaving the Afghan to haul up the rope; led him downstairs to the room in which he had talked with Rai-ul-daula. The Begum was there and rose to receive him.

Having made her a deep bow, he asked with breathless anxiety. 'My wife, your Highness? Is she safe? Is she well?'

The Begum nodded. 'Yes, she is safe.' Then, after a second's hesitation, she added, 'She is still in the harem, and being well cared for.'

'God be thanked!' he exclaimed. 'And your Highness's son, the Wazier? I heard that yesterday he had been deprived of his office. A letter was sent to him which may have caused the trouble, but that was no fault of mine. I hope . . . I trust . . . I should be terribly distressed if anything serious . . .'

She shook her head. 'No; my son has many powerful friends. If Jawahir-ul-daula decreed his death without sufficient cause, from fear for their own lives they would band together and revolt. The young Prince knows that would be the end of himself. He had dared do no more than confine my son to his own house and put guards upon it.'

'He is here, then?'

'No; this is my house. His palace is two streets away. For the present he is safe there among his own people. But for how long, who can say? It is certain that the Venetian will devise some plot to make a pretext for his execution.'

'Your Highness, I am here tonight in an attempt to rescue my wife,' Roger said quickly. 'I have brave men outside who can be brought in to aid me. I owe my life to your son. If it be possible, we will rescue him too.'

'You are a young man of generous heart; also of great courage,' the old lady murmured. 'To penetrate the city is to ask for an evil death. Your wife is at least fortunate to be the object of such love. Tell me, now, how you hope to recover her?'

Roger gave a brief outline of what he proposed to do. Having heard him out she heaved a sigh. 'You may succeed in reaching her, but you will never get her away. Your men may hold the gate for a while; but you will be overwhelmed by numbers before you can get back with her to it.'

'I can only pray that your Highness will prove wrong in that,' he replied gravely. 'Nothing will deter me from making the attempt. But perhaps you can suggest a better way for me to set about it?'

Her still fine eyes searched his face for a moment, striving to assess what other qualities he possessed besides courage. Then she said, 'Show me the palms of your hands.'

Obediently, he held them out to her. For a good two minutes she studied them carefully. When she looked up it was with a faint smile. 'I do not see death in them, yet; and you have audacity without rashness. If left to his own devices my son may overcome his enemies; but at any time he might be murdered. What neither of you could do alone, the two of you may do together. Putting my trust in your stars, I will gamble with his life tonight. By morning he, you, your wife, myself, all of us, will be either dead or safe.'

She paused for a moment, pulled at the dark hair on her upper lip, and went on, 'I have ways of sending messages to him in secret, and he to others. But that will take time.'

'You have ample,' Roger reassured her. 'My troops are not to attack until half an hour before dawn. I did not dare to risk an earlier hour from fear we would lose our way through the streets owing to darkness.'

'That was sensible. Even so, there will be great confusion. To distinguish friend from foe, there must be a password—a battle cry that my son's men will shout so that your soldiers do not attack them. What shall it be?'

'Clarissa,' replied Roger, without a second's hesitation.

'Cla-rissa; Cla-rissa,' the old lady repeated. 'That is the name of the wife of your great love. Yes, it is suitable. I will write now a letter for my son, and my clever Damaji, who brought you here from prison, will get it in to him. Mahmud Ali Kajar shall go up with you now to get your men in before the moon rises.'

For this there was now no time to lose; so, as soon as the Afghan had been summoned, Roger hurried upstairs with him. Leaning from the window, he called softly down to McCloud, 'All's well,' The Cornet called back an acknowledgment and went forward at a crouching run, a vague figure seen only for a moment in the starlight.

Ten minutes later he was back with his men spaced out at intervals behind him. Mahmud Ali had already lowered the rope. A hefty Corporal swarmed up it. After him came the eleven troopers, and finally young McCloud. The second stage of the venture had been accomplished without the alarm Roger so dreaded having sounded.

Roger told the Afghan that, as there were still five hours to go before the attack, he would like his men to be given a chance to doss down during the time of waiting. Mahmud Ali took them through the back quarters of the house, stopping at a larder, from which he handed out the best part of a cold goose, a big bowl of rice mixed with onions and sweet peppers, and a large flat dough-cake; then he led them across a courtyard to a stable in the stalls of which several horses were dozing. Pointing to some bales of clean straw, he indicated that they should make themselves comfortable.

Having seen their men cheerfully settled at their midnight meal, Roger and McCloud accompanied Mahmud Ali back to the Begum's sanctum. After presenting McCloud to her, Roger said that they, too, would like to rest, if it was agreeable to her, until the fateful hour arrived. She agreed that his wish was a wise one, but insisted that they must first eat, and sent the Afghan back to the kitchen quarters. He returned with a dish of quails, a ragout of rice and antelope, and a copper platter on which were piled a variety of sweet cakes.

Young McCloud tucked in as eagerly as at a dormitory feast, but Roger was so keyed up that he could eat hardly anything. When they had done, the Begum told them to make themselves comfortable on the big divan, put out all the lamps but one and, carrying that away, left them.

Soon after four o'clock she returned to rouse them. McCloud was snoring, but Roger had hardly closed an eye. He sat up, instantly alert, to hear the results of her clandestine correspondence with the ex-Wazier. As he listened he became more tense than ever with excitement. His original plan had been limited to a daring raid to seize and carry off Clarissa; later he had offered to include in the enterprise an attempt to rescue Rai-ul-daula. Now the plan had been amplified to nothing less than the capture of the city.

With intense concentration he strove to take in the exact meaning of the sentences spoken by the Begum in Persian. Some he asked her to repeat, until he felt confident that he had a complete grasp of the whole scheme. First, as planned by himself, he must capture the gate and let in the waiting squadron of cavalry. Next, some of them must go, guided by Mahmud Ali, to Rai-ul-daula's palace, slaughter the guards set about it, and restore him to freedom. Roger, meanwhile, guided by Damaji, could go as he had intended to the garden door by which a eunuch had let them out of the palace. But, simultaneously, the great main gate of the palace should also be attacked to draw off the palace guard. Rai-ul-daula's friends commanded the greater part of the Bahna army, and would keep it from intervening; but, in the palace, the Rajah's men were expected to prove loyal to him. There were several hundred of them; unless they could be overcome swiftly, other bodies of troops might decide to disobey their officers, join them, and assist in driving the British out of the city. If, owing to some delay, that were allowed to happen, disaster would overwhelm them all.

Roger and his men were all provided with white native garments and turbans. At a quarter to five, led by Mahmud Ali and Damaji, they filed out of the house into the street. Three minutes' walk brought them to within a few yards of the gate. The majority of the party crouched back in the pitch blackness of an angle made by the walls of the nearest tower, while the two natives went forward. Mahmud Ali spoke to a sentry who was leaning against the door of the gatehouse. After showing some reluctance, the man went inside and returned with his officer. Mahmud Ali whipped a knife from under his robe. In one stroke he severed the officer's throat. At the same moment, Damaji fell upon the sentry. With the side of his palm he struck him sharply under the chin and, as his head went back, plunged a knife in his stomach.

The group waiting in the shadows ran forward. McCloud joined Mahmud Ali at the gate and helped him draw back the immense strong teak beam that, like a huge bolt, held the two halves of the gate shut. The others followed Damaji through a door in the base of the tower into the guardroom. By the light of a single oil lamp a brief, grim tussle ensued. Within three minutes the remainder of the guard were senseless or gasping out their lives. Roger felt it to be a horrible business, but knew that it was necessary. No other course could have prevented a premature alarm ruining his plans; so it was either no quarter for the guard or death for himself and all who were with him.

Needing no bidding, the troopers now flung themselves on the great wooden winch, heaving it round so that the thick hempen hawser coiled about the drum slowly drew the nearest half of the great gate back. As soon as there was an opening wide enough, McCloud slipped through and, as fast as his legs would carry him, raced down the road.

As he did so, a voice called down from the top of the tower above the guard-room. It could not have been McCloud's running off outside that had attracted the attention of the sentry up there, as he was leaning over the inside parapet and his head and shoulders could be seen against the paling sky. He must have heard the creaking of the great winch; but it was still almost pitch dark down in the well between the two towers, so he could not have seen that half the gate was actually open.

At the sound of his voice, Roger's party stopped dead in their tracks; then Mahmud Ali called up something that seemed to reassure the sentry. He drew back from the parapet and half a dozen of the troopers filed quickly into the other gatehouse. Grabbing the spokes of the winch there, they began to drag the other half of the gate open.

For a few minutes Roger waited in breathless suspense, staring out through the open gate along the still dark road. Suddenly he caught the sound of a muted drumming. It was the squadron, with the hoofs of their horses muffled in old rags, coming up at a canter.

The sentry had caught it too. Next moment a shot rang out. Then another and another, from other sentries posted farther off along the wall. Roger could see the squadron now as a black compact mass swiftly approaching.

'Laker!' he shouted. 'Laker! Here I am!'

In a swirl of dust, the Captain pulled up beside him, while the squadron streamed past them under the tall arch. A dozen men of the garrison were shooting now, but the attackers got by almost unharmed. In the last troop, one man was hit in the arm, another had an ear chipped and, with a screaming neigh, a wounded horse pitched its rider. The rest rode on, pulling up in the adjacent streets, the houses in which gave them temporary cover from the sentries on the walls.

To make himself heard above the din of cries, shots and curses, Roger had to shout at Laker but, by an exchange of a dozen quick sentences, they modified the plan they had agreed on; for now, with the help Rai-ul-daula would give them, they could hope to capture the city. It was agreed that No. 1 troop should go with Roger to secure Clarissa; Nos. 2 and 3, under Laker, with Mahmud Ali as guide, were first to free the ex-Wazier, then attack the main gate of the palace; while No. 4 troop should remain there to hold the gate in case they were forced to retreat through it.

While Laker shouted his orders, and passed the recognition battle cry 'Clarissa' to his officers, Damaji, Roger, McCloud and their squad of twelve picked men each took a grip on the stirrup leather of one of the No. 1 troop. Led by the red-jacketed mute they set off up the street, running beside the mounted troopers. Within five minutes they entered the narrow lane, one side of which was formed by the wall of the palace garden. Those running let go their hold and swiftly formed a group outside the door which had been opened by the eunuch on the night of Roger's escape. Meanwhile, the mounted men divided into two sections, each trotting to one end of the street and halting there ready to resist any attempt to interfere with Roger and his party.

Two of the special squad produced canisters of gunpowder that Roger had had them bring in with them, and a third a length of fuse. McCloud placed the canisters against the gate and fixed the fuse. The corporal lit it with his tinder-box, and they all ran back. The fuse spluttered and a small blue flame ran along it; there came a bright flash and a shattering explosion. Without waiting for the smoke to clear, Roger rushed at the door and, followed by his men, flung himself against it. The explosion had shattered the lower part and sprung its hinges. Two minutes' ramming by muscular shoulders and they had forced the wrecked door far enough back to get through.

McCloud blew his whistle to call up the mounted men while Roger, half-blinded by smoke, staggered into the garden. Dawn was not far off and there was now sufficient light for him to get his bearings. When crossing the garden before, he had heard a woman's laughter coming from a long low building that lay to his right. Damaji had come up with him and pointed at it, confirming his belief that it was a part of the harem. Followed by the troopers, now wielding their drawn sabres, they pelted across the garden towards it.

The firing down by the city gate had increased, and lights coming on in the building showed that the sound must have aroused some of its inmates. As Roger raced towards it a door at the top of a shallow flight of steps swung open and the portly form of a eunuch showed framed in it against the light. At the sight of the dark figures running towards him, he gave a shrill cry of fright and quickly shut the door again. But before he could bolt it, Roger was up the steps. With one violent kick he forced it back a foot, then jabbed with his sword through the opening. The point of the blade caught the eunuch in the arm. He gave a screech of pain and, clasping at his wound, staggered aside. A moment later the whole squad was tumbling inside.

They had entered a bare tiled hallway with graceful arches in its walls. Another eunuch was standing in one of them. His eyes wide in their puffy sockets, he turned and fled. Instinctively Roger dashed after him. A dozen strides carried him down a short passage and into a long silk-curtained room. In it there were a score of divans and as many scantily clad houris, just aroused from sleep. They began to scream. Those who were nearest cowered back against the walls; others, at the far end of the apartment, fled like a herd of terrified gazelles, bunching together as they stampeded through a farther archway.

At a glance, Roger had seen that Clarissa was not among them. With flying feet, he pursued the huddle of dark heads, streaming veils, and shapely brown limbs through the archway into another chamber. It was very similar to the first, but occupied by a number of older women, evidently the concubines of the young Rajah's father. Most of them, too, were now screaming, but some showed a bolder face, and one flung a dagger at Roger. It missed him, but struck one of the troopers behind him, gashing his cheek. With a thrust of his left hand, Roger pushed the woman over, and sped on after the younger ones through yet another archway.

It opened onto a passage at one side of which there were a number of curtained doorways. Ripping aside the first curtain he came to he saw beyond it a comfortably furnished room with a tumbled divan from which its occupant had already fled. The next was similarly furnished and also empty. These, evidently, were the apartments of the favourites. One after the other he snatched at the silk curtains, peered for an instant into the abandoned rooms, and hurried on. In the sixth room, lying on its divan, he found Clarissa.

For a moment he thought she was asleep; then he realized that she could not possibly have slept through the piercing screams and clamour made by the other women during the past few minutes. Yet if she was not asleep —an ice-cold hand gripped his heart—she must be dead.

CHAPTER TWENTY

With Death at the Post

Clarissa was lying on her back, covered to the chin. Her eyes were closed, her long pale gold hair, of which she took such care, was tangled on the pillow; but her cheeks had the warm flush of life. Suddenly she groaned.

Calling her name, Roger flung himself down beside her. She did not answer but began to turn her head uneasily from side to side. He saw now that there were little beads of perspiration on her forehead, and that the flush in her cheeks was too hectic to be natural. Her small imperious acquiline nose stood out white, sharp and bony from between them. Each faint breath she drew came with a little rasp. Gently he put his lips to hers, and found them burning. That light caress confirmed the fact that had already dawned upon him. She was in the grip of a high fever.

'Oh, Clarissa!' he cried. 'My sweet, my darling! What have they done to you?'

His anguished cry aroused her from her torpor. The long lashes that made fans on her cheeks fluttered and her eyes opened. As he bent over her, she looked straight up at him but showed no sign of recognition. Then, turning her head from side to side again, she began to babble incoherently.

After a moment, he realized that there was nothing he could immediately do for her. A stool, a bowl of rose-water, and a square of damp linen beside the bed showed that up till a few minutes ago she was being nursed by one of the other women. The nurse must be found as soon as possible, and a doctor. But there was no chance of that until the Rajah's troops had been overcome and order in the palace restored. Meanwhile Malderini, the fiend who had brought his fair love to this sorry pass, might get away.

Coming to his feet he cried to McCloud, 'Stay with her. Bathe her face with that rose-water. I'll be back as quickly as I can. Two of the men I'll leave with you. The rest I'll take. I've a man to kill.'

Urged on by fierce cold hatred, he began his hunt. Even Malderini, he felt certain, would not have been permitted to enter the women's part of the palace; so he wasted no time looking into the other rooms of the seraglio. Coming on another garden entrance beyond the favourites' corridor, he ran through it. No. 1 troop had followed his squad through the blown-in door and were hotly engaged in the middle of the garden with a body of about sixty of the Rajah's soldiers. The natives had the advantage of numbers and that, owing to the trees, lily ponds and beds of shrubs, the mounted men could not form up to charge. But as Roger came on the scene some fifty yards behind the phalanx of Indians, it suddenly broke. The white-robed figures scattered and ran towards him. Putting spurs to their horses, the hussars came in swift pursuit, crashing across the flower-beds and cutting down the yelling brown men with their sabres.

Suddenly Roger realized that he was still wearing a turban and white robe himself, so he might be mistaken for one of the flying enemy. Wrenching them off, he shouted to his men to do the same, and cried out 'Clarissa! Clarissa!' He was only just in time. A burly sergeant was charging down upon them, his sabre raised high to cleave a head. With a shout of recognition he swerved off towards another group.

Damaji led the way to a door in a building at right angles to the harem quarters. With blows and kicks they forced it and entered a wide corridor. The rooms that gave off it were store rooms and workshops. In some of them servants and slaves were in the act of trying to hide themselves; in many instances they fell to their knees, banged their heads on the ground and cried out for mercy. Hurrying through the building, Roger and his band crossed a small courtyard, smashed open another door and found themselves in a pillared hall. There, more servants flung themselves down before them, or scattered and fled. Two minutes later Roger was dashing in and out of another row of rooms, all of which had divans and appeared to be the apartments of some of the courtiers; but none of them had things in them which might have belonged to Malderini.

A shout from his corporal brought him back into the passage. From its far end a body of about twenty of the Rajah's guards were running towards them. Although they were outnumbered, they stood their ground, for the passage was only some eight feet wide and, on so narrow a front, not more than three couples could engage one another at a time. The guards were wearing shining brass helmets and corselets of chain-mail, but the hussars were better swordsmen. In the furious cut and thrust that ensued during the next few minutes, they more than held their own for the loss of one man, killing or grievously wounding five of their attackers. Then, as Roger wrenched his sword point back from out of the muscle of an Indian's neck, he glimpsed another group of guards at the far end of the passage running up to reinforce their comrades.

Knowing that the odds were now too great for them to force their way through, he gave the order to retreat. Still cutting and thrusting furiously as they went, they backed away step by step towards the pillared hall. Next moment he was seized with anxiety as to how they would manage when they reached it, since the greater number of guards would be able to spread out and surround them.

Swiftly he saw that they must again stand and fight until help came. The No. 1 troop had had orders to remain in the garden and hold it; so that should Laker fail in his attempt on the main gate, Roger and his squad, having rescued Clarissa, could be certain of getting out that way. Parrying a pike thrust he shouted to the corporal.

'We must stand here, or we'll be cut up in the hall. Get back to the garden. Bring up half the troop! Tell the rest to keep by the door in the wall. Off now, and quickly. Waste not a minute.'

As the corporal backed out of the scrimmage, another hussar went down beside him. That left only Roger, Damaji and seven of them against at least thirty of the Rajah's guard. Only the narrowness of the passage saved them from being overwhelmed in the next few minutes.

During them, while the sweat poured down Roger's face on account of his exertions, his mind sought frantically for a way out of the desperate situation in which he now found himself as a result of having agreed to the Begum's plot. Had he stuck to his original plan, they might by this time, ill as Clarissa was, have wrapped her in a cocoon of blankets and carried her off on some sort of emergency stretcher.

No sign or sound suggested that Laker had yet forced the main gate, so Roger had good reason to believe that he might have on his hands the majority of the palace troops. Even with the help for which he had sent the corporal, the struggle must now become a fighting retreat. How, if they had to defend themselves all the way back to the garden door, could they possibly manage to construct a rough litter for Clarissa, collect her, and get her away?

Two more of the guards went down and another hussar. Then Roger heard the sound of running feet behind him. Flickering his sword point at a brown moustached face, he suddenly jabbed it into a fierce dark eye, then with a gasp of thankfulness, threw a glance over his shoulder. The gasp turned to one of dismay. It was not the corporal returning with help, but another crowd of yelling natives. He and his men were trapped in the narrow passage.

There was only one thing for it. 'Quick!' he shouted. 'Into the room on the left. We'll barricade the door!'

As the men behind him backed into the room, there suddenly came a cry from the crowd of white-clad figures that had just appeared on the scene. It seemed to him at that moment like angels' music. Above the swift pattering of sandalled feet as they rushed forward, their voices chanted 'Cla-rissa! Cla-rissa!' He knew then that they must be some of Rai-ul-daula's men.

Near exhaustion from ten minutes' unceasing cut and thrust, he backed after his remaining hussars into the room at the side of the passage. The furious onrush of the newcomers swept back the guards. For another ten minutes a frightful struggle raged. The passage was now half blocked by dead and dying, the floor slippery with new-spilt blood. Then the dozen guards who were left standing suddenly panicked, turned and ran, pursued by Rai-ul-daula's yelling men.

Still panting, Roger led his little band out again. They followed the victors at a run. After traversing another long echoing corridor and an empty hall, they burst out into the great forecourt of the palace. Dawn had now come. By its light, Roger saw that the main gate was hanging broken from its hinges. Laker's troopers were inside, sabring little groups of the palace guard that, here and there, were still putting up a resistance. For another ten minutes sporadic fighting continued with its sounds of shots, screams and curses; then they died away.

Laker caught sight of Roger, waved his long curved sword, rode up to him and cried: 'I met with no serious opposition in the city, and the palace is now ours. We have only to round up the prisoners. What of Mrs. Brook?'

'I found her,' Roger replied hoarsely. 'She is ill, desperately ill; but safe. I've been searching for that fiend Malderini.'

At that moment a big palanquin with red curtains came through the gate. Roger ran towards it expecting that it carried Rai-ul-daula; but, as the bearers halted, one of the curtains was drawn aside and the Begum looked down on him.

'I have come,' she said, 'to do what I can for your poor wife.'

He frowned up at her. 'You knew, then, how ill she was?'

The old lady nodded. 'I knew; but it would have been no kindness to tell you. It would have disturbed your mind while all your thoughts should have been on our plan to seize the palace. But be sure that from now on she could not be in better care than mine.'

'I am most grateful to Your Highness,' he murmured. Then he added, 'I pray you excuse me now. I am seeking the man who is responsible for her state.'

She leaned forward and shook her head. 'You will not find him. He is gone from here.'

'Gone!' he repeated, then suppressed a blasphemy that had risen to his lips. 'I understood he had got himself made Wazier in your son's place.'

'He did, two mornings since. But perhaps in some way he got wind of your intended attack. I learned only half an hour ago from a eunuch who is in my pay that the Venetian left the city last night.'

Roger could have wept with fury; but there was nothing he could do about it. Even if the direction that Malderini had taken was known, he must now have six or eight hours' start, and to set off in pursuit of him with Clarissa in her present state was out of the question.

He was still endeavouring to fight down his rage when Rai-ul-daula, surrounded by a little crowd of richly dressed nobles, emerged through an archway from an inner court. On seeing Roger, he hastened towards him, opened his arms, embraced him and cried:

'This day is heaven sent. Last night I believed myself abandoned by gods and men. I was impious, for dawn finds me safe and free. I owe you my life, and vow eternal friendship to you.'

'Excellency,' Roger replied, 'you owe me nothing. Had you not saved my life ten nights ago, how could I have lifted even a finger to aid you. But I joyfully reciprocate your friendship; the more so as I have been appointed a political agent of the Company, and am charged with putting matters to rights in Bahna.'

Rai-ul-daula's eyes, with their awful squint, appeared to be fixed on opposite angles of the courtyard, but the white teeth under his fine upturned moustache flashed in a smile, as he cried, 'No news could be more welcome. Within an hour I will have sorted the sheep from the goats. We will then hold a *diwan*, and you shall make known the Company's pleasure.'

The Begum's palanquin had already moved on. Pointing after it, Roger said hurriedly, 'I thank you. Pray excuse me now; I wish to accompany Her Highness, your mother, to my sick wife.' Then, still followed by the remains of his squad, he ran to catch up the palanquin.

He found Clarissa much as he had left her. Angus McCloud was bathing her face but she was still delirious. The Begum forced a few drops of dark liquid between her teeth from a thin phial, and after a few minutes she ceased her low-voiced babbling. To Roger, the old lady said:

'Her state is much worse than was reported to me. It is her chest. There is inflammation there. It is shown in the manner of her breathing. We must rub her with hot oils. But first we will move her.'

'Move her?' repeated Roger with a quick frown.

'Yes; she must have more light and air, more room for attendants to be with her, and be in a place where she will not be disturbed by the nearness and chatter of other women. It is not far, and she will take no harm. The divan can be lifted and carried without disturbing her.'

Damaji was still with them. The Begum turned and spoke to him. He salaamed then, pointing to the divan, looked at Roger. After only a moment's hesitation, Roger called in his men and told them to pick it up. Following the mute, they carried it down the corridor, through a hall and out into a smaller garden that Roger had not yet seen. On the far side of it there stood an ornate pavilion. On entering it, Roger guessed that it was here that the Rajah had slept, sending when he wished for whichever of his houris he favoured at the moment to be brought to him; for its central room contained a big elaborately carved bed, and there were other rooms off it for guards and servitors.

The Begum rejoined them, now accompanied by several other women who had come out of their hiding places on her calling aloud that they had nothing to fear. She sent Roger and his men outside, and for three-quarters of an hour he paced the small garden, a prey to agonizing suspense; then she came out to the porch of the pavilion and beckoned him inside.

Clarissa had been transferred to the big bed. Her long hair had been done up in plaits round her head and, although she was in a coma, her expression was much more relaxed. The Begum said to him: 'Poor child, she is ill; very ill. But I will remain to do all I can for her. There is an entrance behind this place by which you can come to it without passing through the harem. Damaji will show it to you. I have had the divan on which she was carried here placed in the next room. I know you will wish to be with her. You can sleep there if you wish.'

As Roger was thanking her, he heard McCloud calling him, so he went outside. Mahmud Ali was there. He had come with a message from his master that the *diwan* had assembled and awaited Roger's pleasure. No more could be done for Clarissa for the present, so he accompanied the Afghan through the rambling buildings of the palace to the spacious throne room.

In it were now assembled some hundred people. The throne was empty, but ranged round it stood Rai-ul-daula and his friends. Behind them were several eunuchs, fan bearers and a number of the Rajah's guards. To the right stood Laker, most of his officers and a troop of his hussars; to the left a group of a dozen nobles with their arms bound behind them and, two paces in front of the group, young Jawahir-ul-daula, also bound.

As Roger entered, Rai-ul-daula and his companions salaamed; Laker gave an order, the British drew their sabres and presented arms. Drawing himself erect, Roger walked with a firm tread towards the throne, but did not mount it. On the first step he halted, turned and, taking Sir John Shore's Commission from his pocket, read it in a loud voice in English; then he handed it to Rai-ul-daula and said in Persian:

'Be pleased to have a translation of this document read out.'

A eunuch was called forward and, in a piping falsetto, gave a rendering of the Commission in the dialect of Bahna.

When it was done, Roger turned to Philip Laker. 'Captain, I desire an escort for His Highness the Rajah. A Lieutenant and six of your men. The two leading files will take him by the arms and bring him before me.'

Laker gave the order. Jawahir-ul-daula's sensual mouth was loose and trembling; his eyes flickered wildly, and his face had a faintly bluish tinge under its bronze. When he had been thrust forward by the two leading troopers, Roger said to them:

'Throw him on his knees.'

They did as they were bid, and with such a force that the aigrette in his turban touched the ground. Instead of striving to rise, he grovelled there, whining for mercy. Ignoring his pleas, Roger addressed him loudly in Persian.

'Jawahir-ul-daula. You have broken a solemn treaty made between your country and the Honourable the East India Company. You have repudiated a just debt owing to the Company and mustered your army with intent to wage war against the Company's forces. You have abetted the abduction of a subject of His Majesty King George III and held her prisoner here. In these things you have followed the advice of evil counsellors, and so shown yourself unfitted to rule. By the powers vested in me, I hereby depose you.'

After a moment's impressive pause, he went on. 'That is not all. On my first journey here you had me ambushed and captured. Two of my escort were killed during the fighting; the third surrendered and your men cut his throat in cold blood. A few hours later you told me here in this chamber that your men had acted on your orders; so that no word of my capture should get back to Calcutta, and it would be believed that myself and my escort had fallen victims to a band of robbers. For that triple murder I mean justice to be done.' He paused again, then said in English to the Lieutenant:

'Take this man outside and hang him.'

When the ex-Rajah had been dragged away, Roger turned to Rai-ul-daula and asked, 'Are you willing to pay out of the Bahna treasury the twelve lakhs of rupees owing to the Company, and a sum sufficient to reimburse the Company for having had to send an expedition to Bahna?'

The reply was a clear affirmative, accompanied by a low bow.

'Are you willing to enter into a new treaty with the Company, the provisions of which shall be similar to those in the treaty between it and the Rajah, your late brother, to reinstate the Company's officials for the administration of the finances of the state, and to rule with firmness, justice and mercy?'

Again, Rai-ul-daula pledged his word and made a solemn bow.

Roger waved a hand towards the row of a dozen captive courtiers and said, 'I leave it to Your Highness to dispense justice to these people.' Then he took his cross-eyed friend by the hand, led him up to the throne of elephant tusks, seated him upon it, and cried:

'Let the fate of Jawahir-ul-daula be a warning to you all. I give you a new and wiser ruler, Rai-ul-daula. Long may he reign!'

Even those who could not understand Persian could see what was happening from the ex-Wazier's having seated himself on the throne. The natives all paid homage by prostrating themselves, while Laker again ordered his officers and men to present arms, and give three cheers.

Thankful to have got through the ceremony, Roger had a brief talk with Laker, then hurried back to Clarissa. McCloud and his squad were still on guard outside the pavilion. Having told the men that he would see to it that they were specially rewarded for their yeoman services, he thanked them and told them to rejoin their troops; then he said to the Cornet:

'For the part you played I'll see to it that you are promoted to Lieutenant, even if I have to buy the rank for you. But first, there is one other important service you can render me. I must secure a British doctor for Mrs. Brook, with a minimum of delay. A number of our men have wounds, too, so would fare better in the hands of a qualified man than those of the squadron's barber. There must be a surgeon with Colonel Gunston's force, and it can as yet be only one night's march through the mountains. I wish you to snatch a few hours' sleep, then set out after them and bring their surgeon back here with you.'

The stalwart young man shrugged. 'I slept all through yesterday afternoon, Sir, and had three hours last night; so I need no sleep as yet. I'll take two good men and set off at once.'

Roger did not seek to deter him, but twenty minutes later saw him, well mounted and provisioned, set off on his mission. After that he could only hang about the pavilion in miserable suspense.

It was not until late that night that Clarissa had a short interval of consciousness. At first, she believed the sight of Roger, seated beside her, to be a dream; but, once she was persuaded that it really was him, her joy was unbounded. Yet, as soon as she began to talk, she was seized with such a terrible paroxysm of coughing that he feared she would have a fit. The Begum hurried in, upbraided him and made her swallow some more of the potent black drug, which sent her off again into a coma.

Next morning, she had another period of lucidity, but Roger feared to question her in case by talking she brought on herself another attack; so, after they had exchanged whispered endearments, he kept her quiet by telling her about his two attempts to rescue her.

Late that afternoon, reeling in his saddle from weariness, Angus McCloud returned with Surgeon Pomfrett. After making a thorough examination of Clarissa, the Doctor pronounced her chances far from good. He declared that she was suffering from congestion of the lungs and, producing leeches from a bottle, set the horrid creatures on her back. The treatment appeared to ease her for a time, but the following morning she was weaker.

It was on that day, the Thursday, that Roger was informed that Gunston's force was approaching the city. At the time Clarissa was sleeping; so Roger left her and held a short conference with the new Rajah.

During the past half-century, there had been numerous instances of revolutions in the native states, in which the Company had played a part in deposing an ill-disposed Prince and substituting one whom they hoped would prove more co-operative. In every case, following Eastern custom, the new occupant of the throne had showered gifts upon all those who had helped to set him on it, and British officers and agents had come in for a handsome share in these gratuities. Rai-ul-daula had needed no prompting to follow the practice.

He had not only paid in Indian coin the equivalent of the thousand guineas promised by Roger to the men of the squadron, but doubled that sum. Each of the officers had received a small sack of gold, bales of silk and beautifully chased weapons. Philip Laker was better off by a year's pay, two splendid horses, a jewelled sword, and numerous rich garments. Roger had received special treatment. The cross-eyed Rajah had taken him to the treasury, spread out his hands, and said, 'All this I owe to you. Take of it what you will, my friend, and be welcome.'

Roger had politely demurred; but Rai-ul-daula had thrust upon him rings, strings of pearls and uncut stones that he knew must be worth several thousand pounds. He knew too, that, if Gunston's force entered the city, the new Rajah would feel obliged to make him and his officers considerable presents, and he saw no reason at all why they should share in these benefits.

As a result of Roger's talk with Rai-ul-daula, an order was given for the city's gates to be closed, and he went up to the roof of one of the towers that flanked the main gateway.

Gunston, accompanied by a small staff, was riding at the head of his force. When he had come to within fifty yards of the gate, he looked up, saw Roger, and shouted, with a frown:

'What's the meaning of this, Brook? Why are the gates closed against us?'

'Because your presence here is no longer necessary,' Roger shouted back.

'What the devil d'you mean?' Gunston cried, angrily. 'I'll give it you that capturing the place with only a squadron was a fine piece of work. But you can't hold a city this size permanently with two hundred men.'

'I'll not have to,' Roger told him. 'I had Jawahir-ul-daula hanged on Monday, and made my good friend, Rai-ul-daula, Rajah in his place.'

'So I heard. But though you think him your friend, you can't rely on these fellows.'

Roger leaned over the parapet and gave full vent to his bitter feelings. 'I did better by relying on him than on yourself. Had I left matters to you, Clarissa would have been dead before I got here. You and your men played no part in taking Bahna, and shall derive no benefit from it. Did I let you in, I know well enough what would happen. Your sepoys would treat the place like a captured city. They'd start to loot it and rape the women. I couldn't stop them and you would not try. The new Rajah is my friend and I mean to protect his people. It is I who now command four thousand troops, and you eight hundred. Should you attempt to force this gate, I'll lead them out against you. Now get back to your camp at Bamanghati and skulk there in it as long as you like.'

Turning away, he left Gunston purple with rage and mortification, and with no alternative other than beating a shamefaced retreat. But this triumph over his old enemy gave him no pleasure. He would a thousand times rather that Gunston had placed him eternally in his debt by using, as an excuse to ignore Sir John Shore's orders, the fact that an English woman had been kidnapped; for Clarissa might have been rescued while still in full health had he marched his force on Bahna when first implored to do so.

As it was, her state continued to cause Roger such terrible anxiety that he hardly left the pavilion, from fear that at any moment one of her frightful paroxysms of coughing might end in a fatal convulsion. Being so constantly at her bedside enabled him to exchange a sentence or two with her at times when she became conscious; while, at others, he was perforce harrowed by her ravings during periods of delirium. It was largely from those ravings, confirmed by occasional sentences whispered when she was lucid, that he learned what had happened to her.

It was the news brought in by Jawahir-ul-daula's scouts on the previous Saturday, that Gunston's force was approaching through the mountains, that had evidently caused Malderini to act without waiting for any particular phase of the moon. That night he had had Clarissa and himself carried in a palanquin some two or three miles outside the city, and into a jungle where they had halted at a ruined temple.

Clarissa had only the vaguest impression of the place, as the starlight did not penetrate there and it was lit only by the flickering torches carried by some of Malderini's native servants. Moreover, Roger gathered, ever since the Venetian had kidnapped her he had kept her in a dreamlike state; so that although she was subconsciously unhappy, and occasionally feebly rebellious, she was neither fully aware of what had happened to her, nor of her surroundings. She knew only that the temple was small, partially ruined and overgrown with creepers; and that she had been taken down a broken flight of steps to its crypt.

At the far end of the crypt there sat, cross-legged, a hideous, many-limbed idol, that Roger guessed must have been one of the evil god Siva—the Destroyer—and, below it, a long flat stone altar slab. Down there it was reeking with damp and hideously cold, but Malderini had ordered her to strip. Being completely dominated by his will, she had obeyed.

He had made her stretch herself out flat on her back on the stone, then proceeded with his evil rites, muttering incantations while anointing various parts of her body with an unguent that stank abominably. How long she had lain there naked, she had no idea; only a memory of her teeth chattering violently as the creeping cold paralysed her limbs.

She thought that, for a time, she had fallen into a coma, but had been roused from it by a faint wailing, and the feel of something warm upon her chest. Suddenly, it had penetrated her bemused mind that the thing Malderini had laid upon her was a very young baby. She had attempted to sit up, but his will held her down as firmly as if she had been bound by a dozen cords. He had held the infant's head between her breasts, then cut its throat. Streams of warm blood had run down to her armpits and across the lower part of her neck. Next moment she had felt Malderini's mouth against her flesh as he guzzled up the blood. Then she had fainted.

She remembered nothing more until she had come round, still shivering, as she was being put to bed on her divan in the harem. Malderini had been standing over her, his terrible eyes lit with excited triumph; and he had said to her:

'I have no more use for you, and release you now for the little time you have to live. You have served my purpose. I am confident that the sacrifice was accepted and that I shall become Doge of Venice.'

Utterly exhausted, she had fallen asleep. On waking on the Sunday morning, her mind was clear and, for the first time, she was fully conscious of all that had happened to her since she had been abducted. But her chest pained her, she had begun to cough and, by the afternoon, she was in a fever.

Roger alternately shuddered and cursed silently as he gradually built up this terrible picture. If he could have got at Malderini during those days and nights, he would have torn him limb from limb with his bare hands. Yet, above all, he was tortured by the thought that he might lose Clarissa, and even went the length of making a vow that he would forgo his vengeance if only the God he had long neglected would permit her to recover.

Surgeon Pomfrett and the Begum did everything they could but, by Friday, fever and the awful racking cough had worn Clarissa to a shadow of her former self. Early on Saturday morning she seemed to rally a little, and began to talk with greater ease than she had at any time during her illness. Roger tried to stop her but, with a weak gesture, she waved his remonstrance aside, and said:

'I must talk now, darling. It's my last chance. I'm going to die.'

'No, no!' his cry was agonized. 'You're not. Another day or two and you'll be round the corner.'

She shook her head. 'I am; and you must not grieve for me. Oh, Roger, I've been so fortunate.'

'Fortunate!' he moaned. 'How can you say . . .'

'I have,' her words came low, but clear. 'I've had a wonderful life. Most women have to marry someone they don't like either for position, or just to get a home. Only later—if they're lucky—do they meet a man they really love. I've never had to let myself be loved by anyone but you. From the time I could think of love, you were my heart's desire and—and you became mine.'

After a little pause she went on. 'No woman ever knew greater happiness. The Isle of Spices. It was paradise on earth. Then our long voyage to Calcutta . . . and there . . . the joy of living as your wife. Five . . . five months, darling. Five months of heaven.'

She closed her blue eyes and fell silent for several minutes. Then she spoke again. 'But it couldn't have lasted. Such things never do. I always knew it couldn't. I made up my mind that . . . that sooner or later I'd have to . . . to lose you to some other woman.'

'No, no, Clarissa!' he protested, miserably. 'You're wrong in that. Since we set out from England, I've never given a thought to any woman but yourself.'

'I know,' she murmured. 'That's what's so lovely. You've been all mine. Now I'll never have to face the agony of watching you change. You were my paladin from the beginning. You are my paladin still. You faced death twice to come here for me. What other woman in the world has had her lover take a city for her with . . . with the aid of only a few score men?'

Again she paused, then suddenly she half sat up and cried: 'I die happy! Oh, Roger, be happy for me, and happy too. Bless you . . . bless you for your love.'

She choked, fell back, twisted violently, then went still.

He bowed his head on her shoulder and wept.

CHAPTER TWENTY-ONE

The Wrong Side of the Fence

ROGER was twenty-eight. During the past thirteen years he had loved half a dozen women. Had their lovely faces been represented in an arch, Georgina's would have formed its keystone. With her, he shared an affinity that went to the depths of both their beings; in her single person, she combined for him the rôles of sister, mistress, mother and friend, filling each part according to his need, as he, in turn, played that of brother, lover, father and friend to her. It was she who had made a man of him while still a boy, and he had no doubt that his last thought would be of her when his time came to die.

Then all through his later 'teens, he had suffered the agonies that only the young can feel when stricken with a hopeless passion; for it had never seemed remotely possible that Athénais de Rochambeau could be his. Yet, years later, after she had married, had children, and was in peril of the guillotine, they had, for a few brief months, known great happiness.

To his wife, Natalia Andreovna, he had been attracted by a brief violent passion. She had made no secret of her habitual immorality, and had delighted to gratify her desires with all the abandon of her fierce Russian nature. But he had soon learnt that she was vicious, treacherous and incapable of any decent emotion. The cynical old Empress Catherine had forced him to marry her as the alternative to losing his life; and at her death he had felt only relief.

His affaire with the dark-browed Isabella d'Aranda had begun only as a flirtation and grown with propinquity, during their long journey together through France and Italy. Her education and intelligence had been much superior to those of most women, so added greatly to the attraction of her typically Spanish beauty. But she was by nature a prude, and it was cumulative frustration, more than anything else, which had led to his becoming obsessed with desire for her. In the end, as in the case of Athénais, it was after she was married that she had given him, as a wife, what she had refused him as a maid.

For his second wife, Amanda, he had never been subject to any desperate craving. It had amused him to take her away from George Gunston and, after a while, he had become slightly bewitched by her delightful vagueness, happy, generous disposition and merry laughter. It was Georgina who had insisted that the time had come for him to settle down and that Amanda would make the perfect wife for him. He had allowed himself to be persuaded, and never regretted it. They had, at times, had tiffs, and one serious breach, but their marriage had been a much happier one than most. There had grown up between them that serene companionship, and very deep affection, which are the better parts of love, and it had taken him a long time to get over her loss.

But Clarissa had given him something that none of the others could. He had first met her at his marriage to Amanda. She had then been an awkward, gawky, schoolroom miss. He had watched her grow up into a slim-limbed young goddess; then, under the magic of his own caresses, she had flowered into a divinely beautiful woman. She had thought with love of no man before she met him; cared for no other, even for a brief period, of the many who had pursued her while he was still married to Amanda; faced the hardships of a stowaway in the hope of becoming his mistress, been undaunted by his refusals and even entered on a distasteful mockery of a marriage that she might bind him to his promise to become her lover afterwards. She had given her whole life to her love for him.

She had kept secret her forebodings that, in time, she was certain to lose him to another woman, and such a thought had never crossed his mind. On the contrary, it had been full of plans for their future. He had been waiting only for the Court case with Winters over the marriage settlement to be decided before taking her back to England. The money from that, with which she had insisted on dowering him, together with his own now comfortable fortune, would have made them richer than many people who had quite large estates. He had travelled enough to last him a lifetime, so had meant to settle down in earnest. Instead of appearing to little Susan as an occasional visitor, who always brought presents, he could have become a real father to her. And Clarissa had been determined to give him a son. He would have liked a son. A son of theirs could not have been other than strong-limbed, handsome, blue-eyed, gay and courageous. He had already begun to make half-formed mental pictures of the boy. But now, although barely twenty, the warm loveliness that was to have formed the beating heart round which this new life of contentment was to centre lay cold, rigid, dead.

The Begum, Angus McCloud, Rai-ul-daula, Philip Laker and his officers, all did their utmost to comfort him. But after a few hours he asked them to spare him further marks of their sympathy, and it became clear that his mind was set on one thought—to pursue and be revenged upon Malderini.

As a first move, late that afternoon, he discussed the matter with Rai-ul-daula and Philip Laker. The former told him that the Venetian had already extracted his wife's inheritance from Jawahir-ul-daula, so his purpose in coming to India had been fulfilled. Therefore, as he had disclosed to Clarissa his ambition to become Doge of Venice, it was a hundred to one that he was on his way back there.

He would certainly not have gone down to Calcutta, as the risk of being caught and brought to book there, before he could get a ship, would have been far too great. Besides, as Rai-ul-daula pointed out, it was only the people who lived on the borders of the great ocean—English, Portuguese, Dutch and French—who habitually used the long sea route to India. Arab, Greek, Levantine, Venetian and Genoese merchants had for centuries accomplished a great part of the journey overland, always entering India by her western ports, or by way of Persia. In some parts, such travellers had to risk attack by brigands; but, in the main, they could count on the protection of the native Princes, and were welcomed at their courts. It was known that Malderini had arrived at Bahna from the interior, and there could be little doubt that he was now on his way back through it.

Roger felt that there should be no great difficulty in tracing the Venetian and that, though he had a week's start, by hard riding there would be a good chance of catching him up about a fortnight hence. Laker promptly offered a troop of his hussars to participate in this man-hunt; but the cross-eyed Rajah shook his head.

He said that to rely on horses at all would be a great mistake, as the stages between towns with good inns were often more than one day's journey, and to be benighted on horseback meant having nowhere to sleep; whereas a palanquin served also as a bedroom. Moreover, in many places it was impossible to get remounts, but relays of ryots could be hired at every village to carry palanquins at a trot to the next; so, if one was prepared to put up with the jolting by night as well as by day, one could cover great distances each twenty-four hours. He added that, to make the most of his start and get well clear of the British, Malderini would probably have travelled at top speed like that for the first few days; so that even on horse-back, without remounts, it would now prove impossible to catch up with him.

Much disappointed, Roger had to resign himself to the thought of a long chase across India and perhaps right back to Europe; so he refused Laker's offer of a troop, but gladly accepted Rai-ul-daula's offer to take Mahmud Ali as his guide. There remained only the question of money for the journey, and Roger asked the Rajah if he would change some of his bills on London for gold. The last thing he had meant to do was to invite a further gift, but Rai-ul-daula said at once that he should have all the gold he needed, and that, if he was so lacking in delicacy as to produce paper in payment, it should be burnt before his eyes.

That Saturday night he wrote a long letter to Hickey, telling him of all that had happened and stating that he did not intend to return to Calcutta. He had always been averse to trading on Clarissa's marriage to extract money from Winters, but, as that unpleasant young man had accused Clarissa and himself of being a pair of incestuous crooks, he felt that, having come into a fortune, Winters should at least be made to disgorge a moderate sum, somewhat larger than the contemplated costs of the case. Accordingly he made over his rights to Hickey, suggesting that he should settle the matter out of court while Winters was still unaware that neither Clarissa nor himself would now appear at the hearing. Winters, he felt sure, would jump at the chance of settling for a few thousand pounds, a portion of which could be used to pay off the servants and other liabilities of the Brook household, while the greater part would both cover legal expenses and provide a handsome acknowledgment to Hickey of his many friendly services.

This missive Roger sent off by fast messenger the following day. Another, his report to Sir John Shore, he held over to be taken by the officer whose troop was to escort the belated payment of the twelve lakhs of rupees down to Calcutta. In it he informed the Governor that urgent personal affairs necessitated his return to Europe; so he was handing over his responsibilities as the Company's agent to Captain Philip Laker.

Having despatched his letter to Hickey, Roger went to make his last farewells to Clarissa, as her funeral was to take place that morning. Her bandaged face was peaceful, and although now very thin, the ravages of the disease had passed from it. After kneeling by her silently for a while, he left the pavilion. Outside, in its garden, he found the Begum waiting for him; holding out a large handsome casket, she said:

'I was told you were here; so I came to give you this. It is your lady's hair. She wished you to have it.'

Thanking the Begum gravely, Roger took the casket and opened it. Inside, there was a thick two-foot-long coil of pale gold tresses, still shimmering with life. He guessed that Clarissa had intended only a lock to be cut off and given him to put in a locket, or wear in a mourning ring, as was the fashion of the times; but, evidently, she had been misunderstood, so they had shaved her head. Many Indians wore beautifully plaited, gold-adorned, bracelets of human hair, and that gave him an idea.

'I should like,' he said, 'to wear it. Could Your Highness have it made up into a rope for me?'

She looked a little surprised, but nodded. 'If you wish. But there is a lot of it. Unless it is to be very thick, such a rope would be nearly as long as you are tall.'

'That is as I would like it. I leave tomorrow morning, though. Could it be done by then?'

'Yes; I will summon my jewellers at once, and set them to work on it.'

Having handed her back the casket and thanked her, he walked through the palace to Laker's quarters to settle final arrangements about the funeral. He had naturally intended to have Clarissa buried in the normal way, but that could be done only outside the city, and Surgeon Pomfrett had persuaded him against it on the grounds that the grave would almost certainly be violated by robbers hoping to find jewels; so he had agreed that, like those of a Hindu lady of high caste, Clarissa's remains should be burnt.

With Laker, he went out to inspect the funeral pyre that had been built in one of the courtyards, and soon afterwards the squadron began to form up in it. All the nobles of the court collected there; then Rai-ul-daula arrived in stately procession with his guards. To the beating of muffled drums, Clarissa's body, draped in gorgeous silks, was borne into the court on a litter carried by sixteen bearers and placed reverently on the incense-scattered pyre. Surgeon Pomfrett read the Church of England service for the burial of the dead, the fire was lit, and so, with all the pomp appropriate to a Princess, the loveliness that had been Clarissa Marsham ascended in perfumed smoke towards the eternal gods.

That night her hair was brought to Roger, now as a plaited cord, half an inch thick and secured at its ends in jewelled tassels. Undoing his cravat, he put it loosely twice round his neck, then tucked the ends in under his shirt, so that the whole of it was next to his skin.

Next morning he went to take leave of the Begum, then of his good friends, Rai-ul-daula, Philip Laker and Angus McCloud. Then the other officers of the squadron, and many of the Rajah's people assembled to see him off. On March 25th he had been brought into Bahna as a prisoner; now, on April 12th, he left it with every mark of honour that its ruler could pay him, but with a heart of lead.

Rai-ul-daula had provided him with two palanquins; in one he was to travel with Mahmud Ali, the other was to carry a cook, paraphernalia for camping and stores. At night he would sleep in one and the two natives in the other. As there was virtually no hope of catching Malderini in the early stages of the journey, he had decided not to martyr himself by nightly joltings but to camp each evening; and this made it possible to trail two chargers on long leads behind the rear palanquin, so that he and Mahmud Ali could break the monotony of the daily trek by riding part of the time.

The best road led south-westward through Singhbhum to Saranda and Jharsuguda. Enquiries in the villages through which they passed confirmed that Malderini had taken that way and, as Rai-ul-daula had supposed, was halting only to purchase food and have meals cooked; so, in this first stage, he had gained a further three days on them. But that did not now unduly trouble Roger as, in the long journey back to Europe, his enemy might meet with many unavoidable delays which would bring them up with him.

From Jharsuguda the main artery for traffic ran due west through the heart of the Maratha country to the city of Raipur, then on to Nagpur, the great metropolis of central India. Day after day the palanquins lumbered on, sometimes through dense jungle and at others through low pastures along the banks of rivers. Frequently, among the bearers who trotted them from village to village, there were men who had helped carry Malderini's palanquins, and after reaching Raipur they learned that he had dropped to a slower pace, halting to sleep at nights; but by then he was a fortnight ahead of them.

On most nights they camped beside a river, so that after the long day Roger could refresh himself with a dip; but he soon decided to give up shaving. Now and then, Mahmud Ali shot a buck; but generally they did not dare to venture far from their camp for fear of wild animals, and sometimes they had to build a ring of fires as protection against them.

Their pace varied greatly. There were days when over flat country they covered as much as forty miles between dawn and dusk, but, on others, hills and rough going slowed them down to fifteen, and at times they lost the greater part of a day owing to the armed retainers of local potentates insisting on taking them before their masters. Sometimes they were received with veiled hostility, and forced to pay a tribute before being allowed to proceed; at others, they were treated with great politeness and, to avoid giving offence, Roger had to allow himself to be entertained for the night. None of these petty Princes could understand his anxiety to push on, and it was only by the exercise of great tact that he could resume his journey after a break of anything from twelve to eighteen hours.

In no way could he have better seen the teeming life of India and the splendid evidence of its ancient civilization. Behind the walls of each city narrow streets seethed with jostling multitudes. Richly curtained palanquins borne by slaves lumbered their way through crowds of hucksters, beggars, shouting naked children, and soberly robed women carrying water jars on their heads. At every street corner there was a juggler, holy man, snake charmer or brothel tout. In the villages the evidences of poverty were shocking to behold. Goats and cattle shared the flimsy habitations, and rickety scrofulous youngsters fought over pieces of water-melon. By contrast, every twenty miles or so, they came upon temples carved with superb artistry and served by dignified, shaven priests, or fairy-like palaces with fountains playing in their courts, carefully tended gardens, and domes and turrets that stood out as though carved from ivory against the azure sky.

It was after leaving Nagpur that they lost track of Malderini, but that did not greatly worry Roger, as it could now hardly be doubted that the Venetian was heading for a western port on his way back to Venice; so they pushed on through the great state of Badndara to Badnera, and thence to another great city, Malkapur.

There, Roger decided to sell the palanquins and horses and take to the great water highway formed by the rivers Sonala and Tapti, which flowed right down to the Indian Ocean. The transfer to a big gaily painted barge with sixteen rowers proved advantageous in more ways than one. Overland they had averaged only a little more than twenty miles a day, whereas by water they were doing nearer thirty. At nights Roger had the barge moored well out from the river banks, which kept them much freer from the myriads of flies, mosquitoes and other pests that had plagued them unmercifully during the past seven weeks. The heat, too, with the advance of summer had become almost unbearable, and on the water he felt it slightly less. All the same, it was with heartfelt relief that he breathed in the sea breeze at Surat when they arrived there on May 26th.

Having financed the return to Bahna of the invaluable Mahmud Ali and his cook, and made them both handsome presents, Roger went in search of a ship. His enquiries led him to an Arab vessel that was loading for Berbera and due to sail in three days' time. He made an arrangement with her captain for himself and a servant. In the latter capacity he engaged, on the recommendation of a banker with whom he had changed money, a merry-looking rascal named Hassan Abu ben Oman.

It was, too, on the banker's advice that he decided to make himself less conspicuous on the next stages of his journey by wearing Arab garments. The Sheiks of the Red Sea lands, and the Turkish government in Egypt, were not openly hostile to Europeans, but in strictly Mohammedan countries there was always a risk that some fanatical mullah might raise a mob against an obvious Christian; so the change was a sound precaution. His ten months in the tropics had made him very bronzed and, during the past seven weeks, he had grown a good beard so, when he had dyed it black and put on robes and turban, he was able to pass easily as a fair-skinned Arab.

While in Zanzibar he had picked up a smattering of Arabic, and as soon as they sailed he began to practise speaking it regularly with his new servant. From Surat they had a most fortunate passage and docked at Berbera in the Gulf of Aden on June 12th.

There he was held up for only two days before Hassan Abu found for them another ship which was about to sail up the Red Sea for Suez; but, in this part of Roger's journey, luck was against him. The vessel was not only dirty and uncomfortable, but proved much slower than the one in which he had spent fourteen days between Surat and Berbera. Worse still, four days north of the straits of Bab-el-Mandeb she became becalmed for a whole week.

The heat was intolerable. It had been bad enough during the middle of the day when crossing central India but, hot as that had been, it was no more than a gentle warmth compared to this. The sails hung slack, the sun blazed down, thinning the stagnant air into a degree at which it lacked all reviving properties when breathed in and, instead, felt like a draught of molten copper. The deck was so hot that even the hardened feet of the Arab sailors would have blistered had they crossed it, and the only moving things in the vessel for hours on end were the hordes of flies, which enjoyed a happy immunity because their victims were too exhausted by the heat to drive them off.

At last a light breeze enabled the ship to make headway again, but their progress continued to be slow, and the heat so sweltering, that Roger reckoned he must have lost a stone in weight during the best part of the month it took him to journey up the Red Sea.

After a night in Suez, Hassan Abu secured camels for them and they joined the daily caravan that was about to set out for Cairo. Again, it proved a slow and uncomfortable method of travelling, so, after an hour or so, Roger suggested to Hassan that they should let their ungainly beasts trot and press on alone. But the young Arab would not hear of it, insisting that, if they left the protection provided by the caravan, desert robbers would certainly capture and hold them to ransom, if not kill them. In consequence, the journey took them three gruelling days and it was not until July 10th that they reached Cairo.

On arriving in that fabulous city, Roger was torn between the desire to remain there a while, so that he could see some of its marvels, and the urge to settle his account with Malderini. It was now over three months since Clarissa had died, so his mind was no longer numb with the ache of losing her; but he still wore the rope of her hair round his neck and had vowed not to take it off until he had killed the fiend who, by his abominable rites, had brought about her death.

The question was decided for him by a most unpleasant bout of stomach upset that laid him out entirely for twenty-four hours. After it he was so exhausted that he felt it would be foolish not to allow himself a few days to recover. During them, by carefully observing and following the behaviour of the Mohammedans, he was able to mingle unsuspected with the crowds of worshippers in several of the great mosques and so see their beautiful interiors. He also made an excursion out to the Pyramids and another down the Nile to Memphis, the ancient capital of the Pharaohs.

As the Delta was highly populated, there was little fear of two travellers being attacked by robbers while riding through it; and, having had more than enough of the discomfort of travelling by camel, Roger bought two horses on which, on the 16th, they set out for Alexandria. Two nights later they reached that splendid city by the sea, and next morning, having at last exhausted the gold that Rai-ul-daula had pressed upon him, he went to a Greek banker named Sarodopulous to change one of his bills on London.

A clerk took the bill into an inner office and the banker himself came out holding it. He was a handsome middle-aged man, with a greying beard. Giving Roger a suspicious glance he asked him how it had come into his possession.

'It was issued to me by Messrs. Hoare's bank in London against my own account,' Roger replied. Then, knowing that most educated Greeks were multi-lingual, he added in English, 'I may not look it at the moment, but I am an Englishman.'

'Forgive me, Sir,' Sarodopulous bowed, 'but until you spoke I would not have known it. And it is unusual for Arabs to present bills drawn on London. I thought perhaps . . .'

'No,' Roger smiled, 'it's not stolen. I am wearing these clothes only because I have travelled up from Berbera. Now that I am once more in a cosmopolitan city, I must get myself something more in keeping with my nationality.'

'Perhaps I can be of service to you?' offered the Greek.

Roger thanked him and went on to compliment the banker on the exceptionally fluent way in which he spoke English.

'For that there is a simple explanation,' Sarodopulous showed two rows of fine white teeth in a quick laugh. 'My wife is English.' Then, after a moment's hesitation, he added, 'There is nothing she enjoys more than conversing with her countrymen, and I should be honoured if you would care to dine with us.'

Having gladly accepted, that afternoon Roger presented himself at a large white villa, set among palm trees and having a fine view over the lovely bay. Mrs. Emily Sarodopulous proved to be a woman of about forty who evidently had been very good-looking, but she was now enormously fat. Judging by the richness of the dinner she provided, and the way she tucked into it herself, the reason for her bulk was not far to seek; but she had retained an active mind and a passionate attachment to the country of her birth.

Roger soon learned that she was a Suffolk woman, and the daughter of a sea-captain. Some twenty years earlier her father had taken her with him on a voyage and their ship had been wrecked off the coast of Libya. Sarodopulous's firm had been the agents for the ship's owners and, while taking care of her survivors, the young Alexandrian Greek had fallen in love with the pretty English castaway. Their attitude to one another showed that neither had ever regretted it.

As Roger was ten months behind with events in Europe, he naturally plied his host and hostess with many eager questions; and, owing to Sarodopulous's banking connections all over the Mediterranean, he could not have found a better man in Alexandria to bring him up to date.

In October the Archduke Charles had severely defeated the French armies on the Rhine, and this had enabled him to send strong reinforcements down to Italy in the hope of relieving General Würmser, who was besieged in Mantua by General Buonaparte. But the new Austrian Commander-in-Chief, General Alvintzy, had not proved equal to the task.

Early in November Buonaparte, by a series of swift unexpected moves, had tempted Alvintzy into giving battle in an unfavourable position. Würmser, in a sortie from Mantua, and General Davidovich, with a third Austrian army had both attempted to come to the assistance of their Commander-in-Chief, but the youthful Corsican had outgeneralled all three old men. There had been three days of desperate fighting at the bridge and across the dykes at Arcola, resulting in a great French victory.

In the depths of winter, Alvintzy had made another bid to relieve Mantua by a strong feint across the lower Adige and attacking with his main force farther north-west at Rivoli. This led to complete disaster for the Austrians. Having utterly shattered their main army on January 13th, Buonaparte did a lightning swing which compelled the surrender of the lesser. On February 2nd, Würmser surrendered Mantua with a further 18,000 men, 315 cannon and an immense quantity of munitions.

Meanwhile, stung into open hostility by the outrageous demands of France's atheist Government, the Pope had sent his army marching northwards. Having dealt with the Austrians, Buonaparte turned upon it. At the sight of the French bayonets, the Papal forces fled. On February 19th, His Holiness had been forced to buy peace by the payment of a heavy indemnity and the giving up of many of his finest art treasures.

During these months, too, the French agents had been looting all the great cities of Italy of pictures, statues, manuscripts and plate, and sending hundreds of wagonloads of them back to Paris; so that after the surrender of the Pope, Buonaparte had been able to write to the Directory that his victories would yield to France 'almost every fine thing in Italy, except a few objects at Turin and Naples'.

After Alvintzy's defeat at Rivoli, the Archduke Charles had taken over from him, but even his ability and prestige could not restore Austria's fortunes. Hoche's final pacification of La Vendée the preceding autumn had enabled large reinforcements to be sent to Buonaparte, so he now commanded an army of 70,000 men, led by many of the brilliant soldiers who were to be his future Marshals—among them Berthier, Masséna, Augereau, Sérurier, Lannes, Marmont and Bernadotte. With the confidence imbued by the many victories in which they had participated under their young commander, they swept irresistibly forward, driving the Austrians before them out of the Venetian lands and right round the head of the Adriatic.

By the end of March, they had penetrated both the Tyrol and Carinthia. On the 30th of that month, Buonaparte drove the Archduke out of Klagenfurt and established his headquarters there, while his spearheads were advancing through Austria. By April 7th he had pushed on to Judenburg, barely a hundred miles from Vienna.

But by then his army was almost as exhausted as that of the Archduke's; so they agreed to a week's truce. Had the French armies on the Rhine been able to play their part in Buonaparte's great plan, and join him in the Tyrol, there could be no doubt that he would have dictated peace in the Austrian capital; but they had failed him lamentably. Rather than risk defeat at the very end of his brilliant campaign, without deigning to consult his nominal masters in Paris, he had on April 18th signed peace preliminaries with Austria at Leoben.

When the Greek had concluded his account of Buonaparte's victories,

Roger asked if negotiations were in progress for a general peace; and on learning that they were not, he said glumly, 'Hard pressed as Austria was, one would have expected the Emperor to make some effort towards that end before abandoning the alliance. We could long since have made peace had we not stuck out for the return to him of his Belgian lands; and now we're left to fight the French on our own.'

'The Austrians excuse themselves by maintaining that the British abandoned them. No doubt you will not have heard it; but the Fleet was withdrawn from the Mediterranean last November.'

'Hell's bells!' Roger exclaimed in dismay. 'Then things are come to a pretty pass. What caused this pusillanimous decision?'

'We count Admiral Hotham mainly to blame,' Mrs. Sarodopulous told him. 'He had numerous chances to smash the French while they were still weak, but failed to take them. Then the entry of Spain into the war gave our enemies a big superiority in ships, if not in their fighting power. Admiral Jervis superseded Hotham, and might have retrieved the situation, but Admiral Mann, who commanded the supporting squadron, and was to join him off Corsica, arrived there without stores, so had to return to Gibraltar. There he lost his nerve, and was chased home by the Spaniards. Jervis was by then so heavily outnumbered that he had no option but to take his fleet out into the Atlantic.'

'At least, my dear,' put in her husband, 'we can cheer Mr. Brook a little by telling him of Admiral Jervis's splendid victory over the Spaniards off Cape St. Vincent, last February. With fifteen ships, he defeated twenty-five Spaniards so severely that the Spanish fleet will not dare another encounter for a long time yet. I'm told he's been made Earl St. Vincent for it, though half the glory should to to his second in command, little Commodore Nelson, for having boldly left station at a critical moment of the battle and broken right through the Spanish line.'

'Thank God for that,' Roger sighed. 'Such a crippling blow to the Spanish Fleet makes the invasion of England somewhat less likely.'

'I'd not be sure of that,' the Greek replied soberly. 'There is great discontent in Ireland, and last December the French attempted an invasion of that country, counting upon being well received there, and hoping to make it a base for an attack on England. A fleet of forty-five vessels was despatched from Brest under Admiral Morad de Galles, with General Hoche in command of the troops they carried. They dodged Lord Bridport's fleet and got clear away into the Atlantic. But God intervened. Only some half of the French ships reached Bantry Bay; the rest, and among them that carrying Hoche, the Irish leader Wolf Tone, the money and the plans, were dispersed by a great storm. Many were wrecked; the rest crept back into Brest during January.'

Roger nodded. 'That was truly a merciful deliverance. What a pity though that, with so many troops on board, our Channel Fleet failed to catch them.'

Mrs. Sarodopulous gave him a troubled glance. 'All has been far from well with the Channel Fleet. In April, on returning to Spithead, it mutinied.'

'At that I am not altogether surprised,' Roger said after a moment, 'an outbreak of the kind has long threatened. My father is a Rear-Admiral, and he has often told me of the inhumanity with which the common sea-men are treated. When the pay of the troops was raised, theirs was not; should they become incapacitated from wounds, they are frequently turned off to starve; the food given them is often scarcely fit for animals; many Captains treat their men with great brutality; and such major punishments as a flogging round the fleet are little less than murder. Their grievances are many and well founded. Yet, with Britain's fortunes at so low an ebb, this could hardly have happened at a worse time.'

'On both counts you are right,' agreed the Greek. 'And, alas, from my latest intelligence, things have become worse instead of better. In May, the mutiny spread to the Nore and some crews there, having put their officers ashore, even went to the length of running up the red flag. Yet more alarming still is Britain's financial state. Her shipments of gold in recent years to her allies on the Continent have so impoverished her that last February there were fears for the solvency of the Bank of England. For some days, Mr. Pitt was faced with the worst financial crisis London has known for many years. He has temporarily restored the situation by the issue of a Patriotic Loan, to which there was a fine response, but all over Europe the confidence of bankers in Britain's stability has been badly shaken.'

After listening to all this news of defeat and disaster, Roger felt that, short of collapse, he could not have returned to find his country in a worse mess. Shying away from this depressing thought, when they had left the dining-room and settled themselves on a terrace to enjoy the sea-breeze after the long hot day, he asked:

'What part, if any, has the Serene Republic played in these events?'

Sarodopulous shrugged. 'None. Who could have expected otherwise? The Venetians of old were a great and proud people, but for a century past they have been unworthy of their ancestors. Too much money from great estates on the mainland which they have long neglected, gambling, women, music, the playhouse, dabbling with the occult; all these have drained away their courage, patriotism and pride. At General Buonaparte's bidding the *Serenissima* handed over all its strong places and disbanded its famous Slavonian levies. But they have since paid the price for their poltroonery.'

'The fools might have known from Buonaparte's treatment of the people of Milan that licking his boots would not save them.' Roger gave a short, hard laugh. 'Can one imagine that Corsican brigand refraining from despoiling so fabulously rich a city once it had opened its gates to him? I'll wager there is hardly a Titian, Tintoretto or Bellini left in it by now.'

'His hand fell on them far more heavily than that,' remarked Mrs. Sarodopulous quickly. 'He abolished the *Serenissima!*'

'What say you, Madame?' Roger stared at her in amazement. 'I'd not have thought that even he would go to such lengths. The Serene Republic has lasted a thousand years. It was as much a permanent feature of Europe as Portugal, the Netherlands or Sweden. Surely you cannot mean that, even subject to his will, it no longer has a government?'

'There is no longer a Doge; the Senate is no more. Instead, General Buonaparte has given the city a Municipality on the French lines, made up of criminals and atheists.'

'On what excuse did he do this terrible thing?'

'The people on the mainland were driven to desperation by pillaging and raping by his troops. On Easter Monday the men of Verona rose and massacred the French garrison. The rising was, of course, swiftly put down; but General Buonaparte charged the Senate with having inspired it. Rather than take up arms while they still had them, they agreed to his demand that the ancient State should commit suicide by voting themselves out of existence.'

'When was this?'

'In mid-May. Since then the city has been ruled by its Municipals, dancing to the tune of their French masters; and all the Venetian lands west of the Adriatic have been split up into Communes on the French model.'

'This suits me ill,' Roger said thoughtfully. 'I am on my way to Venice, and, now the French control the place, for me to enter it as an Englishman would be to invite arrest.'

'Why, then, not go there as an Arab?' Sarodopulous suggested.

Roger passed his hand over the beard that he had not yet had an opportunity to shave off. 'Perhaps; but no! I wish to avoid notice as much as possible. As an Arab in a European city I should be much too conspicuous.'

'Not in Venice,' countered the Greek. 'The Queen of the Adriatic has for so many centuries been the gateway into Europe from the East that its population is more mixed than that of any other city. As slaves, seamen, or traders, as many coloured men have found their way there as there are Europeans in Alexandria. If you took a cargo of some sort with you, and arrived as an Arab merchant, the port officials would not give you a second glance.'

'I am no merchant,' Roger smiled, 'and I would, at least, have to make a pretence of disposing of the goods I had brought. I fear my fumbling efforts to do so would soon arouse the suspicions of the Venetian merchants to whom I tried to sell them.'

Sarodopulous remained silent for a moment; then he said, 'I have it. You could go as a perfume seller. Such a cargo would take little space and Eastern perfumes always find a ready sale in Europe, so you might even make a handsome profit on your investment. You would stand no risk of dickering with Venetian merchants, either; for you could dispose of your wares by making a round of the palaces and selling them direct to ladies of fashion.'

Roger's eyes lit up. 'You've hit upon the very thing! I will adopt your idea and could not be more grateful for it.'

They then discussed possible ways for Roger to proceed on his journey, and Sarodopulous said that, rather than wait, perhaps a week or more, for a ship sailing to Brindisi or Naples, and thence travelling overland to Venice, he thought it would be quicker to take a local Greek trader across to Crete, where it should be easy to pick up a Venetian vessel homeward bound. On Roger's accepting this advice, the banker promised to make all arrangements, and his wife suggested that, until a trader could be found to take Roger to Crete, he might prefer to stay with them instead of at an inn. He at once expressed his delight at her kindness; so a servant was sent to fetch his few belongings and Hassan.

The next two days passed all too quickly, as for the past three months he had spoken hardly a word of English, and had suffered great loneliness from having no one to whom he could talk as an equal. To be able to do so again, freely, and in his own tongue, proved a wonderful tonic for him; so it was with real regret that on July 21st he parted from his kind host and hostess to go aboard a Greek trader.

She was quite a small ship, and one of several that plied regularly between Alexandria and Crete, carrying corn one way and olive oil the other. He was still wearing the costume of a respectable Arab and had with him a hundred pounds' worth of scent that Sarodopulous had got for him from the Alexandria *muski* at trade rates; but Hassan he had paid off with a suitable gift before leaving.

This stage of his journey proved ill-starred. On the first night out, they were caught in a violent storm which abated as suddenly as it had arisen, but, even so, the crossing took eight days instead of the usual four or five.

Crete had belonged to Venice for over four hundred years and, even after it had fallen to the Turks in 1669, the Venetians had been allowed to retain two fortified ports there to within living memory; so its people still had strong ties with the Serene Republic, which continued to carry most of the island's trade. In consequence, on arriving in Candia Roger had no difficulty in finding a captain, one Gulio Battista, who was sailing in a few days and would take him direct to Venice.

Battista was a fine-looking, bearded, middle-aged seaman, and Roger would have found him a most pleasant companion had he not been so depressed by the fate that had overtaken his country. From him, as the ship ploughed her way through the Ionian sea, Roger learned the full story of the fall of the *Serenissima*.

In Battista's opinion, the ancient oligarchy had, to a large extent, brought its troubles on itself. Although they ruled the greater part of north-east Italy and territories that extended right down the Dalmatian coast of the Adriatic, they had always refused the people of these lands any share in the government. Only nobles of the city itself, the names of whose families were inscribed in the Golden Book, could be elected to the Senate. Not unnaturally, both the nobility and the cities of the mainland had long resented this, and Buonaparte had used them as his cat's-paw.

Already, in the previous October, he had sponsored the creation of one new state, the Cispadane Republic—which had been formed from the Duchy of Modena together with the Papal territories of Bologna and Ferrara —and during the spring there had been talk of turning the Duchy of Milan into another Republic, also modelled on that of France. The western frontier of Venetia ran with the Milanese and a large area on the Venetian side was mainly populated by Lombards. These, having no reason for loyalty to the *Serenissima*, had promptly begun to agitate for inclusion with their fellow Lombards of the Milanese in the new Republic. In mid-March, incited by Buonaparte's agents, the inhabitants of Bergamo, Brescia and Salo had revolted and proclaimed themselves independent municipalities, upon which the French garrisons had prevented the Venetian authorities from suppressing these revolts, then driven them out.

The Senate had appealed to Buonaparte, who had hypocritically declared that it was not for him to interfere in the domestic affairs of a neutral, but if the Serene Republic would become the ally of France, he would then bring the revolted cities back to their duty. But, having fresh in mind the way in which he had dealt with the Milanese when they became his allies, the Senate had nervously declined his invitation.

To goad the *Serenissima* further, towards the end of the month a body of French cavalry entered the city of Crema by a trick, disarmed the garrison and declared the place a free municipality. This time, matters were taken out of the supine Senate's hands. By their rapacious exactions and brutal lawlessness, the French soldiery had already earned themselves the bitter hatred of the peasantry throughout all northern Italy. Those in the Crema territory rushed down from their mountains, attacked Buonaparte's troops and killed a number of them. This was just the sort of thing the unscrupulous Corsican had been angling for. It enabled him to pretend that his army was in danger from the whole country rising behind it. He dictated a violent diatribe against the Senate, in which he accused them of conspiring against him, and declared that all the Venetian provinces must be delivered from their tyranny; then he despatched his chief aide-de-camp, Junot, to read it to them.

On April 15th Junot had done so. On the 17th had come the rising in Verona. For three days the population of the city and its surrounding district massacred every Frenchman they could lay hands on, including the wounded in the hospital. Only those in the fortress survived, and they added to the carnage by turning its guns on the town.

On the 19th fuel was added to the flames by yet another incident, this time in Venice herself. It was an age-old law that no foreign armed vessel should be allowed to enter the harbour. A small French warship defied the ban and ignored an order to leave. The forts then opened fire, killing several of her crew.

Buonaparte now had all the ammunition he wanted. With a great show of righteous anger, he declared war on the Serene Republic. Rather than fight, the Senate humbly agreed to accept his terms. On May 4th, they handed over their three senior Inquisitors and the Commander of the Port to his Commissioners, and disarmed and sent back to Dalmatia their trusty Slavonian troops. In the meantime, the French *Chargé d'Affaires*, Villetard, had been intensely active in forming a party of so-called 'patriots' on the traditional revolutionary lines.

Ten days later, the final scenes of degradation took place. In the vain hope that Buonaparte might treat Venice better as a democracy than as an oligarchy, the Grand Council voted, by 512 against only 20, its own abolition, and the transfer of its authority to a Municipality selected by Villetard. The aged Doge, Manin, fell in a dead faint from shame as he took off his bonnet of office. This, his other insignia, and the Golden Book, were publicly burned. Trees of Liberty were set up in the Square of St. Mark, the Venetian fleet was handed over, and a ghastly pretence was made of welcoming the French troops into the city as the bringers of liberty.

Roger was deeply sensible of the terrible distress that these happenings must have caused Captain Battista, and many other Venetians like him, who would willingly have fought for their country; but it was inescapable that enervating luxury had rendered the Venetian nobility rotten to the core, and that this, coupled with cowardly inaction, or rather lack of a demand for it, on the part of the majority of the citizens, was responsible for the fall of the ancient Republic.

The voyage up the Adriatic proved a pleasant one, and on August 15th they entered the thirty-mile-long lagoon, with its many islands. For two hours, Roger enjoyed the spectacle of the beautiful city rising from the sea, with the lofty campanile and the domes of Sta Giorgio Maggiore, Sta Maria del Salute, and those of a score of other great churches, gradually coming nearer.

They docked at the Zattere allo Spirito Santo and, after Roger had paid the dues on his scents, Battista took him to an auberge in a narrow street just behind the church of that name, that catered for Eastern merchants. After arranging for his accommodation, they parted on most friendly terms, and Roger, pretending deafness so as to avoid talking with the land-lord and other lodgers at the place, took up his abode in a small, but clean, apartment on the second floor.

To reach Venice from Bahna had taken him four and a half months and, for the greater part of the six thousand miles between them, he had suffered loneliness and great discomfort. But, had he gone back to Calcutta, returned from there by ship to England, or even to Gibraltar, and then done the last stage through the western Mediterranean, it could well have taken him much longer; and, by the route he had followed, with its many hazards of delay by weather or waiting for ships to sail, there had always been the chance that he might catch up with Malderini.

Roger would not have been surprised if it turned out that he had by-passed his enemy and arrived first; but he thought that unlikely. In any case, Malderini had no reason to hide his return, and it would soon become widely known because he was a prominent citizen of Venice. That also meant, though, that it would be far from easy to kill him without arousing a big hue and cry, and, while Roger was determined to have his life, he had no intention of paying for it with his own, if that could possibly be avoided. He therefore decided that, whether or not Malderini had yet arrived, he would do well to spend his first few days in Venice familiarizing himself with the city.

During the long August evening and all the following day, on foot and by gondola, he explored the maze of canals crossed by scores of little bridges and a labyrinth of narrow streets, alleys and small squares that make Venice so unlike any other city. By night, while drinking coffee at a café in the crowded Piazza San Marco and listening to the band of a French Chasseur regiment, he delighted in the fairy-like beauty of the Byzantine Cathedral. Filling one end of the huge open space, its innumer-able coloured marble pillars, lit by the hundreds of lamps in the arcades along the other three sides, and its five cupolas standing out against the deep blue starlit sky, gave it the appearance of a painted back-drop on some gargantuan stage. By day, he admired the great square Palace of the Doges, the world-famous Rialto Bridge and the scores of stately palaces on the Grand Canal.

That afternoon, he learned by tactful enquiries that, on the fall of the *Serenissima*, the British Ambassador, Sir Richard Worsley, Bart., had demanded his papers and left Venice; but that the Consul, Mr. John Watson, had remained on as *Chargé d'Affaires*, and lived in the Calle del Sansovino, just behind the Dario Palace.

Next morning he went there in the guise of a perfume seller, supporting by a strap round his neck a box-like covered tray, holding a score of small square glass bottles, each containing a different scent. Although not large, like nearly all the houses in the better quarters of Venice that of the Consul had a handsome pillared doorway of carved stone, and the windows of its ground-floor rooms were protected by iron grilles, wrought by a craftsman. Roger pulled down the long iron bell-pull, and waited.

The door was opened by a footman in undress livery, who had the dark eyes and complexion of a typical Italian. Immediately he saw that Roger was a huckster he made to close it again; but speaking in broken Italian Roger said quickly:

'Scent, very special, for your master. Scent from London. English Lavender. You tell him, English Lavender. He very pleased with you. English Lavender.' And, as he was speaking, he swiftly thrust a sequin into the servant's hand.

The man hesitated a moment, then, evidently reluctant to return such a handsome bribe, nodded and shut the door. Five minutes later he returned and let Roger into a small stone-flagged hall with a row of four pillars at its far end. Between two of them, a tall thin man of about fifty was standing. He had blue eyes and was wearing his own hair which had been a fiery red, but was now streaked with grey.

Roger had no doubt that he was Mr. Watson. After making a grave salaam, he went forward muttering his Italian patter, repeating 'English Lavender' and lifting the lid of the box of perfumes. The Consul made a pretence of looking at them and smelt the back of his hand on which Roger had smeared the wet stopper of one of the little bottles. As soon as the servant had disappeared, he said:

'This is not lavender.'

'No,' Roger replied in a low voice. 'But I am English. When can I see you on private business. I have a letter from Mr. Pitt.'

After a surprised lift of his thick eyebrows, the Consul whispered back: 'There is a side door in the wall to the left. Be there at eleven o'clock tonight and give three sharp knocks.' Then talking loudly in Italian again, he led Roger back across the hall and let him out.

A little over twelve hours later, he let him in by the side door. It gave onto a small court, having in it a single old magnolia tree, some tubs of flowers, and a marble table with an inlaid top upon which were an oil-lamp and some papers. The August night was very sultry and evidently the Consul had been working out there. Motioning Roger to an iron garden-chair, he said at once:

'I never expected to be honoured by a letter from the Prime Minister, but . . .'

'Forgive me,' Roger interrupted. 'I fear I misled you. The letter is to myself; and I wished to show it you only as evidence of my *bona fides*. Here it is.'

'Ah, well!' Mr. Watson hid his disappointment with a little shrug, took the letter that Colonel Wesley had delivered to Roger in Calcutta, read it through by the light of the lamp, and said: 'This makes it clear that you are in the Prime Minister's confidence, Mr. Brook. In what way can I be of service to you?'

Roger bowed. 'I thank you, Sir. In the first place, do you know anything of a Signor Rinaldo Malderini?'

'Yes. He is, I think, the sole survivor of a noble Venetian family, and married to an Indian Princess. His is not an attractive personality and he is said to dabble in the Black Art. He is reputed to be rich and is interested in theatrical productions, acting frequently as backer for them. But he has also, at times, been employed by the government. He went on a mission to London for the *Serenissima* last summer; an unfortunate choice for us, as his sympathies are pro-French. He has since been absent from Venice for many months; but where, I do not know. He reappeared here about three weeks ago.'

'Ah!' exclaimed Roger. 'He is back, then. Where does he live?'

'He has a palace on the Grand Canal on the corner where the Canal San Barnaba runs into it. Anyone will point it out to you. If your business with him is secret, though, have a care of the gondolier who takes you there. Under the old régime, all gondoliers had to report nightly to the police on the trips they made and any conversations of interest between their passengers that they had overheard. That was one of the principal ways in which the Inquisitors were kept informed of everyone's doings, and the French have been quick to avail themselves of it.'

'I thank you for the warning. It must be, though, one of the few things which have not changed with the coming of the French.'

'Alas, yes. Venice was a delightful city. Provided one did not meddle in politics, there was no city in which greater liberty was enjoyed. I have been Consul here since '91 and had hoped never to be transferred to another post. Whether I shall be allowed to remain depends now on how Venice is disposed of in the peace treaty.'

'Since the preliminaries were agreed last April, I find it surprising the final terms have not yet been settled!'

'It is the Austrians who have held things up. They are playing a waiting game, in the hope that events in Paris will enable them to exact better terms from General Buonaparte.'

'I have been long abroad, Sir,' Roger informed his companion. 'In fact, to India and back; so I am completely out of touch. Pray tell me how matters stand in Paris now?'

Mr. Watson sat back and crossed his long legs. 'The Directory still rules the roost and is as corrupt as ever. But it is having a hard fight to hold its own. Of the five, Rewbell, Barras and Larevellière-Lépeaux are all rabid revolutionaries; Carnot and Barthélemy, who replaced Letourneur last March, are moderates. As Rewbell and Co. are in the majority, they are able to out-vote the other two on every measure; so the proscription of émigrés and the persecution of priests continue unchanged, although the vast majority of the French people would gladly see an end to the state of things they have inherited from the Terror.

'That this is so was clearly shown by the first re-election of the *Corps Législatif*, which was held last March. Of the two hundred and sixteen members from the old Terrorist Convention who had to offer themselves for re-election, only eleven were returned. They were replaced almost entirely by Deputies who favour a restitution of the Constitution of '91. Few, if any, of them desire a king, of course; but they would like to see real liberty restored under just laws and religious toleration. Yet, with the Directory as it is still constituted, they are powerless.

'In January there was a Royalist conspiracy led by the Abbé Brottier. It was badly handled, so swiftly suppressed. But I don't doubt that, seeing the general state of France, the Austrians are procrastinating in the hope of another which will prove successful. Buonaparte and the Directory now form an uneasy partnership. His victories have so increased his stature that they are now frightened of him. On the other hand, he was Barras's protégé and is tarred with the same brush; so the overthrow of the Directory might lead to his recall, or anyway weaken his hand to an extent that would enable the Austrians to get better terms from him.'

'So that's how things stand,' Roger nodded. 'The fact that the Austrians are making peace at all, though, throws the whole burden of the war onto us, and our situation was bad enough already. Knowing how anxious Mr. Pitt was to obtain peace, before I left England last summer I wonder greatly that he, too, is not endeavouring to negotiate a settlement with the French.'

'He did so endeavour, by sending my Lord Malmesbury to Paris last December. But at that time, of course, he was still bound by our understanding with the Austrians that their Belgian lands should be returned to them, and the French would not hear of it. They put a pistol to his

Lordship's head, and told him to accept their own terms in full or quit Paris within forty-eight hours. Our Ambassador here, Sir Richard Worsley, when placing our affairs in my hands before he left, told me that the French Constitutional party are actually eager for peace, but the Directory regards Britain as the most implacable of all its enemies. They showed it by their insulting treatment of my Lord Malmesbury, and no doubt Mr. Pitt feels that, while they remain in power, to go hat in hand to them again would be too great a humiliation. Like the Austrians, he must be hoping for their downfall.'

'I'd not count on it,' Roger remarked, with a shake of his head. 'If they do fall, it will mean the dry guillotine for them—a one-way trip to Cayenne —so they'll fight to the last ditch. Besides, I greatly doubt if their overthrow would bring about any permanent change to our advantage. I am well acquainted with General Buonaparte. Unless I much misjudge the man, now he has proved himself by such a tale of victories he would march on Paris, throw the whole Chamber of Deputies into prison and restore the Directory—or something very like it. No. To my mind, instead of banking on such flimsy hopes, Mr. Pitt would be better advised to endeavour to rebuild the Coalition.'

'How can he, with Spain and Holland gone over to the enemy, Italy overrun, and Austria about to sign a peace?'

'There is still Prussia; she might be drawn in again. And Sweden, and Russia. What of the last? A year ago the old Empress Catherine was on the verge of making an alliance with us. Is she still havering?'

'We'll get no help there. She died last November.'

'The devil she did!' exclaimed Roger. 'Well, God rest her soul. She once played me a scurvy trick by forcing me to take a hell-cat as my wife. But she was a great woman for all that. Who has succeeded her?'

'Her son, as Paul I. He so hated his mother that he has reversed all her policies, good or bad, as though he hoped to spite her in her grave.'

'I'm not surprised by that. He is a weak-kneed imbecile.'

'At all events, he has become pro-French. Prussia is still occupied in holding down her share of Poland's carcase, and, since King Gustavus's assassination, there has been little hope of persuading the Swedes to fight.'

Roger sighed. ''Tis a plaguey poor look-out for Britain, then, I doubt though if Austria will accept as final this set-back she has sustained. She has a mighty reservoir of men and, can we but hang on, after she has licked her wounds a while she might come in with us again. I pray only that her diplomats will succeed in securing a peace that will leave her comparatively strong. Have you any idea of the terms under discussion?'

'I know those agreed in the preliminaries at Leoben. Austria was to surrender all rights to her Belgian territories and the Duchy of Milan and receive in compensation the Venetian lands in Dalmatia, Istria and on this side of the Adriatic as far south as the river Po. She was also to recognize the French frontiers as proclaimed by the Republic. Venice was to be compensated, if you can call it that, by receiving the Papal States of Romagna, Ferrara and Bologna.'

'The last would mean Buonaparte's committing infanticide on his young Cispadane Republic.'

Mr. Watson smiled. 'As you have admitted, Mr. Brook, you are behind the times. He did so a month ago, but at its own request. In July he founded another Republic, the Cisalpine, formed from the Duchy of Milan, and the Cispadanes begged so hard for union with this more powerful young sister that he let them have their way.'

'Surely that makes it even less likely that he would now tear a large limb from it to please Venice?'

'I agree. But remember the preliminaries of Leoben were settled before he quarrelled openly with the Serene Republic.'

'True. So it looks now as if Venice will not possess any mainland territories in the future.'

'I think it likely; but she has only herself to blame. Sir Richard Worsley did his utmost to get the *Serenissima* to fight and, had he succeeded, what a different picture there might be. They had 13,000 devoted Slavonian troops here in the city alone. They could have armed the Veronese and others loyal to the Republic, called on the Tyrolese and Croats for help and launched a formidable army in Buonaparte's rear while he was at death grips with the Austrians up in the Styrian Alps. His supplies would have been cut off and by now, instead of his being the master of all Italy, his whole campaign might have been brought to ruin.'

Roger nodded. 'That I know was Mr. Pitt's hope. And even if she had failed, the Serene Republic would have made an end worthy of her. But I felt convinced from the beginning that the *Serenissima* would not have the guts to fight. What now, though? Do you think Buonaparte will leave the city its independence?'

'I certainly hope so; and so does our Government at home.'

'In that I disagree,' Roger said firmly. 'I would like to see it given to Austria. So rich and populous a city would prove a great asset under firm rule. Should there be a resumption of the war, the possession of such a place could make a vast difference.'

'Buonaparte must know that, so, although the Austrians may press for it, I greatly doubt if he will let them have it.'

They fell silent for a minute, then Roger said, 'Given that they are allowed to retain their independence, I take it that when the French have withdrawn there is a possibility that the Municipality may be overthrown and the *Serenissima* revived? If it was your ambition to become Doge in such a new government, how would you set about it?'

Without a second's hesitation, the Consul replied, 'I should become a leader in the resistance movement which has already started, and hope to make a name for myself by some shrewd blow against the French.'

'I see,' said Roger thoughtfully. 'There are then still a few Venetians left who have some stomach for a fight.'

'Yes; and the man you enquired about has, since his return, become their leader.'

'What!' cried Roger, springing up. 'Malderini! But I thought you said he was pro-French?'

'He was, a year ago; but he has now changed his tune. I much dislike the man but needs must collaborate with him. Only a few days ago I received instructions from the Foreign Office to render these conspirators all the aid in my power.'

Roger suddenly hit the table with his fist. 'Ten thousand devils! What a plaguey twist of Fate! To think that, now I've run my most deadly enemy to earth, I should find him on my side of the fence!'

CHAPTER TWENTY-TWO

Within the Enemy's Gates

ROGER had found himself confronted with many a tricky problem in the past, but never one in which his private interests were so diametrically opposed to his duty to his country.

Before letting him out of the side door of the Consulate, Mr. Watson had made it plain that he believed the secret resistance movement in Venice would become a force to be reckoned with, because among the conspirators who formed its council there were representatives of all classes; and, when considering the matter later, Roger was forced to concede that the Consul was probably right. He had already seen enough of the city to realize that three months had been ample to take the gilt off the gingerbread for even the poorer classes, as far as the new French brand of 'Liberty' was concerned.

Like all the other proletariats in the cities of the Rhine, Belgium, Holland, and Northern Italy, into which the Republic had sent its agitators, they had eagerly drunk in the fine-sounding phrases about 'equality' and a new 'brotherhood of man' in which the nobles and the priests must disgorge their wealth and surrender their age-old privileges. But, instead of their taxes becoming less, they had been made far heavier by the crushing indemnity that Buonaparte had imposed upon the city. Food, wine and all other commodities, which had always been so cheap as long as the Serene Republic controlled its great mainland territories, had now become scarce and expensive, owing to the endless requisitions—and the French paid for nothing. The French troops proved no 'brothers', but lorded it everywhere as conquerors, ousting the citizens from the best tables at the cafés, and beating up shopkeepers who refused to sell them goods for only a fraction of their value, while after dark no woman, even if escorted by a man, was safe from them. Buonaparte's Commissioners had stripped the Doge's Palace of its finest paintings, commandeered the Venetian Fleet and, bitterest blow of all to Venetian hearts, even made off with the *Bucentaur*—the magnificent gilded barge in which with splendid pageantry the Doge had, each year, celebrated the immemorial festival of the marriage of the city to the sea.

Now that it was August, the people danced no more round the Trees of Liberty that they had set up with such enthusiasm in May.

Whether they would have the courage to rise and massacre their oppressors was another question. As Roger considered it and the possible result of such a rising he wondered if after all Mr. Pitt might not have been right in his contention that if Venice could have been won over in the previous autumn she would have made a valuable ally. From what Mr. Watson had said, it was clear that had the *Serenissima* decided to fight, even in the last stage, the city would have proved a terrible thorn in Buonaparte's flank. He had had no fleet so could have attacked only from the landward side, from which it was separated by three miles of water, rendered most treacherous by innumerable shoals and shallows to all who did not know the channels. In the face of the many forts that protected it, and with a garrison of 13,000 hardy Slavonians, even Buonaparte's veterans might have found it too hard a nut to crack. Yet, in the event, Roger's estimate of the decadent nobility that then ruled the city had proved correct; they had not had a kick left in them.

Now, however, the situation was entirely different. By surrendering the Three Inquisitors—the chosen of the Ten, who had been the real rulers of Venice, with power even to search the Doge's pockets—the *Serenissima* had committed suicide; but the Municipality which had replaced them was only a rabble of puppets who could be thrown out tomorrow had they not been maintained in office by the French. A dozen members of the Great Council had had the courage to vote against surrender, and there must be many lawyers, merchants, doctors and so on who would have resisted if given the chance. The oppression would bring the best among them to the fore and if they led a rising they would find ready backing from a great part of the population.

On the other hand, Buonaparte now held the city and had taken over the Venetian fleet. In view of that, and knowing the ruthlessness with which the French would act, Roger felt that a rising could have little hope of success. Yet the fact remained that, from distant London, Mr. Pitt was doing all he could to bring about a rising, and the ambitious Malderini, aided no doubt by the power of his hypnotic glance, had swiftly established himself as the head of the conspiracy; so to kill him now would be equivalent to killing the General of an allied force.

Considering the matter further, after getting into bed in his lodging, Roger began to wonder if Mr. Pitt's policy was the right one. Should the rising take place and be crushed, as he felt certain it would be, Buonaparte would exact a merciless vengeance. There would be no question of Venice being left as an independent City State after that; or of his letting the Austrians have it, as they were apparently pressing him to do. It would probably be first given over by him to his troops to sack and, after that, incorporated into his new Cisalpine Republic, which would remain permanently under the domination of France. Then, if the Austrians could be persuaded to resume hostilities next spring, and they attempted the reconquest of northern Italy, they would have it as an almost impregnable base for enemy operations on their flank.

The more Roger thought over the situation, the more convinced he became that a rising in Venice was both against the interests of the Venetians themselves and against the long-term interests of Britain. If that was so, it followed that one of the best ways of checking the movement would be to kill its leader.

Having reached that, to him, satisfactory conclusion, he at last drifted off to sleep; but not until the early hours of the morning. In consequence, next day he woke late, and even lay for another hour in bed debating with himself possible ways of putting an end to Malderini without being caught.

The result of his deliberations was a mid-morning outing for a box of paints, a canvas, an easel and a camp stool. To find what he wanted he had had to cross the Grand Canal and walk through a score of tortuous alleys until he hit upon the Merceria, one of the few footways in Venice broad enough to be called a street, and in which were situated some of the best shops.

When making his way back, as he thought, he lost himself completely, but came upon a little square, one side of which was occupied by the Fenice theatre. He recalled having heard Malderini say, when at Stillwaters, that although small it was one of the loveliest in Europe; so he would have liked to see its interior. For a moment he was tempted by the idea of returning there for the performance that evening; but he was still dressed as an Arab and, although there were quite a number of traders and sailors wearing Eastern costumes to be seen among the kaleidoscopic crowds, it seemed very unlikely that any of them would patronize a European theatre; so he decided that to do so would make him undesirably conspicuous.

Nearby there was a tavern with tables on the pavement under a creeper-covered trellis. It was not yet the dinner-hour, but the sight of the place made him feel hungry, so he sat down and enjoyed a meal of fried scampi, delicious canneloni and fresh apricots. Again, to act in accordance with his appearance as a Mohammedan, he had to deny himself wine to wash down this most enjoyable meal; but on his long journey from Berbera to Alexandria he had become accustomed to going without it.

On leaving the tavern, he picked up a gondola on the Albero Canal and had himself taken up the Grand Canal to the steps leading up to the Salizzada San Samuele, which was exactly opposite the entrance to the Canal San Barnaba. He then set up his easel in the broad passageway at the top of the steps, got out his paints, and began a painting of the Malderini palace.

It was a handsome building with a tall pillared portico above the water-lapped steps of its front entrance and a graceful carved stone balcony along the first floor, both on its Grand Canal side and also that looking out on the Barnaba. In the latter there was a much smaller waterport for the use of servants and tradesmen, as in Venice goods were delivered only by boat. That, Roger suddenly realized, was one of the things which made the city so unlike any other and so delightful. Coaches would have been too wide to pass down many of the streets, but carts of all kinds, horses, mules and donkeys were all also forbidden. In consequence there was no perpetual clatter of wheels and iron-shod hoofs on cobbles; a restful quiet reigned, broken only by the musical calls of the gondoliers to one another, by which they avoided collisions, and, by night, the strains of violins as family parties glided along the canals taking the air in the soft starlight.

As it was mid-afternoon, it was quite a time before Roger saw any activity at all in the Palazzo Malderini, but in due course servants made brief appearances from time to time in some of the upper windows. Then, a little before five o'clock, his heart gave a sudden bound. A tall slim figure that, even in the distance, he recognized instantly as that of the Princess Sirīsha had come out onto the balcony. Another shorter, plumper woman was with her, but was evidently a maid since, having arranged some cushions in a chair while the Princess leaned for a few minutes on the balustrade of the balcony, she retired.

For about an hour and a half the Princess sat up there idly watching the lively, ever-changing scene below her in the Grand Canal, then she went in. Roger stayed on for a while, hoping to catch a glimpse of Malderini, but when the light began to fail his painting no longer provided an excuse for his remaining; so he called up a gondola, which took him down the Barnaba and through several small canals to some steps near his lodging, where he got rid of his artist's impedimenta.

He had already discovered that in Venice there were scores of small taverns that, despite the steep rise in prices of which the inhabitants complained so bitterly, gave one very good food for quite a moderate price. So he had an evening meal at one of them on the Zattere al Ponte Lungo. Then he crossed again to that only great open space in the whole city, the vast Square of St. Mark, where it seemed at least half its citizens congregated every night to stroll, gossip, flirt, drink at the cafés and listen to the band.

But that night nature spoilt it for him. One of the thunderstorms that so frequently afflict Venice in the summer months broke soon after ten o'clock. The lightning flashed, the thunder rumbled and the rain streaked down in torrents. The crowds rushed for shelter in the long arcades that formed three sides of the Piazza and huddled in them but, even after a downpour of an hour, it lessened only to a steady soaking rain; so, when he got back to his inn, he was wet through and in an ill humour.

But next morning he was up early, set off cheerfully again for the San Samuele steps, and was seated at his easel by eight o'clock. In the *Minerva* on the way to Cape Town, he had done a little painting, but while in Calcutta he had been far too occupied with other matters to indulge in his hobby; so he was deriving considerable pleasure by combining it with his watch on the Palazzo Malderini.

At a little before nine, two wide, low doors at water level, on the Barnaba side of the palace, opened and from an enclosed dock a gondola emerged. Until the coming of the French, the cabins of all gondolas had been painted black and their gondoliers had worn plain sailor's costume, except in the sole case of the Doge, whose men had worn his livery. Now, anyone could brighten up their conveyances as they would, and Roger noted that Malderini's men wore the same bright colours as those of the great striped mooring posts, like bigger editions of barbers' poles, that stuck up out of the water in front of the palace steps.

The gondola was brought round alongside the steps, the short, heavy figure of Malderini emerged from the front door, was bowed into it by several servants, and the craft set off downstream.

Half an hour later it returned. Soon afterwards the Princess Sirīsha came out, accompanied by a tall dark bony man whom Roger recognized as Malderini's valet, Pietro. He got into the gondola with her and it brought them across to the San Samuele steps, where they both landed, then tied up there. Close on midday they returned and it ferried them back to the palace. About two o'clock it went down stream again and brought back Malderini.

By that time Roger was extremely hungry so he walked through to the little square behind the Palazzo Morosini, and had a good meal of minestrone, ossobuco and wood-strawberries at a tavern there. Satisfied with the progress he had made so far, he decided that it would be unwise to overplay the part of an amateur painter; so he arranged with the proprietor of the tavern to leave his painting things there, and spent the rest of the afternoon sightseeing. First he visited a jewel of the Renaissance, the Church of the Miracoli, next the Rialto bridge, by which he crossed and went on to the huge cathedral-like church of the Frari; then he idled away the evening.

The following day, events provided for him a programme that differed little from that of its predecessor. He took up his station at eight o'clock, saw Malderini go out at nine and return shortly after two—this time accompanied by two other well-dressed men—and the Princess go out for her walk, accompanied by Pietro, between ten and twelve.

Later in the day, he strolled along to Venice's waterside promenade, the broad Riva degli Schiavoni, on one side of which rose the square Palace of the Doges, supported so miraculously upon its ground-floor range of arches, and on the other a long row of booths where cheap-jacks of all kinds plied their trades against a background of masts rising from the scores of small ships moored alongside the quay. He walked on as far as the great gates of the Arsenal, behind which lay the dockyards of the Venetian fleet, where, in the great days of Venice, 16,000 men had laboured on her ships week in, week out. On his return he left the quay to visit the tiny church of San Giorgio degli Schiavoni and admired the wonderful series of paintings by Carpaccio, which at least the French could not steal, because they were painted on its walls.

Before settling down for the evening again in the Piazza San Marco there was one grimmer sight at which he paused to look. It was a little enclosed bridge—almost the shape of an inverted V—high up over the narrow canal between the Doge's Palace and the city prison. It had been named the Bridge of Sighs because so many men had passed over it never to return, for the prison, which was known as the 'Leads', had a reputation as sinister as that of the Bastille.

On his sixth morning in Venice, he took with him to the San Samuele steps his tray of scent samples as well as his paints and canvas, as he felt that, should events follow the same course as on the two preceding days, they would have established a pattern, and he might risk acting upon it. Since Malderini was involved in a conspiracy, it seemed certain that he must often go out by night as well as by day, so Roger had considered lying in wait for him after dark. But to attack him on the water would have necessitated difficult and dangerous negotiations to find a gondolier prepared to accept a heavy bribe to become an accessory to murder; while to attack him on land was to risk a hue and cry being raised with the almost inevitable result that the attacker would get lost in a maze of alley-ways and find himself cornered in one of the cul-de-sacs in which Venice abounded. In consequence, Roger had decided that the deed must be done in Malderini's own palace, and as a first step, he had prepared a plan by which he hoped to get inside it.

Malderini left in his colourful gondola as usual soon after nine, then it returned and, an hour later, ferried the Princess and Pietro across the Grand Canal. Roger continued his painting for some twenty minutes, then he went to the little tavern in the Campo Morosini, where he had had two midday meals, and left his artist's paraphernalia with the proprietor. From there he walked back to the Grand Canal, picked up a gondola near the Palazzo Cavalli, and had himself taken to the landing steps of the Palazzo Malderini.

He did not attempt to land but had his man keep the gondola close in to the steps so that he could do so at any moment. After a wait of nearly half an hour, all the church bells of Venice began to chime midday. They were still pealing when Roger saw the Princess coming down the San Samuele steps. Two minutes later her gondola had ferried her across. By that time Roger had stepped onto the landing place and, as Pietro handed her ashore, he salaamed, presented his tray of scents and said, 'Gracious lady! Perfumes from the East! Very beautiful but price modest. Please to accept samples.'

To his dismay she gave him only a glance and walked on, while the skull-faced Pietro turned to hustle him off the steps. He had meant to whisper a few sentences to her as she was examining his scents. In another moment she would be gone. It was now or never; so had to take a chance and call aloud after her.

He had before used broken Italian. Now he used a different language for each short sentence—French, Arabic, Italian again, then Persian—and in the last he cried, 'I come from Bahna. I must talk with you.'

Her steps suddenly slowed. In the doorway she halted, turned and beck-oned to him. With the eager smile of the trader who has intrigued a possible buyer, his white teeth flashing between his black beard and moustache, he ran up the steps and presented his tray, once more breaking into a multi-lingual patter.

After smelling the stoppers from a few of his little bottles, she said in Italian, 'Come with me upstairs.'

Ignoring Pietro's scowl, he followed her through a lofty pillared hall and up a curved staircase guarded by a beautiful balustrade of wrought and gilded ironwork, to a room on the first floor with tall windows overlooking the Barnaba canal. It was evidently her boudoir and much of its furnishings were of Indian design. Pietro had followed them up, but with a quick word she dismissed him. He gave Roger a suspicious glance and went with obvious reluctance. As soon as the door had closed behind him, she turned to Roger and asked in Persian, in a whisper:

'Did I . . . did I hear you aright?'

He nodded, but put a finger to his lips, again broke into his mixed Italian-Arabic sales-talk, and offered her his tray.

She came close to him and made a pretence of examining the scents. Her long fingers were trembling so violently that she could hardly hold the little bottles as he handed them to her, and her great dark eyes stared into his with an expression that was half excitement, half terror. After a minute he said in a low voice:

'Fear nothing. I come to help you. Go now and make sure that Pietro is not listening at the door.'

Controlling her agitation with an effort, she did as he had told her. Pietro was not there. Shutting the door again, she ran back to him and cried, 'What is the meaning of this? Who are you?'

He smiled. 'My disguise must be good, since you fail to recognize me at close quarters. But you will remember your visit to Lady St. Ermins's house down in Surrey, when you were in England; and the Englishman who fought a duel with your husband.'

She gave a little gasp. 'Yes, yes. I know you now. I felt sure I had seen those blue eyes and long eyelashes of yours somewhere before. It is not true, then, that you come from Bahna?'

'I do,' he assured her. 'I arrived in Venice a week ago. But there is one question I must ask you without delay. The night before my duel with Malderini, we met at the bottom of the staircase. You said that he was the most evil of men and asked me to kill him. Do you still desire his death?'

Her hand jerked up to her mouth to suppress a cry, and she threw a terrified look over her shoulder. Then, in a fierce whisper, she replied, 'Yes, yes, yes!'

'Then I will rid you of him,' Roger said firmly. 'But I shall need your help.'

'I . . . I . . .' she faltered, 'I will give it you if . . . if I am able. But he has the mastery of my mind. He can turn my will to water. When we are with other people he imposes silence on me. There are often times when I do not know what I am doing. And . . . and he can read my thoughts. That is why I have never succeeded in running away from him.'

'He did not take you with him to India. Surely you could have found an opportunity to do so during all those months he was away?'

She shook her head. 'No. Before he left, he hypnotized me into following a set routine. I never left the house. Pietro remained here as watch-dog. Even if I had made a supreme effort and broken the spell, Pietro would have prevented my escape. Now that I am allowed out again for a morning's walk he accompanies me everywhere. It has always been so. I am never permitted to be alone, even for five minutes, with anyone who might help me.'

'You imply that you could make a supreme effort. If I am to free you, this is the time to do so. You must arrange some means by which I can get into the house at night. Or come downstairs and let me in yourself. Does he still sleep with you?'

'Ner . . . ner . . . no.' Again she jerked up her hand, but this time to smother a hysterical laugh. 'No; my marriage is a mockery. He married me to get possession of my fortune, and because he knew that he could make a good medium out of me. He came to India when I was a child and got my poor father into his toils. I was very young. Too young to be a wife, but he made me his slave. Then he brought me to Europe. It was only later I realized . . .'

She broke off, suddenly shaken by a fit of sobs. Then, dashing the tears from her eyes, she began to babble semi-hysterically about her life with Malderini. Roger was shocked and amazed, but her voice had risen to so high a pitch that he feared someone would hear her and come running to see what was the matter. Grasping her by the arms, he gave her a quick shake and said:

'Quiet! For God's sake lower your voice or someone will think I am maltreating you. What you say is terrible: but it all fits in with what I heard in Bahna.'

After a moment she got control of herself and said in a more nearly normal voice, 'Bahna! What were you doing in Bahna? And what led you to come in pursuit of Malderini?'

It took him several minutes to tell her, and having to give an account of Clarissa's end re-aroused his hatred of her killer to fever pitch. She listened, her great brown eyes swimming in tears; but she made no comment until he had finished, then she said:

'I understand now why you are set on killing Malderini. The lovely young lady who became your wife I remember well. That she should have died of a chill caught in such a way is especially terrible. I have suffered the same thing at his hands. Five times he has killed cats, and three times human infants, on my body. The first time I thought I should go mad, but he threw me into a trance afterwards which dulled my memory of it; and at least I am still alive.'

'Would you swear to that in front of a magistrate?' Roger asked quickly.

'If so, we'll break out together now. I've a pistol so could hold off the servants. We'll get a warrant and return with the municipals to search the
palace. Somewhere in it there is bound to be corroborative evidence: an
altar to the Devil, perhaps, books on Satanism, robes with . . .'

'No! No! No!' She shrank away from him in terror. 'I dare not! Even to
attempt it would be useless. His familiar spirits would warn him of what
we were about to do. He would strike me dumb from afar.'

'I cannot believe that he has the power to do that.'

'He has! He has! The evil gods give it to him in return for those blood
sacrifices he makes to them. You believe him to be a charlatan because you
caught him out in a trick. He is greedy for money and has used it success-
fully several times to win wagers. Yet he can levitate me. He has done so
several times. He learnt how from the fakirs in Bahna. But to perform the
feat requires weeks of patient preparation.'

Roger shook his head. 'He only made you believe solely by his will-
power that he raised you from the ground. That he has extraordinarily
strong hypnotic powers I admit. I have had personal experience of them.
But all this Black Magic hocus-pocus, and the abominable rites he practises,
do no more than give him immense confidence that, by one means or
another, he will achieve his ends.'

'You are wrong!' she cried. 'Wrong! He can overlook people from a
distance. Of that I am certain. He is the Devil incarnate, the very embodi-
ment of evil, and has become the recipient of many strange powers. He
may be overlooking us at this very moment, and listening to us conspiring
against him.'

As though to confirm her terrified apprehensions, the tall, gilded double
doors of the apartment were thrown open, and Malderini stood framed
between them.

CHAPTER TWENTY-THREE

Patriot or Spy?

IMMEDIATELY behind Malderini, and towering above him, stood the
lank-haired Pietro. Farther back there was a group of half a dozen
men servants.

Malderini advanced a few paces into the room. His malevolent glance
fixed itself on Roger, who had instinctively looked straight at him. Then,
without shifting his gaze, he said, presumably to Pietro:

'You were right. He is the Englishman.'

R.V.—10

Again Roger felt the impact of those terrible soulless eyes which fastened on his own, seemed to dissolve his will and bear him down. But he had come prepared for the possibility that Malderini might return earlier than he had on the past two days and catch him in the palace. Swiftly his left hand went inside his robe, fastened on a small packet and drew it out. Tearing his eyes from Malderini's riveting stare, he shook the contents of the packet out into the palm of his right hand, then, springing forward, he flung it into his enemy's face.

It was red pepper. Malderini's grey eyes blinked for a second then he shut them with an agonized cry. Next moment he was sneezing violently. His big fleshy face distorted by pain and rage, he staggered forward blindly. With his hands clutching like talons at the empty air, he cried in his thin, high voice:

'Seize him! Seize him! Pietro! Stefano! Bimbo! A hundred sequins to the man who brings him down.'

They needed no bidding. Barely a second after Roger had flung the pepper, Pietro dodged out from behind his master, and the other men started forward after him. Roger had barely time to pull out his pistol, and not enough to cock it and hold them up as he had hoped. The weapon was dashed from his hand by Pietro's onslaught.

Swivelling round, Roger overturned a small table. The long-legged valet tripped over it and went crashing onto the parquet floor. The Princess screamed, but got in the way of the next man to make a grab at Roger. He threw a quick glance at the double doors. There were five men between him and them. Even having rendered Malderini *hors de combat*, without a sword he knew he could not possibly fight his way out. Driving his right fist into the stomach of a fat bald man, with his left he fended off a blow from another. A third man dived for his legs, seized his ankles and, with a jerk, threw him over backwards. His bottom hit the floor with an awful bump, but his head was saved by coming down on the cushioned seat of a chair some feet behind him. He kicked out savagely, freeing his legs; then, by a lucky stroke, he landed a kick on the chin of the man who had thrown him.

Imprecations and wailing filled the air. Malderini still had his clenched fists pressed against his eyes. He reeled about, sneezing, choking, and getting in the way of the others. Sirīsha, with the shrill fluency natural to Eastern ladies when wrought up to a high pitch of distress, continued to scream as though she was being beaten. The fat man who had been winded made awful noises as he strove to draw in breath, and the fellow who had been kicked under the chin emitted long heart-rending groans. But Pietro was up again. Followed by the three still uninjured men, he flung himself at Roger.

His dive missed only by inches. Just in time Roger threw his body sideways and rolled over and over across the polished floor. He was brought to rest by a wrought-iron jardinière containing half a dozen pots of flowers. Squirming round it, he got to his knees, seized it by its slender legs and, as he rose, brought them up with him to chest level. As Pietro and the other men came charging across the floor at him, he used all his strength to hurl it at them.

Pietro, his eyes distended by sudden fear, went over backwards. The end of the jardinère caught the man beside him on the arm and threw him off his balance. But the other two continued to come on.

By that time, Roger was through the open window and out on the balcony. Without looking over he knew that the drop to the canal was a good thirty feet; but if he let himself be captured in the Palace he knew that he would never come out of it alive. Without a second's hesitation he flung one leg across the stone balustrade. But the two men ran at him and seized him.

Up till then he had not had a second to draw the knife that he carried on the belt beneath his robe. As they grabbed his shoulders, he wrenched it out and jabbed it into the ribs of the nearest. The man gave a piercing cry and, as he doubled up, thrust automatically with his arms at Roger. The violence of the push overbalanced him. The other man had grasped his robe at the back of the neck. As he fell backwards over the stone balustrade the man hung on. For a moment he swung, his legs kicking frantically in the air, suspended by his robe. Suddenly there came a sharp rending sound. The stitching round the collar of the robe gave and it ripped. A ragged remnant of the collar was left dangling from the clutching hand. Roger fell, feet first, like a plummet, into the canal below.

He struck the water with a terrific splash and plunged through it with scarcely less speed. His feet hit mud and went into it as though it were butter. For an instant he panicked, fearing that it would trap him; but his knees had bent double and, as he jerked himself erect, with one wild wriggle he also freed his feet. Automatically he drew in breath. The water gushed up his nostrils, causing him acute pain at the back of his nose. He choked and took in another mouthful of the horrid sewage-tainted water. Then with bulging eyes and straining lungs he came to the surface.

As his head bobbed up its appearance was greeted with a chorus of excited shouts. At this middle-day hour the Grand Canal was full of traffic. Although he had fallen into the Barnaba Canal, scores of people had seen him. Malderini's people were leaning over the balcony yelling, 'Stop thief! Stop thief!' and half a dozen boats had already turned in his direction.

Desperately he struck out up the narrower canal. Fifty yards ahead, where the Malderini Palace ended, he could see a flight of steps leading up onto the canal's side-walk. If he could reach them and land there was still a chance that he might escape from his pursuers.

But a broad-bottomed boat, loaded high with vegetables, was coming down the canal towards him. The man who was steering the boat gave a swift twist with his long sweep and its prow veered round, barring Roger's passage. Glancing over his shoulder he saw that Malderini's gondola, with its two liveried men urged on by their fellow servants craning over the balcony, was bearing down upon him.

Caught between the two, he temporarily accepted the lesser evil and allowed a thick-necked peasant to haul him onto the vegetable boat. No sooner was he on it than he gave his rescuer a violent shove, which sent him over backwards upon a great pile of artichokes, then dived back into the canal on the boat's far side.

As he came up again, once more shaking the foul water from his eyes, he realized that the odds were hopelessly against him. He was now like a bear in a bear-pit surrounded by a pack of fierce dogs. With swift strokes, craft of all sorts had moved up from both directions. They were full of excited shouting people and their boats now formed a solid ring only ten feet away all round him.

The Malderini gondola shot out from the circle that hemmed him in. Stooping, the liveried servant in its prow seized him by the arm. He resisted wildly, but someone threw an empty bottle that hit him on the head. It did not stun him but temporarily dazed him to a degree that robbed him of the strength to break free.

Muzzy, panting, soaking and exhausted he was dragged on board. The excitement now being over, the other craft disengaged themselves and the mass of boats began to break up. Overhead from the balcony Pietro was shouting down to Malderini's gondoliers, 'Don't let him escape! Have a care that he does not escape! Bring him into the palace! Quickly! Quickly!'

Roger's bemused brain took in the shouted order. Again it was borne in upon him that once he became a captive inside the palace, there would be little chance of his getting out of it alive. Desperately he looked round for some means of saving himself. Suddenly his glance fell on a gondola not far off which had as passengers four French soldiers. Struggling into a sitting position he called to them:

'*À moi! À moi! C'est un Français qui vous appel! Au secours! Mes braves! Au secours!*'

Hearing his cries the soldiers immediately took a renewed interest. Shouting back to him, they had their gondola turned in his direction. It arrived at the same moment as Malderini's at the steps of the palace. Still half dazed, Roger was hauled out onto the landing place by the two gondoliers, but while struggling with them he called again to the Frenchmen:

'Help, comrades; help! I am a Frenchman! Don't let them take me inside the palace. They mean to murder me.'

The soldiers promptly jumped ashore, and their leader, a sergeant, cried in execrable Italian, 'Let this man go. Take your hands off him.'

Pietro, meanwhile, had run downstairs, and now appeared with three of the other servants at his heels. At a glance he took in the situation. Pointing at Roger he shouted in French as execrable as the sergeant's Italian, 'This man is an Englishman, an assassin and a thief. He has stolen jewels from my mistress. We must take him in and search him for them.'

Roger was getting his wits back. Swiftly he denied the charge and offered to be searched there and then.

A heated wrangle ensued during which most of those participating could understand less than half of what the others said. But one thing at least appeared beyond dispute to the soldiers—Roger spoke French with the fluency and accent of a native; so he must be a Frenchman. Therefore, whether he was a thief or not, they were not going to let him be maltreated by a bunch of Italians. They insisted that he should be taken to the Municipality, and that they would accompany him to see fair play.

Forced to give in, Pietro, now brandishing a stiletto as a threat to Roger should he make a further attempt to escape, made him get back into the gondola and got in beside him. The soldiers reboarded theirs, and the two craft set off side by side down the canal.

The Municipality had taken over the administrative offices in the Doge's Palace, and, owing to the epidemic of lawlessness that had swept the city since the fall of the old régime, a magistrate's court was maintained in perpetual session there.

Roger was marched through the great courtyard of the palace to the part of it in which the court sat and handed over to its officers. Pietro having charged him with theft, he was taken to a cell and searched. During the process he thanked his gods that while in Venice he had followed his usual practice, when living under an assumed identity, of hiding his papers and most of his money under a floor-board in his room; for the discovery of his Bills on London and, above all, Mr. Pitt's letter, would have been the end of him. His one chance of regaining his freedom was, he felt sure, to continue to maintain that he was a Frenchman, in the hope that he would reap the benefit of the licence which the French forced the Venetians to extend to their nationals whenever one of them committed a crime that was not of a really serious nature.

Twenty minutes later he was taken into the court, and he saw at a glance that it inspired little more confidence in the dispensation of strict justice than had the tribunals he had often attended in Paris during the Revolution. It differed only in that there was no crowd of *sans-culottes* and shrewish women to throw gibes at the unfortunate prisoners. But a group of French soldiers leaned against one wall smoking short clay pipes and frequently spitting, a handful of lawyers, some unshaven and others with their feet up, lounged on the benches, the straw on the floor did not look as though it had been changed for a month, and the place smelled foul.

Three men sat up on a dais behind a table littered with papers. Two wore tricolour sashes of office in the new Italian colours. One of them was a quite young man with the burning eyes of a fanatic, and wearing a workman's blouse; the other who, as he sat in the centre, was evidently the President, was much older, well but untidily dressed, and with a mean little pursed-up mouth. The third, to Roger's great relief, was a French Captain, evidently acting as a Provost-Marshal.

Pietro gave evidence that Roger had got into the Malderini Palace on the pretence of being an Arab perfume seller; but that he was, in fact, an Englishman, and a thief who had been caught in the act of robbing the Signora Malderini of her jewels. Further, that he had attacked the Signor Malderini, doing him serious injury by throwing pepper in his eyes and wounded one of the servants with a knife. The fact that no jewels had been found on Roger, Pietro argued, was no defence, as he must have dropped them when he fell into the canal.

For the past hour Roger had been frantically exercising his wits for the best defence he could put up, and had decided on romance. The charge that he was an Englishman and a thief he declared to be sheer malice, and addressing himself to the Provost-Marshal broke into fluent French. He admitted having got into the palace under false pretences, but said he had fallen violently in love with the Signora Malderini, and had disguised himself as an Arab scent merchant so that he might see her alone and declare his love for her. Upon being surprised by her husband, he had naturally defended himself, and done so by throwing at him a sample of pepper which he happened to have in his tray because the merchant from whom he had bought it dealt in spices as well as perfumes.

To the Captain's questions he replied that his name was Breuc, that he had been born in Strasbourg but had lived the greater part of his life in Paris, and he had little difficulty in convincing his questioner that he was a Frenchman.

This relieved him of his worst anxiety, and he felt that he was now well on the way to getting out of the very nasty scrape in which he had landed himself. But, next moment, to his dismay and alarm, he heard the Provost-Marshal say to the two magistrates that, as the accused was not a member of the French armed forces, the case was outside his province.

The two Italians then took over, and a sharp argument ensued between them. Again Roger's hopes were raised for a moment, by hearing the young magistrate with the fanatical eyes declare that they were not there to protect the wives of rich ex-senators from their would-be lovers and that the prisoner had been punished enough for his prank. But the older man retorted sharply that, all men being equal, all had a right to equal protection from the law. Then, with what Roger felt sure was special pleasure in for once having a free hand to punish a Frenchman, he snapped at him:

'The charge of theft remains unproved. Your method of pursuing your amorous designs, although reprehensible, is no business of this court; but that you have wantonly assaulted a peaceful citizen and his servant is beyond dispute. We order that you be confined to prison during the pleasure of the Municipality.'

Shaken to the core by the possible implications of such a sentence, Roger was led away. He had escaped death at Malderini's hands by calling on the soldiers for help, but was to be imprisoned for an indefinite period. There raced through his mind the awful fate that had in certain cases befallen men so condemned. Without friends to petition for their release, they had been forgotten and left for years to rot in the dungeons of such prisons as the Bastille and the Leads. Many must have died from debility or despair, but some, owing to a new Governor of the prison being unable to even learn the crime for which they had long ago been incarcerated, had been released, old, feeble, half-blind and with beards down to their waists.

This nightmare possibility filled him with such dread that he hardly noticed where he was being taken until his guards, having marched him up a long flight of stairs, turned with him into a narrow passage with an abrupt upward slope. It was only by noticing that both walls had perpendicular slits in them to let in daylight, and that on reaching the top of the slope, the passage beyond sloped downward with equal steepness, that he realized that he was crossing the Bridge of Sighs.

Two minutes later he had entered the Leads. He was taken down a spiral staircase and along a gloomy passage made from rough-hewn stone blocks; a stout wooden door was opened, and he was thrust inside a cell. He glimpsed a wooden bench, some rusty chains fixed to staples in the wall, then the door was swung to and locked, leaving him in total darkness.

Groping his way to the bench, he sat down upon it and sank his head in his hands. He felt now that he might have done better to take his chance with Malderini. Death, even a painful one, would have been better than the appalling empty, hopeless future which he felt now faced him.

Suddenly he began to shiver. His clothes had still been wringing wet when he had been brought to the Doge's Palace. The midday heat of August which penetrated its courts and rooms had been sufficient to prevent

his feeling any discomfort during the hour he had been in them. But down
in the dungeons there reigned the cold of a perpetual winter. It dawned on
him that if he let his damp clothes dry on him he would catch a chill which
would probably result in his death from pneumonia within a week. Urged
to it by the instinct of self-preservation he stripped to the skin, laid out
his clothes on the dusty floor, then flailed his arms and beat his body all
over with the flat of his palms to restore his circulation.

He kept at it until he was exhausted, and the violent activity took his
mind temporarily off his frightful situation. But as he sank down on the
bench again, the high-lights of the trap in which he had helped to catch
himself impinged upon him with renewed force.

He had no friends in Venice to whom he could appeal for help, even if
he could get a message out, except John Watson; and to have disclosed his
association with the British Consul would have been fatal. The Municipality had no reason to accord him a quick release. On the contrary, as he
was believed to be a Frenchman, spite would influence them to leave him
there indefinitely. There remained Malderini. It seemed just possible that
when he had recovered his sight, he might press for some more definite
penalty. That would lead to the prisoner being brought before the court
again, and at least give him another chance to appeal to the French authorities for protection. But why should Malderini take such a step? What
better revenge could he hope for than to have his enemy left to rot in one
of the lower dungeons of the Leads? Surely he would use such influence as
he had to prevent the case ever being raised again, so that after a few months
the prisoner would become only a number in a cell and all else about him
be forgotten.

Some hours later, the door of the dungeon opened, a bearded jailer set
down inside it a jug of water, a hunk of bread and a crock containing a few
spoonfuls of luke-warm vegetable stew. By then, although from time to
time Roger had endeavoured to warm himself up, he was blue with cold;
so he eagerly snatched at the blanket that the jailer, with a surprised look at
his nakedness, threw to him. The door slammed and once more the
darkness of perpetual night shut out his grim surroundings.

After rubbing himself fiercely with the blanket, as though it were a
towel, he wrapped it round him, and cautiously felt about until he could
find and eat his meagre supper. His clothes, he found, were nearly but not
quite dry; so, still wrapped in the blanket, he lay down on the bench and
pulled them on top of him for extra warmth.

The night seemed endless. At times he dozed, but he never fell properly
asleep and for hour after hour remained semi-conscious of his physical
discomfort and hopeless situation. It was not until the jailer brought
another skimpy meal that he realized morning had at last come. After

eating it he dressed again in his now dry clothes, then sat huddled on the bench staring into the darkness.

Hours later, as it seemed to him, but actually about nine o'clock, he received a visit from the head turnkey. This functionary knew nothing of the crime for which he was imprisoned or of how long he was likely to remain; his sole interest being in whether Roger had money, or friends who would find it on his behalf, to pay for various privileges such as better food, a light, writing materials and books to read.

When Roger had been searched his money-belt had not been taken from him, and in it were twenty-six sequins, so he felt a natural impulse to jump at the chance of securing these amenities; but the caution inherited from his Scots mother saved him from being too badly swindled. By hard bargaining he reduced the turnkey's extortionate demands to the still extravagant figure of a sequin—which was about nine shillings—a day for better food, rushlights that would last eight hours, two extra blankets, and a book to be changed twice a week.

The book brought to him was Dante's *Divina Commedia*, which was long enough to hold his interest for many hours, and his improved ration was to include a litre a day of cheap wine; so at the thought of this new dispensation his spirits revived a little. But only temporarily, as these small comforts could do nothing to improve his future prospects, and those filled him with abysmal depression. There seemed no reason why the Municipality should release him and every reason why Malderini should use all the influence he had to keep him there. In less than a month, unless he were to forgo the better food and books so that he could prolong his purchase of rush lights, the awful darkness would close about him for good.

He had already several times considered his chances of making an escape and been compelled to dismiss them as negligible. It was well known that only one prisoner had ever succeeded in escaping from the Leads, and that had been the notorious adventurer Casanova, some forty years earlier. How he had succeeded was common knowledge because for years afterwards he had entertained people in half the capitals in Europe by telling them the tale. He had been confined in a cell up on the top storey immediately under the great lead roof that gave the prison its name; had managed to squeeze himself through a small window and, risking death from a single slip, had, with extraordinary courage, walked fifty yards along a nine-inch ledge to freedom. But Roger was in a windowless dungeon in the depths of the prison and, even if by a bribe he could have got himself transferred to the top floor, he knew that his head for heights was not good enough to have emulated Casanova's remarkable feat.

The only other possibilities were either to bribe the jailer to leave the dungeon door unlocked, or spring upon and overcome him. But many

other prisoners in the past must have got so far with their attempts only
to be caught at one of the check-posts before they could escape from the
building; otherwise, Casanova's claim that he was the only prisoner ever
to have got away would have been disputed.

Eventually Roger came to the conclusion that his one and only hope
lay in writing to the French *Chargé d'Affaires*. He was most reluctant to do
so because that meant he would have to substantiate his claim to French
citizenship. That, he felt, should not be difficult, for during the Revolution
he had been an original member of the Commune of Paris, had undertaken
missions for the Committee of Public Safety as *Citizen Representant* Breuc
and after the fall of Robespierre had become a Colonel on Barras's staff.
He had, therefore, been quite a prominent figure and could claim the
friendship of Carnot, Buonaparte and numerous other highly placed
Frenchmen. But doing so was certain to result in his having to provide an
account of his activities for the past seventeen months, and to cover such
a lengthy period with a chronicle composed of plausible lies was going
to be anything but easy.

Nevertheless, the risk of being caught out was one that he must now take
as the only alternative to remaining where he was; so, when the jailer brought
his afternoon meal, he asked to see the head turnkey again, as he had decided
after all that he would like to buy some writing materials from him.

An hour later the turnkey arrived with them, and, having parted with
another of his sequins, Roger asked him how much he wanted to deliver a
letter. For this service the man demanded ten sequins, and this time Roger
tried in vain to beat him down. If he paid that price it would at one stroke
deprive him of half his capital, and there was the awful risk that the
avaricious ruffian might tear the letter up instead of delivering it. Tortured
by this thought, he managed to strike a bargain to the effect that, should
the letter not result in his being again brought before the court, he would receive books and light free for a month. That having been agreed to, the man
promised to come back for the letter in an hour and to deliver it that evening.

When he had gone, Roger thought out his letter with great care, sentence
by sentence, until he was satisfied that he had composed one on lines that
were most likely to be effective. It was not an appeal but a most vigorous
protest. Having given particulars of himself as Citizen Breuc, he displayed
intense indignation that the French authorities in Venice should allow
any Frenchman to be treated in the way he had been. He claimed that his
conduct in the Malderini Palace had at worst been no more than a minor
offence, then hinted that his real reason for entering it had been in connection with a mission he had undertaken for a person of importance in
Paris. Finally, he said that, if steps were not taken to secure his release
at once, he would bring the matter to the attention of General Buonaparte.

Soon after the turnkey had collected the letter, his rush light burnt out and he spent another fourteen hours of misery and anxiety in pitch-black darkness. All the following day he waited, hoping to be sent for and trying to distract his mind with Dante's masterpiece; but he did both in vain. Another night crawled by, during which he was tortured by the fear that the turnkey had, after all, cheated him and taken his ten precious sequins for nothing. Then, on his third day in the Leads, at about ten o'clock in the morning, to his unutterable relief two officials of the court came to fetch him.

Now full of confidence that he was about to be released, he accompanied them with buoyant steps back across the Bridge of Sighs, down the long staircase and across the great open courtyard to the court room. There were many more people in it than there had been three days before and, as Roger was put into the dock, he caught sight of Malderini, the Princess Sirīsha and Pietro, sitting together on one of the benches. Their presence caused him a sudden uneasiness.

He had thought it unlikely that Malderini would be informed of his demand to be brought before the court again, or that the original case would again be gone into, and anticipated that he would have only to convince the French authorities that in Paris he was regarded as a person of some importance; but the presence of the Malderini party suggested that they were to be called on to give evidence and, if so, it was certain that his enemy would do everything in his power to prevent his release.

The same elderly man with the pursed-up mouth was acting as President, but his younger colleague had been replaced by a neatly dressed little man with a bulbous nose on the end of which was balanced a pair of steel-rimmed spectacles. The Provost-Marshal was also changed: an elderly Colonel with a bristling red moustache. It was he who conducted the enquiry from the beginning, and the two Italians remained silent throughout. Picking up a paper that Roger recognized as his letter, the Colonel gave a loud cough, and said:

'You state in this that you are the Citizen Breuc, who by various acts in the glorious Revolution deserves well of your country.'

'I am,' replied Roger firmly. 'And were we in Paris, I would have no difficulty in producing a hundred people to prove it.'

'Perhaps; but we are not in Paris.' The Provost-Marshal again held up the letter. 'In this you imply that you were sent here on a secret mission. How long is it since you left Paris?'

Roger was quick to see the need for caution, so he answered, 'A considerable time. Other work for the Republic has since necessitated my going on a long journey.'

'First witness,' snapped the Colonel and Roger saw Gulio Battista emerge from the crowd. The stout sea captain gave him a friendly look and was obviously reluctant to give evidence that might prove to his detriment; but when questioned he admitted that he had carried Roger as a passenger from Crete.

As he stood down, the Provost-Marshal asked, 'Where did you come from before you arrived in Crete?'

Not daring to lie in case he was caught out, Roger replied. 'Alexandria.'

'And you expect us to believe that you were sent on a mission to Venice via Alexandria and Crete?' The Colonel brushed up his fiery moustache. 'Well, we shall see. There are good reasons for believing you to be an impostor. Second witness!'

Roger moistened his lips. The enquiry had opened far from well, and as the Princess Sirīsha was brought forward he had no reason at all to hope that she would improve matters. Although at first she appeared slightly confused, that was no more than any Eastern woman might have been in such unfamiliar surroundings, and was certainly not sufficient evidence on which to allege that she was acting under her husband's hypnotic influence, despite Roger's certainty that she was.

After a hesitant beginning she told her story clearly. Believing Roger to be an Arab perfume-seller she had taken him up to her boudoir. He had then disclosed his true identity and she recognized him as an Englishman whom she had met in England when there with her husband, the previous summer. He had told her that he had been sent from England by Mr. Pitt to stir up trouble in Venice for the French, but had been robbed of his funds so wanted her to help him with money. She knew her husband to be a loyal supporter of the new Government so naturally she had refused. Thereupon Roger had snatched a valuable ring from her finger; but before he could get away, her husband and the servants had arrived on the scene.

The diabolical cunning with which Malderini had elaborated the original charge filled Roger with considerable alarm. In an attempt to spike his guns once and for all, he cried loudly to the Princess:

'Tell the truth, *Madame*! In God's name make an effort. Tell the court the truth about your husband. Show him up for what he is. Free yourself from this evil . . .'

He got no further. The President hammered furiously on his desk with his gavel, the Colonel, the other magistrate and two ushers all shouted at him to be silent, drowning his words. Meanwhile, the Princess had given him one terrified look, then half collapsed against Malderini who had come swiftly up behind her.

Pietro was the next witness called. He substantiated his mistress's story, then described the weekend party at Stillwaters where he had first seen Roger in his true colours as an English aristocrat.

Malderini followed. He was wearing a dark shade over his eyes, so evidently the pepper had inflamed them seriously; but that was little consolation to Roger at the moment with all this sworn testimony piling up against him. His enemy skilfully embroidered the statements of the other two, then produced a trump card in support of his verbal assertions. It was a printed paper which, he asserted, must have fallen from one of Roger's pockets during his struggle to escape, as, he said, it had been found on the floor of the Princess's room immediately afterwards.

After the Provost-Marshal had examined it and it had been explained to him, it was handed to Roger. On the one side of the paper was a printed plan of Vauxhall Gardens; on the other a programme of music and price list of wines. There were also two addresses scribbled on it in different shades of ink. One, in an educated hand, read—Lucy Cresswell, at Mrs. Goosens, three doors from the Cock Tavern, Drury Lane—the other, in printed letters, was that of the British Consul in Venice.

The writing of the first was vaguely familiar to Roger and, after a moment, he recognized it as that of Richard Sheridan; then he guessed at once how the programme had come into Malderini's possession. Evidently the playwright had taken him to Vauxhall one evening and scribbled on it the address of some lady of the town that he had picked up there; then later, by which time Sheridan had probably become fairly drunk, Malderini had pocketed the programme as a souvenir. The Consul's address he would have added that morning.

But to the court, the implication was clear. Roger had kept the paper for the young woman's address, and jotted down that of the Consul's upon it. As the latter was in capitals, he could not prove that he had not written it, and his having had it on him was the strongest possible support for the contention that he was a British spy.

The case against him was now extremely black, but he knew that any sign of weakness would be fatal; so he launched a violent attack on his enemy. With some skill he argued that the three last witnesses must all be taken as one, and that one was inspired by jealous hatred. The servant, Pietro, naturally said what his master had told him to say; the unfortunate wife was completely under her husband's domination and had, no doubt, been persuaded to perjure herself from fear of him; while he had hatched this iniquitous plot in an attempt to revenge himself on a man he believed he had found on the point of seducing his wife.

In swift trenchant French, Roger went on to call the shades of Lafayette, Mirabeau and Danton to witness that he was no British spy, but Citizen Breuc, patriot of the Revolution. He had just got to the point of demanding to be sent before General Buonaparte, who would vouch for him, when there was a stir at the back of the court, and a youngish, thin-faced man, with a very long sharp nose, thrust his way through the crowd.

Silencing Roger, the Colonel addressed the newcomer. 'Citizen Villetard, your arrival is most opportune. You can settle this question for us.'

Roger shot a swift glance at the thin-faced man. Villetard was, he knew, the clever and indefatigable French *Chargé d'Affaires* who had stirred up the Venice mob in May and engineered the downfall of the *Serenissima*.

With a bow to the magistrates, Villetard said, 'Citizens, I must apologize for being late, but the many preparations for today's festivities delayed me.'

The Provost-Marshal returned his bow and said, 'Citizen Minister, am I right in believing that all agents sent from Paris on missions to Venice are under obligation to report to you on their arrival?'

Villetard nodded. 'Yes, that is so.'

'Very well then. The prisoner claims to be one Citizen Breuc, who has deserved well of the Republic, and asserts that he came here on such a mission. Is that the truth, or is he lying?'

After one glance at Roger, Villetard replied promptly, 'He is lying. There was a Citizen Breuc who was at times employed by Citizen Carnot, and stood in high favour with Citizen Barras; but I have heard nothing of him for a year at least. For him to have dropped out of things suggests that he is probably dead, and this man, having learnt that, has endeavoured to make use of his identity. He is unquestionably an impostor.'

The Provost-Marshal bowed again. 'I thank you, Citizen Minister.' Then he signed to a Sergeant, pointed at Roger, and added. 'Take him down to the Arsenal and tell my deputy to deal with him.'

'I protest!' cried Roger. 'I demand to be sent before General Buonaparte!'

With a shrug and a twirl of his red moustache, the Colonel retorted roughly, 'The General-in-Chief is far too occupied with matters of importance to be troubled with English spies.'

The President rapped with his gavel, stood up and declared the sitting closed. The people began to crowd out of the court. Two French soldiers took Roger by the arms and with him between them followed the Sergeant out into a long draughty corridor. Some way along it the Sergeant unlocked a door. Roger was thrust through it into a cell. As he turned, the Sergeant, a real grizzled old soldier with a walrus moustache, said:

'You can cool yer 'eels 'ere fer a bit while we 'ave our midday grub; then we'll take you fer a little walk dahn to the Arsenal.'

'Why am I being taken there?' Roger asked anxiously. 'Is part of it used as a military prison?'

The Sergeant gave a throaty chuckle. 'Not likely, chum. We're takin' you there ter be shot.'

CHAPTER TWENTY-FOUR

Half an Hour to Live

ROGER had known the answer before he asked the question. For a few moments he had tried to persuade himself that he was being transferred to a different prison and had clutched, as at a straw, at the thought that, spies being a matter for the military, he was only being removed from the custody of the civil authorities. But convicted spies were shot. And he had been convicted. There were no convenient walls in the Doge's Palace, or the solid block of the Leads against which a man might be shot out of sight of the public; whereas, in the many acres covered by the great Arsenal, there were plenty. Instinct had told him what to expect immediately the Provost-Marshal had given the order for him to be taken there.

In the past ten years he had had a dozen narrow escapes, and a wonderful run for his money; but now the game was up. It was the normal end to anyone who plied his trade long enough and he had taken the pitcher to the well once too often. Yet it was a bitter pill that his downfall had been brought about through his private vendetta against Malderini. Death at the hands of a firing squad would at least have been more acceptable as the penalty of failure in some worth-while *coup* planned in the service of his country and Mr. Pitt.

It galled him terribly to think that Malderini had outwitted him, and he wondered if he could have played his cards better. Perhaps, after all, the Municipality would have released him after a few weeks, had he had the fortitude to endure misery and uncertainty for a while in the Leads. He might at least have held his hand for a month before taking the step by which he had burnt his boats. But on second thoughts, he felt again that the dice had been loaded against such a hope. Malderini had known that he was in the Leads and would have spared no pains or bribes to have had him kept there.

Again, he might have addressed his letter to General Buonaparte instead of to the French *Chargé d'Affaires*. But, if he had, would it ever have reached that immensely busy, and now great, man? He thought it very unlikely. No, for once the stars had been against him in his knowing no one in Venice who could vouch for him as the Citizen Breuc, and the damnable cunning of Malderini had prevented him being given the benefit of the doubt.

For three-quarters of an hour he sat on a three-legged stool in the cell, striving to regard his situation philosophically; then the Sergeant and two soldiers returned for him. One of the soldiers had a length of cord and with it proceeded to tie his arms behind his back, while the Sergeant remarked:

'Don't want you tryin' no tricks on us while we take our little walk along the Plagegio Schiavonio. Lots of people about ter day, an' it wouldn't do us no good with our officer if we was to let you make a bolt for it among that crawd.'

When his arms had been tied, there was enough cord over for each of the soldiers to take a long loose end and they attached these to their belts, so that if he did take to his heels he would only drag them after him.

'Here we go,' said the Sergeant. 'Nice day for a stroll, though a bit 'ot out in the sunshine.' Then he led the way from the cell with his men bringing Roger along between them.

It was just on midday and outside the sun was blazing down; but that fact passed unnoticed by Roger as they came out of the great gateway of the palace. The Piazza was packed with people and he was able to advance only because a broad lane was being kept clear from the gateway down to the landing steps on the Grand Canal. Soldiers posted every few feet on both sides were having difficulty in keeping back the solid masses of men, women and children.

'Speshul fer you,' remarked the grimly jovial Sergeant. 'Turned out the guard, they 'ave, an' done yer proper.'

Roger, looking twice his age, his hair a mop, his beard uncombed, his soiled and torn Arab garments flapping about him, was far from presenting the type of spectacle calculated to bring tears to the eyes of onlookers; and from the crowd he received as many jeers as looks of pity. But he walked forward with a firm step, and, on lifting his chin, noticed that flags were flying from every point of vantage. He had naturally not taken the Sergeant seriously, and Villetard's having said that the delay in his arriving at the court had been owing to arranging 'the festivities', he assumed that one of the new Republican holidays—perhaps a Feast to the Goddess of Reason—was being celebrated.

Twenty feet from the gateway, the lane through the crowd made a curve, then ran straight on between the two lofty columns, one topped by a figure of St. Mark and the other by the Winged Lion of Venice, to the quay-side. As Roger rounded the bend, he saw that a little crowd of richly dressed officials was standing at the top of the steps, and that a great gilded barge had just drawn up to them. Everyone was now craning their necks in that direction, but at that moment an officer caught sight of Roger's party. Waving his drawn sword, he shouted angrily to the Sergeant to get off the route. Hastily, and greatly to the annoyance of some members of the crowd, Roger was bundled sideways into its front rank; for, instead of thrusting through it, the Sergeant said to his men, with a grin:

'Timed it nicely, didn't I, boys? Couldn't 'ave a better view, not if we was the Directors themselves awearin' their plumes an' cocked 'ats.'

In spite of the tumultuous agitation that seethed in Roger's mind, instinct impelled him to ask, 'What's happening? What is all the excitement about?'

'It's the Little Corporal's Missus,' the Sergeant told him. "'E's sent 'er 'ere on a visit.'

That meant nothing to Roger, and he remained silent for a minute; then, a vague interest aroused again, he enquired, 'Who is the Little Corporal?'

'Well, of all the ignorance!' exclaimed the Sergeant. 'You must 'ave been dead six months already not ter know that. It's our name for 'op-o'-me-thumb—the little General. We give 'im 'is stripes fer the way he led us to all our victories.'

Instantly Roger became as still as a ramrod. Next moment he saw her. The group of officials forty yards away had parted. Carrying a great bouquet of flowers, *La belle Creole*, as she was called—Josephine, widow of the Vicomte de Beauharnais and now Madame Buonaparte—was still nodding to right and left, acknowledging their homage. Then she began to walk forward and the crowd burst into cheers.

Like a cannonball with a double charge of powder behind it, Roger launched himself towards her. Taken completely by surprise, the two soldiers were dragged after him. At the top of his lungs, he yelled.

'Madame Buonaparte! It is I. Citizen Breuc. Help! Help! They are going to shoot me! Help!'

The cheers ceased abruptly. Every face was turned towards him. He had already covered half the distance that separated him from Josephine before the soldiers, tugging on the cords that bound his arms, brought him to a halt. She too had halted. She gave him a look of compassion, but shook her head. She was the kindest of women and spent half her life interceding with her normally ruthless husband to secure mercy for enemies upon whom he was about to vent his wrath; and more often than not saving them from imprisonment or death. But this was Venice, and the matter evidently one in which she felt she had no right to interfere.

Roger's guards were handicapped by their muskets, but several of the soldiers who had been lining the route came to their assistance. One of them hit him a savage blow on the side of the head. It temporarily silenced and half stunned him, and he was hauled back through the crowd into its fringe. Bowing to right and left, Josephine walked on. The people began to cheer again. Somewhere in the distance a salute of guns was still booming out. A band in the Piazza struck up the Marseillaise.

The Sergeant, furious at the thought that he would be called to account for this untimely scene, smacked Roger's face hard several times with the flat of his hand. The blows had the effect of bringing him out of his temporary stupor. Josephine was then passing within fifteen feet of him. As he glimpsed the standards that were being carried aloft behind her, he let out a last despairing shout:

'Fouché! Your diary! William de Kay! Help!'

Josephine's footsteps faltered. She had gone suddenly pale under her rouge. She halted and gave a loud cry. 'That man! Who is he? Please . . . please bring him here.'

Anxious to earn merit in her eyes, half a dozen officers sprang forward. The crowd melted before them. Roger was torn from his captors, turned about and shoved by them to within a yard of her.

Half fainting, he fell on his knees, but turned his face up and managed to gasp out, 'Madame, I am the Citizen Breuc. You remember me! You must! I implore you to save me!'

She stared down at his grimy face, with its tangled hair and beard. 'No, no! You cannot be. You bear no resemblance.'

'I swear I am.' He staggered to his feet, so that he was facing her. 'I was here on a secret mission; that's why I am disguised. But look in my eyes, Madame. Look in my eyes, and you will know me.'

For a moment her soft brown eyes looked into his deep blue ones, then she whispered, 'It is! It is!'

'You are right, Madame,' said a deep voice behind her. 'It is indeed the Citizen Breuc. I, too, now recognize him.'

Shifting his glance for a second, Roger saw that the speaker was Andoche Junot, an old friend of his, and General Buonaparte's first aide-de-camp.

Josephine had turned to the Mayor of the new Municipality of Venice, who was doing the honours of the city for her. In Italian, which she could speak a little, she said, 'Citizen Mayor, this man is well-known to me and in the past rendered me a service which I shall never forget. I do not know of what crime he is accused, but whatever it may be I beg his pardon of you, and that you will give him to me.'

The Mayor bowed so low that the big old-fashioned wig he was wearing came down almost to the level of Josephine's waist. As he lifted his fat face he replied with a servile smile, 'Madame, your illustrious husband has bestowed liberty on Venice, and liberty is worth more than life; so the lives of everyone in this city are yours to dispose of.'

Without even waiting for the Mayor's reply, General Baraguay d'Hilliers, the Commander of the French troops in Venice, who was standing beside him, cried, 'Free this man! And be quick about it.'

Roger's escort hastened to obey. As his arms were being untied, the Sergeant grinned at him. 'Your lucky day, chum. But I were right, weren't I? Didn't I say they'd turned out the guard speshul fer you?'

The irrepressible humour of the old soldier released the tension of Roger's overstrained emotions. He found himself laughing, and saying, 'If you hadn't delayed to see the procession, I'd be dead by now. Find me later through Colonel Junot and I'll make you a handsome present to drink my health.'

As the procession moved on Roger fell in behind Junot, an incongruous figure among this splendid array of gorgeously clad officials and the bevy of beautiful women who were in attendance on Josephine. A moment later, at a touch on his shoulder, he turned to find that the clever-looking Citizen Villetard had sidled up to him. In an anxious voice the Chargé d'Affaires said:

'Citizen Breuc, I am desolated at the thought of the part I played in Court this morning. At any other time I should have gone into such a matter more fully. I should have sent for you and questioned you myself. But for the past few days I have been overwhelmed with the work of preparing for Madame Buonaparte's reception. And the Signor Malderini had already denounced you as a British spy before your letter was received. He seemed so positive of his facts. I can hardly hope for your immediate forgiveness; but if there is any way in which I can be of service to you, you have only to command me.'

Roger was much too shrewd to show malice to a man who might prove useful to him, so he replied at once, 'Even the most conscientious of us makes mistakes at times, Citizen; and my narrow escape this morning was one of the risks inseparable from my work. In that I may later accept your offer of assistance. For the present, I require only a certificate of civicism, as a protection against any further mistakes of the same kind, and decent quarters where I can exchange this now useless Arab disguise for more suitable garments.'

Villetard gave a sigh of relief. 'Nothing could be simpler, Citizen. When our Ambassador was withdrawn in April, I took over the Embassy, and in it there is ample accommodation. I beg that you will allow me to become your host, and everything you may require shall be furnished you.'

The invitation suited Roger admirably; so he graciously accepted and they walked on side by side, across the great courtyard of the Palace, up the broad stairway, now flanked by Venetian halberdiers, and through the enormous hall in which the Grand Council had elected the Doges. It had a frieze of their portraits going right back to the year 810 and, at one end, forming a twenty-foot high background for the seventy-foot-long dais, Tintoretto's vast painting—the largest in the world.

It was from the dais, three months earlier, that Junot had read to the cringing Senate, Buonaparte's threatening message, which had led to the fall of the thousand-year-old Republic. Now he stood behind Josephine, a resplendent figure, square chinned, curly haired, smiling amiably, while the Mayor made a long speech of servile adulation about the benefits the conqueror had bestowed upon the city, and Josephine replied in her halting Italian that only urgent affairs had caused him to send her, instead of coming himself, to say how greatly he valued their friendship.

Afterwards she was conducted to the Doge's private apartments, which had been made ready for her, so that she might rest through the heat of the afternoon. Roger then accompanied Villetard to the French Embassy, where his host installed him in a comfortable room, provided him with a valet and sent for a barber and clothiers. As a further gesture of amends the long-nosed diplomat then begged his acceptance of a silver-hilted sword and a purse of five hundred sequins for present expenses. Roger saw no reason to refuse them and, to the delight of Citizen Villetard, promised to speak well of him to Madame Buonaparte.

Four hours later, bathed, rested, his beard shaved off, and dressed in ready-made, but not too ill-fitting, clothes, he returned with Villetard to the Palace for the banquet which was being given in Josephine's honour. When he kissed her hand at the reception and thanked her for his life, she said:

'People may reproach me for laziness and love of pleasure, Monsieur, but not for forgetting my friends; and I shall ever count you one of them. But I am all agog to learn what brought you to so sorry a pass. Please come here tomorrow morning and tell me all about yourself.'

Junot, too, was eager to hear his story, and later in the evening, after the first formal quadrille had been danced, the two men sat down together over glasses of wine. Roger had always found it good policy to tell as much of the truth as possible about his doings and, since he had to account for his long absence from France, he had decided to make no secret of his voyage to India.

When last in Paris, he had succeeded in blending various rôles he had played in the past into one coherent story which was now generally accepted in the *salons* of the French capital. By then there were plenty of people who had once graced the halls of Versailles, but having liberal principles had stretched them far enough to the Left to survive the Terror and, after the fall of Robespierre, they had emerged, either from prison or a caution-dictated obscurity, to form with the new masters of France a revived upper-class of wealth and fashion; so to them there was nothing at all strange in the *ci-devant* Chevalier de Breuc having kept his life and liberty by fooling the *sans-culottes* into believing him to be a dyed-in-the-wool revolutionary. He had, too, so skilfully dovetailed his French and English identities that the Buonapartes, Barras, Junot and everyone else with whom he was well acquainted as Citizen Breuc, thought him only half French by birth and brought up in England, but entirely French in sympathies, and a patriot who had rendered France many useful services.

In consequence he led Junot to believe that, since he could pass with ease as an Englishman, he had been sent to India by the French Government to assess the possibilities of the French regaining a hold on the territories they had lost there, and of the wealth they might hope to gain if they could succeed in ousting the British from Bengal. He then showed equal eagerness to hear from the young Colonel an account of General Buonaparte's remarkable campaign.

Junot had the heart of a lion, but no great brain, and it had been his conspicuous bravery while a Sergeant at the siege of Toulon that had led the little Corsican to promote him to Lieutenant and make him his A.D.C. Afterwards, he had accompanied his new master to Paris where, during Buonaparte's dark days, when he was out of employment, they had shared a room in a back-street hotel, and, by various shifts, Junot had managed to support them both. When the *coup d'état* of 13th Vendémiaire had brought Buonaparte with one bound from obscurity to Military Governor of Paris, he had not been slow to show his gratitude, and Junot, who regarded him as little short of God, was delighted to plunge into a panegyric about his triumphs.

'When we arrived in Nice towards the end of March '96,' he said, 'I will confess that I was just a shade anxious about the sort of reception our General would have when he took over the command. He had brought with him from Paris Berthier, to be his Chief of Staff, Marmont, Murat and myself. Naturally we all had absolute faith in him, but he had never before commanded even as much as a Brigade in the field; so we couldn't help wondering how the old hands would like his appointment.

'Sérurier was one Divisional Commander. He is a *ci-devant* Count, you know. He spent years in the old army and only joined the revolution because he had been treated so shabbily; a conscientious man and good at looking after his men, but stuck fast in all the old traditions about setpiece wars. Augereau was another; a *sans-culotte* if ever there was one, and vain as a peacock, but a skilful tactician and a tremendous fighter. Masséna was the third; a dour silent fellow, but by far the ablest of the lot. All of them had victories to their credit, and a much better claim to be appointed General-in-Chief than our little man; but in no time at all they were eating out of his hand.

'You know his immense energy. He gave them no time to talk or grumble. The Army was short of everything, but all the same, within a fortnight of his taking over, we were up in the Ligurian Alps firing our first shots at the village of Montenotte.'

With uncheckable enthusiasm, Junot talked on for over an hour, describing victory after victory fought in the summer heats across the rivers Adda, Po, Mincio and Adige, then during the desperate winter campaign up through the snow-clad Alps into Austria.

Then he spoke of the new army that Buonaparte had forged. 'You'll find it very different from that with which we served at Toulon. It hadn't altered much when the little man took it over. The troops were still just ill-disciplined cut-throats who thought themselves as good as their officers. They got no pay and had few clothes; many of them had rags wrapped round their feet because there were no boots. Only a flaming belief that they were fighting to save the revolution kept them going. But the General has altered all that. Money and paintings aren't the only things we've had out of Italy. Every tailor, cobbler and saddler in the country has been made to sweat blood. You'll have seen some of our smart new uniforms in Venice, though.

'Another thing: from the beginning he abandoned the practice of calling them "Citizens" and instead always addresses them as "Soldiers". Among the officers, too, the word "Monsieur" has come back, and woe betide the rough-neck who dares any longer to question an order. All that old business of soldiers' committees that had to have the situation explained to them and be argued round before they would agree to attack, has long since gone by the board.

'Buonaparte has changed too. Even his oldest friends no longer dare "thee" and "thou" him. He keeps himself very much aloof, and rightly so. He is no longer interested in Corsica, either. You'll remember how passionately he used to discourse on the island's right to independence. Now, for him, it has become just one of the Departments of France, and he looks upon himself as a Frenchman. He has even changed the spelling of his name so that it now sounds more French, and signs everything "Bonaparte".'

Roger listened, fascinated, to all this, but he was desperately tired; so, when Junot went off again to dance, he left the Palace, had himself taken back to the French Embassy and there flopped into bed.

Next morning, his face still lined and his eyes deeply shadowed from his recent ordeal, but in excellent heart, he went to his old lodging near the church of the Spirito Santo. The landlord, naturally, did not at first recognize him, but he told him that he had been living there in disguise, spoke of Captain Battista and the previous day's trial, of which the man had heard, and soon convinced him of his identity. Up in the room he had occupied he retrieved, from under the floor-boards, his Bills of Exchange on London, the equivalent of fifty guineas in gold, a small silk bag containing the jewels that the Rai-ul-daula had given him, and the letter from Mr. Pitt.

The first, if his luck turned again, and it was found upon him, he would be able to account for, but the last he certainly could not. The letter had served him well, and he was loath to part with it, but to keep it was a risk that he felt he could not afford to take; so, using his tinder box, he burnt it to ashes.

From among the jewels, he selected a star sapphire as big as a hazel nut which, set in a surround of small diamonds, had been used as a hair ornament but could be made into a very unusual brooch, and slipped it into his waistcoat pocket. The other items he disposed of about his person; then he paid the landlord what was due to him and crossed the Grand Canal to wait upon Madame Boneparte in the Doge's Palace.

She received him as an old friend, in négligé, lying on a gilt day-bed while her hair was being dressed and coiled with ribbons high on her head, á la Grecque. With the abandonment fashionable under the Directory, she was wearing only the most flimsy garments, through which he could see a good part of her well-rounded limbs. Her retroussé nose deprived her of real beauty, but her brown eyes were large and luminous, and there was a voluptuousness about her that drew many men to her like a lodestone.

After he had kissed her hand, he went down on one knee and offered her the jewel. Never having seen one like it before, she examined it with delight, but then refused to take it, saying that she was still his debtor rather than he hers.

But, knowing her love of pretty things, he insisted that she should, telling the glib lie that he had brought it all the way from India for her.

At that she exclaimed with astonishment and begged him to tell her about that distant land. For half an hour he entertained her with accounts of Rajah's palaces, snake-charmers, hunting tiger from the back of an elephant, and other true travellers' tales, then she said:

'The General-in-Chief will be enthralled to have an eye-witness account of such matters, Monsieur. He has always been intrigued by the East and, as you may know, once contemplated leaving the French service for that of the Grand Turk. No doubt, now that you are returned, he will offer you suitable employment. He always prefers to have familiar faces about him, and in recent months he has displayed a special preference for those whose breeding distinguishes them by their good manners. You fulfil both of those requirements so I am sure he will give you a warm welcome. Meanwhile, I should be most happy if you would accept a post as one of my equerries.'

Roger's hesitation was hardly perceptible. Willy-nilly, he had been pitched back into the tortuous maze of international intrigue, and the offer of the appointment led right to the heart of it. Smiling, he expressed his thanks and the pleasure he would derive from becoming one of her personal entourage.

Having kissed her plump hand again, he left her and returned to the Embassy. Villetard was out, but an hour later he came in and Roger asked him for a quarter of an hour's private conversation. He readily assented and they went into his office.

Since his rescue the previous morning, Roger had had no opportunity to take any steps against Malderini, but he had found time to consider how best to deal with him. His own position as the friend of Madame Boneparte was now unassailable, and his identity as a Frenchman having been proved beyond dispute automatically convicted Malderini of deliberate perjury with intent to secure the death of a French citizen. He might, in the past twenty-four hours, Roger realized, have fled the city; but, if he had, he could not have got far, and with all Northern Italy now virtually a French province, it should not be difficult to have him hunted down.

Roger's first thought had been to get Villetard to have him arrested, and clapped in the Leads, and have strict orders given that he should receive no money; as, for a man of his age and poor physique on short rations, that would almost inevitably mean a lingering death in the darkness. But it might be many months, or even several years, before he finally gave up the ghost; and, whereas he could have seen to it that Roger was kept there indefinitely, the reverse did not apply, as Roger would be leaving Venice and, if the city was to be restored to independence, soon after peace was signed the French would leave it too.

On consideration, he decided that the best way of making certain of his object was to get Villetard to have Malderini brought to the Embassy and confined in one of its cellars on the pretext that he was withholding valuable information. He could then go down at night to 'question him', and he would be found dead in the morning. Even if it was suspected that Roger had put an end to him, no action would be taken. Plenty of people had met their deaths in similar ways in Venice these past few months. His body would be thrown into the canal the following night, and that would be the end of the matter.

In consequence, as soon as they were seated in Villetard's room, he confirmed what he had hinted in his letter—that his reason for getting into the Malderini Palace had been not a romantic one, but in connection with secret work for the Republic about which he was not at liberty to speak—and asked that Malderini should be arrested, brought to the Embassy as soon as possible, and locked up in a cellar.

As Villetard listened to this request, he began to look uncomfortable and, when Roger had done, he said, 'Citizen, you know how eager I am to be of service to you, but I greatly fear this is a matter in which I cannot do as you wish. Quite apart from your desire to question Malderini in connection with this work you speak of, you must naturally be feeling an intense resentment against him for having so nearly brought about your death, and it would be no more than a mild revenge to keep him here or, better still, in the Leads, for some months on bread and water. But, unfortunately, I could not agree to either, because he is one of my most valuable agents.'

CHAPTER TWENTY-FIVE

The Uncrowned King

HAVING learned from Mr. Watson that Malderini had established himself as the head of a conspiracy which aimed, at the first opportunity, to oust French influence from Venice, Villetard's disclosure showed that the Venetian was playing a double game. That did not surprise Roger, but he could not reveal the source of his information, so could do no more than throw suspicion on his enemy; and he said with a frown:

'You surprise me greatly. After all, he is an ex-Senator, so he must be strongly antagonistic to the new Republican régime. In fact, I heard a rumour a few days ago which led me to believe that he is actually involved in a conspiracy to overthrow it. If we had him here we might find means to get the truth out of him; and it may well transpire that he is double-crossing you.'

Villetard put a finger to his long nose and smiled. 'Such a proceeding is quite unnecessary, Citizen. Trust me to know what goes on in Venice. Between us two, the rumour you heard has substance. Since his return from India he has made himself the head of a resistance movement and he keeps me informed about it. He is hard at work encouraging all the disaffected elements here to unite. When the time is ripe, they will prepare a rising. He will let me know shortly before it is to take place, and we shall pounce. Thus, in one swoop, we shall net all our most dangerous enemies. You see now how, for the time being, it is absolutely essential that he should be left at liberty.'

This complete check to Roger's plans filled him with intense annoyance, but clearly there was no way in which he could overcome it; so, after a moment, he asked, 'And after this fine *coup* has taken place? What then?'

'Oh, he will claim his reward.' Villetard shrugged. 'If Venice retains her independence, he hopes to persuade General Boneparte to agree to some modification of its Government. It would have to remain a People's Republic, of course, with an elected Chamber of Deputies, but the office of Doge might be revived as a substitute for Mayor, and it is that which he hopes for. But once a traitor, always a traitor. We'd be fools to leave such a man here as First Magistrate. Far better throw him to the lions—or, in this case, to you. Once he has served his purpose, I'd have no difficulty in finding an excuse to put him in the Leads for as long as you like, or, if you prefer, have him knifed for you one dark night.'

Roger would have much preferred to see the business concluded within the next few days, but that would have meant his seeking out and killing Malderini himself and, strong as his position now was, he was greatly averse to risking being charged with murder, particularly as the deliberate wrecking of Villetard's plans might jeopardize the extent of French protection he could otherwise have relied on. After only a moment's thought he decided that he must leave Malderini a few more weeks of life, and rely on Villetard's promise to ensure having his revenge after the *coup* had taken place.

That afternoon, he was one of the gilded throng that attended Madame Boneparte on a water procession up the Grand Canal, but unfortunately the splendid spectacle was spoiled by one of the terrific thunderstorms to which Venice is subject. In the evening there were further festivities at the Doge's Palace, and a fine display of fireworks. Then on the following morning, August 26th, having acted as her husband's Ambassador and conveyed to the people of Venice his most friendly feelings and deep concern for their future welfare, she set out on her return journey to his headquarters.

As one of her suite, Roger accompanied her and, now that he was again a free man with no immediate problems to worry him, he thoroughly enjoyed taking part in this semi-royal progress. The procession of barges left Venice to the roar of cannon and were received by the forts at Mestre with another volley of salutes, but their passengers did not land there. Instead, they continued on by the Brenta canal, past graceful Palladian villas and between smiling vineyards and cherry orchards up to Padua, where they spent the night.

Next day the journey was resumed with the ladies in coaches, the gentle-men riding beside them, and with a full regiment of Chasseurs clattering along before and behind as escort. They travelled by Vicenza, Verona and Brescia, at each being lodged in the sumptuous apartments of some great palace and being lavishly entertained by the authorities of the city. The fifth day was their longest stage, but relays of horses were always ready for them every few miles, and as twilight fell they arrived at the imposing Chateau Montebello, three miles outside Milan, which Boneparte had made his permanent residence since the cessation of the fighting.

Soon after the arrival of Josephine's cortège, Junot spoke to Duroc, the Master of the Household, about accommodation for Roger, but the Château was so crowded that only an attic could be found for him. Having freshened himself up as well as he could there, he went down to the great chambers of the building, and mingled with the many people who were lounging and gossiping in them, until the General made his appearance with Josephine on his arm on their way to supper.

From what Junot had said, and various remarks made on the journey, Roger had been prepared to find a big change between Buonaparte, as he had known him in Paris, and Boneparte the conqueror; but, even so, it far exceeded his expectations.

The change was not so much in the man himself as in the state of things he had created round him. In Paris he had only recently become acknowledged as a young General who might well have a future, and been somewhat feared for his sharp tongue. Here, he moved in an aura of adulation and glory, even grizzled veterans hanging on his words with bated breath whenever he spoke of war. Then, he had not long acquired his first coach, or been able to afford to replace his shabby clothes with such luxuries as an enormous hat laced with a three-inch deep band of gold galloon. Now, although quietly dressed himself, he was the pivot around which revolved an amazing scene of pomp and splendour.

Roger had seen many Great Headquarters; not only those of Revolutionary Generals such as Dumouriez and Pichegru, but also those of the Prince de Condé on the Rhine, and of King Gustavus in Sweden. Compared with this, they were all as cottages to a mansion; for this was the Court of a mighty potentate. It was thronged not only with scores of officers in brilliant uniforms and lovely women, but also with ambassadors from many of the German States, the Swiss Cantons and the lands to the east of the Adriatic, and notabilities from every city in Italy. The presence of these last brought home to Roger more than anything else the fact that from Nice to Venice, and from Rome to the Brenner Pass, the young Corsican, who had celebrated his twenty-eighth birthday only a fortnight before, ruled with supreme power and that, throughout all these many lands, his least word was law.

Nominally he was still the servant of the Directory, but even if he wished to consult them it took the best part of three weeks to get from Paris the answer to a question, and he rarely asked one. Meanwhile he acted like an absolute monarch, and played the part of a king as though he had been born to it.

During the campaign he had fed in private with his staff, and any of his senior officers who had been in the neighbourhood of his headquarters had always been welcome at his table. Now, like royalty, he had his meals served in public, in the great banqueting hall of the Château, with two or three hundred people looking on, and his Generals and other persons of importance were invited to eat with him only as a favour. Whenever he emerged from his private apartments, lanes of bowing courtiers formed for him to pass through, no one sat in his presence unless he indicated that they could, men removed their hats when he appeared, and only a very limited number of people enjoyed the privilege of addressing him unless he had spoken to them first.

To augment the semblance of a royal family, he had sent for his mother and his two eldest sisters, Eliza and Pauline. His features had a closer resemblance to those of Lætitia Boneparte than those of any of her other seven living children, and it was from her that he got all his strongest traits of character. His father, Carlo, had given him only a dash of gentle blood, a love of display and an openhandedness with money. The mother was of near-peasant stock. She had lost her husband twelve years before and had had a desperate struggle to bring up her large family. Honest, virtuous, strict and frugal, she had done so in a way that did her great credit; but her natural limitations deprived her of much of the pleasure she might now have derived from her son's rise to fortune. Tall, gaunt and plainly dressed, her very presence was a censure on the frivolity of Josephine and her circle. Tight-lipped and frowning she showed her disapproval of the adulation paid to Napoleon, whom she continued to regard as an uncertain-tempered young scatterbrain. Years of scraping had made her chronically mean, and his extravagance appalled her. But she had her principles, and remained the rock upon which the whole family was founded. For that he loved and honoured her.

Eliza was twenty; cold, hard, and snobbish from having been educated, although by Royal charity, at an academy for young ladies near Paris. She had recently married a Corsican noble, named Pasquale Baciocchi. Her mother had been pleased with the match and permitted it without consulting Napoleon. When he had heard of it, he had been furious as he had intended to provide her with a husband having better brains and fortune.

His elder brother, the pedestrian-minded, yet industrious, Joseph, he had had appointed Ambassador to Rome, but he had already usurped the headship of the family from him, and on that account been even more enraged with his second brother, Lucien, than with Eliza. This young man was such a rabid revolutionary that he had changed his name to Brutus, and some time before, in true democratic style, married a girl named

Christine Boyer who acted as barmaid in her father's inn at St. Maxime. In the spring of '96, Roger had bought a property in the South of France not far from that little town, to enable him to give out in Paris that he was going to stay there for a while, as cover for secret returns to England; so it chanced that he knew the girl slightly. He thought her pretty, honest and reasonably intelligent, but that did not make up for her lack of birth and fortune in the eyes of Robespierre's old protégé—the poverty-stricken little Captain of Artillery—now that he had become the uncrowned King of Italy.

Pauline, however, was admirably sustaining her new rôle as a Princess. She was the beauty of the family, a lovely young creature of seventeen, gay, flirtatious and always surrounded by a group of admirers, although she too was married, and had been so only for a few months. But she had married, under Napoleon's auspices, the handsome and gallant General Charles Leclerc.

Louis, Lætitia's third son, was also there. As the only possible means of giving him an education Napoleon had, after a leave in Corsica as a young Lieutenant, taken him back to France. He had shared with Louis his modest lodging, kept him on his meagre pay and tutored him at nights; so he looked on Louis as a son rather than as a brother. Louis was now nineteen; he had served through the Italian campaign on Napoleon's staff and worshipped him.

Jerome, the youngest boy, as yet only thirteen, was at school under Joseph's care in Rome, and Caroline, the youngest girl, aged sixteen, was with Hortense de Beauharnais, Josephine's only daughter, at Madam Campan's, a smart finishing school for young ladies outside Paris.

Josephine's son Eugene was also doing his step-father credit. He was short, sturdy and had a waddling walk, but was full of fun, generous and, although still in his 'teens, had proved his courage in several battles as Napoleon's youngest A.D.C.

Lastly, this semi-royal family circle was completed by Joseph Fesch, Lætitia's half-brother: a mild-mannered little priest. He had inherited nothing of her forceful, narrow, but clear-cut views and iron will to maintain her old principles, yet was already being fawned upon by the bishops and cardinals who came to pay court to his pale, young, dynamic, and terribly explosive nephew.

After supper on Roger's first evening at Montebello, Josephine beckoned him to her and told Napoleon how she had rescued this old friend of theirs in Venice. Close to, Roger found him little changed either physically or in manner. He was as thin as ever, an undersized wisp of a man; yet his feats of endurance, and his having played a bold part in the hand-to-hand fighting on several critical occasions during the campaign, testified to his actual fitness, and the strength that lay concealed in his slender body. His skin seemed a little less yellow but it was stretched as tightly as ever over his high cheekbones, and his prominent nose stood out sharply from them. The greater part of his broad forehead was hidden under a fringe and long lank 'ocks of hair fell down to his collar on either side of his immensely strong jaw. He seemed a little listless and disinterested as Josephine spoke to him of Roger, but his fine eyes had already shown friendly recognition and, when she had done, his mobile mouth breaking into a sudden smile, he said quickly:

'I am pleased that Madame my wife should have arrived so opportunely to save you. Sometime you must tell me what you have been up to for all these months. When I have a moment I will send for you.'

For the next few days, Roger mingled with the Court, renewing some acquaintances and making many new ones. Joachim Murat he already knew. It was this handsome, dashing Gascon who, in the pouring rain on the night of 12th Vendémiaire, had fetched the guns from Les Sablons and so enabled Buonaparte to give the Paris mob 'a whiff of grape shot' on the morning of the 13th. Since, starting with a brilliant charge at Borghetto, he had established himself as Bonaparte's finest cavalry leader, and now decked himself out in uniforms of his own invention of which the cloth could hardly be seen for gold. Marmont, a young gunner who was Bonaparte's special protégé, he had also met, and Alexander Berthier, the Chief of Staff, as ugly as Murat was handsome and rivalling him only in the splendour of his uniforms.

Among his new acquaintances were stolid old Sérurier, tall, stern, gloomy, with a big scar on his lip; Joubert, a young General who had greatly distinguished himself and in a very short time become one of the most trusted leaders of the army; André Masséna, tall, dark, thin, Jewish-looking, who seemed a dull man socially, but was said to be a living flame of inspiration on a battlefield. It was he who, in the final advance across the Alps, had stormed the Col de Terwis, and at Rivoli he had led his division in a way which had already earned him immortal glory. Desaix was also there. From discontent at the lack of initiative shown by the Army of the Rhine, he had left it and come down to Italy to offer his homage to Boneparte. His request for employment had been accepted and soon this brilliant soldier was being looked on by the General-in-Chief as one of the ablest of his lieutenants. Lannes was another; as yet only a Brigadier, and still suffering from terrible wounds received in the campaign, but he had been the first man to cross the river Adda and was already regarded as the most audacious leader of infantry assaults.

It was on the third morning that Roger was sent for, and he found the General-in-Chief in one of his tempers. He had been reading some newssheets financed by the extreme Right which had articles in them deliberately belittling his achievements, because he was regarded as a die-hard republican.

As Roger was shown in, he threw the papers on the ground, trampled on them and cried in his harsh French, with its atrocious Italian accent, 'Lies! Lies! Lies! How dare they say that all my plans are made for me by Berthier, and that old Carnot sends me day-to-day orders from his Cabinet in the Luxemburg.'

Pausing for a moment, he stared at Roger, then went on angrily, 'But you know the truth, Monsieur Breuc; you know the truth. When we had that long talk together in my room at the Rue des Capucines, I told you my intentions, did I not?'

'Indeed you did, *mon Général*,' Roger replied enthusiastically, 'and you have carried them out most brilliantly.'

'All but; all but. We should be in Vienna now, had my colleagues accomplished a tenth of what I have done. Four times the Austrians have put armies in the field much greater than mine, and four times I have defeated them.

'And what with, I ask you? What with? When I came to it the army was no more than a rabble. I spoke to the men. I said: "Soldiers, you are naked, badly fed. The Government owes you much; it can give you nothing. Your long suffering, the courage you show among these crags, are splendid, but they bring you no glory; not a ray is reflected upon you. I wish to lead you into the most fertile plains in the world. Rich provinces, great towns, will be in your power; there you will find honour, glory, riches. Soldiers of the Army of Italy, can you be found lacking in honour, courage and constancy?"'

As Roger listened, he realized what such a declaration must have meant. Up till then, France had been fighting against a Monarchist coalition to save the Revolution—to defend herself from invasion and having a king put back on her throne by force of arms—and, where her legions had carried the war into other countries, Belgium, Holland and Piedmont, it had been with the proclaimed ideal of liberating these peoples from the tyranny of autocratic rulers. But Bonaparte had thrown all that overboard. He had altered the whole policy of the war to one of open aggression, declaring it upon peaceful states that in no way threatened France, and inciting his troops to follow him by promises of a free hand to loot and pillage them.

Roger's face remained impassive, but he realized now that the small thin man, dressed so quietly in white breeches, tricolour sash and green coat, who ranted at him, was another Attila who, for his own glory, would stop at nothing and prove a terrible scourge to mankind. Meanwhile the tirade went on:

'I marched them and fought them until they could no longer stand. In eleven days, I forced the Piedmontese out of the war. In a campaign of fourteen days I conquered the Milanese. In fifteen days I forced the Pope to sue for peace. Within thirty-six days of leaving Mantua I was only seventy miles from Vienna. Had I consulted my own interest, and the comfort of the army, I should have remained in Italy. But I threw myself into Germany to extricate the armies of the Rhine. I crossed the Julien and Nordic Alps in three feet of snow. I brought my artillery by roads where not even a cart had ever been and everyone said it was impossible. Had Moreau crossed the Rhine to meet me, we should be in a position to dictate the conditions of peace as masters. As it is, I am left to bluster and intrigue to hold the half of what I have won. Meanwhile, these gentlemen in Paris have the insolence to criticize my treatment of the Milanese and the Venetians. But I shall show them. Yes, I shall show them. I have sent Augereau to Paris and he will know how to deal with such traitors.'

Suddenly he broke off, gave Roger a long stare and snapped: 'And you? What have you been doing?'

Roger told him that knowing that one of his greatest ambitions was to conquer England, he had in the spring of '96 had himself smuggled over to renew his contacts there and to be the better able to report on the chances of a successful invasion.

At first he seemed to be only half listening and thinking of something else; but when Roger went on to say that a chance had arisen for him to go to India, Bonaparte's large luminous eyes suddenly lit up.

'India!' he exclaimed. 'The East has always fascinated me. You must tell me about it. Every detail. But not now. Tell them to lay a cover for you at my table. Over dinner I shall have time to please myself in listening to you.'

Among Roger's greatest assets was the ability both to write and talk well; so at dinner he was able to hold his audience enthralled by accounts of the wealth of Calcutta, fairy palaces, tiger shoots, temples, bazaars, and native Princes dripping with jewels. But Bonaparte never took long over his meals; so afterwards he carried Roger off to a big room, the walls of which were covered with maps.

At a large desk in it a man was working who had been pointed out to Roger as Fauvelet de Bourrienne. He had known Bonaparte from the age of eight and been his only intimate friend while they were cadets together in the Military Academy at Brienne. Later he had held a diplomatic post in Germany and, as he was an aristocrat, had wisely refused to leave it when recalled to Paris during the Terror. In consequence, had been listed as an émigré and only after considerable pressure by Bonaparte been granted permission to come to his headquarters. He had arrived on the day that the peace preliminaries at Leoben had been signed, and Bonaparte, knowing his great abilities, had at once made him his Chef de Cabinet.

The maps on the wall were all of Italy or Germany, but Bourrienne produced one of India and, knowing his master's habits, spread it out on the floor. Boneparte flopped down in his favourite position at full length on his stomach and Roger knelt beside him.

It was not until Roger began to trace his homeward journey that Boneparte realized that he had returned by way of the Red Sea and Egypt and, at this, his mood changed from that of interested listener to eager questioner.

'If I ever go to India, that is the road I shall take,' he declared after a while. 'The Revolution played the very devil with our fleet, and sailors cannot be made like soldiers in a few months of hard campaigning. It will take years yet before the new officers of our Navy become expert at their business and discipline among the seamen is fully restored. Meanwhile, at sea the British will continue to have the advantage of us. It would be suicide to try to transport an army round the Cape. Besides, there are no lands on which we could live on the way.'

As Roger talked on about Cairo, the Pyramids and the Nile, it emerged that the young conqueror's mind had already been moving in that direction, for he said, 'The Austrians thought themselves clever when in June they anticipated one of the proposals for a peace, by occupying the Venetian territories on the Dalmatian coast; but that gave me just the excuse I needed for seizing Corfu and the Ionian Isles. We took them by clever stratagem, too. I sent General Gentilli to tell the Venetians in the forts that, as the friend and protector of Venice, I was sending French troops to strengthen their garrisons. The fools believed him and admitted our men. We collected most of the Venetian Navy, five hundred cannon and immense stores. But I'd meant to have the Islands anyhow, because they are the first stepping-stone should we decide to go east.'

'Now that you have become of such importance to France, surely the Directory would not agree to your leaving Europe?' Roger hazarded, to draw him out.

'What, those fellows!' He gave a quick laugh. 'They would give an eye apiece to see me go. And they have often toyed with schemes for getting back our lost foothold in India. It must be that next or the conquest of England, and if the English make peace we will go to Egypt. I'll not see my soldiers disbanded or starving. I owe it to them to find them fresh employment.'

After a moment he went on, 'And whichever it is, you must come with us. Your antecedents, and the knowledge you have acquired of places, will prove most useful. Bourrienne—Bourrienne; do you hear me?'

The *Chef de Cabinet* had all this time been writing letter after letter at incredible speed. Now he looked up and asked, 'What is it, *mon Général?*'

Boneparte got to his feet, dusted his bony knees, and said, 'Breuc, here, is half an Englishman and can pass as one anywhere. If we had invaded the island in '96, I should have taken him with me. I shall do so if fate assigns that to us as our next task. But I find now that he has spent the past year in the East, and has added Persian and Arabic to the several European tongues he speaks; so he could prove equally valuable to us on the Nile. Besides, he was with me at Toulon, and on 13th Vendémiaire, and I like to have about me faces I know. I shall make him an extra A.D.C., but at one time he was a journalist; so while we have no fighting to do, he could help you.'

Bourrienne stood up, bowed and said, as he and Roger cordially shook hands, 'I have work enough here for ten, and most of the staff are more able at handling a sword than a pen; so I shall be delighted to have Monsieur Breuc's assistance.'

Thus it transpired that, without any striving on Roger's part, the long chain of his previous activities opened wide to him all Bonaparte's secrets.

The Corsican's reference to the possibility of England making peace led Roger to take an early opportunity next day of questioning Bourrienne on the subject. He then learnt that despite their humiliation in December, the British Government had again opened negotiations. Of their last attempt, owing to the severe winter weather, Lord Malmesbury's progress to Paris had been so exceptionally slow that Edmund Burke had caustically remarked that 'he must have gone all the way on his knees'. This malicious jibe had been printed in all the Whig news-sheets and so reached France, where it had caused much delighted laughter. Nevertheless, in spite, so French intelligence reported, of strong opposition from King George and a threat by the Foreign Secretary, Lord Grenville, to resign, Mr. Pitt had decided to eat humble pie and try again.

The Directors, fearing that, if Malmesbury came to Paris, now that the Right had become so strong it might be strengthened by him to overthrow them, had decreed that the negotiations should be conducted in Lille. Malmesbury had arrived there in July and the key man among those sent to treat with him was Hugues Bernard Maret, a gifted diplomat who was anxious to agree a peace, as also were the French Constitutionalists, who now formed the great bulk of the Deputies. Owing to the wretched conditions that prevailed in the interior of France, they would have even met Britain half-way. Carnot and Barthélemy were also strongly of the opinion that now that France could negotiate from strength, owing to her victories in Italy, she should seize the opportunity to get good terms and bring an end to the war. But they were outvoted by their three die-hard Republican colleagues. These insisted that Britain should not be left even a rag to cover the shame of her surrender.

Now that the Austrians were negotiating separately, Mr. Pitt was no longer under any obligation to insist on the return to them of their Belgian territories. He was even willing to give up all the West Indian islands that Britain had taken from the French, and to assist them in suppressing the negro revolt in the richest of all their old colonies—San Domingo. But the Jacobin Directors were now sticking out for the return of colonies lost to their allies. They demanded back Trinidad for Spain and the Cape for Holland, knowing that if these were conceded they could make them their own. Realizing this, Mr. Pitt had dug his toes in about the Cape, since without it the British route to India would no longer be secure. There the matter rested.

As a by-product of this discussion, Roger learned that Talleyrand had returned from exile in America and, owing to the influence of that brilliant intriguer, his old friend Madame de Staël, the French wife of the Swedish Ambassador, been given the Foreign Office. At that Roger was delighted, for he knew Talleyrand always to have favoured an alliance with England against the growing power of Prussia. Moreover, although Talleyrand was one of the only two Frenchmen who knew that Roger was the son of an English Admiral, he owed to him both his life and the preservation of his house from confiscation during the Terror, and he was not the man to betray a friend who had rendered him such services.

The other, who knew Roger for a true Englishman, was Joseph Fouché, a most dangerous and vindictive Terrorist who, to save his own skin, had assisted in bringing about Robespierre's downfall. But the reaction had caught up with him and, by tactful enquiry, Roger learnt that for a long time past nothing had been heard of him; so, presumably, he had submerged himself in the masses from fear that he might yet be called to account for his many crimes.

Very soon, too, Roger was able to get a firm grasp of the situation in Paris. The Royalists there had practically come out into the open. They were few, but very active, and well supplied with money. All their resources were applied to rousing the Constitutionalists, who had not only a majority in both Chambers, but now represented the greater part of the French people, to action. General Pichegru was the man upon whom they relied to lead them; but although already secretly sold, as Roger knew, to the Royalist cause, he was too cautious to risk an attempt to overthrow the Directory until he could be certain of strong military backing.

Despairing of him, the Clichyans, as the Royalists were termed from having a Club where they brewed these plots up in Clichy, had turned to Carnot. But he and his respectable colleague, the diplomat Barthélemy, would have no truck with any movement for a restoration, although they were for peace and a new era of justice and toleration, which the moderates wanted.

Opposed to them stood the remnant of the Terrorists who still controlled the executive power: Rewbell, the German-born apostle of equality through the murder of the whole of the upper class; Larevellière-Lepeaux, who would have liked to see every priest crucified; and Barras, brave, dissolute and utterly corrupt, who cared only for women and gold; together with all the minor Jacobins who had succeeded in keeping their heads after the fall of Robespierre and feared that they still might lose them should the reaction triumph.

Each week, motions were now being passed by large majorities in the Chamber of the Five Hundred that favoured such measures as the resumption of ringing of church bells, that the relatives of *émigrés* should no longer be debarred from holding Government appointments, and that certain categories of *émigrés* should be allowed to return. Above all, they agitated for the re-establishment of the Paris National Guard; and on this hinged everything. By far the greater part of the National Guard was drawn from the *bourgeois*, who were heart and soul with the moderates. It was their attempt to assert themselves that Barras, with the aid of Bonaparte, had crushed on 13th Vendémiaire and after it the National Guard had been disbanded. Under the Constitution no troops, other than the 1,500 guards of the two Chambers, were allowed within twelve leagues of Paris; therefore, if the National Guard was re-created and armed, it would have Paris at its mercy, and could be used to overthrow the Directory. It was for that Pichegru was waiting.

The Directory had behaved far from well to Bonaparte. Jealous of the name he was making for himself they had, until almost the end of his campaign, starved him of reinforcements, and it was largely their withholding funds from General Moreau which had rendered him unable to set his army in motion across the Rhine to make a junction with that of Italy.

Bonaparte, on the other hand, had ignored their instructions in so flagrant a manner that it would have cost any less successful General his command. To start with, he had been told to turn Piedmont into a Republic; instead he had, on his own authority, signed a peace with the old King Victor Amadeus. Then he had been ordered to march his army south through Central Italy so that it might, in turn, crush the Kingdom of Naples; instead, he had risked it in the north against an Austrian Army of far greater numbers.

His policy had been right. The Austrians were the only major land-power in arms against France. If they could be defeated, all the lesser enemies must collapse like a house of cards. By making a quick peace with Piedmont, he had freed his army so that it might be turned swiftly against the Austrians before they could become still stronger. Their defeats had led in turn to the fall of Parma, Modena, Milan, Mantua, the disintegration of the Supreme Republic, and Naples abandoning the Coalition to become neutral.

Again, the Directory had urged him to have no mercy on Rome and to abolish the Papacy. He had thrown that order away, too, and dealt with the matter in a way about which they could not complain but also enormously to his own personal advantage. He had deprived the Pope of the greater part of his territories, exacted from him a huge indemnity and robbed him of many great works of art; but he had left Rome free and not interfered in any way with His Holiness's spiritual authority. Such restraint by the representative of a Government of anarchists and atheists had been so unexpected that the Pope had written to him as 'My dear son', the Cardinals had blessed him while handing over their gold plate, and he had enormously enhanced his own popularity in France, where there were millions of Catholics still practising their religion in secret, who now began to look on him as a possible champion of their faith.

The Directory had, too, given him a Political Commissar—one General Clarke—without whose sanction he was not supposed to enter into any negotiations with the enemies of the Republic, let alone agree terms of peace. But this Franco-Irish diplomat-soldier proved no match for the wily Corsican. On plausible pretexts Clarke was always got out of the way to handle small matters in distant cities, to find on his return that Bonaparte had already settled some big one according to his own fancy. When the Directors protested, he pretended surprise, wrote that he was tired and ill, and offered to resign his Command. They fumed with rage but dared not recall him because of his obvious ability and ever-increasing popularity.

Nevertheless, his own interests demanded that he should support them against the Clichyans, and early in the summer he had sent his personal Adjutant, the *ci-devant* Count de Lavalette, off to Paris to keep him secretly informed of the situation. Lavalette had reported that unless some drastic step was taken, the Directory was almost certain to be overthrown; but he had advised against Bonaparte himself coming to Paris if it could possibly be avoided, because the moderates formed such a high proportion of the population that if he took any direct action against them his own popularity was bound to suffer.

With his usual cunning, he had got round that by making Augereau his cat's-paw. The Army of Italy was rabidly republican and on July 14th it had celebrated the anniversary of the fall of the Bastille with tremendous enthusiasm. Bonaparte had issued a stirring proclamation calling on it to demonstrate its adherence to the principles of the Revolution by loyal addresses to the Government. Each Division had done so in no uncertain manner. Augereau's men, the reddest of the reds, had, in referring to the new measures for moderation being advocated in the two Chambers, even gone to the length of including a passage which read:

'Tremble, O conspirators! From the Adige and the Rhine to the Seine is but a step. Tremble! Your iniquities are numbered, and the price of them is at the point of our bayonets!'

These were open threats against the legally elected Legislature that should it go too far the troops would march on Paris and bring about a renewal of the Terror. On the pretext of sending a number of captured enemy flags to Paris, Bonaparte had then sent Augereau there with instructions to see to it that the loyal addresses from the Army of Italy were published. He was now sitting back, quietly confident that the fierce swashbuckling General would take any steps necessary to pull his chestnuts out of the fire for him.

Roger gained all this inside information while assisting Bourrienne, mainly in translating documents and writing *précis* of confidential reports. He would have given a great deal to be able to send a report himself to Mr. Pitt, but for the time being he had no means of doing so. He could only wait until an opportunity arose for him to return to Venice and hope to get one through by one of the secret couriers who must, he knew, be keeping Mr. Watson in touch with London.

Meanwhile, as one of the personal entourage, he saw Napoleon and Josephine every day and sometimes was invited to spend the evening with them. The former never tired of hearing more about Egypt and India, and the latter found him an asset to the family's amusements. She loved amateur theatricals, charades and childish games, and in private the great man was by no means averse to looking on or joining in the games, provided always that he was allowed to be the winner.

It was some ten days after Roger's arrival at the Château Montebello that chance revealed to him that childish games were by no means the only ones played there by the General-in-Chief. Having woken early one morning, he went down from his attic in a chamber robe and soft slippers to Bourrienne's office to collect some papers with the intention of reading them in bed. As he walked noiselessly along a corridor on the first floor, he passed a door that was not quite closed, and heard someone on the other side of it say:

'You saw the General come out of her room. Do not deny it.'

He recognized the voice as that of Constant, the General's valet, and, halting in his tracks, he listened intently to catch the rest of the conversation. From it he learned that Bonaparte was having an *affaire* with one of Josephine's ladies-in-waiting and going to her room by stealth at night. On this occasion they had fallen asleep so Constant had gone to her door and tapped on it to wake him. Some minutes later, he had hurried back to his own apartments and had caught sight of a housemaid watching him from a window that overlooked the corridor. Believing her to be a spy placed there by his wife, he had sent Constant to warn her that if she breathed a word she would be instantly dismissed.

Roger had soon discovered that the immorality rampant in the Paris of the Directory had arrived with the dozens of beautiful and fashionable women who now graced the General-in-Chief's court at Montebello, and that nearly all of them had become the mistress of one, if not more, of the gallant blades who trailed their sabres in its splendid *salons*. Several of them had, in fact, made him quite open overtures; but he still wore the rope of Clarissa's golden hair round his neck, and had taken a vow not to kiss another woman until he had revenged her. Yet, in this gilded brothel, Napoleon and Josephine appeared to be a couple apart, and a model of connubial bliss; so he was both surprised and intrigued to find that this was not so.

During the day he made tactful enquiries of several men with whom he had become fairly intimate and soon learned what he would have learned much earlier had his mind not been too occupied with other matters.

The intensity of Bonaparte's first passion for Josephine could not be doubted and only the glamour of at last having an army to command had caused him to tear himself away from her within a few days of their marriage. That marriage, to her, had so far been only an episode into which she had been persuaded to secure a promising future for her children; so on his departure she swiftly slid back into her old way of life.

She was a voluptuous, lazy creature and without being in the least vicious quite naturally accepted the immoral way of life led by her friends. Bonaparte had written again and again, covering reams of paper with passionate pleas for her to join him, but she had lingered on for many months in Paris before at last doing so, and he had had ample grounds for believing that during them she was being unfaithful to him.

His love for her had not cooled, but his physical passion could at times be as demanding as his craving for glory; so quite early in their separation he had spent occasional nights with other women.

When she had eventually arrived at Mantua the violence of his passion had again frightened her, and to such a degree that she had become cold towards him. Feeling certain that she had given herself freely to other lovers, this had driven him into a frenzy of fury, and a climax had been reached when he intercepted a letter to her from Lazare Hoche whom he knew to have paid her marked attention in Paris. As that brilliant young General was his only serious rival to fame, and the letter was decidedly more than affectionate, his rage had known no bounds. He kicked a pug-dog that Hoche had given her to death before her eyes, and the fact that he had later had a memorial erected to it in the garden was small consolation in view of her passionate love of animals.

From that point the urgency of his physical desire for her appeared to have cooled somewhat, but she still inspired in him a strong affection, and he showed great kindness and thoughtfulness towards her. It was this which caused him to exercise caution in his amours, as both of them continued to be jealous where the other was concerned, and he went to great lengths to spare her the knowledge of his infidelities.

All this gave Roger much food for thought, and that night a plan evolved in his mind by which he might both serve his country well and bring Malderini to book in a highly suitable manner. He had to bide his time for a further day and a half until chance left him alone with Boneparte in the map-room and the General was not engaged on any matter of importance. Then he said, casually:

'Mon Général. In view of the great interest you take in all things connected with the East, I have been wondering if it would amuse you to dine, tête-à-tête, one night with a very beautiful Indian Princess?'

CHAPTER TWENTY-SIX

The Rape of Venice

'AN Indian Princess,' Boneparte repeated. 'That would certainly be an experience. But surely there is not such a woman here in Milan, or I would have heard of her?'

'No. She lives in Venice. I thought perhaps when you next go on one of your tours of inspection. . . .'

'Yes, I could arrange to spend a night there. Tell me more of her. Would she prove readily complaisant?'

'That I cannot guarantee,' Roger smiled. 'But I should have thought, mon Général, that you would have found women as easy to conquer as enemy fortresses. I can only vouch for it that she is in her early twenties, has beauty and a noble carriage, speaks Italian and French fluently, and hates her husband.'

'Presumably, then, she has had numerous lovers.'

'I doubt that. Her husband is a Venetian ex-Senator and he keeps her like a bird in a gilded cage. The poor lady has had no more chance to succumb to temptation than if she had continued to live as the inmate of a seraglio in her native India.'

'Pst!' Boneparte exclaimed with annoyance. 'That makes her ten times more alluring, yet rules her out for me. Why arouse my interest when you must know well enough that it means the sort of adventure which can so easily end in scandal and that, for the sake of Madame my wife, I am determined to have no scandal attaching to my name.'

'There will be no scandal if you leave the matter to me.'

'How can you be sure of that? Husbands have an uncanny knack of returning unexpectedly when a lover has been introduced into the house.'

'I should get her out of it to sup with you in some place where there was no risk of your being disturbed.'

'Since she is so jealously guarded, even if she were willing, that savours of abduction. Were it discovered that I had connived at the abduction of an ex-Senator's wife for my pleasure, it would set all Venice by the ears. Policy made it necessary for me to despoil Venice of all her mainland territories, but I have brought freedom to the people of the city, and they bless me for it. They rely upon me now to maintain their independence, and look on me as their protector. To have raped the Serene Republic politically was one thing. To as good as rape the wife of one of its leading citizens is quite another. Did it become known, I would at once lose their esteem and be accounted a villain.'

Roger shrugged. 'Your fears are needless. I can so arrange matters that there will be no scandal, and am prepared to guarantee that the husband shall be given no grounds for complaint. All you have to do is to give me a chit to Villetard ordering him to carry out my instructions. Only a handful of people need ever know that you have spent the night in Venice and, unless you distrust your personal staff, none of them will afterwards bear word to Madame Boneparte that you supped with the Princess. On that I pledge my head. But, if this little project of mine for providing you with a few hours' interesting relaxation from your immense labours has no real appeal to you, let us say no more about it.'

'An Indian Princess,' Boneparte muttered, and he began to walk up and down the room with his hands clasped behind his back. 'An Indian Princess. Yes, well, why not, if you are so certain that the matter can be arranged discreetly? You are prepared to take complete responsibility for that, eh?'

'I am. I'll answer for it with my head,' Roger repeated.

'Very well then. When next I go on a journey which will bring me within easy distance of Venice, remind me of it.'

Roger gave a secret sigh of satisfaction. It had required skilful handling to lure the lean, lank-haired panther, even with such an attractive piece of meat. But he had felt that Boneparte's snobbishness would prove a helpful factor; for, despite his passion for Josephine, he had gone to the length of marrying her only because a union with her, as the widow of a nobleman of the *ancien régime*, would lift his own social status, and his rise to greatness was still recent enough for a Princess to have, in his mind, a mystic superiority over any ordinary woman. That, combined with the way in which anything to do with the East held a special fascination for him, had done the trick.

In these September days there was an atmosphere of suppressed excitement among the small intimate circle surrounding the General-in-Chief, as they awaited the resolving of the crisis in Paris which could not be long delayed.

It was one of the great weaknesses in the Constitution of the Year III that Ministers, instead of being selected from the Five Hundred and the Ancients, were outside them and appointed or dismissed entirely at the will of the Directors. Recently the majorities in the two Chambers had been pressing hard for a reshuffle, in the hope that men of more moderate views might be put into several of the key posts, but their intrigues to that end had weakened instead of strengthened their position. Rewbell, Larevellière and Barras had not only retained the men the Moderates wished to oust, but had seized the opportunity to get rid of Cochon, the Minister of Police, and Petiet, the Minister of War, both of whom were devoted to Carnot, and replace them with old revolutionaries.

At this, the resentment of the Moderates, egged on by the Clichyan Royalists, had become definitely threatening, so Barras had sent to Hoche for armed support. Some months before Jourdan, having long failed to maintain the reputation he had achieved as a General during the early wars of the Revolution, had been relieved of his command of the Army of the Sambre and Meuse, and been replaced by Hoche. On the excuse of moving troops towards Brest in preparation for another attempt against Ireland, Hoche had marched some fifteen thousand men to the neighbourhood of Paris, and a body of his cavalry had overrun the limit beyond which troops, other than the Constitutional Guard, were forbidden to approach the capital. The result was a frightful outcry in the two Chambers, and Carnot and Barthèlemy had vigorously protested to their co-Directors; but as they were in the minority no action was taken against Hoche.

In the meantime, definite evidence had come to light that General Pichegru had sold out to the Royalists. On the French entering Venice, they had arrested a Royalist agent named Comte d'Entraigues and seized his papers. Among them was an account of Pichegru's treacherous agreement, while commanding the Army of the Rhine, with two other royalist agents, the Comte de Montgailliard and M. Fauche-Borel, who were acting on behalf of the Prince de Condé.

When Roger learned of this his heart had, for a moment, stopped beating, for he too had been deeply involved in the affair and had actually bought Pichegru, on Mr. Pitt's behalf, for a million francs in gold, obtained against British Treasury bills from the house of Rothschild in Frankfurt. But fortunately he had known Montgailliard to be a rogue before taking any part in the matter, so had refused to have anything to do with him; and he had swiftly got over his fright on realizing that, had any mention been made of him in d'Entraigues's documents, Bourrienne would certainly have known about it and already had him arrested.

Bonaparte had sent the papers to Paris, and their contents had since been confirmed from another quarter. It transpired that General Moreau had also known of Pichegru's treacherous dealings with the Prince de Condé, but out of friendship for his brother General had not reported the matter. But Moreau was a staunch Republican, and now that the Directory was in danger had come to Paris and denounced Pichegru to it. Yet, even so, presumably from fear of Pichegru's arrest proving the signal for a general rising against them, they had so far taken no action against him.

Thus matters stood at the moment, and everyone at Montebello was anxiously waiting to see if Pichegru, possibly supported by Carnot, would launch a counter-revolution, and, if so, whether Barras and Co. supported by Hoche and Augereau, would succeed in suppressing it.

Roger had never met Pierre Augereau, but he had heard a great deal about him. He was the son of a working mason, and a typical gamin of the Paris gutters. As a young footman, then as a waiter, he had been dismissed from both posts for seducing young women, then he had gone into the Army and soon become the best swordsman in the Royal cavalry. The number of his fellow N.C.O.s that he had seriously wounded or killed in duels was legendary; and when a young officer struck him with his cane, he had promptly killed him too, which had necessitated his bolting to Switzerland on a stolen horse.

From there, as a traveller in watches, he had gone to Constantinople and on to Odessa where, finding a war in progress, he had enlisted in the Russian Army. Not liking the Russians, he had deserted, worked his way via Poland to Prussia and enlisted in the army of Frederick the Great. Not liking the Prussians either, he had deserted again and, the penalty being death, had protected himself from capture by taking sixty other troopers with him; they had fought their way over the frontier into Saxony.

For a while he had earned his living as a dancing-master, then drifted to Athens, whence he had eloped with a beautiful Greek girl to Lisbon. There, the French Revolution having broken out, his violent advocacy of revolutionary principles had led the Portuguese Government to put him in prison; but, with the aid of a French merchant captain, he had got back to France, where he had enlisted in a volunteer regiment and fought the

Whites in La Vendée with such ruthless ferocity that he had soon been elected *Chef de Bataillon*. By '93 he had been made a Divisional Commander.

He was now forty years of age, a huge hawk-nosed brute of a man, licentious, foul-mouthed, quarrelsome; but a magnificent soldier. His division was the best cared for and the most reliable in the Army of Italy. It was always where it was wanted, he had a marvellous flair for timing its attacks and led them with complete disregard for personal danger.

He had moral courage, too, and, although he had become a loyal admirer of Boneparte, was not afraid to stand up to him. In fact, on the one occasion during the campaign when the little Corsican had lost his nerve, or at least appeared to have done so, it was Augereau who had taken charge and pulled him through.

That had been at Castiglione. With his usual daring he had placed himself between the three Austrian armies commanded by Generals Würmser, Quosdanovich and Davidovich, but one of his own Generals, Valette, had practically thrown away a key position, thus rendering the situation of the French army extremely precarious. This had sent Boneparte into such a transport of fury that, apart from reducing the wretched Valette to the ranks, his mind had seemed to lose the faculty of forming any decision. At a night conference of Generals he had talked vaguely of a retreat to the Adda. Augereau had violently opposed retreat and eventually stamped out of the meeting in a passion. Next morning another conference was called and the argument recommenced. This time, on Augereau's again pressing for a vigorous attack, it was Boneparte who had walked out, simply remarking, 'Well, I wash my hands of it, and I am going away.' The astonished circle were stricken dumb, except for Augereau, who shouted after him, 'If you go, who is to command?' The reply, called back over Boneparte's shoulder, was 'You'.

Augereau had promptly given battle, leading the first charge himself. Soon afterwards Boneparte had resumed the direction of operations, but Augereau had also delivered the final stroke that had routed the Austrians, so it was undoubtedly his victory. Nevertheless, it was the opinion of some people that Boneparte's apparent temporary mental collapse was simply a cunning ruse, and that the wily Corsican, finding himself in a position which threatened to mar his unbroken record of victories, had deliberately left the decision, either to fight or retreat, to someone else, so that if things did go wrong he could escape being blamed for it. Having regard to the extraordinary duplicity of Boneparte's character, that was certainly a possibility; but, even so, Roger did not see how by just walking out, a General-in-Chief could shrug off his responsibility. The fact remained, too, that Boneparte was most generous in his praise of Augereau, and for years afterwards whenever anyone complained to him about the great swashbuckling gamin, he would reply: 'Ah, but look what he did for us at Castiglione.'

A few weeks after despatching Augereau to Paris, Boneparte had sent Bernadotte after him with some more captured flags; but that was a very different story. Charles Jean Bernadotte was, like Murat, a Gascon, and later as the sovereigns of Naples and Sweden they became known as the 'Gascon Kings'. But Bernadotte, although in appearance another splendid-looking, large-nosed swashbuckler, had a subtle and treacherous brain. He was a great flatterer, greatly liked by his troops and junior officers, and always charming to civilians, but universally hated by his brother Generals, and to that feeling Boneparte was no exception.

Bernadotte had won his fame with the army of the Sambre-et-Meuse and had expected to succeed Jourdan on his retirement. Instead, the Directory, at last acceding to Boneparte's plea for reinforcements for his final drive into Austria, had ordered Bernadotte to march his division down to Milan. The result had not been a happy one.

The French armies of the North were still practising the old war technique of ponderous march and counter march, with plenty of prolonged periods in between for drill and sprucing themselves up. Bernadotte's division were good fighters when they actually got into a battle, but when they joined the Army of Italy neither they nor their General sought to hide their contempt for the slovenly mobs which had performed such prodigies of valour under Augereau and Masséna. The latter were largely ex-sans-culottes, the former moderates, and as soon as the campaign was over open strife broke out between them. Brune, who was temporarily commanding Masséna's division, had called on Bernadotte's Chief of Staff and asked him to forbid the use of the word 'Monsieur' among his officers. The Chief of Staff had refused and challenged Brune to a duel. Officers and men had taken up their leaders' quarrel with the result that, within twenty-four hours, fifty men had been killed and three hundred wounded.

Boneparte and Bernadotte had disliked one another on sight, and the former's Chief of Staff, Berthier, had developed a positive hatred for the handsome, long-nosed supercilious Gascon. But at least they had good reason to believe him loyal to the Directory; so they had got rid of him by pushing him off to Paris after Augereau.

Couriers came galloping in from Paris night and day, but even with the best speed they could make, their news was over a week old before it got to Montebello. It was therefore not until September 13th that Boneparte and his staff had first particulars of events on 18th of the month in the revolutionary calendar named Fructidor.

This date, by the old reckoning September 4th, 1797, was to rank with 13th Vendémiaire, and later 18th Brumaire, as key dates in the short life of the Directory. The corrupt but courageous Barras, and the brutal but bold Augereau, managed everything between them. The former did not even tell his colleagues Rewbell and Larevellière what was planned until a few hours before the blow was struck.

Augereau's troops surrounded the two Chambers and demanded the surrender of the Constitutional Guard, a large part of which had been suborned beforehand. When asked by what right he did so, he had grinned, drawn his huge sabre, and declared: 'By that of the sword.'

Next day the Five Hundred and the Ancients were summoned to meet in the Odeon Theatre and the School of Medicine, respectively. Few who were not partisans of the Left dared to do so. To these were put resolutions that Barras and his friends had drafted overnight. The principle of these was the completely arbitrary cancellation of the recent elections in forty-eight Departments, thus throwing out at one stroke the greater part of the Deputies who represented the moderate views now held by a majority of the people of France.

After this first news of the *coup d'état* couriers arrived almost every hour at Montebello bringing further details. Some fifty members of the two Chambers, among them Generals Pichegru and Willot and such famous anti-Terrorists as Boissy d'Anglas, Bourdon of the Oise and Barbé-Marbois, had been placed under arrest and condemned to transportation; so, too, had the able and honest Director, Barthèlemy, to whom, as a diplomat, France owed the withdrawal of Prussia from among her active enemies. Carnot's arrest had also been ordered, but he had taken the precaution of hiding in his bedroom at the Luxembourg a spare key to a small gate in the garden and, warned only just in time by his brother, he had escaped through it.

No one could have been more pleased at this last piece of news than Roger. Although Carnot had been one of Robespierre's colleagues, he had taken no part in the Terror and, as a professional soldier, concerned himself only with the defence of France. He had not only raised, armed and trained her great new armies, but for five years been solely responsible for the strategy by which she had kept her many enemies at bay. He had, too, been in a large part personally responsible for the great republican victory at Wattignies; for, having planned the battle with Jourdan at his field-headquarters, he had later, on seeing a wing of the French front break, leapt into the fray, rallied the retreating *sans-culottes* and, waving his hat on the end of his cane, himself led them back in a victorious charge. He was a great man in every sense, honourable, generous, courageous, compassionate, and with high ideals for the real betterment of the masses; and Roger regarded him with more respect than he had for any other revolutionary leader.

After a further week or so, to the relief of most people, it became apparent that the Left did not intend to use its triumph to launch a renewal of the Terror. With shocking barbarity the shilly-shallying Pichegru, the unfortunate Barthèlemy, and a number of others were transported in iron cages through France to La Rochelle, before being shipped off to 'la guillotine sec', as exiles in the fever-ridden swamps of Cayenne. Apart from this, no acts of tyranny were indulged in and Paris, although trembling, remained quiet. But the laws against émigrés and priests were once more rigidly enforced, the Royalist Clubs were closed, and a heavy censorship was placed upon the press. Merlin of Douai and Françoise de Neuf-château were elected as Directors to replace Carnot and Barthélemy, much to Augereau's annoyance, as he had hoped to become a Director himself; but to console him he was made General-in-Chief of the Armies of the Rhine.

News of a further result of the coup d'état reached Peschiera, on Lake Garda, to which Boneparte had moved at the end of September. The peace negotiations at Lille had dragged on since July, because Mr. Pitt, although willing to buy peace by giving the French practically everything for which they asked, still refused to give up the Cape of Good Hope. The French were, it is true, demanding its return to the Dutch, but everyone knew that now they dominated Holland so completely it would be turned into a French naval base, and with the French at the Cape it would not be long before they cut Britain's invaluable shipping route to India.

The French Republicans had always regarded Britain as their most deadly enemy and had no desire for peace with her. Now that they had succeeded in crushing the Moderates, who favoured peace, they broke off the negotiations and, on September 17th, Lord Malmesbury had been told in the most cavalier fashion that he must leave France within twenty-four hours.

Roger had hated the thought of Britain making such a humiliating peace after all the years of effort, thousands of lives and millions in treasure that she had poured into the war; yet he needed no telling how black her future looked now that, once the Austrian business was settled, she must fight on alone. The only escape from invasion and the annihilation he could see for his country was that, by hook or by crook, she must once more arouse Europe against France and provide her again with enemies on the Continent.

The greatest hope for that lay in the fact that France was still bankrupt. Only the huge indemnities that Boneparte had been extracting from the Italian States had kept her going during the past eighteen months. And Boneparte had altered the whole aspect of the war to one of open aggression and plunder. If that policy was continued, and it must be unless France was to collapse, the next victims would be the small German states on the far side of the Rhine. At that Prussia and Russia would become alarmed and might be drawn in to Britain's assistance. Austria too was very far from being down and out. She now had Dalmatia, with its hardy population of Croat and Slovene fighting men to draw upon, as well as Hungary and her other vast dominions. With such a huge reservoir of manpower, given a few months to recover from the blow Boneparte had dealt her, she could again put great armies in the field.

That, Roger felt, made it all the more imperative that nothing possible should be left undone which would strengthen Austria's hand in launching a new campaign, and his mind turned once more to Venice.

From Bourrienne he had learned the inner history of Boneparte's rape of the Serene Republic. The Austrians had long had trouble in ruling their Flemish subjects so that, now France had a secure hold on Belgium, they were prepared to give up their claim to it, but only provided that they were compensated with equally valuable territory nearer home. Boneparte had already made his plans for forming the Italian Duchies into one or more Republics under French influence so that, as he had written to the Directory, in any future war France would be able to menace the rest of Italy through them; therefore, they could not be given up. But what about the broad fertile lands ruled by the *Serenissima*?

There lay Venice: a great, fat, golden calf, that had only to be killed and cut up. But Venice had declared her neutrality. She would not even act like a very small bull and put up the sort of token resistance that had served to justify Boneparte's deposing the rulers of the Duchies, and even he could not bring himself to face the opprobrium with which all Europe would have regarded him had he cut the calf's throat while it licked his hand. It had to be made to bite.

On his instructions, his agents had stopped at nothing that might goad the mild beast into a protesting bleat. They had set the nobles of the mainland against those of the city, used the separatist ambitions of minorities and fostered a revolutionary spirit in the mobs of the towns. He had given his brutal soldiery *carte blanche* to do as they liked while quartered in Venetian territory, and been far more harsh in his exactions and requisitions from this neutral state than in any of the lands he had conquered.

In spite of all this the *Serenissima* had remained with bended knee; but, outside its control, unceasing deliberate torment had at last aroused sporadic resistance. That had been enough. With sickening hypocrisy the little Corsican had told the *Serenissima*'s envoys, sent to express regret and offer handsome compensation, that he 'could not discuss matters with men whose hands were dripping with blood'.

Even before that the fate of the Serene Republic as a nation had been sealed and, when rumours of his intention had got about, he had temporarily masked his true character as a brigand by throwing out the suggestion that, if Venice would give up her northern provinces to Austria, she should receive as compensation Bologna, Ferrara and the Romagna. But he had not meant one word of it; these ex-Papal States had already been earmarked by him as part of his new Cispadine Republic.

The 'Easter Vespers', as the massacre of the French in Verona had come to be called, was the fruit of all his efforts. After it he no longer needed to talk of compensation. He had his long-desired pretext for declaring war on Venice. The spineless *Serenissima* collapsed, enabling him to cut chunks of meat from the living body of the calf and chuck them at will to the Austrians.

But the Austrians were greedy, and clever enough to know that France needed peace as badly as they did. Their envoys, M. de Merveldt and the Marquis di Gallo, had shilly-shallied for months at Montebello putting off the agreement of definite terms while watching events in Paris and hoping for a change of Government that would be to their advantage.

It had not matured. On the contrary, the *coup d'état* of 18th Fructidor had settled the Directory in the saddle more firmly than ever. Boneparte's hand was strengthened. He was able to threaten now that if matters were not concluded soon he would resume the offensive and, after all, conclude them in Vienna.

The Emperor felt disinclined to call his bluff and Thugut, the Austrian Chancellor, sent his most able diplomat, Count Cobenzl, to enter on really serious negotiations. Early in October, Boneparte, accompanied by his personal staff, moved up to Passeriano, south of Udine, to meet the new Austrian Plenipotentiary. In addition to Venice's territories on the east of the Adriatic, which Austria had already grabbed, he wanted her mainland territories as far west as the river Adige and the city itself. In return Austria was prepared to give up all claim to Belgium, to exchange the city of Mayence for that of Venice and to accept France's boundary as the Rhine. The Directory wanted the boundary, but was so strongly averse to giving the Austrians all they wanted that it threatened to order the Armies of the Rhine to take the field again.

This possibility of a resumption of hostilities caught Boneparte at an awkward time. The Austrians had cleverly talked away the summer and the idea of waging another winter campaign through the Alps did not appeal to him at all. Moreover, he wanted the Austrians out of the war so that he could develop new schemes he had in mind. He therefore decided to ignore the Directory's orders and make the best peace he could get behind their backs.

Venice was clearly the main bone of contention. The Emperor was set on having it, and the Directory were set on incorporating it in the new

French-controlled Cisalpine Republic. Boneparte, on the contrary, while stripping it to its shirt, had all along posed as its protector. He liked the rôle, and from mixed motives wished to continue playing it. At times he enjoyed making generous gestures and this was a chance to make one. If, too, he allowed the city to retain its independence, that meant that the thousand-year-old Republic would survive; so, although he had reduced it to a puppet state he would, instead of being regarded as her assassin, be hailed as her champion. He had raped Venice, but would save her from murder.

Having got rid of General Clarke, Boneparte ignored the Directory's orders and put his own terms to Count Cobenzl. Berthier, meanwhile, was told to get out the maps and, as a precaution, start planning a new campaign, and was given several officers, Roger among them, to assist him.

The Chief of Staff was an ugly little man with a head far too big for his body. The splendour of the uniforms he designed for himself could not disguise the ungainliness of his movements, or his enormous red hands with their finger nails bitten to the quick. His speech was as awkward as his body and he was incapable of showing natural affability. But, under his frizzy hair, he had a quite exceptional brain.

Not that he was an original thinker and, although he did not lack for courage, on his own he would not have made even a passable General. His forte was his extraordinary capacity for memorizing detail. He could at any time give the approximate strength, the position, and the name of the commander, of every unit in the Army of Italy. He was a living card-index, carrying every sort of information about fortresses, topography, munitions, supplies, hospitals, transport and the enemy. His value to Boneparte was trebled by two other factors: he positively worshipped the General-in-Chief and was capable of working swiftly, yet carefully, for far longer hours than any other man could possibly have sustained. At critical times in the campaign he had often gone for several days without sleep and appeared no whit the worse for it.

For some days Roger devilled for him, while he worked out with meticulous care the routes which should be taken by infantry, cavalry, artillery and transport of each division, should it become necessary to resume the war. It was on October 11th that, after a morning session with Berthier, Roger met Boneparte in a corridor, and the little Corsican said to him abruptly:

'You seem to have forgotten your suggestion about my spending a night in Venice, to meet an Indian Princess.'

Roger was very far from having forgotten, but he had felt that, although they were now within a day's ride of Venice, it would be tactless to reopen the matter while this new period of intense activity continued, and he said so.

Boneparte grunted. 'I told you to remind me, so you should have. But I've thought of it more than once. It promises to be an interesting experience. Cobenzl will not receive from the Emperor any reply to my latest proposals for some days; so now is the time. How soon can you arrange it?'

'To manage the matter with discretion I'll need two clear days in Venice,' Roger replied. 'If all is going well, I could get a courier back to you here the day after tomorrow; then, if you go down to Mestre on the fourteenth, I'll report to you there that evening with everything in readiness for you to dine with the lady that night.'

'Good; see to it, then.'

'*Mon Général*, I will leave at once; but there is one thing I must take with me. I need a line of authority from you to Villetard, instructing him to give me any assistance I may require.'

'Why should you need that?'

'There are such matters as suitable accommodation to arrange. Far too many tongues would wag if I brought the Princess to the French Embassy and you dined with her there. At such short notice . . .'

'You are right. Come with me.' Boneparte took Roger into his cabinet, scribbled the line of authority and, as he handed it over, said: 'No scandal, mind. There is no reason why Madame, my wife, should ever know that I have left here except on a short journey to inspect troops, but I am bound to be recognized in Mestre, and I want no rumours running round among the Venetians that I slipped into the city by night in order to seduce an ex-Senator's wife.'

'You may rely on me,' Roger declared firmly, and half an hour later he set off with high hopes that, at long last, his chance had come to be revenged on the villainous Malderini.

CHAPTER TWENTY-SEVEN

The Trap is Set

IN the early hours of the morning, Roger reached Mestre. It had been a long and tiring ride, but during it he had matured his plans and, although they entailed great risk to himself, he was now more than ever determined to go through with them.

The French Headquarters at Mestre was in a large villa on the outskirts of the town and, as one of the General-in-Chief's A.D.C.s, he had no difficulty in getting a shake-down there for what remained of the night.

Next morning he had himself ferried across the three-mile-wide stretch of shallow water to Venice and by half-past nine was closeted with Villetard at the French Embassy.

When he had confirmed that Malderini was still in Venice and keeping the Embassy secretly informed about the anti-French conspiracy, he asked, 'Is there any prospect of a rising taking place in the near future?'

'No, none,' Villetard replied. 'It could not possibly succeed, and they know that. They will do nothing until after the Peace, and then not for several months; anyway, until the greater part of the Army of Italy has returned to France and the garrison here been reduced to a token force.'

'If the City's independence were restored no garrison would be left here.'

Villetard shrugged. 'If it were, the conspiracy would no longer have an object, and Malderini have lost the chance of achieving his ambitions through having made use of it. But surely that is most unlikely? All the information that has reached me points to the Directory's insisting that the city should be incorporated into the Cisalpine Republic; and that it will be so is the opinion generally accepted by the people of Venice.'

'Then they put no trust in General Boneparte's promises that Venice shall survive as a City State?'

'No. Why should they? He has played ducks and drakes with all the other States of Northern Italy and altered the arrangements for their future from month to month, according to his whim. From the beginning he spoke fair words to the Serene Republic, yet acted towards it as a whip of scorpions. Why should he suddenly change his tune? What has he to gain by preserving a remnant of it? Those are the questions that the Venetians are asking themselves. Go into the cafés and a dozen times a day you will hear the opinion asked, "Will he make us citizens of his new Cisalpine Republic or, far worse, give us to the Austrians?" '

'Should he do the latter the prospects of the conspirators would be no better after the peace than before it; for 'tis certain that, as the French troops moved out, the Austrians would move in, and they would never reduce their garrison to so low a state that it would be overcome by a popular revolt.'

'True. The Venetians' only real hope of regaining their independence is that, having been made Cisalpines, they will succeed in breaking away after the French have gone.'

'They will be given one other.' Roger suddenly held Villetard's eyes with an intent glance. 'The General-in-Chief is coming here on a brief visit. If they captured him they might extort their own terms as a ransom.'

Villetard sat forward with a jerk. 'What! Surely you are not suggesting . . .'

'This is no suggestion. It is a plan already agreed on. General Boneparte is anxious to exterminate this nest of vipers before the peace terms are declared, so that they will no longer be able to rouse the population in a revolt against them.' Having calmly told this thumping lie, Roger produced his note of authority and went on.

'Here is my warrant for requiring your assistance. There can be no risk of their attempting to assassinate him, because even a child would know that, did they succeed, we should burn the whole city about their ears. But, if they are secretly informed of his coming, and it is made apparently easy for them to kidnap him while he is here, it seems to me that they would hardly be likely to forgo such a temptation.'

'The hot-heads would jump at such a chance,' Villetard agreed, 'but I rather doubt if the more level-headed would risk taking part in a gamble of that kind. After all, whatever they might force General Bonaparte to sign as the price of his liberty would not be worth the paper it was printed on. The moment he was free he would not hesitate to repudiate it and, like as not, in one of his fine rages, turn his troops loose to sack the city.'

With a smile, Roger shook his head. 'No. Malderini and his friends could do better than that. They could first demand from him a declaration restoring to the City of Venice her independence. Once that had been published, as though emanating from him at some headquarters on the mainland, it would be natural that the withdrawal of the French garrison should follow. They would make him sign another order to that effect and wait until there was not a single French soldier left in Venice before releasing him. If things had gone to that length, he could not repudiate his declaration and order the re-occupation of the city without suffering great loss of face; because his kidnappers would have warned him that, should he attempt to do so, they would disclose the fact that he had been abducted and coerced. For it to become known that a General-in-Chief had allowed himself to be captured by a handful of civilians would make him the laughing-stock of Europe. Can you see our little Bonaparte putting himself in such a position?'

'I certainly cannot.'

'Then I wish you to see Malderini as soon as possible and instruct him to prepare his fellow-conspirators to take part in a plot on those lines.'

'I take it you have no intention of allowing General Bonaparte to be captured; but intend to ambush his would-be kidnappers when they make their attempt.'

'Exactly.'

'But how does Malderini come into this? He might be killed, or anyway would be among the captured. If General Bonaparte decided to reward him afterwards by enabling us to bag these malcontents, by making him First Magistrate, all Venice would realize the truth—that it was he who had betrayed his companions. In such a case his life would not be worth a month's purchase. It's certain that some relative of one of the men he had betrayed would assassinate him.'

'He will be killed, because I intend to kill him. But it will be for you to still his fears and flatter his ambitions. Tell him that there will be no shooting unless his friends shoot first, and that the strictest orders will be given that none of his party are to be fired upon unless they use a weapon. Tell him that he must make some excuse not to act as leader and spokesman, but keep in the background, where he should be safe even from a stray bullet. Tell him that all the others will be executed to ensure their silence about his having been one of them, and that he will be allowed to escape. No Venetian need ever know that he took part in the attempt. Finally, promise him on General Boneparte's behalf that, if all goes well, a clause shall be inserted in the peace treaty reviving the ancient office of Doge, and that he shall be installed in it.'

Villetard nodded. 'Yes. Given an assurance of such measures for his own protection both during and after the *coup*, I doubt if he could resist walking into so well-baited a trap. I see one possibility, though, which might, temporarily at least, deprive you of your personal revenge.'

'What is it?'

'If he is not to act as leader, why should he go at all? Providing he gets his friends to make the attempt and furnishes us with full particulars of their arrangements, he will have played his part. To avoid all risk to himself he could pretend illness at the last moment as an excuse not to accompany them.'

'I had thought of that,' Roger smiled, 'so I intend to provide him with a special reason for being of the party; a reason which no normal illness would excuse in the eyes of his companions. Have you ever met his wife?'

'No. Few people have. He keeps her, as they term it in the East, in purdah. But I know her well by sight. Everybody does, because she makes such a distinctive figure. She is often to be seen accompanied by Malderini's lanky manservant walking in the city in the morning, and whenever the weather is clement she sits on the balcony of the Palace watching the traffic in the Grand Canal for an hour or two in the afternoon. Why do you ask?'

'Only because it is my intention to kidnap her.'

'How will that assist your plan?'

'Anything to do with the East holds a particular attraction for the General-in-Chief. His reason for coming to Venice is that I have told him about her and the idea of a *tête-à-tête* supper with an Indian Princess greatly appealed to him.'

Without the quiver of an eyelid, Roger went on to tell another thumping lie. 'It was that which led me to suggest to him that this secret visit of his would provide us with an excellent opportunity to ensnare the potential trouble-makers of Venice. He approved my idea and has sent me to arrange matters.'

Villetard ran his finger down his long nose. 'You certainly have a fertile mind for such schemes, Citizen Breuc, and I am fortunate to have your co-operation in clearing out these vipers. Have you worked out your plan in detail?'

Roger bowed. 'Thank you, Citizen Minister. Yes. I take it you have plenty of people at your disposal who can put rumours into circulation?'

'Plenty. I often have to use such methods.'

'Then first I would like you to have it put about as soon as possible that General Boneparte is already in the city and has been living here for several days incognito, and that having on several occasions seen the Princess Sirisha he has expressed great interest in her, so that it gets to Malderini's ears and those of his fellow conspirators.'

'Yes. I will do that. What then?'

'I want you to find for me by tonight a suitable house for this tête-à-tête supper; so that I can make all arrangements there tomorrow. It will, of course, be during the supper that the kidnapping attempt will take place; so it must be one in which I can conceal a score of troops, yet have them handy. The difficulty is that it should be somewhere fairly isolated, in case shooting does occur; because in no circumstances can we have a night-patrol arriving on the scene and discovering the General-in-Chief in such a situation.'

'I appreciate that,' Villetard nodded, 'and I think I know the very place to suit you. It is an island about three miles distant, called Portillo. On it there is a little casino, a charming place, beautifully furnished. It was the property of the last French Ambassador here before the Revolution, so was taken over by us at the same time as the Embassy. Many of the Venetian nobles own such casinos and, as was the Ambassador's custom, use them for entertaining the ladies of the Opera.'

'Nothing could be better. Then today you will see Malderini and put to him this project for kidnapping General Boneparte. You will also get the rumours going about his being in the city and the interest he has expressed in the Princess. Tomorrow I shall require a few of the Embassy servants who can be relied on to keep their mouths shut to come out with me to Portillo and prepare the casino there for the General's reception. The following day I propose to kidnap the Princess and take her there. I shall do it publicly and in such a manner that everyone will know that she has been abducted by the French. If the rumours do their work, Malderini and his friends will believe that she had been carried off by Boneparte's orders. In consequence, he will not have the face to back out from accompanying them in a bid to kidnap the General and rescue her. Is that all clear?'

'Perfectly; but this business of kidnapping the Princess does raise one other point. Has it occurred to you that at times love can prove stronger than ambition? If Malderini believes that General Boneparte has seduced her, he might be filled with jealous rage to such a degree that he may attempt to kill him.'

Roger smiled. 'Seductions usually take place after supper, not before; so he would expect to arrive on the scene in time to save her from the General—or herself. But you have no need for anxiety on that score. I shall be there, and it is Malderini who is going to be killed.'

'Very well then. Everything shall be done as you wish it.'

'I thank you, Citizen Minister. You will not, of course, disclose to Malderini until the last moment the place at which the General-in-Chief is to be on the night of the 14th. It is important, too, that he should not learn that I am back in Venice; otherwise, knowing my enmity to him, and that having been rescued by Madame Boneparte I must also be a friend of her husband, he might suspect a trap. I must, therefore, go about my business here in some disguise. Have you anything to suggest?'

'Nothing could be simpler. The Venetians follow the strange custom of holding carnival for six months every year. They do not, of course, have their processions and actual fiesta until the last few weeks; but in this most licentious of cities a degree of licence has long been permitted from October 1st. From then on anyone who wishes may go about masked without question, which makes it easier to conduct clandestine love affairs. You have only to change that smart uniform for civilian clothes, wear a long cloak and a mask, and even if you came face to face with Malderini he would have no idea who you were.'

Everything having been satisfactorily settled, as Roger had been riding for a good part of the night he said that he would like a few hours' sleep; so Villetard took him to the room he had previously occupied while at the Embassy, and promised to provide him later with a suitable costume in which to go out.

At three o'clock he was called by a valet who had brought up a variety of clothes for him to choose from. Instead of his military boots he donned buckled shoes and white stockings, with a pair of nankeen breeches to go above them, then selected a wine-coloured tail-coat that was a little large for him, but would serve well enough. The cloaks were light in weight but enormous garments that would wrap twice round a man, had to be kept from trailing on the ground and had deep double collars. The masks were grotesque, covering the whole face, and having long hideous noses. As the Venetian nobility had not yet taken to the fashions brought in by the Revolution, they still wore high-sided, richly decorated tricorne hats, and the one that fitted Roger best was edged with ostrich feathers round its rim.

When he had finished dressing, carrying the cloak, mask and hat, he went down to dine with Villetard, who told him that as the season of masks now enabled anyone to come to the Embassy in daylight with no more risk of being recognized than at night, he was expecting Malderini at five o'clock. That suited Roger, as he had work to do and it gave him an excuse to make himself scarce immediately after the meal.

Having collected everything necessary from Villetard's secretary, he went up to his room, locked himself in and sat down to write a report for Mr. Pitt. He could send no piece of information that was of startling value but during the past six weeks he had acquired a great quantity of miscellaneous data about Boneparte, his political trickery, and the people round him, which would be read with much interest in Whitehall. His final page was on the present situation, and he said that, although he had been given to understand that Mr. Pitt favoured an independent Venice, his own conviction was that the future prospects of England could be better served if the city was handed over to the Austrians; and that, while he had no great hope of influencing events, even at the risk of his master's displeasure he intended to work for that end.

In it he had given no indication that he was on Boneparte's staff, or had been living at his headquarters, and he did not sign it; so if it was captured, even the similarity between the English and French versions of his name would not give a clue to the identity of the writer. Only his handwriting could give him away, and the odds against both the report falling into French hands and his writing being recognized were sufficiently long to be an acceptable risk; or at least one which he had to take in the service of his country.

When he had addressed and sealed the document, he wrapped a second parchment cover round it and, having sealed that too, wrote 'John Watson Esquire, Personal' on it. Then, putting the bulky package in an inner pocket, he buttoned his coat over it, put on his cloak and mask, and went downstairs.

The report had taken three hours to write, so it was now a quarter-past eight o'clock. He was told that Villetard had gone out about an hour before and was not expected back until his usual hour for supper, which was half-past ten. Roger told the doorkeeper that he had a mind to spend an hour in the Piazza San Marco, so one of the Embassy gondolas was whistled up to take him there. The weather, as is customary in Venice in October, was still mild; so a band was playing in the Piazza and the usual crowd sauntering, flirting, and exchanging greetings or gossip.

For half an hour he sat at a table outside Florian's, immune from recognition behind his hideous mask, sipping strong black coffee and a golden liqueur. Then he had a gondola take him to the first bridge over the Trovaso

Canal. From there, on foot, he twisted his way back, temporarily losing his way twice, through a score of narrow turnings, until he reached the British Consulate. After he had pulled the bell it clanged hollowly, but before the clanging ceased the door was opened by the same footman who had answered it to him before. This time he did not tip the man. His richly feathered three-cornered hat had made that unnecessary. In Italian he brusquely demanded speech with the Consul.

The man bowed him into the low pillared hall, and asked him to be seated. Two minutes later Mr. Watson came out to him. For the servant's benefit, as he bowed he announced himself as the Marchese di Piomboli. Mr. Watson returned his bow and asked what he could do for him. As soon as the servant had gone, Roger removed his mask for a moment and said in a whisper, 'I am the Arab perfume seller. Can you get a despatch to London for me?'

The lanky, red-haired Mr. Watson nodded, and whispered back, 'I trust so. Our people are still getting through. If all goes well, it should be there in under three weeks.'

Roger quickly passed him the despatch, pressed his hand and turned towards the door. With no further word said, Mr. Watson let him out. In a nearby canal he picked up a gondola and had it take him again to the San Marco. After strolling there for ten minutes he got another which took him back to the French Embassy. He had timed things excellently and arrived just as Villetard was sitting down to supper.

Over the meal, Roger learned to his delight that Malderini had swallowed the bait. He had gone home to summon the conspirators to a conference for that night, and had expressed no doubt about their being prepared to risk everything on this chance to secure Bonaparte's person.

For them, the prospect of coercing him into signing documents upon which he would not be able to go back without looking a fool was far better than anything they could ever have hoped for. Malderini's knowledge that the General-in-Chief was already in the city, and the promise of information about a place at which he could easily be captured a few nights hence, they would believe to have been obtained by heavy bribery from an official at the French Embassy; so the principal matters for discussion at the conference would be, who should act as spokesman to General Bonaparte in order to obtain his signature to the required documents, and where should they hold him prisoner while the orders extorted from him were being carried out.

Roger went to bed feeling soberly satisfied with the progress he had made to date. It was a great relief to have got his report off to Mr. Pitt, as there could be no telling when, if ever, he would be able to send another. But he kept on examining his plan from every angle, for one could never be quite sure that every possibility had been thought of, or that some unforeseen factor would not suddenly arise to throw everything out of gear. And he had one very serious cause for worry. Bonaparte had stipulated 'no scandal', but to make certain of getting Malderini into the trap he had been compelled to have rumours circulated that the General was making a visit incognito to Venice, and take steps to ensure that when the Princess Sirīsha was kidnapped his name should be linked with hers. To have used the authority Bonaparte had given him over Villetard for his own ends, and entirely contrary to the General's interests, was a flagrant breach of trust. When the little Corsican learned about that, as he was bound to do, unless it could be justified by a motive that he would accept, he would fly into one of his terrible rages and Roger might find himself back in the Leads.

Another matter that worried Roger considerably was the fate of Malderini's co-conspirators. The great majority of the Venetian upper class had conclusively proved themselves to be spineless decadents, but these people must surely be the exception to the rule. Some might be ambitious men, prepared to gamble their lives against a chance of power should they succeed in bringing about a restoration of the old régime; others no doubt were fanatics, egged on by their father-confessors to strike a blow at the new government of atheists; but among them there must be a number of real patriots, and all of them must be accounted men of courage. That they, of all Venetians—just because they had allowed themselves to be caught in the web of the treacherous Malderini, and because Roger, in the hope of serving his country and to revenge himself, had to smash it—should be the ones who had to be sacrificed, seemed a gross injustice. He could see no way to avoid that and the thought of it plagued his conscience severely.

Yet, as so often happens, sleep brought a possible solution to the problem. Soon after waking next morning, an idea in connection with the carnival took form in his mind, and by developing it there seemed a chance that when Malderini's associates had served their purpose he might be able to save them from the worst consequences of their attempt upon Bonaparte.

To put it in train, as soon as he had dressed and breakfasted he donned his cloak and mask and went out shopping. His purchases consisted of one of the huge gold-laced hats that Bonaparte had taken to wearing and the smallest sizes available in the second-hand shops of hessian boots, white breeches and plain uniform coat, by which the General's figure had become so well known. To these he added a tricolour sash, white stock, spurs, cloak and one of the grotesque carnival masks.

With all these packed in two boxes, he returned to the Embassy where he found a small party ready to accompany him to Portillo. It consisted of Villetard's steward, Citizen Crozier, a valet, a porter and two cleaning women, all of whom, as was the case with the whole of the staff at the Embassy, were French. Roger transferred his packages to the six-oared barge in which they were waiting, and it pulled away.

Leaving the Grand Canal it turned into the Canal San Felice, which led into the basin of the Misericordia on the northern waterfront of the city, then headed north through one of the pole-marked channels across the open water. As Venice and its innumerable adjacent islands lie in a thirty-mile-long lagoon, they are protected from the rollers of the Adriatic and, being a fine sunny day, the inland sea was as smooth as a millpond. A half-mile out they passed the island of San Michele, the cemetery of Venice, above the walls of which the tall cypresses rose like green candles, then some distance farther on the much bigger island of Murano with its quite considerable town, famous for its centuries-old glass factories. Beyond it, in the distance, lay another large but less populous island, Barano, and between them to either side were scattered a number of small islets. Crozier pointed out one of these to Roger as Portillo, and the barge's crew soon brought them to it.

The islet was about an acre in extent and the only building on it was the casino, a charming little one-storeyed pavilion set picturesquely among cypress trees. They landed on a wide stone wharf and at Crozier's shout a bent old man, who was the caretaker, hobbled out to meet them. He let them in through the front door and Roger set about making a thorough inspection of the place.

It had only two main rooms, a salon and a bedroom; both were spacious and lofty. Beyond the former lay a kitchen and two small bedrooms for servants. To that side of the main building, a short ditance from it, was a big woodshed well stocked with fuel, and on the other a boat-house, in the rear part of which was stored garden furniture. Behind the casino, surrounded by cypresses, lay a small garden containing only some flowering shrubs and a few pieces of statuary. The furniture in the main rooms had been stacked in their centres under dust sheets and the place smelt musty from disuse; but, even so, Roger saw at a glance that when in proper order it made a perfect retreat for lovers.

All the windows were thrown open, and Crozier began to unpack from hampers he had brought bed-linen, plate, glasses and bottles; his men set about unstacking the furniture, and the women about their cleaning. Having satisfied himself that the place could be made entirely suitable for his purpose, Roger returned to the barge and had himself rowed the four miles into Mestre.

On landing he took off his mask, hired a carrotza to take him to the French headquarters just outside the town and introduced himself to the garrison Commander's adjutant. At that officer's desk he wrote a note for Bourrienne informing him that everything had been arranged for the visit of the General-in-Chief on the following night, and had it sent off by galloper.

As he watched the man go he realized that he had burnt his boats and that, although his own arrangements for trapping Malderini were well in train, that was by no means the case with the entertainment he had promised Bonaparte; as he had yet to kidnap the Princess Sirīsha. But to have done so before the day of the *coup* might have ruined his own plan, and if he had delayed in sending his despatch to Bonaparte, there were no means of getting him to the rendezvous by the night of the 14th.

At the adjutant's invitation, he dined that afternoon in the mess, then had himself rowed back to Portillo. During his absence a most pleasing transformation had taken place. The big rooms had been thoroughly cleaned, the air scented, and the fine gilt and ormolu furniture of the period of Louis XV set out. As he looked at the magnificent bed, with its silk curtains falling gracefully from a coronet held by two gilded cupids, his imagination swiftly conjured up the images of the satin-clad, powdered-haired noblemen who must, in the past, have led beautiful women in crinolines and patches to give and receive amorous joys in it. For a moment he wondered if the skinny lank-haired little Corsican would succeed, after the *coup* was over on the following night, in persuading the lovely Indian Princess to let him have his way with her there. But that was a matter for them.

An hour later all the preparations, except for the supper which must be brought next day, were completed; so the party returned to Venice, taking the old caretaker with them.

That evening Roger arranged through Villetard that next morning at nine o'clock a fast barge, with at least eight oarsmen, should be at the Embassy steps. It was to be manned by French sailors and carry six troopers, all picked men who could be relied on to keep their mouths shut and under orders to obey him without question.

Later that night, Villetard told him that he had again seen Malderini, and that his side of the affair was all in order. The hot-heads among the conspirators had shown immediate enthusiasm at this chance to kidnap their great enemy, and even the more cautious had soon been persuaded that, if he could be coerced into ordering the evacuation of Venice by the French, the fact that a few civilians had done so would be sufficient hold over him to ensure that he did not rescind the order after they had released him.

They had decided to take him to one of the distant islands about twelve miles away at the south end of the lagoon, as from it he could not possibly escape, and that, too, would eliminate any risk of the French finding him should they institute a house-to-house search throughout the city. One of

Malderini's lieutenants was a lawyer named Ottoboni, an inveterate talker, who also prided himself on his ability as a negotiator; so when Malderini expressed some misgivings about being capable of arguing such a forceful character as Bonaparte into doing as they wished, the lawyer had promptly volunteered to handle that side of the business, which would leave the arch-conspirator free to keep out of personal danger in the rear of the party.

Malderini had pressed Villetard to tell him whereabouts Bonaparte was lodging in the city, so that the conspirators could make detailed plans for their *coup*. But Villetard had replied that he was actually in Mestre and coming over only from time to time. It was, however, certain that he would sup in Venice the following night, although where was not yet definitely settled. That would be known by about seven o'clock; so Malderini was to come to the Embassy shortly before half-past, and Villetard would be able to give him full particulars of the General-in-Chief's plans for the evening.

By this arrangement, Roger reckoned that the kidnappers could not arrive at Portillo much before nine o'clock, by which time he expected to have Napoleon and Sirīsha comfortably settled down at supper. Only one fence now remained to be got over—the kidnapping of the Princess; but everything else had so far gone according to plan and, buoyed up by his natural optimism, Roger went cheerfully to bed.

Next morning, punctually at nine o'clock, he went out to the French-manned barge, which had been brought to the Embassy under the command of a tough-looking middle-aged naval lieutenant named Bouvard. First, Roger made sure that its crew and the half-dozen soldiers had been warned that they were to be engaged in a special undertaking and that in no circumstances were they to talk about it afterwards; then he explained what he intended to do. As he proceeded, broad grins spread over the faces of most of the men and a few began to mutter ribald comments; but he soon reduced them to order by saying that this was no affair of gallantry—it was a step that had to be taken in the political interests of the Republic.

Having made certain that the Lieutenant fully understood what was required of him, he gave the order to cast off and had the barge rowed down the Grand Canal as far as the Canal de Duca, which was on the opposite side to the Malderini Palace and about two hundred yards below it. He then had the barge backed into the Duca Canal and made fast to one side of its entrance, so that all of it except its bow was concealed by the house on the corner. Climbing across the thwarts he settled down in the bow to keep watch on the Palace.

It was by then twenty-past nine, and it had been the Princess Sirīsha's custom to go out for her morning walk at about ten o'clock; so he had taken up his position to watch for her to come out of the Palace in ample time—provided that she had not changed her habits. On that point Ville-tard had been unable to give him any information, and the possibility that she had made his wait an anxious one. Now that autumn was here, she might not go out for a walk every day, and he was working to a strict time-table. To have abducted her the day before would have sprung his mine under Malderini too early and perhaps provoked him into some act which would have upset everything previously agreed on; but Sirīsha had to be given time to recover from the shock she would sustain, so must be carried off by midday at the latest. Fortunately it was again a lovely sunny day, so the prospect of her coming out seemed good; but Roger was un-comfortably aware that, should she fail to do so, he would have to go in and get her.

His uncertainty about how matters would develop made his forty-minute wait seem very much longer, but at last the many bells of Venice chimed ten, and he sat forward with renewed eagerness, his eyes riveted on the portico of the Palace two hundred yards away.

Five minutes passed, ten, but there were no signs of activity. The gondola was tied up to one of the mooring poles striped, like a gargantuan barber's pole, with the Malderini colours, but the gondoliers had not come out to it. On the other hand, the Princess had not come onto her balcony, which would have suggested that she meant to take the morning air up there instead of during a walk.

Suddenly the panic thought struck Roger that she might no longer be living in the Palace. Perhaps, by having those rumours spread about Boneparte's expressing an interest in her, he had overplayed his hand. It was just possible that Malderini had decided to remove her temporarily to some place where the General-in-Chief would see her no more and so be deprived of any opportunity of endeavouring to make her acquaintance. If so, he was in the very devil of a mess. The rage that Boneparte would fly into that evening when he learned that he had been brought all the way down to Venice for nothing was something that Roger did not care to dwell upon.

It looked now as if he would have to force his way into the Palace anyhow. If she was there, with six strong troopers to aid him he did not doubt his ability to carry her off. If she was not, then he would have to do his utmost to bribe or terrify the servants into telling him where she had been taken. The minutes, instead of dragging, were racing now, and he had just decided that, in case he had to go some distance to find her, he dare not put off raiding the Palace after half-past, when the bells tolled the quarter. At that moment the gondoliers appeared, and the Princess and Pietro followed them out almost immediately afterwards.

Catching his breath with relief, Roger gave the word to untie the barge and scrambled back across the thwarts into its stern. He had no need to give any further orders; Lieutenant Bouvard knew what had to be done. The barge shot out from its lurking place and turned up the Grand Canal. Sirīsha was just settling down in the cabin of the gondola. It pushed off and headed for the San Samuele steps opposite. By the time it reached mid-canal, the barge was only twenty yards from it, coming on fast and heading for its beam. The gondoliers gave their recognized long-drawn cries to take care. Seeing that no notice was taken of them, they shouted frantic warnings. The barge held its course until six feet from the gondola, then Bouvard threw his tiller right over. The bow veered sharply round and struck the gondola hard just abaft its high key-like prow. The shock caused the gondolier standing on its peak, with the boat-hook ready in his hands to pull her into the steps, to lose his balance. Shouting vitriolic abuse at the clumsiness of Frenchmen, he went over backwards; his spate of words was suddenly cut off as his head went under water.

Next moment the two craft swung round side by side. The French sailors nearest the gondola seized it and held it. A soldier in the stern raised his musket and gave the gondolier holding the sweep a sharp prod with the end of its barrel; he too went overboard. Roger and two more of the soldiers jumped into the gondola amidships. Pietro had been sitting just outside the cabin. He had had the sense to remain seated until after the shock, but now he was on his feet and had whipped a stiletto out from his waistband. One of the soldiers clubbed his musket and swiped sideways with it at Pietro's arm. With a howl of pain he dropped the long glittering blade. Roger was tempted to kill him, but decided to give him the benefit of a chance, because he had had the courage to show fight in defence of his master's wife. With all his force, he drove his fist into Pietro's stomach. Malderini's skull-headed servitor doubled up and, his eyes starting from his head, collapsed backwards, heels over head, into the water. With not a breath of air left in his lungs, he might come up, or he might not. Roger wasted no time in waiting to see; he plunged into the cabin.

Sirīsha had already risen, as far as its low roof would allow her to. She was crouching inside it, with a terrified expression on her face. This was no time to offer any explanation. Roger seized her by the arm and dragged her into the well of the gondola. She began to scream, but he did not attempt to stop her. Picking her up bodily, he lurched back with her into the stern of the barge. The sailors let go the now empty gondola, thrust it off with their oars, and began to pull vigorously towards the entrance of the Canal Trovaso, which was on the same side as the Malderini Palace but a little farther down.

At that hour the Grand Canal was teeming with gondolas and provision boats. From fifty of them, at least, the occurrence must have been witnessed, or had their attention called to it by Sirīsha's screams; but the barge was manned by French sailors and had French troops on board. The air was filled with curses and shouts of protest and abuse, but none of the Venetians dared to attempt to block its progress. Now, rowing all out, and in excellent rhythm, the crew of the barge sent it speeding round into the Canal Torvaso and along it to the bridge that spanned its far end, linking the Quai al Ponte Lungo with the Quai al Gesuati. There Roger had it pulled in at the steps and landed the six soldiers with orders to return direct to their barracks and remain there for twenty-four hours. He had brought them only in case he had to raid the Palace, and now had no wish to let more people than was absolutely necessary into the secret of where he was taking the Princess.

Telling them that he would secure them all a month's exemption from fatigues, he waved them away. The barge pushed off, pulled out some distance from the wharfside, then headed west, towards the mainland. He had purposely left Venice from its south side to lessen the risk of chance observers getting any idea of its destination, although this meant a long row right round the city before it could head towards Portillo.

By this time Sirīsha's screams for help had subsided into a tearful sobbing. Roger's cloak and mask had prevented her from even guessing who he might be and, as yet, he had had no time to talk to her. But now he took her hand, patted it, and whispered in Persian:

'You have nothing to fear. This is part of a plot to free you from your evil husband. This is no place to tell you of it; but I am an old friend and I swear that you can trust me.' As he spoke he lifted the side of his mask a little so that she could glimpse his features.

When she did so, she gave a little gasp. 'I . . . I thought you dead! How . . .? Oh, I am glad. But I will be patient.'

It took two hours' steady rowing to reach Portillo. On their arrival there, Roger told Lieutenant Bouvard that his men were not to come near the casino, but could eat the rations with which they had come provided, and take an easy among the cypresses, until he should be ready, late in the afternoon, for them to take him back to Venice. Then, giving the Princess his arm, he escorted her up the steps to the casino.

The steward Crozier received them. He reported that in accordance with his instructions he had brought out an ample supply of food prepared by the Embassy chef that morning, then sent the barge back and remained alone there to serve it when required. Roger told him that they would like a light meal in about twenty minutes, dismissed him, led Sirīsha to a couch, and sat down beside her.

Removing his mask, he said: 'Since you thought me dead, I had best explain how my lucky star averted your husband's design to have me shot. As we first met in England and I speak English perfectly, you naturally supposed me to be an Englishman; but I am not. At least, I am only half English by blood and, although I have a number of relatives and friends there, I have lived most of my life in France and regard myself as a Frenchman. Fortunately, among my French friends I can count General and Madame Boneparte. It was the latter's recognition of me on her most opportune arrival in Venice, just as I was being marched off to be shot, that saved me and procured my release. I have since been made one of General Boneparte's aides-de-camp, and it is at his wish that I have brought you to this casino.'

Her eyes were round with astonishment. 'But . . . but I have never even set eyes on the General. And you said this was a plot to rid me of my husband.'

'It is.' Roger smiled. 'The two matters have a bearing on one another. Are you aware that Malderini is the head of a conspiracy to overthrow the French-sponsored régime in Venice?'

'No. He tells me nothing. Of such things I know only what I read in the news-sheets.'

'Well, that is the case; and for some time we have been anxious to nip this conspiracy in the bud before the conspirators can give us serious trouble. We have therefore laid a trap for them. Tonight, General Boneparte is coming here; they mean to attempt to kidnap him, but it is they who will be caught instead, and disposed of.'

'You mean that Malderini will be caught and . . . and killed?'

'Yes. I take it that you have not changed your mind about wishing for his death?'

'No, no! He is horrible, malefic, evil! I would have killed him myself a hundred times, had he not this terrible power over me that makes me helpless in his presence.'

'Then you may rest easy. Within six hours he will be dead. I intend to settle accounts with him myself.'

'Oh, if only I could believe it!' she burst out. 'To be free! To be free at last after all these years. But it won't happen. He'll find some way to prevent it. He'll know by now that you have carried me off. He'll follow me here.'

'He cannot. He can have no possible means of finding out where I have taken you.'

'He has! He will! He'll use his crystal to overlook me.'

'I do not believe it. At half-past seven this evening, he will be told where you are, but not before. He should arrive here with his fellow conspirators about nine o'clock. By that time, this casino will be surrounded by guards and you will be supping in it with General Boneparte; so you will be absolutely safe, and I . . .'

'I don't understand,' she burst out again. 'Why should I sup with this great General. He means nothing to me or I to him.'

'I've had no chance yet to explain,' Roger said quickly. 'This is the way of it. General Boneparte is the bait in the trap to draw Malderini and his fellow-conspirators to it. But I also had to dangle some bait to induce the General to come to Venice. You are that bait.'

'I! But why? I tell you he has never even seen me.'

'I am aware of that. But everything to do with the East holds an extra-ordinary fascination for him. He has never met an Indian lady of noble birth. I told him about you and suggested that I should arrange for you to sup together. The idea delighted him, and . . .'

She held up a slim coffee-coloured hand. 'To sup. What do you mean by that? Although Malderini has kept me in purdah I am no longer a child. Speak plainly, please.'

Roger made a little bow. 'I am glad that you should wish me to. General Boneparte asked me your circumstances. I told him only that you were so jealously guarded that I thought it unlikely that you had had any lovers, but that you hated your husband and would not repulse him on that account. I promised that I would arrange for you to sup with him; but no more. Should you refuse to allow him to kiss more than the tips of your fingers, he will have no grounds for complaint against either of us.'

'He may endeavour to force me against my will. What then? Do you promise to come to my assistance?'

Again, Roger was entirely frank with her. 'This, Madame, is our pro-gramme. Unless Malderini delays for some reason, he and his friends will make their attempt to kidnap General Boneparte while you are supping with him. Under my orders the guards, who will have been disposed about the casino in an ambush, will suddenly appear on the scene and defeat the attempt. Having killed Malderini, I shall then convey the other prisoners under escort back to Venice, leaving you alone with the General.'

'Then it is your intention to leave me at his mercy.'

'Permit me to observe,' replied Roger quietly, 'that you are a well-made woman, whereas he is much below the size of an average man. He is, in fact, shorter than yourself, although admittedly more muscular. Moreover, I am inclined to the belief that few men, large or small, derive much pleasure from taking a woman against her will. He has great personality. I should not be at all surprised if you find yourself strongly attracted to him. If so, well and good. If not, then you must risk the other thing, or accept the alternative.'

'The alternative,' she repeated. 'What is that?'

Roger stood up. 'Why, that since I brought you here without your permission I am responsible for you. As I shall not be here at the time when General Boneparte might seek to take advantage of you, it is for me to prevent such a situation ever arising.'

'What do you mean? I do not understand.'

'Simply that, should you not be prepared either to grant the General certain favours in the event of your finding him attractive, or repulse him if you do not, then I must take you back to the Malderini Palace this afternoon.'

'No!' she exclaimed. 'No, no! Not that!'

He shrugged. 'The choice is yours, Princess. The rôle that I am playing at the moment is repugnant to me. But I'll not have it on my conscience that I acted the pimp for Boneparte to the extent of procuring a woman for him against her will. You are no child and, if you find his attentions distasteful, you should be capable of dealing with him. But either you face up to that as the price of being rid of the husband you hate before morning, or all I have done so far must go for nothing. I'll have to face the General's wrath when he finds I have disappointed him, and you will continue to be the slave of Malderini.'

She hesitated only an instant, then looked him squarely in the face. 'Nothing could equal the horrors to which he has subjected me. I would give myself to a sweeper rather than return to him.'

'There is no question of your being called on to do anything so disagreeable,' Roger smiled. 'I cannot vouch for the attitude General Boneparte will adopt towards you, any more than I could vouch for the attitude you will adopt towards him. I had, though, as a matter of fairness, to assure myself that you understood the most unpleasant turn that events might take. But the General is by no means lacking in chivalry, and if you play your cards skilfully the game should remain in your own hands. And now, I think we might partake of some refreshment.'

At his call, Crozier wheeled in a small two-tier table loaded with all sorts of cold delicacies, fruit and wine. When he had withdrawn, Roger served the Princess and resumed the conversation in a lighter vein. He told her about Boneparte's background as a young man, and of his better side: of his care to spare his wife pain from knowledge of his infidelities, of his great generosity to his family who did little but cause him annoyance, of his loyalty to his friends, his thoughtfulness for his servants, and that, while he would wither with his viperish tongue men of the first rank of whose actions he disapproved, he was invariably courteous to women.

When they had finished their meal, Roger suggested that she should spend the afternoon resting in the bedroom. Then he added that he had some work to do which would take him an hour or so, after which he must return to Venice; so he would not disturb her but take leave of her now.

Instantly, she became panic-stricken and implored him to remain with her. Again she insisted that Malderini would use his crystal to find out where she was, and come out to the island to regain possession of her before Roger returned. In vain he tried to still her fears. He had intended to take the whole crew of the naval barge back to Venice and dismiss it there, so that none of them should become aware of Boneparte's visit to the casino. But now, feeling that it was just possible that there were some grounds for her fears, he decided to leave Lieutenant Bouvard and two of the sailors, as well as Crozier, as a guard; and on his promising to do that, she reluctantly agreed to his leaving her.

When he had seen her into the bedroom, in which everything necessary to a lady's toilette had been set out, he went round to the back of the boathouse. The previous day he had left there the two parcels of clothes he had bought. Having unpacked them, he collected from the boats a number of cushions and, slitting them open, used the stuffing from them to stuff the stockings, breeches, coat and hat on a framework of sticks. When he had done, he had a quite unmistakable effigy of Boneparte wearing a carnival mask. Wrapping it up in the big cloak, he hid it behind some garden chairs, then went to summon the crew of the barge.

He told Bouvard that he was leaving him there with two men and that the three of them were each to patrol a third of the islet's coast until his return. In no circumstances was anyone to be allowed to land and, if anyone attempted to, they were to be shot on sight. He then put on his mask and had the remainder of the crew row him back to Venice.

At the Embassy steps he gave each of the crew five sequins, cautioned them against talking and sent them back to the dockyard. Villetard was in his office and greeted him with much concern. All Venice was talking of the Princess Sirīsha's kidnapping and, owing to the rumours which had already been spread, assumed that it had been done on General Boneparte's orders. The resentment was intense, that he should abuse his power to have carried off in broad daylight a woman to whom he had taken a fancy, and Villetard made no secret of his opinion that, unless Roger had some means of justifying his act, the General-in-Chief's rage would be unbounded when he learned that he had been made the central figure of such a scandal.

Roger needed no telling about that. He knew that to be revenged on Malderini he had taken a terrible gamble, and that there was many a slip 'twixt the cup and the lip. If a single hitch occurred in his intricate plans now, by midnight he would be dead, on his way back to the Leads, or flying for his life. But what gave him greater concern at the moment was what Villetard had to say of a call that Malderini had paid him an hour earlier.

Malderini's pudgy face had been quivering with anger as he had demanded to know why, when there were a thousand other beautiful women in Venice, General Bonaparte should have shown such lack of decent feeling as to have carried off the wife of a man who was on the point of rendering France an important service.

In vain Villetard had attempted to soothe him by telling him that, for his own protection, he had observed the strictest secrecy about his being a French agent; and that the General-in-Chief was as yet unaware that it was he who would lead the conspirators into the trap that night. Malderini had talked of cancelling all his arrangements and, instead, going in pursuit of his wife.

Greatly surprised that he might be able to do so, Villetard had asked how he had found out where she was. To that he had replied that he was not quite certain, but he was sure she had been taken to an island with a casino on it. He had seen her there in his crystal with a tall masked man. He had yet to discover which of the many islands with casinos on them it was; but another session with his crystal might reveal that to him.

Villetard had urged him most strongly not to ruin everything by acting precipitantly, and argued that he had only to wait till evening to recover his wife unharmed, as it was certain that General Bonaparte would return her to him when he knew that it was to him they would owe the capture of the conspirators. Villetard had also pointed out that unless he did wait and carry things through as arranged, he might get himself killed by whoever was guarding his wife, and in any case lose his reward. Even so, he had gone off still in a high dudgeon and refusing to promise anything.

At this news, Roger's spirits sank to zero. Sirīsha's worst fears had been realized and, crystal or no crystal, Malderini had now only to become aware of the fact that the French Embassy owned an island with a casino on it, to realize that she had been taken to Portillo. Roger thanked his stars he had left Bouvard on guard there, but Malderini was as cunning as a serpent, so might think of some way to fool him. In any case, if Malderini's rage drove him to go out there within the next few hours, the whole plot would be blown sky high. It could only be hoped that the thought of losing his chance to beome Doge would restrain him. In any case, there was nothing that Roger could do about it; so he took leave of Villetard and, once more a prey to acute anxiety, had himself rowed into Mestre.

For mid-October the weather was very hot and it looked like thunder. Vaguely he noticed it and hoped that there would not be a downpour which would drench Boneparte and himself when they were rowed out to

Portillo, but his mind was too full of other matters for him to think much about it.

He reached the headquarters outside Mestre soon after five o'clock and learned from the adjutant there that the General-in-Chief was expected at about six. He then asked for a guard of twenty picked men who could be relied on to preserve secrecy to act as escort to the General on an evening excursion. Half an hour later they were paraded for him and he spoke to each of them individually, first questioning them about their service, then telling them that the General's life would be in their hands; so they must obey any order given to them without a moment's hesitation. He then arranged for boats to be ready down at the wharf at seven o'clock to take the whole party to one of the islands in the lagoon, and sent the men on ahead to the wharf.

These final details had only just been settled when Boneparte's travelling carriage, escorted by a troop of cuirassiers, clattered into the yard. General Baraguay d'Hilliers received him, and he inspected the guard of honour, pausing here and there to speak to an old soldier and giving his ear a tweak. Then, without a glance at Roger, he went inside with the General.

The handsome curly-haired Junot was with him and, dropping behind, gave Roger a grin, winked and whispered, 'All well for this evening?'

Roger had good cause to fear that by this time all might be far from well, but he showed no sign of his anxiety and replied in a low voice, with a grin, 'Yes, the lady awaits his pleasure. What sort of a mood is the little man in?'

Junot pulled a face. 'Bad. The first snow was to be seen on the mountains up there this morning, and if we mean to break the armistice we are under obligation to give the Austrians twenty-five days' notice. That would mean another campaign in deep snow and after the soft living the troops have had this past six months they're not up to it.'

'Then he's no alternative but to agree to a peace pretty quickly now.'

'That's just the rub. I think he'd give a lot to, but these damned Austrians have dug their toes in over Venice. A despatch reached Cobenzl last night. The Emperor has agreed everything except that he insists on being given the city.'

They went into the mess together, had a glass of wine and talked to the officers there for an hour while Boneparte was in d'Hilliers's office shooting questions at him about the state of his command. Shortly after seven the two Generals emerged. The guard presented arms, Boneparte gave a glance round, beckoned to Roger and strutted to his carriage. Roger and Junot followed him, got in, and took the seat opposite to him. As the carriage drove off, he frowned at Roger and said:

'Well?'

'All is arranged, *mon Général*,' smiled Roger, with a cheerfulness he was very far from feeling. 'The Princess Sirīsha awaits you in a charming casino on one of the smaller islands named Portillo.'

'What! We are not going to Venice then?'

'No. I thought it unwise for you to take the risk of going into Venice in case you were recognized and attacked.'

'Nonsense! Who would wish to attack me? The Venetians have much to thank me for.'

'Perhaps; but I learned from Villetard that some of them are showing base ingratitude, and even conspiring to overthrow the Republican régime you gave them.'

Bonaparte grunted. 'A few malcontents. There are such in every city.'

'In any case, *mon Général*, for you to spend the night on this island will be more discreet.'

'True. And that is important. I only hope this Princess proves up to my expectations. I am badly in need of a little relaxation.'

The drive to the wharf was a short one. A few minutes later the carriage pulled up and they descended from it. Twilight had fallen but there was still sufficient light to see some distance, and it was still hot and oppressive. The Embassy barge was drawn up at the bottom of some steps about thirty yards from where the coach had halted. In front and behind it were two other barges in which were seated the guard of twenty men that Roger had sent ahead. As the General-in-Chief appeared, a sharp order rang out, everyone in the barges stood up and came stiffly to attention.

Bonaparte gave them a glance, halted, and swung round on Roger. 'What are those men of the Hundred and Thirty-First doing in barges?'

'They are your escort, *mon Général*,' replied Roger promptly.

'Escort! I want no escort!'

Roger was as stricken as if he had had a heart attack. Before he had recovered sufficiently to speak, Bonaparte went on peevishly:

'Do you think I want the whole Army of Italy to know how I am spending the night?'

'No,' Roger stammered. 'No. But you must have an escort—you must?'

'Must! Who in thunder are you to tell me what I must or must not do? Tonight, I need you. Tomorrow, I shan't. On our return in the morning you will consider yourself under arrest.'

'Yes. Very well. As you wish.' Roger held up a protesting hand. 'Do what you will with me in the morning. I don't care. But I implore you to take an escort tonight in case . . . in case . . .'

'In case what?'

'Well, the Venetians. The conspirators I was speaking about in the coach. They might find out that you were on Portillo and try to kidnap or kill you.'

'Fiddlesticks! How can they find out? You are behaving like an old woman.'

'But . . . but . . .'

'Stop acting like a fool, Breuc. All the escort I require is yourself and my orderly sergeant. Dismiss those men in the barges at once, and take me to this island.'

CHAPTER TWENTY-EIGHT

In the Trap

FOR a moment Roger's mind went blank with sheer horror at the thought of the position in which he had landed Boneparte and himself; then it began to work with a speed at which it had rarely worked before. Somehow, he must get them both out of this terrible mess; but how? And he had only seconds in which to think. If Boneparte were given his way, they would be seven on the island, including Crozier and the three sailors. As the conspirators would expect to have to overcome a guard, they would be many more than that. The little Corsican was brave as a lion and would not submit tamely to being kidnapped. He would put up a desperate fight; so the odds were they would all get killed or seriously wounded.

There seemed only two ways to prevent that: either by stopping the conspirators from carrying out their plan, or by stopping Boneparte going to the island. For a second Roger wondered if he could get a message through to Villetard, telling him that there had been a hitch and that he must send Malderini off on a wild-goose chase by giving him the name of some island other than Portillo. But it was already past seven. It would take the best part of an hour for a messenger to get to Venice and Malderini was to be given the place of Boneparte's rendezvous within the next half-hour; so he would be on his way to Portillo before the message reached Villetard.

Then Boneparte must be stopped. But how could he be unless he was told the truth? If he was, would he accept the situation, agree to take the escort and see the matter through? No, he would not, because it would have to be disclosed to him that his intention to spend the night at the casino with a lovely woman had got out; otherwise the conspirators would not know about it. And he had been insistent that there should be no scandal. His only means of scotching it would be to dine with the officers in the mess at Mestre and spend the night there.

With lightning speed, Roger assessed the results of confessing the truth. An end to his prospects of revenging himself on Malderini; the poor Princess Sirīsha left, after all, in her evil husband's clutches; himself clapped into a fortress for a term of years; and all chance gone of using the conspiracy, as he had hoped to do, as a pawn for England in the great game of international statecraft.

It was this last, more than anything else, that made him suddenly decide to take a final gamble. He had taken so many to bring his plans up to their present state; why not one more? Boneparte was already walking towards the steps. Junot took a pace forward to follow and see him off. Roger grabbed him by the arm, pulled him back, and whispered:

'One moment!'

'What is it?' Junot said, testily. 'You seem in a great state today.'

'I've reason to be. I've no time to explain; but you must take charge of the escort and come after us.'

'Sacré bleu! Disobey his orders! Is it likely?'

'You love him, do you not?'

'Of course. If I had nine lives, like a cat, I'd give them all for him.'

'Very well then. Tonight his life may be in danger.'

Junot's hand jumped to his sword hilt. 'If anyone dares . . .'

'Listen!' Roger cut him short. 'I have only a moment. We are going to the island of Portillo. You must follow with . . .'

'How can I? It's still light enough to see several hundred yards. If he turns his head he'll catch sight of us. I'll be ordered back, and he'll have my hide off me into the bargain.'

'Breuc!' The angry cry came from Boneparte, who had just stepped into the barge. 'Breuc! Stop gossiping with Junot. What the devil d'you mean by keeping me waiting?'

'Give us a quarter of an hour's start,' Roger gasped. 'It will be near dark by then. Portillo. Come in on the garden side. I'll be waiting for you.'

Turning away from Junot he ran across the quay, down the steps and jumped into the barge.

That Boneparte happened to be in one of his black moods made the journey even more of an ordeal for Roger. When the Corsican was talkative whoever was with him had to drive their wits hard to keep up with his agile mind, but now he sat with his arms folded and his chin down on his chest, obviously plunged in gloomy thoughts; so Roger's mind was free to roam over a score of unpleasant possibilities.

That Junot would follow them he had no doubt; but how long would he delay before doing so? Malderini and his friends would leave Venice at about eight so should arrive at Portillo by nine, or perhaps even a little before that. But it was a good mile farther to Portillo from Mestre than it was from Venice; so Junot could not be expected before half-past eight, as the barges with the troops in were more cumbersome and slower than the Embassy barge. Half an hour should be margin enough, but none too much in which to make sound dispositions to receive the conspirators.

On that score he now felt fairly safe. The thing that really worried him was the possibility that Malderini had decided to put the rescue of his wife before all else and had got to the island before them. If he had, and had managed to trick, hypnotize, or overcome Bouvard and his men, the love-nest would now be empty. What Boneparte would have to say about that in his present ill humour passed beyond imagination.

There was, too, another and even more frightening possibility. Malderini might have brought the whole body of conspirators to Portillo with him. If so, they could easily have overpowered the guard and would still be there, in ambush, lying in wait for Boneparte.

That thought made Roger close his eyes and bite his lip. It was not that he felt the same deep affection for the little Corsican as did Junot and several other people among the entourage; it was a matter of his personal honour. The fact that Boneparte's death might well prove to the advantage of England in the long run had no bearing on the matter. Had Roger met him on a battlefield, he would have killed him without hesitation, but, as things stood, this brilliant, mercurial wisp of a man had befriended and trusted him; so to deliberately lead him into a trap was a shameful thing to do.

Yet Roger could not escape the fact that that was exactly what he might be doing. The knowledge forced him to consider again if he ought not to confess to the tangled web he had spun and have the barge turned back to Mestre. Had his personal concerns alone been in the balance, he would now have accepted defeat and done so; but there was one matter outside them, and it was that which constrained him to remain silent.

Junot had said that now the snow had come it was too late in the year for Boneparte to have any hope of launching another successful campaign, and that he was anxious to conclude a peace as soon as possible; but the Emperor of Austria still insisted on being given Venice. Tonight, there was just a chance that the Corsican might be persuaded to abandon his self-chosen rôle of protector of the city. To manœuvre him into doing that, Roger believed, would, in the long run, be just as much a victory for England as one gained in battle. This was not simply a personal issue; he was, in fact, facing the French General-in-Chief on a battlefield. So the battle must go on.

There were no stars or moon; heavy thunder clouds rolled low overhead, blotting out the sky. By the time they picked up Portillo, darkness had fallen, and they were within a few hundred yards of the island before the

denser blackness of its tall cypresses showed its position. His hopes mingled
with misgivings, Roger sent out a hail. To his immense relief it was Bouvard
who replied to it.

The barge drew into the steps. Boneparte sprang lightly ashore and Roger
after him. Bouvard was unable to surpress an exclamation of surprise as he
recognized the General-in-Chief; then he reported all well. Boneparte asked
him his name and how many men he had there. When he had replied he was
told to collect his two men, get in the barge with them and return with it
to Mestre.

Roger would have given a great deal to retain the sailors and the barge's
crew, as their departure would leave only himself, Crozier and the orderly
sergeant on the island with Boneparte; but he felt that any attempt to
intervene would be useless, and the thought that Junot must by now be well
on the way to Portillo made him considerably easier in his mind; so he
remained silent while his companion, with his harsh Italian-accented French,
adjured the men in the barge to preserve silence about having brought him
to the island and gave an order that the barge was to return for him at
seven o'clock in the morning.

While he was addressing the sailors, Roger had a quick word with the
orderly sergeant, telling him to remain there on the steps and challenge
any boat that might approach loudly enough to be heard in the casino; then
he accompanied Boneparte up to it. On entering the *salon* they found
Sirīsha sitting on a sofa looking at an album of water colours. Putting it
aside she stood up.

Bowing deeply to her, he returned to Boneparte and said, 'Mon *Général*,
this is Her Highness Princess Sirīsha of Bahna.' Turning back to her, he
added, 'Your Highness, permit me to present Citizen Napoleon Boneparte,
General-in-Chief of the Army of Italy and the most renowned soldier of
modern times.'

Sirīsha smiled, made a slight inclination of her head and extended her
hand. Boneparte returned her smile, bowed, took her hand, kissed it, then
led her back to the sofa, sat down beside her and began to talk with lively
animation. Within a few minutes he had become a different man from the
ill-tempered little autocrat who had stepped out of the barge.

Roger gave a discreet cough and said, 'When you wish for supper, you have
only to call for it,' bowed again, and slipped out of the salon into the kitchen.
Crozier was there with everything arranged on his two-tier wheeled table;
cups of jellied consommé, a cold lobster, breast of duck spread with foie
gras and garnished with cherries, a cannon made out of pressed marron,
half concealed by a smoke cloud of spun sugar, slices of pineapple in
Kirsch, late fresh peaches, champagne, Château Yquem and old cognac.

After nodding approval of it, Roger glanced at the clock. The hands stood at twenty minutes to nine. He checked it with his turnip watch and, to his consternation, found it right. They must have left Mestre later than he had thought. But Junot should be arriving soon. Cramming his hat on his head, he went out of the back door into the garden. It was now fully dark, and as he made his way across it, he could make out the pieces of statuary only just in time to avoid walking into them. A hundred paces brought him to the far shore of the islet at the back of the casino. For some five minutes he stood there peering out over the inky water, looking in vain for signs of Junot.

There came a sudden sharp pit-a-pat on his hat and shoulders. It had begun to rain. A long roll of distant thunder seemed to run round the great lagoon. The heavy drops fell faster. Another minute and it was sheeting down. All that could previously have been seen of the darkened landscape was blotted out. Even the tops of the cypress were now engulfed in an impenetrable blackness.

With a furious curse, already half drenched, Roger swung about and ran for the house. It looked now as if Fate had led him on only to crush him more certainly at the finish. Finding Sirīsha still there, safe and sound, had for the past quarter of an hour led him into a fool's paradise. But the game was not played yet out. In this torrential downpour all the odds were against the French coxswains of Junot's barges finding the island. Yet those of the conspirators might. From boyhood onward, every Venetian fished these waters or traversed them on picnics.

As he staggered through the deluge, he ran slap into a small fountain, tripped on its rim, bashed his shoulder against the figure in its centre and fell sprawling in its basin. Blaspheming, he picked himself up only to find that he had lost his sense of direction. Next moment a vivid streak of lightning gave it to him again. The thunder rumbled, nearer now. The rain came sheeting down as though poured out of some gigantic cistern.

Groping his way forward, he reached the back of the casino. Along it ran a three-foot wide iron canopy with a scalloped edge. Under it, now protected from the cloudburst, he fought to regain his breath. After a moment he saw, within a yard of him, a chink of light. It was coming from a window behind which the curtains had not been completely drawn. His stockinged feet squelched in his shoes as he took a pace sideways, bent down and peered through the inch-wide opening.

He found that he was looking into the *salon*. By twisting his head a little he could see Boneparte and Sirīsha. They were still seated side by side on the sofa, but now had napkins and plates on a low table and had started supper. The Corsican's face had an expression that Roger had rarely seen on it. His over-wide, incredibly forceful jaw was relaxed, his sensitive mouth was curved in a charming smile, and his big grey eyes were alight with laughter as he waved his fork in the air, evidently demonstrating one of the thrilling stories that he so much enjoyed telling. That the Princess no longer felt the least constraint with him was obvious, as Roger watched, she suddenly threw her head back and very faintly he caught the sound of her delighted laughter.

Roger groaned. What could have been more fortunate than that they should like one another. But they, too, were floating like bubbles in a paradise of fools. Junot should have arrived with the troops a good twenty minutes ago. The fact that he had not showed conclusively that in the storm he must be hopelessly lost. The conspirators were far more likely to find their way through it and land on the island at any moment. It was, too, more probable than not that they would erupt onto the scene without warning. The orderly sergeant had been ordered to stay on guard, so he would not disobey; but he had not been warned to expect an enemy, so he might have taken shelter in the kitchen and be keeping watch through its window. If so, owing to the rain, it was unlikely that he would see anyone approaching until they had actually landed.

Every few moments the lightning made terrifying zigzags, rending the sky and throwing everything up in a flash of blinding brilliance. The thunder no longer rolled but crashed in a series of earsplitting detonations, as though the heavens were cannonading the earth in an attempt to destroy it. Roger, soaked to the skin, continued to peer between the chink in the curtains. Bonaparte was feeding Sirīsha with titbits of lobster from his fork, when the thing that Roger was dreading happened.

His range of vision did not include the door of the *salon*, so he did not see it burst open. He saw Bonaparte suddenly start, drop his fork, spring to his feet and snatch up the light sword that he had thrown down on a nearby chair; then the room was full of angry shouting people. Unchallenged owing to the downpour, the conspirators had landed on the island and forced their way into the casino. Roger's hand instinctively went to his own sword hilt. If Bonaparte meant to fight, the least he could do, having led him into this trap, was to go to his aid. Yet if he did, what hope would the two of them have against the score or more Ventians? It was not muscle but wits that were needed if there was to be any chance of saving the situation. Junot could not be far off. Surely there was some way in which he could be brought to the rescue?

Bonaparte had drawn his sword and stood behind the supper table, ready to defend himself. Packed close together, the Venetians enclosed him in a semi-circle. They were a mixed lot. A few were wearing the rich brocaded coats and powdered wigs that the Venetian nobles still went about in as a gesture of contempt for the 'new order'; but most of them looked like prosperous bourgeois, and two wore fishermen's jerseys. A tall man with high cheekbones and thick lips, in the centre of the group, appeared to be haranguing Boneparte. That would be the lawyer Ottoboni. Roger could not see Malderini, so assumed that, according to plan, he was keeping well in the background.

Frantically Roger racked his wits for a way to signal Junot. He had a pistol in his belt so could have fired it, but dismissed the idea at once. With the thunder and the storm it would never be heard at any distance. The storm seemed to be easing slightly. There had been no flash of lightning for several minutes. He wondered now that Junot had not picked up the island by the light of the flashes. Perhaps he had, but lost it again and gone past it in the darkness. It would be easy to miss such a small piece of land when one could hardly see one's hand before one's face.

Light! The inspiration struck Roger's mind like a comet, following his thought of flashes. Turning, he raced along the covered way to the kitchen window. It had no blind and one glance through it told him all he wanted to know. It was occupied only by Crozier who, bent almost double, was peering through the keyhole of the door into the *salon*. Roger thanked all his gods at finding that he was pitted against amateurs. In a *coup* such as this, men who knew their work would have surrounded the house before breaking in, then made certain of securing any servants and all the doorways to the place. But Crozier's still being free, showed that the fools had all crowded into the *salon*.

Quickly now, he slipped through the back door into the kitchen. Crozier came upright with a jerk, turned a frightened face to him and gasped:

'The General! What are we to do? Oh, what are we to do?'

Roger stepped past him, shot the bolt on the *salon* door, and answered in a low voice, 'Fire! I want to make a fire. Oil, paper, sugar, get me anything you can that will light wood quickly.'

As he spoke, he ran to the stove. Three large kettles of water and a coffee pot were simmering on it. Below them the wood fire glowed red. Grabbing an iron bucket from under the sink, he seized a pair of tongs, fished out some large lumps of burning wood and dropped them into it. Crozier had collected on the table a canister of lamp oil, a bottle of brandy and two bundles of faggots.

'Do them up in the table-cloth and take them to the wood shed,' Roger ordered. Then he wrapped a towel round his hand to prevent it being scorched, picked up the bucket and hurried out after the steward. When they reached the wood shed, he scattered the faggots at the foot of the big pile of logs, threw the oil over them, poured the brandy onto the table-cloth and added it to the pile. Then he waved Crozier back and from the open doorway pitched the glowing embers from the bucket onto the oil-soaked faggots. There was a sudden spurt of flame and in a moment the whole heap was on fire.

'Keep it going,' he cried to Crozier. 'Fetch from the kitchen anything that will burn. Make as big a blaze as you can.'

Turning, he ran back along the covered way to the *salon* window. To light the bonfire which he hoped would show the position of the island to Junot, even through the teeming rain, had taken only five minutes. He found the scene in the *salon* scarcely changed. Boneparte was still standing behind the table, sword in hand, but Ottoboni was now holding up a long scroll of parchment and evidently reading from it the conditions guaranteeing the restoration and independence of the Serene Republic that they meant to force him to sign.

Roger felt certain that he would refuse. They would get his signature only by carrying him off and starving him until he gave it. That sent another flash of inspiration darting through Roger's mind. The boats! If he could kill the guard they must have left on them, and turn them adrift, the conspirators would have no means of leaving Portillo. They would be caught there with their prisoner. Junot *must* find the island soon, then the situation would be saved.

Running to the other end of the casino, Roger crept round the boat-shed and peered out at the wharf. Once more he thanked his gods that he had to deal with amateurs. The fools had not even left a guard on their boats.

It was still raining hard but not so heavily. Darting out from his hiding place, he raced across the wharf. As he did so he caught sight of a figure seated, head in hands. It was the orderly sergeant. In spite of the storm he had not left his post, but in the darkness must have been taken by surprise, knocked on the head and left for dead.

Seizing him by the arm, Roger dragged him to his feet and shouted in his ear, 'Pull yourself together. Help me untie the boats.'

There were three barges tied to the tall striped mooring posts. The rain had saturated their painters making them stiff and the knots difficult to undo. The sergeant, still half-dazed, fumbled with one while Roger wrenched at another, but he had burnt his left hand badly on the bottom of the pail when he had tipped out the burning wood from it. His scorched fingers made the job painful and more difficult.

At last he got it free, and pushed the barge off with his foot, but after it had drifted a yard it came to rest in the tideless water. Hurrying over to the sergeant, he helped him free the second barge, then he cried:

'Get in it. Push off, then find the boat-hook and pull the barge I've freed well clear of the steps.' The man stumbled in, grasped an oar, lifted it with an effort and thrust the barge out.

Four swift paces brought Roger to the post to which the third barge was moored. At least he now had light to see by. The whole wood shed was roaring up in flames, making a splendid beacon and lighting up the whole front of the casino with a lurid glare. With his burnt hand paining him abominably he strove to undo the painter.

Suddenly there was a shout behind him. Swinging round, he saw that the conspirators were crowding out from the main door of the casino. Two of them had Boneparte by the arms and were dragging him along between them. By now the sergeant had managed to get the two barges well away from the wharf. But there remained the third and the knot of its painter still held fast.

At the sight of their boats being cast adrift a yell of anger went up from the conspirators. Three of them drew their swords and came running at Roger. He had just time to swing his cloak and twist it twice round his left arm, then he whipped out his own blade and threw himself on guard. It was as well that he was one of the finest swordsmen in Europe, or he would have been dead within the next two minutes.

Individually his attackers were no match for him, but there were three of them and others were coming up behind. Only two factors favoured his survival against such odds for even a brief space. He had his back to the edge of the wharf, so they could not get round to attack him in the rear and, whereas they were armed with rapiers, his sword was a much heavier double-edged army weapon.

The first three lunged at him almost simultaneously. With one harsh, clashing stroke he swept their three blades aside, brought up his own and, curving it back high, flicked its point across the face of the man on his right. It slit his nose through the bridge. He gave a screech of agony. It gushed blood and he fell back out of the fight.

The other two lunged again. The middle man was very tall. Roger caught his thrust from below, forced his blade high up in the air, sprang forward and kicked him in the groin. With an awful groan he went over backwards. It was Roger's forward move that had saved him from the man on the left. His thrust missed Roger's heart and passed beneath his arm, piercing his clothes and taking the skin off his ribs. Turning upon him, Roger lunged but, still slightly off-balance from his kick, missed. His blade passed over the man's shoulder. Both stepped back, but now two other men came dashing into the fray.

One, a big man in a woollen jersey, wielding a long curved knife, slipped on the spilt blood from the nose of the man Roger had slashed. His mouth flew open in a curse, his head jerked back and his feet flew up. His left boot struck Roger low down on the right thigh, causing him to stagger sideways. That saved him from death by the lunge of the other newcomer. Instead of the sword point entering his body it barely pinked his right shoulder.

His blade was still engaged with that of the survivor of the first three. With a violent twist of the wrist he slid his blade under that of his opponent. It pierced his heart. His sword fell from his hand and clattered on the wet stones. His face contorted in a spasm and he collapsed.

Some thirty feet away, Boneparte was still struggling with his captors. 'Well done, Breuc!' he shouted. 'Well done! You shall have a diamond in your sword-hilt for every one of these traitors you can kill.'

Roger bared his teeth in a sardonic grin, for it looked at the moment as if gold nails in his coffin would be a more appropriate tribute. The man whose nose he had slit was coming at him with a maniacal glare in his eyes; the one whose sword had pinked his shoulder had drawn back his weapon for another lunge, and the man in the jersey was on his feet again waiting with his curved knife for a chance to run in; but yet another new-comer with a drawn sword had pushed him aside to get space enough to join in the attack.

For two terrible minutes the four thin shafts of steel clanged and slithered, rasping on one another for a second then flickering like writhing snakes in the light of the flames as they swept in swift arcs from head high down to knee level and back. With three blades against him, Roger dare not use his skill in feints or tricks as he would have in a duel; neither could he give back, and he had no room to use swift footwork to his advantage. It was all he could do to parry the lunges and keep his opponents off by making sudden jabs at the eyes of one or other of them every few moments.

Stooping suddenly, the man on the right ducked down, got past Roger's guard with a low thrust and pierced his left leg half-way up the thigh. Before the blade could be withdrawn. Roger's had entered the man's throat. He fell, gurgling horribly. But the man in the jersey sheathed his knife and, snatching up the fallen man's sword, took his place.

The pace of the swordplay to keep three men at bay was so furious that Roger was tiring now. His sword arm felt as heavy as lead, his wrist was aching; so, too, was his burnt hand. So far none of his wounds had been serious and in the heat of the conflict he hardly felt them; but he was losing blood from three places. Sweat was pouring from him and mingling with the rain that still pattered on his face.

The odds were still three to one against him and he knew that he could not keep it up much longer. Yet every moment that he could remain on his feet meant just a shade better chance that the kidnappers would not get away with their captive. From the first he had realized that they might do so by getting out of the boat-house one of the boats belonging to the casino, but in the excitement none of them had yet thought of that. And if they did, its caulking might have become so dry from long disuse, that it would prove unserviceable. He could only pray that that would be so if the idea occurred to any of them, and in the meantime continue to defend the one boat by which they could be certain of carrying Boneparte off if only they could get him into it.

Desperately he fought on, cutting, thrusting, slashing, always threatening the eyes of his attackers, and using his left arm wrapped in its sodden cloak as a buckler to parry the thrusts that came at him from that side.

Suddenly he saw an opening. His sword point darted forward ripping open the cheek of the man in front of him. With a loud cry his victim reeled sideways, cannoning into the man in the jersey and knocking his blade aside. Next second Roger had driven his blade through the jersey into the man's stomach. The third man, now aghast at finding himself alone against so terrible an antagonist, sprang away. Hastily, he and his companion with the slit cheek retreated several yards to join two others who had been standing in the background with their swords drawn but irresolute expressions on their faces.

For a moment Roger stood there gasping and panting, the bodies of the men he had slain or injured in a ring before him, the point of his sword dripping blood on the ground. In the glare of the flames his face looked like a death-mask lit by the hard, glinting, jewelled eyes of an idol. His heart was beating furiously. Borne up on a sudden wave of triumph he rasped out defiantly:

'Come on, you bastards! Come and get your gizzards slit!'

Had they accepted his challenge, he was so exhausted that he could hardly again have lifted his sword arm; but his daring in making it saved him. Believing that he still had plenty of fight left in him, none of them had the courage to renew the attack. Instead, with the wounded who were still on their feet, and the still less warlike who were crowded round Boneparte, they broke into a heated argument upon what they should do next.

Their querulous dispute ended as quickly as it had begun. Like angels' music in Roger's ears, there suddenly came shouts of '*Vive la Republic! Vive Boneparte! Vive Boneparte!*' and a surge of men swept round the corner of the casino.

The beacon made by the blazing wood shed had brought Andoche Junot to Portillo and he had arrived on the garden side. A magnificent figure, his sword held high, the flames glittering on the gold of his pelisse, the future Duc d'Abrantês came hurtling across the wharf to the rescue of his future Emperor, and after him streamed the picked men of the Hundred and Thirty-first.

The Venetians scattered like chaff before the wind; the soldiers pursued and seized them. Boneparte was left standing alone. Suddenly he strode forward, put his arms behind his back, confronted Roger, and said:

'Colonel Breuc, your sword-play was magnificent. You shall be mentioned in an order to the Army. But I require explanations. I do not understand how these people could have known that I was here. Tell Junot to have all those who can walk brought into the *salon*.'

Turning away abruptly, he stalked back to the casino and disappeared through its doorway.

Ten minutes later his order had been obeyed. The conspirators had been rounded up and herded inside. Bonaparte again stood behind the supper table. Sirīsha, pale but composed, was seated to one side of him on the sofa. Roger and Junot stood on the other. On entering the room Roger had looked quickly about for Malderini, and spotted him standing in a corner near the door to the kitchen. The sides of the room, all but that adjacent to the bedroom, were now lined with troops; so, knowing that Malderini could not get away for the moment, Roger took no special action.

The noise of shuffling, low moans from the wounded, and apprehensive murmurs, filled the room. Bonaparte called sharply for silence, then turned to Roger and asked, 'How did these conspirators know that I was here? You were insistent that I should take an escort, and must have told Junot to follow us. You must have known there would be an attempt to kidnap me. What have you to say?'

Now had come the awful moment that Roger had known all along he would have to face. He replied boldly, '*Mon Général*, I am entirely to blame. I learned from Villetard that in Venice a conspiracy was being hatched against French interests. When the Peace had been signed and the bulk of our troops withdrawn from Italy, the conspirators intended to launch a *coup d'état* to overthrow the new pro-French Government and re-establish the *Serenissima*. I decided that the best means of averting such a menace to the interests of France in Italy was to induce the conspirators to show their hand prematurely, then crush them.'

'You mean that, with this in mind, you used me to bait a trap?'

'I confess it. Had you not upset my plans at the last moment by refusing to take an escort, you would have been in no danger. Even then, had it not been for the storm, Colonel Junot would have arrived on Portillo before the conspirators and saved you from the indignities to which you have been subjected.'

'Your arrogance is almost unbelievable.' Bonaparte struck the table with his fist. 'Risk or no risk, that one of my aides-de-camp should have dared to use his General-in-Chief like a piece of cheese for these miserable mice robs me of words with which to blast you.'

Without flinching, Roger faced the blazing anger in the Corsican's eyes. Sadly he shook his head. '*Mon Général*, you do me a great injustice. It was not merely to trap these miserable people that I hatched this plot. You have mentioned to me many times that the people of Venice love and honour you; that they are grateful to you for the freedom you brought them; that they are to be relied on when you are gone back to France to maintain an independent City State, governed on the principles of Liberty, Equality, Fraternity. It may have been presumptuous of me, but I wished you to see for yourself how ill-founded was your belief. Look at them! There are not only noble ex-Senators here. There are also men of the robe, *bourgeoisie*, and even members of the proletariat. They are representative of Venice. For France and yourself they have only hatred. My object was to unmask them before you.'

With a quick gesture Bonaparte waved Roger aside and began to walk up and down, his hands clasped behind him. Six paces forward, six paces back. For a full two minutes he strode back and forth, deep in thought. Suddenly he halted facing Roger, and cried:

'You are right! They attempted to force me to sign a document re-creating the *Serenissima* with a Doge and all their other outworn trappings. They threatened to carry me off and starve me into ordering the withdrawal of our garrison.' Swinging round upon the Venetians he stormed at them: 'You are a miserable, cowardly people, unfit for liberty. You no longer have land or water of your own. I will take all your ships, despoil your arsenal, remove all your cannon and wreck your bank. Then I will hand you over to the Austrians.'

A wail went up. The Venetians fell upon their knees shouting cries and pleas. 'No! No! Anything but that! Have mercy on us. We will do whatever you wish. Anything. Anything. We will be loyal to France. We swear it!'

'Silence!' he snapped. 'You are incapable of loyalty! I have delayed signing a peace only for your sakes, but I'll delay no longer. The Emperor wants your city; he shall have it. You would make slaves of one another. Very well then; you shall all become the slaves of Austria.'

Roger's heart warmed within him. Whatever might happen now he had cleared the big fence. He had preserved Venice from domination by France. In any future combination of the Powers against her, it would prove a valuable bulwark. By patient intrigue, coupled with audacity, he had once more struck a mighty blow for England.

To Bonaparte he said, '*Mon Général*, you should know that there is one man here more treacherous than all the rest. He joined this conspiracy only to make use of it for his own ends. He has kept in touch with Villetard with the object of betraying his friends to us when the time was ripe and claiming as his reward that you should make him First Magistrate of Venice. Any man so despicable deserves death. He is my personal enemy, and I ask from you the right to execute him.'

Malderini had taken no part in the fighting or in seizing Bonaparte. He had watched the *coup* develop with great satisfaction and, when Junot had arrived with the troops, remained undisturbed. He had been expecting events to take exactly that course and that, when the other conspirators were arrested and led away, Villetard would appear to present him to Boneparte and praise the part he had played. Then, on seeing Roger enter the *salon*, he had suddenly been seized with fear that even if his enemy's presence there were pure chance, it might bring about the wrecking of all his plans. Since, he had been watching the proceedings with mounting dismay and apprehension.

Now, as Roger denounced him, he turned, dived between two soldiers, seized the door-knob of the kitchen door and strove to open it. But it was still bolted on the other side. The two soldiers grabbed him by the shoulders and swung him round.

Pointing at him, Roger cried, 'That is the arch-traitor! Bring him here!' Malderini was thrust forward through the murmuring crowd until he was only a yard from Boneparte. His sagging, old-woman's face was grey with terror, but with a great effort he pulled himself together and cried:

'General, you must hear me. This accusation is false. It is made by a man who bears me a grudge because, believing him to be an English spy, I had him imprisoned in the Leads. But that is not all. As a man you owe me some consideration. What will be said of you if you condemn to death a man whose wife you have stolen.'

'You must be mad,' Boneparte snapped. 'I do not know your wife.'

With a bitter, high-pitched laugh, Malderini pointed at Sirīsha. 'Not know her! Why, there she sits. She was brought here for your pleasure. On our entering this room, we surprised you having supper with her.'

Boneparte jerked his head round and fixed his eyes on Roger. 'Is this true? Have you made use of a political situation to get the best of this man in some private quarrel you have with him?'

'Yes,' Roger admitted. 'The Princess is his wife; but it was only by bringing her here I could make quite certain that he would come here with the others. If I had not, he might have betrayed their intention while himself remaining in Venice.'

'No, no!' Malderini cried. 'You are right, General. He has abused your confidence to pursue a private feud. And he has dragged your name in the mud to do it. All Venice knows that for the past few days you have been paying visits in secret to the city, and . . .'

'What nonsense is this?' Boneparte burst out. 'I have never been near the place.'

A sudden murmur arose from the Venetians. 'Oh, oh!' 'We are at your mercy; why deny it?' 'That you have been in the city is common knowledge.'

'Yes,' Malderini hurried on. 'And my enemy must have pointed out my wife to you. It is said everywhere that you had displayed an interest in her. Then, this morning, he abducted her in broad daylight to bring her here.'

'Breuc! What have you to say?' The Corsican's words cracked like pistol shots.

'I do not deny it.' Roger replied tersely. 'Rumours that you were in Venice had to be put round to induce the conspirators to plan this attempt to kidnap you. I abducted his wife with the help of a boat-load of French sailors to blaze the trail more surely. Only by so doing could I make certain of luring him here tonight.'

Malderini gave a sudden chuckle. 'See, General, where this fool's personal thirst for revenge has landed you. We cannot stop you throwing us all into Leads, but what will Venice say? What will the world say? No one will believe that we came here to kidnap you. They will believe that I came here with my friends to rescue my wife from dishonour. They will say that you are a mean, unscrupulous tyrant. That you abused your power to have my wife abducted. That when discovered and reproached, instead of restoring her to me, you were so furious at being actually caught out in your evil design that you decided to do your best to silence us. In the hope of doing so you falsely accused us of this plot, so that you could send us all to prison. And that, to give credence to a serious plot having existed, you have gone to the length of punishing all Venice by throwing her to the Austrians.'

The Venetians had hung breathlessly upon his words, and now, seeing a hope of escaping the penalty for their night's work, they cried: 'Yes, yes!' 'He is right!' 'Everyone will believe that we came here to rescue her.' 'They'll hold your name infamous.' 'They'll say you gave us to the Austrians to cover up a plot that never existed.' 'Italy has hailed you as the new Caesar; tomorrow you'll be known as another Heilogabolus.'

Bonaparte's pale face had gone chalk-white. Once more he turned to Roger, and snarled. 'You got me into this! Get me out or I'll have you chained for life to an oar in a galley!'

Epilogue

'AND then?' exclaimed Georgina, eagerly, 'And then?'

Roger had paused in his story to refill her goblet and his own with champagne. Giving a light shrug, he replied, 'Why, m'dear, being much averse to spending the rest of my life as a galley slave, I was under the necessity of persuading him that he need have no fears for his reputation.'

'Wretch that you are to tantalize me so!' She stamped a small foot.

'Unless you had somehow escaped the Corsican's wrath you would not be here. But how? By what trickery? Tell me this moment.'

The 'here' that Georgina referred to was her boudoir in the Berkeley Square mansion that, as the mother of the young Earl of St. Ermins, she occupied when in London. It was mid-December, very cold and snowing outside; but in the small boudoir, with a good log fire flickering on the ceiling, and the silk-covered walls patterned with Chinese junks, pheasants and pagodas, it was warm and cosy. Instead of having supper served in the chilly dining-room, they had it sent up there, and now sat at their ease on a deep sofa before the fire.

Roger had arrived in London from the Continent only the day before. After the desperate stand he had made against the Venetian conspirators on Portillo, he had been laid up for a fortnight with his wounds. Meanwhile, on October 17th, Boneparte had signed with Austria the famous peace of Campo Formio.

Later, before he went on to Rastadt to ratify it, Roger had made his wounds the excuse for asking for long leave, stating that he proposed to convalesce in the winter sunshine at his little château near St. Raphael. The General-in-Chief, having no immediate use for him, had granted it but stipulated that he should report again by the end of January, as by then the Directory would have decided whether he should be given an army for the invasion of England or be allowed to follow his own inclination of leading a French army to conquest in the glamorous East; and in either case he felt that Roger would be valuable to him. Roger had then gone to the South of France, and spent a month there building himself up locally as one of the new post-revolution landed proprietors and an aide-de-camp to the now world-famous conqueror of Italy.

Early in December, Boneparte had returned to Paris to receive formal thanks for his amazing victories. The Directory feared him but had to do him honour. To the public he was a national hero and amidst delirious scenes of welcome they acclaimed him as another Caesar. Roger ostensibly left St. Raphael to participate in the triumph of his Chief, but, in fact, he journeyed quietly to Brittany and, through one of his old connections there, had himself landed by smugglers only two nights before in a quiet Sussex cove.

That morning he had spent an hour with Mr. Pitt, reporting his own activities and giving his views on probable French intentions for the further-ance of their war against Britain, now the sole champion remaining in arms against the mighty power that, as a result of the Revolution, was spreading communism and atheism across Europe.

The Prime Minister had been plunged in even greater gloom than when Roger had last seen him. During Roger's absence, Britain had suffered one of the most terrible financial crises in her history, and had survived it only owing to Mr. Pitt's ability and the patriotism with which her monied classes had supported the new loans. The financial situation was still a cause for grave anxiety and the signing by the Austrians of the Peace of Campo Formio had been an appalling blow. As a would-be upholder of the Old Order in Europe, Mr. Pitt was naturally much distressed by the total elimination of the Serene Republic, but Roger had quoted Boneparte's own words to him about the Venetians: 'This miserable, cowardly people unfit for liberty.' And he had had to agree that Roger had done well to get them handed over to the Austrians, rather than to leave the wealthy and populous city as a pawn in the possession of the French.

Georgina too had been distressed at the sad fate of Venice, and had appreciated the significance of its value in a possible renewal of the Coalition against France only when Roger had explained it to her that evening. She at once agreed the soundness of the policy he had adopted, but reproached him for having sacrificed to gain his ends the little group of Venetians who had had the courage to enter on a conspiracy aimed at freeing their city from the French.

At that he laughed, and now he told her how, in one move, he had saved both them and Boneparte's reputation.

'You will remember,' he said, 'how, that afternoon, I had made an effigy of Boneparte, and left it hidden under some garden chairs? When the Corsican threatened me with the galleys, I sent Crozier to get it and displayed it to them all. The mask was the conventional Venetian long-nosed hideous affair, but, apart from that, the effigy was a good one. In size and appearance it was Boneparte's double, and would certainly have been taken for him had it been seen propped up in a sitting position at anything over a few yards' distance. I then obtained his permission to make my explanation to him in the form of an address to the conspirators, and this is what I said to them:

' "You have been led to believe that, for some days past, General Boneparte has been living incognito in Venice. The fact is that he has never entered your city. He left the mainland only this evening, and has been resident for the past week at his Headquarters, which are a good day's travel distant from Venice. This can be proved beyond all shadow of doubt. The rumours about his presence in the city are due to people having glimpsed this effigy of him in the cabin of a gondola as it was taken up and down the Grand Canal.

' "Why, you may ask, did we display this effigy? The answer is that we knew that a group of reactionaries was conspiring to overthrow the new Republican régime. The effigy enabled us to bait the trap which has brought you out into the open; and the rumours about General Boneparte's interest in Signor Malderini's wife, followed by her kidnapping, were a part of the same successful plot. That ensured that this arch-traitor would come here with you. Now you have shown your hand you are at the General's mercy.

' "Yet, you are right that a stigma might attach to him for the part played by his effigy. That, we cannot permit; and the remedy is to make public to all Venice the manner in which you have been fooled. Given his permission, I propose that you shall all be lodged in the Leads, but, every evening during the next fortnight, you will be paraded for an hour round the Piazza of St. Mark, in chains, and carrying in your midst the effigy of the General, which you so skilfully and bravely kidnapped." '

'Oh!' murmured Georgina. 'Oh, Roger, what a truly marvellous idea for making those poor wretches appear ridiculous. Did the Corsican see the humour of it?'

Roger laughed. 'Yes, and the sense. He is shrewd enough to realize that making martyrs of people only strengthens their cause, whereas ridicule can kill it. He agreed at once and to my suggestion that the final touch of contempt could be put upon the whole movement by restoring the conspirators to liberty after having been exposed to the mockery of the crowd for fourteen nights.'

'Well done, my dear! It is greatly to your credit that you saved them from the miserable fate which otherwise would have been theirs. I wonder, though, at this clever piece of trickery having saved yourself. The production of the effigy could kill the rumours that the Corsican had been in Venice; but not that he had been supping with the Princess Sirīsha on Portillo, for the conspirators had seen him there with their own eyes, and when released could swear to it.'

'They were warned that a mention of his presence on Portillo traced to any of them would cost the babbler his life; but we had a protection far better than that. Had they sworn until they were blue in the face to having seen him, who would have believed them? It would have been thought only a belated attempt to bluff people into thinking that the conspiracy had, after all, nearly succeeded. No. Had Bonaparte refused to let me handle matters my way, a scandal could not have been avoided. But I had promised him that there should be no scandal and provided the means to carry out my promise. He had to admit that. Moreover, my having revealed the true feeling of the Venetians towards France had saved him from making, in his view, a false step by giving them their independence. Last, but not least, although my plot had threatened to go awry, it had not done so in the end, because I had thrown my life into the scales to prevent him being kidnapped before Junot arrived; and, harsh disciplinarian though he is, anyone can win his pardon for a fault if they show courage on his behalf.'

'What of that poor Princess?' Georgina asked. 'How did she come out of this?'

'When the prisoners were taken off I went with them, so that I could have my wounds looked to as soon as possible in Venice. Boneparte resumed his interrupted supper with Sirīsha, while Junot, with a handful of men, remained to guard him and convey him back to Mestre in the morning.'

Georgina raised one of her beautifully arched eyebrows. 'Did you ever hear, er . . . if the party was a success?'

'It depends what you mean by a success,' Roger smiled. 'Both of them told me afterwards that they had found the other most interesting, but what form their interest in one another took it was not for me to enquire. However, the Princess is now revelling in her freedom, and she is very rich. Venice has only unpleasant associations for her, so she plans to leave it; and, as she liked England, it is possible that she may come here to live. If so, perhaps one day she may confide in you whether Boneparte is as irresistible as a lover as he is a general.'

'You imply that Malderini is dead.'

'He is. Boneparte gave him to me.' Roger's face suddenly became grim. 'I had him taken outside and seated on a stone bench in the garden. I took out the thin plaited rope of Clarissa's hair from under my shirt, and showed it to him. Then I went behind him and threw a loop of it round his neck. As I drew it tight, his cries were silenced. For a few minutes his feet made a horrid drumming on the stone paving while I twisted the rope tighter and tighter, then held it fast. Afterwards I had his body thrown into the lagoon.'

For the space of a few heartbeats they were silent. Then, to distract Roger's thoughts from the awful duty he had fulfilled, Georgina said, 'Since poor Clarissa has been dead nine months, and you have kept your oath, maybe you now feel both free and inclined to savour again a woman's caresses?'

'Why, yes.' He turned to smile at her, then put an arm about her shoulders and drew her to him. 'And it's just as well that I went direct to Venice instead of returning first to England; for I vow the sight of your sweet lips and eyes would have sadly tempted me to break my oath.'

'Dear Roger. But wait one moment!' She threw up a hand as he bent his head to kiss her. 'There remains a point on which I wonder the Corsican did not call you to account. He stipulated that he'd have nought to do with the Princess should it mean that he could be accused afterwards of stealing her from her husband. Yet that is what happened. Malderini denounced him as a seducer before both his fellow Venetians and Junot's soldiers. I'd not have thought Boneparte a man to let that pass.'

'Nor did he; and that last fence could have queered my pitch when I as good as had the whole game in my hands. When I asked him to give me

Malderini, he refused. Mark you, it was not that he has scruples about married women. His stipulation was only a precaution against being accused of misusing his power for such an end should anything have got out; and I had already convinced him that the production of the effigy would dispose of the rumours that he had left the mainland. But he snapped at me that, as it was I who had led him unwittingly to wrong Malderini, I should not benefit by his capture, and that he should suffer no worse punishment than his co-conspirators.'

'How, then, did you get over that?'

'I reminded him that when I had offered to arrange for him to sup *tête-à-tête* with the Princess, I had guaranteed that her doing so should give her husband no grounds for complaint.'

'But it had, and he did complain, most bitterly.'

'True,' Roger smiled. 'But he had no grounds for doing so. Can you not guess the answer to this riddle? I began to suspect it in India; Sirīsha confirmed my suspicions when I got into the Malderini Palace as an Arab perfume seller. My reply to Boneparte was to step up to Malderini. Keeping my eyes lowered, I seized his coat and shirt, close up to the neck with both hands, and tore them apart with all my strength. He struggled wildly but the two soldiers who had brought him forward held his arms. Wrenching and tearing, in less than a minute I had him near naked to the waist, revealing two great ugly sagging witch's breasts. Of the two Malderini twins who had gone to India ten years before, it was the sister who had murdered her brother and taken his identity. The evil creature who had forced upon me this nightmare vendetta was a woman!'

VENICE IN THE

① *Piazza San Marco*

② *San Giorgio Maggiore*

③ *Zattere alto Spirito Santo*

④ *The Palace of the Doges*

⑤ *Palazzo Dario*

⑥ *Canal San Barnaba*

⑦ *Salizzada San Samuele*

⑧ *Palazzo Malderini*